I am doing

Rory regarded Hex, feeling sick as he realized what he had to do. Finally he nodded. "You can come. But one wrong move and it's over. You can't hurt me, remember? I'm protected."

"I know," Hex said even as Fritz and Bridget both cried their disapproval.

"You can't trust him!" Bridget screamed.

"This is a mistake," Fritz told him.

"What else can we do?" Rory asked them. "We will need magic, I know it."

"Soka's spell—" Bridget began, but Rory cut her off.

"Is not enough. I'll do anything to save Mom, even deal with the devil."

OTHER BOOKS YOU MAY ENJOY

SCOTT MEBUS

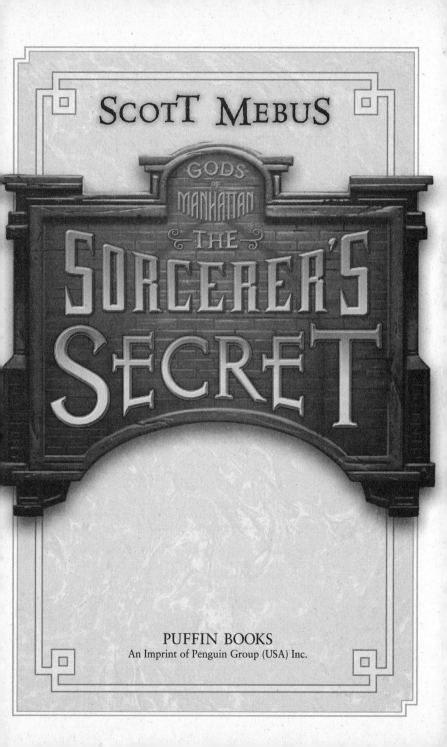

GODS OF MANHATTAN

THE SORCERER'S SECRET

PUFFIN BOOKS
An Imprint of Penguin Group (USA) Inc.

PUFFIN BOOKS

Published by the Penguin Group

Penguin Young Readers Group, 345 Hudson Street, New York, New York 10014, U.S.A.

Penguin Group (Canada), 90 Eglinton Avenue East, Suite 700, Toronto, Ontario, Canada M4P 2Y3

(a division of Pearson Penguin Canada Inc.)

Penguin Books Ltd, 80 Strand, London WC2R 0RL, England

Penguin Ireland, 25 St Stephen's Green, Dublin 2, Ireland (a division of Penguin Books Ltd)

Penguin Group (Australia), 250 Camberwell Road, Camberwell, Victoria 3124, Australia

(a division of Pearson Australia Group Pty Ltd)

Penguin Books India Pvt Ltd, 11 Community Centre, Panchsheel Park, New Delhi - 110 017, India

Penguin Group (NZ), 67 Apollo Drive, Rosedale, Auckland 0632, New Zealand

(a division of Pearson New Zealand Ltd.)

Penguin Books (South Africa) (Pty) Ltd, 24 Sturdee Avenue,

Rosebank, Johannesburg 2196, South Africa

Registered Offices: Penguin Books Ltd, 80 Strand, London WC2R 0RL, England

First published in the United States of America by Dutton Children's Books,
a division of Penguin Young Readers Group, 2010
Published by Puffin Books, a division of Penguin Young Readers Group, 2011

1 3 5 7 9 10 8 6 4 2

LIBRARY OF CONGRESS CATALOGING-IN-PUBLICATION DATA IS AVAILABLE.
ISBN: 978-0-525-42240-2 (hardcover)
Puffin Books ISBN 978-0-14-241878-9

Designed by Jason Henry
Set in Cg Cloister

Printed in the United States of America

To Brian,
who always has my back

·CONTENTS·

CAST OF CHARACTERS

Rory Hennessy—*A thirteen-year-old boy; the last Light in New York City*
Bridget Hennessy—*Younger sister to Rory Hennessy*
Lillian Hennessy—*Mother to Rory and Bridget Hennessy*
Peter Hennessy—*Rory and Bridget's father; missing for past ten years*

· THE RATTLE WATCH ·

Nicholas Stuyvesant—*Son of Peter Stuyvesant*
Alexa van der Donck—*Daughter of Adriaen van der Donck*
Simon Astor—*Son of John Jacob Astor*
Lincoln Douglass—*Son of Frederick Douglass*

· THE M'GAROTH CLAN ·

Fritz M'Garoth—*Lieutenant-Captain and Rat Rider of M'Garoth Clan*
Liv M'Garoth—*Captain and Rat Rider of M'Garoth Clan. Wife of Fritz*

· GODS OF MANHATTAN ·

Mayor Alexander Hamilton—*God of Finance; Mayor of the Gods of Manhattan*
Willem Kieft—*First Adviser to Mayor*
Peter Stuyvesant—*God of Things Were Better in the Old Days*
Caesar Prince—*God of Under the Streets*
T. R. Tobias—*God of Banking*
Walt Whitman—*God of Optimism*
Dorthy Parker—*Goddess of Wit*
Boss Tweed—*God of Rabble Politics and Back Alley Deals*
William Randolph Hearst—*God of Yellow Journalism*
Mrs. Astor—*Goddess of Society*
Alfred Beach—*God of Subway Trains*
Jimmy Walker—*God of Leaders Who Look the Other Way*
Nathan Hale—*God of Martyrs*
Robert Townsend—*God of Ornamental Handkerchiefs*
Teddy Roosevelt—*God of Valor*
Aaron Burr—*A fallen god*

· MUNSEES ·

Wampage—*Only Munsee to escape the Trap*

Tackapausha—*Sachem of the Munsees*

Sooleawa—*Daughter of Penhawitz; sister of Tackapausha; Medicine Woman*

Sokanen (Soka for short)—*Daughter of Sooleawa; Sister of Tammand*

Tammand—*Son of Sooleawa; Brother of Soka*

Askook—*A magician*

Buckongahelas—*Murdered son of Tackapausha*

· GODS OF QUEENS ·

Rufus King—*God of Also-Rans*

Robert Moses—*God of Power-Hungry Politicians*

· GODS OF BROOKLYN ·

Washington Roebling—*God of Dangerous Projects*

Emily Roebling—*Goddess of Finishing What Others Have Started*

· GODS OF STATEN ISLAND ·

David de Vries—*God of Just Causes*

Cornelis Melyn—*God Wishing Life Were Fair*

· OTHER SPIRITS OF NOTE ·

The Abbess—*Founder of the convent on Swinburne Island*

Sly Jimmy—*Member of the B'wry Boys*

James DeLancey—*Leader of the Cowboys*

Colonel Smallwood—*Leader of the Marylanders*

Colonel Wood—*Leader of the Red Legged Devils*

Perewyn—*A Raritan medicine man*

Admiral Howe—*Leader of the Redcoats on Staten Island*

IMPORTANT TERMS

Blood (Bronx, Manhattan, Brooklyn, etc.)—*The restriction of a divine being to the boroughs where his or her mortal self was known to dwell. For example, a god whose mortal self lived on a farm in the Bronx possesses "Bronx blood."*

pau wau—*Munsee word for medicine man or woman*

patroon—*Dutch word for landowner*

GODS OF MANHATTAN

THE

SORCERER'S
SECRET

Caesar Prince had a bad feeling about this.

He'd been called into the bowels of City Hall, deep into the maze of hallways that zigzagged beneath the ancient seat of the gods' power. All the gods had their own rooms down here, and the older the god, the deeper the room. Prince's own room was not easy to find, which was just as he liked it. But even he'd never been *this* deep before. The rooms down here were old, so old that most of their owners had faded away, left behind and forgotten as the city above moved ahead without them. But Willem Kieft never forgot.

It was Kieft who had called him to this place, into what appeared to be the room of the long-gone God of Barrel-making. Metal hoops hung on the wall, coated with dust; rotting wooden slats lay in cobweb-covered piles in the corner. The room's owner had fallen victim to the changing times, leaving behind only this musty place and a dead-eyed painting in the Portrait Room upstairs. No god felt comfortable standing in a dead god's room—and causing discomfort was obviously Kieft's intent.

Prince glanced around at the others whom Kieft had called. There were Kieft's staunchest allies, of course: Tobias the banker, Boss Tweed the rabble-rouser, and Jimmy Walker the look-the-other-way politician. Tobias was flanked by two large green Brokers of Tobias, the metallic monsters who guarded his bank; both Brokers had scorch marks and metal drips across their broad green bodies, as if they'd recently been in a fire. Curious. Leaning against the wall, William Randolph Hearst nodded at Prince with a smirk when Caesar inadvertently caught his eye. Prince was always on edge around the God of Yellow Journalism, as Hearst seemed to know everything about everyone, and wasn't shy about using his knowledge to his advantage. Finally, the Goddess of Society, Mrs. Astor, stood haughtily by the door, barely consenting to associate with the riffraff. They all kept their distance from the strange Munsee Indian across the room, he of the twin snake tattoos practically crawling across his face. There was something profoundly wrong with this man who called himself Askook, and they all studiously avoided his oily gaze as they waited uncomfortably for their master to arrive.

Finally, Kieft strolled into the room, a thin smile playing across his lips as he surveyed his coconspirators. With a shock, Prince realized that the black-eyed god was actually here in person. Normally, the First Adviser would inhabit some unfortunate spirit's body for a meeting such as this. Prince's stomach clenched as his bad feeling got worse.

"So kind of you to take the time out of your busy evening to join me," Kieft told them drily, as if any of them would refuse a summons from him. "As you can see, I've decided to grace you all with my actual presence, as what I have to show you is too important to trust to an avatar."

As those black eyes swept over him, Prince carefully kept his face still. He was playing a dangerous game here, with powers he freely admitted he did not understand. But he was willing to risk everything to make amends.

"Why did you drag us all down to this horrid place?" Mrs. Astor demanded.

"Because some things must be done in secret," Kieft answered, his cold gaze causing her to glance away, humbled. "Some things must be done far from the light, in the bowels of the earth, where there is no one to witness the rules we bend. Am I right, Mr. Prince?"

Kieft was talking about the Trap, which Caesar had built so many years ago. Caesar forced himself to grin and nod back, as if he didn't regret every minute he'd spent in the dark, building that monstrosity.

"What are we doing, exactly?" Hearst asked. He nodded at Askook. "And why is *he* here?"

"Askook will be helping in the demonstration," Kieft said. The Munsee's dead-eyed gaze slid over them as his snakes slithered across his cheeks.

"What kind of demonstration?" Mrs. Astor asked, her haughty tone replaced by a thin whine.

"I'm pleased you asked, Mrs. Astor," Kieft replied, turning to the dapper Jimmy Walker. "Mr. Walker? Could you come over here? I'd be most grateful for your assistance."

"Sure!" Walker hopped forward like a trained puppy, falling over himself in his eagerness to help. "What do I need to do?"

"You've done quite enough, already," Kieft said, nodding at Askook. "Kill him." The snake-Munsee stepped forward, quickly pulling out a knife, and slid the blade across Jimmy Walker's throat. The God of Leaders Who Look the Other Way didn't even have time to react; he soundlessly fell to the floor in a lifeless heap, blood pooling beneath his neck.

The room was shocked silent as Askook pulled out a piece of tanned hide and began to wipe his knife clean. "Jimmy Walker was a traitor to me and all of us," Kieft calmly informed them. "He helped Nicholas Stuyvesant escape my assassins. Thus is disloyalty rewarded." He kicked the body of the dead god with a black boot, rolling Walker's corpse onto its back. Kneeling down, Kieft began to pull at something around Walker's neck.

Glancing at his fellow spectators, Caesar could see the fear plain on their faces. This was impossible; no god could kill another god, or even order another god's death—that was the unbreakable rule. Except they'd just witnessed Kieft's direct order to the Munsee: *Kill him.* No one seemed to want to say anything, so Caesar spoke up.

"How can this be?" he asked. Though he hated to call attention to himself, this was too important to let slide. "The law can't be broken. No god may commit murder by deed or order. It's always been that way."

Kieft glanced up at him, smiling coldly. "Has it? Well, did I not mention that rules would be bent today?" A shiver ran down Caesar's back as the level of fear in the room doubled in an instant. How could Kieft break such a fundamental law? This changed everything. Caesar's task became even more vital; he just had to survive long enough to fulfill it. Kieft grunted with satisfaction as he yanked Walker's locket free.

"You all know what this is," Kieft said, the glittering trinket hanging from his clenched fist. Caesar noticed that more than one god's hand went reflexively to his or her own locket as the black-eyed god continued. "Normally, when a god fades away, their locket fades with them. Only murder disrupts that natural process. And while the Munsees have killed gods before, during our many wars of yesteryear, no one thought to touch the lockets of the fallen. So those lockets would crumble to dust, freeing other gods to take on certain of the dead gods' responsibilities, or allowing new gods to eventually rise in their place. But it doesn't have to be that way."

Caesar immediately knew where this was going, and he did not like it one bit. A sigh from Tweed meant the God of Rabble Politics had also grasped Kieft's meaning.

"You're not saying one of us could wear that?" Tweed said, eyes glinting with greed.

"*Imagine it,*" Kieft whispered, the locket swinging from his hand hypnotically. "More power than you have any right to possess. That is what I offer you."

"Are we a band of murderers now?" Mrs. Astor asked in a huff, though her eyes tracked the locket's swing hungrily.

"Not murder," Kieft assured her. His black eyes glittered in the firelight of the dead god's room. "I will bring war. Righteous war against our ancient enemies. What is more natural than that?"

"Are you sure the Munsees will fight?" Hearst asked. "My sources tell me the old fire for revenge has dwindled some in Tackapausha since his son's return."

"Don't worry about the Munsees," Kieft said. "They will dance to my tune, though they won't know it. But they are only a small piece of my plan. I am bringing you a war like you have never seen. And by the end of it, each of you will have more power than you can stand."

Kieft had them, Caesar could tell. He didn't know what kind of war Kieft had in mind, but a few mysteries he'd been puzzled by had suddenly become clearer. And if he was right, then no one was prepared for what was to come. No one . . .

"So who gets that one?" Tweed asked, his eyes on the prize. Kieft smiled.

"This first locket goes to a man who has only recently offered me aid. But that aid has been invaluable. Mr. Prince, I give this first of many to you."

Kieft reached out and dropped the locket in Caesar's hand. Caesar was taken aback. Was this a trick? Why would Kieft give this treasure to someone he, by all rights, shouldn't fully trust? Kieft's face was still, a picture of calm. Caesar had no other choice. He placed the locket around his neck, gasping as the power flowed through him. It felt so good, yet he couldn't help but think that somehow Kieft had gotten the best of him tonight.

"Why does he get one?" Mrs. Astor complained. "He's a nobody!"

"Don't worry," Kieft said, his eyes flashing. "I brought enough for everyone."

With these words, the door opened to admit a group of terrified minor gods, herded into the room by a pair of the green-skinned Brokers of Tobias. Struggling to hide his horror, Caesar looked away as Askook pulled out his knife. If this really was the start of a new kind of war, Caesar feared for them all.

A BAD DREAM

The city lay dead all around him.

Of course, at first glance, everything seemed fine. The soaring skyscrapers surrounding him gleamed in the sun, while the apartment buildings and storefronts lined each block as always, repeating ad infinitum into the distance. But while the buildings and sidewalks were clean and unblemished, they were completely sterile, and no hint of life could be seen in any direction. The air was eerily quiet—this was a metropolis that looked as though it hadn't been lived in for decades. The cars sat neatly parked along the shining sidewalks, washed and ready for drivers who never came to claim them. Those majestic skyscrapers stood tall but empty, like metal gravestones for a long-dead people. And nowhere could he find a single tree, or bush, or even a blade of grass. The city was nothing but a well-preserved corpse.

A voice came from behind him. "Do you like it?" The boy spun to see a medium-size man in a severe black coat and wide white collar standing on the street corner.

"I know you," the boy said, backing away from the man's deep black eyes.

"Do you?" the man asked. He did not budge from his spot on the corner. "I am glad to finally meet you, in person, so to speak. It is strange to realize I have been guiding your steps without ever seeing your face. But Askook showed me the way to your dreams. I've made a few changes, of course. A taste of the city that *I* dream about."

"Where are the people?" the boy asked, glancing around, and the black-eyed man shrugged.

"Does it matter? *I* am here, and I hold all the memory this place will ever need."

"Did you come to kill me?" the boy asked, his stomach jumping.

"Not today, no," the black-eyed man said, smiling at him with just a flash of teeth. "Today, I wanted to see your face, to catch a glimpse of that pain in your eyes. I believe my friend Typhoid Mary completed her visit to your mother, did she not?" The boy could barely keep the tears at bay as the man continued mercilessly. "She will die, of course—there is no true cure for Mary's gift, sad to say. Not for a mortal."

"I'm gonna kill you!" the boy hissed through gritted teeth. "You've already failed, you know. I freed the Munsees and brought down your Trap. It's all over for you now."

The man with the black eyes began to laugh, and he appeared truly amused. "Is that what you think? That you could ever hurt me? From the Trap falling to that ridiculous Simon Astor boy donning the locket—every move you've made has *helped* further my plan, my vision of what this city must become.

People are more frightened then ever, and with the Munsees back in their lives reminding them of their guilt, they're more willing to act on that fear. You might say that I could not have done it without you."

For a moment the boy reeled, overcome by the thought that he might be assisting this madman in any way. But he couldn't bring himself to believe it.

"You're lying!" he accused the man. "You're nothing but a liar! If I'm such a big help to you, then why did you hurt my mother? Why bother with me at all? I'm just a fly to you. A mortal, a little nothing. So why are you here? Why even waste your time on me? Why not just kill me already?"

The man with the black eyes abruptly turned away. "You should see to your mother. After all, she'll be dead soon."

He walked away as the boy screamed after him, "Why are you running away? What are you so . . ."

". . . scared of?"

Rory woke up with a start, those words on his lips. He was lying on the forest floor in the middle of Inwood Hill Park, not far from his family's apartment. Above him, the trees swayed softly in the late August breeze as the cool air riffled through the leaves. The ground he lay upon was littered with branches and fallen foliage—a remnant of the violent storm that had recently battered the island of Manhattan. But most of the great trees had survived. It would take more than bad weather to destroy this small forest oasis.

He closed his eyes, struggling to remember his dream, but

it was already slipping away. A rustle nearby caught his attention.

"What are you doing here, all by yourself?" a voice asked by his ear. Rory sat up quickly, embarrassed to be caught unawares. A small figure stood on a log near his head, gazing compassionately at him. Fritz M'Garoth, battle roach and rat rider, placed his roach helmet carefully on the log and sat down next to it as he waited for Rory's answer.

"Nothing," Rory replied. "I couldn't stand waiting by her body anymore, so I walked over here to just . . . get away. I think I'm going crazy, Fritz. I can't take doing nothing."

"Rory—" Fritz began, but he was interrupted by the sound of dogs barking in the distance. "I think they're back with Sooleawa," he said before whistling. His rat steed, Clarence, emerged from the underbrush, waiting patiently as Fritz climbed into the saddle.

"Rory, we're going to fix this," Fritz promised. "She's going to be all right. You haven't let us down and we're not going to let you down, either. Okay?"

Rory nodded and Fritz guided Clarence around, riding the rat back into the trees. Rory followed, the hope in his heart barely holding off the guilt that threatened to take him over completely. His mother's illness was his fault, he knew that. And if his mom didn't recover, he'd never forgive himself.

Never.

The sounds of dogs barking had quieted by the time Rory and Fritz finally reached Wampage's cave. They stepped out into the small clearing before the cave, which was dominated by a glowing white mound at its center. This was the last shell pit—a repository of wampum, a source of Munsee magic. Wampage had protected this shell pit ever since the Trap was sprung over a century earlier, living with the Munsee spirit dogs in his cave as they awaited their people's return. These dogs were gathered around their master's feet as Wampage nodded his greeting.

"Sooleawa is doing what she can," he told them, stepping aside to reveal the silver-haired medicine woman kneeling beside the still form of poor Mrs. Hennessy. With a hand on Rory's mother's forehead, the Munsee woman's eyes were closed as she muttered to herself.

"She's not tossing and turning anymore!" Rory exclaimed, taking an excited step forward.

"Don't get too excited," his sister's voice advised him, thick with misery. Bridget sat slumped against a tree at the outer edge of the clearing, their spirit dog, Tucket, lying at her feet, licking her wooden hand in sympathy. She looked exhausted with her arms wrapped around the good-natured dog's thick neck. "I got excited, too, but Soka said she's not *better* or anything. Sooleawa showed up and put her hand on Mom's head to stop her from shaking and moaning, but she still won't wake up."

"My mother is doing everything she can," a light voice said, and Rory turned to see Sooleawa's daughter, Soka, walking up to him, absently stroking her long, thick braid as she gave him a look filled with sympathy. "You must be patient."

To Rory's embarrassment, he felt his heart jump at the sight of the pretty Munsee girl. He told himself sternly that he had no time for thoughts like this, not with his mother lying sick a few feet away. "We're glad she agreed to come," he said, trying to sound casual. But he couldn't help himself from adding: "And I'm . . . glad you came, too."

"Yes, well . . ." Soka trailed off, looking away uncomfortably. She noticed something lying next to Mrs. Hennessy. "Is that your mortal body, Bridget?"

Bridget's flesh-and-blood body did, in fact, lie next to their mother's, it, too, appearing to be in a deep sleep.

"Nicholas and the others brought the body up with them before you got here," Rory explained, nodding at Nicholas Stuyvesant and the rest of the Rattle Watch, who were standing by the cave speaking with Fritz. "We'd left her back in Washington Irving's house when we went to meet you in the park at the fountain."

"Why aren't you in that body, then?" Soka asked Bridget. "You know how dangerous this paper body can be."

"I tried!" Bridget protested. "I leaned over and breathed out and everything! But nothing happened! Alexa thinks I might be too worked up or something. I'll try again later."

"You must," Soka told her sternly. "You can't live in this paper body forever. It isn't safe for your soul." She suddenly swayed on her feet, reaching out to grab a nearby tree trunk to steady herself.

"Are you okay?" Rory asked her, worried. "You look a little green."

"Ever since the Trap fell I've been a little . . . under the weather," Soka told them, swallowing hard. Now that he wasn't blinded by his happiness in seeing her, Rory noticed the circles under her eyes and the sickly cast to her skin. Soka noticed his concern and waved him off. "Don't worry. Mother believes it has something to do with feeling the land for the first time, since I was born in the Trap. Though I seem to be the only one affected . . ."

Rory was about to say something else when Sooleawa climbed to her feet, demanding all their attention with her presence.

"I can do nothing more for her," she told them.

"What?" Rory asked, running up to the medicine woman. "Why not? You can do anything! Use your magic. Please!"

"I have done what I can, but I can go no further," Sooleawa told him sadly. "The power to heal such damage as this illness has wreaked is beyond me. Not since my mother, Alsoomse, left us has any of our people wielded such power."

"Are you saying it's hopeless?" Rory asked, his heart sick and heavy beyond belief.

"No!" Sooleawa told him firmly. "I was able to put her body into a special trance that keeps her temporarily free from the passage of time. She will not worsen for at least a little while. It is not much, but it gives us time to discover a way to save her."

"How?" Rory begged her. "How do we save her?"

Nicholas Stuyvesant stepped forward.

"There's only one place to go when you don't know what to do," he said. "The Fortune Teller."

Wampage shook his head. "You are fooling with magic no one understands," he said. "I remember someone like this Fortune Teller, though we had a different name for her. She was not to be trusted."

"She's the one who told us that Rory was going to help free your people," Simon Astor offered. "Not bad for a shifty dame, right?"

"I still do not like it," Wampage continued, glancing at Sooleawa. She stayed silent, even as Fritz cut in.

"I don't like it, either," he said. "From what you have told me, Nicholas, what you give up is not always worth the information you receive." At this, Nicholas glanced away, unable to meet the battle roach's eyes. Rory wondered what the immortal teen had handed to the Fortune Teller in order to find him. What would Rory be forced to give in order to save his mother? It didn't matter. Rory was tired of standing around, feeling useless. It was time to act.

"I'm going," he said firmly. "Just show me the way, Nicholas."

Wampage and Fritz tried to dissuade him, but finally, Sooleawa put an end to the argument.

"If you are willing to sacrifice, we must respect that," she said. "I, myself, must return to the village. Soka?"

"I . . ." Soka glanced at Rory. "I would like to see this Fortune Teller, if I may. I have a question for her myself."

Sooleawa shook her head. "You will not always be able to so easily shirk your duties, my daughter. Wampage, we must talk. You can leave the fortune-telling to others, today."

She turned away, walking toward the cave. Wampage gave Rory an encouraging pat on the shoulder before following his medicine woman into the dark. Rory took a deep breath, daring to feel a little more hopeful. He didn't care what the Fortune Teller asked for; he'd give anything to have his mother back, healthy and whole. Anything at all.

THE HERRING MAN

alt Whitman glanced around the room, trying to gauge the mood of his fellow council members. Though Tobias had called the meeting of the Council of Twelve, everyone knew that Kieft was behind it. As First Adviser, Kieft technically had no authority over the council, though if anyone really believed that, Whitman had a bridge to sell them. Kieft didn't need a vote to push the council in whichever direction he wished. Or at least, that had been the case when he stood firmly at Mayor Hamilton's right hand (though someone less charitable might say that Kieft's hand was the true power in that relationship). But that was before Hamilton broke with Kieft, refusing to fight the Munsees and even offering his own life as compensation for his role in the Trap. Now no one knew what would happen or where the true power lay.

Hamilton sat at the head of the table, looking tired. Ever since his long-lost daughter, Abigail, had emerged from the park, the Mayor had begun to stand up to Kieft. But Mrs. Dorothy Parker, the Goddess of Wit and Whitman's best friend on the council, thought he still couldn't be trusted not to fold when push came to shove. However, Whitman had hope that Hamilton would surprise them. Of course, as God of Optimism, he could hardly think otherwise.

The rest of the council split along its typical lines: Whitman himself, Peter Stuyvesant, Mrs. Parker, Zelda Fitzgerald, and James Bennett on one side; Tobias, Boss Tweed, and Horace Greeley on the other; with the rest drifting somewhere in the middle. The battle lines had never seemed more clear than when Whitman and his friends—and they alone—began to get sick during the final days of the Trap. Whitman knew that Kieft had used Typhoid Mary to poison them. Peter Stuyvesant insisted that Caesar Prince was also somehow in on it. Indeed, Peter was staring a hole into the back of Caesar's head, muttering under his breath. Whitman hoped Peter was wrong; Caesar had always seemed like someone with his heart in the right place. Of course, as Mrs. Parker put it, Whitman could point out a serial killer's good qualities, so maybe he wasn't the best judge.

All conversation in the room died as the doors to the council room opened, admitting a grim-faced Willem Kieft. Before Hamilton could say a word to bring the meeting to order, the First Adviser began to speak.

"Luis Fredo, God of Sanitary Street Vendors," he said. Whitman's brow furrowed—what was this? Kieft continued. "Molly O'Sullivan, Goddess of Big Tips. Saul Rabinowitz, God of Garmentos. Samantha Yip, Goddess of Good Parking Spaces. Cornelis van Tienhoven, God of Untrustworthy Friends. Jimmy Walker, God of Leaders Who Look the Other Way."

"What about them?" Mrs. Parker demanded. "Have they all been deluded by your lies?"

"They were all murdered last night," Kieft said. A shock ran through the council chamber.

"That's impossible!" Babe Ruth announced. "We took the knife. Without that, who can kill gods?"

"The Munsees," Tobias answered in a bored voice, barely looking up from his ledgers.

"That's ridiculous," Whitman maintained. "These are more lies and innuendo."

"Their bodies lie in the outer chambers," Kieft said, a slight sneer twitching at the edge of his mouth. "If you'd like to see."

Whitman glanced at his friends, uncertain. Stuyvesant, however, did not bother to second-guess, standing up and pointing at Kieft.

"You killed them, you murderous dog!" he shouted. Kieft stared back at him steadily as both sides of the table erupted. Hamilton rose.

"Order!" he commanded, and turned to Stuyvesant, whose large nose was bright red with fury. "Peter, you know this cannot be true. We all know the rules. They cannot be broken, as many have proven through their failures."

"Indeed!" Kieft agreed. "So, someone else must be at fault here, and the Munsees are the only possible suspects."

"Now, that is a stretch, Willem," Hamilton began, but Kieft coldly cut him off.

"They have reason to hate us, as we all saw the other day when the Trap fell, and they have the ability. How can the people of Mannahatta feel safe with such murderers running about?"

"Feel safe?" Mrs. Parker was incredulous. "If anyone should be worried about their safety, it's the Munsees. The last time they took their eyes off us, they ended up stuck between the same trees for a hundred years."

"And now they are exacting their revenge," Kieft replied, his eyes glinting. "They must be . . . dealt with."

"You mean war!" Mrs. Parker exclaimed. "I won't let you do it! We will vote you down!"

"You misunderstand me," Kieft said. "The battle is beginning whether *you* want it to or not."

"Are you threatening this council?" Hamilton asked, his eyes narrowing. Whitman was glad to hear a hint of steel in his tone.

"I wouldn't dream of it," Kieft said, eyebrow raised as he stared down his former protégé. "I'm merely stating that someone has to take a stand against the Munsees and do what needs to be done. In the absence of anyone else coming forward, I will humbly take on those duties. Anyone who wishes may join me. Anyone who doesn't may step aside. But stand in my way . . ."

"I don't like what you're implying," Stuyvesant said, rising to his full height atop his good leg and his peg leg. "It sounds to me like you're forming an army!"

"No army, I assure you," Kieft said. "Just a collection of concerned citizens, much like the patriots who fought in your sacred Revolution. You are welcome to join me, but be warned, I will not tolerate interference. And now I must leave you, for good. This council has served its purpose, but times have changed, and a new leadership structure is needed. I cannot stand to the side any longer, not with my city under attack. Feel free to come with me if you wish to help; we have much to prepare for."

With one last contemptuous glance at a shocked Hamilton, Kieft spun about and strode out of the room. As expected, Tweed, Tobias, and Greeley followed him. But then, to Whitman's utter shock, Caesar Prince pushed himself to his feet, tipped his fedora at the remaining council members, and followed Kieft out the door. Stuyvesant nodded in cold satisfaction.

"I knew it," Peter said. "It was him that poisoned me. I thought I knew him, but I never did."

The door shut behind Caesar and then the council room exploded into frenzied conversation. Whitman sat back heavily in his chair, shell-shocked. A war was coming, all right, and it looked to be bigger than any of them had thought. Already, Kieft was building his army. The only question was: Would anyone stand with the Munsees, or would they all step aside?

***

This is not the way we left it."

Nicholas stared despondently at the mound of rubble, crouching down to sift halfheartedly through the pieces of broken mortar at his feet while the others helplessly looked on. They'd confidently come south to the Lower East Side, where Nicholas and Alexa had found the Fortune Teller's door a few months earlier. But there was no door in this dark alley, or even a wall—only rubble. A heavy bluish mist covered the ground, rising up around their ankles as if they were walking on dry ice. Rory felt uneasy standing in it, as if the ground beneath the mist had somehow become incredibly thin and fragile, covered with cracks he couldn't see. He had the disconcerting impression that if he were to stamp down hard, he'd break right through and fall helplessly forever into the depths of the earth. Glancing around, he noticed that everyone looked a bit green, Soka most of all. Her sickness seemed to be rearing its ugly head again and she had to cover her mouth to hold back her coughs. He took a step toward her in order to escort her back to the sidewalk, but she waved him off. Tucket trotted over to her, his big paws disappearing into the blue mist, and gave her a lick on the hand. She smiled, finally getting her coughing under control enough to give the big dog a pat.

Fritz rode his rat over the fallen bricks and concrete, the blue mist clinging to his armor like sticky puffs of cotton candy as he searched for some clue as to what had happened. "Was this fog here before?" he asked Nicholas.

"No," Alexa answered for the despondent Stuyvesant. "It was creepy around here, true. But not *this* creepy."

"Are you certain the door was here?" Soka asked, swallowing as she tried to keep her composure.

"I promise you, it was," Alexa explained, frustrated. "It was one of the three doors, right there."

"Three doors?" Soka asked. "There are others?"

"Yes, there are three entrances to the Fortune Teller's, and any one person can only pass through each entrance one time. So, essentially, you can ask the Fortune Teller three questions, one per door."

"If you can find them," Lincoln Douglass added. He kicked

a pebble, which popped in and out of the heavy mist like a skipping stone as it went skidding off down an alleyway.

"Only one person ever did find all three, as far as we know," Simon said, irritably waving away the mist from his bright aqua tunic.

"Who?" Bridget asked, her eyes wide.

"My father," Alexa answered. "I discovered from studying his diaries that he'd found all three doors and asked his three questions. But I could only find a mention of the location of one of the doors—this one. Whole chunks of his journals are missing and I can't seem to find those lost pages in any of his old haunts. It's so frustrating. I know he wrote about his past; he told me time and again. But I guess the past is forever forgotten, now." She sighed heavily, regretting the loss of her father's thoughts and memories. "It's gone, like this door."

Rory felt just as defeated. The atmosphere of the neighborhood around them didn't help. Here in Mannahatta, the Lower East Side was populated with ghostly memories of the old tenements built in the latter part of the nineteenth century. Known for their poverty and criminal element, with many of the dingy old structures pressed together so tightly that their mostly immigrant inhabitants could go days without seeing the sun, they had finally been torn down and the neighborhood rescued from squalor by the turn of the twentieth century. But the stain of those days remained in Mannahatta, and as Rory looked around at all the dismal, rickety buildings on every side, he could feel the tension creeping up his spine. Lincoln had spent the trip down happily informing him of all the evil spirits of sadistic gang leaders and murderers who made their home here, not to mention the hopeless souls who'd died within the tenements, condemned to haunt their decaying halls. Indeed, ever since they'd entered the neighborhood, Rory couldn't stop shivering. He knew it was afternoon, but the alleys between the old, creaking buildings were as dark as night. Rory could hear moaning and other creepy sounds in the distance. They'd all hoped to be in and out without wasting much time.

But now they were staring at a pile of rubble where a wall used to be. There wasn't a room on the other side of the ruined wall; instead the broken stones seemed to separate a small, muddy backyard from the alley. But Nicholas and Alexa swore that they had stepped through a door here to find the Fortune Teller.

"Maybe Kieft tore it down," Lincoln suggested. "One stick of dynamite and BOOM!"

"Maybe," Nicholas answered absently, rubbing his chin as he took in the devastation. "But that doesn't explain the mist."

"Or the fact that I want to jump out of my skin," Alexa said.

"Maybe that's just the Tenements," Lincoln offered. "I always feel weird down here."

"Not like this," Nicholas said firmly. Rory opened his mouth to ask a question when suddenly Soka dropped to her knees, throwing up all over the mist-covered rubble. Everyone stood by, shocked, as Soka regained control of herself, tears running down her cheeks. Bridget immediately ran to Soka's side and rubbed her back.

"You are not okay!" she scolded the shaking Munsee girl.

"No, it's all right," Soka insisted. "I'm better now. I don't know what's happening to me."

"We're all lucky that mist is covering up the sick," Simon declared, turning away with a wince. "Otherwise I'd be joining her. That was the grossest—"

"Shh!" Soka cut him off, wiping her mouth as she scrambled to her feet. "Something is out there."

The Munsee girl's warning shut them all up, and they unconsciously huddled together as they listened. Rory imagined all the horrible creatures out in the dark and repressed a shiver.

"I can hear something," Simon muttered, nervously straining to listen. Tucket began to growl, his ears flattening back. After a minute, Rory could hear it, too. A creaking, as if something big were coming. Finally, a long shadow appeared at the end of the alley, and they prepared to face whatever danger approached.

"HERRING!" A voice cried out from the darkness, scaring them out of their wits. Terrified, Simon immediately leaped away—only Nicholas's quick hand kept Simon from running off down another alley.

"GET YOUR HERRING, HERE!" the voice cried again, the shadow almost upon them. Nicholas and Alexa exchanged confused glances. By now, only Bridget still looked frightened.

"*Fish?*" she whispered, horrified. "I hate fish!"

The shadow stepped into the light, transforming from a creature of doom into a bent old man pushing a cart of fish.

"Hello, young people," he said brightly, a strong Yiddish accent coloring his words. "Who wants a little pickled herring to last you till supper? I got deals here like you wouldn't believe!"

Nicholas relaxed, shaking his head with a smile.

"You scared the daylights out of us, Mr. Russ," he said.

"If it isn't young Mr. Stuyvesant," Mr. Russ said, smiling. "And you troublemakers are his Rattle Watch! I've heard such stories about you. How could *I* scare *you*? I'm just an old man with a barrel of fish to sell. How could I scare anyone?"

"It is a rough neighborhood," Alexa pointed out.

"This was *my* neighborhood," Mr. Russ said proudly. "I made my fortune here. What is there to be afraid of?"

"You tell me," Simon said, nodding toward the blue mist. "This looks like a horror film."

Mr. Russ wasn't listening. Instead, his eyes had widened as he noticed Rory standing between Soka and Bridget.

"You," he said, pointing a bony finger at the boy. "I know you."

"What do you mean, you know him?" Alexa asked as the others gathered around Rory protectively. Rory felt a little irritated—he could handle himself against an old man, at least.

"It's in my head," the old man said. "She put it there."

"She? Who is she?" Nicholas looked alarmed.

"The Fortune Teller."

"You spoke to her?" Fritz asked intently. "Did you know her door was here?"

"Please, little fellow, this is my neighborhood," Mr. Russ said, waving his hand dismissively at the roach. "The day something happens here I don't know about? That's the day I hand over my cart and get into the button business with my brother-in-law. But this was more dumb luck than anything. I was just doing my rounds when I happened upon . . . well, I guess I should show you. Now, how did she say to do it? Oh yes." Mr. Russ began to mutter as he twirled his hand in the air. Air began to move around them, blowing through their hair as the mist began to move. The bluish fog sent tendrils up into the air, rising up like smoky fingers reaching for the sky. Those fingers expanded, gradually forming into ghostly figures right before their eyes. Tucket began to bark, leaning forward to snap at the images in the fog, forcing Rory to hold him back. More mist floated up, re-creating a foggy version of the now-destroyed wall. A ghostly door formed in the center of the wall, and the bluish figures solidified, their color becoming closer to green as they advanced on the mist wall. Rory could still see right through them as they moved, but they became solid enough to be recognizable. And with a start, Rory realized that he did, in fact, recognize them.

"Those are Brokers of Tobias!" Bridget whispered at his side. Indeed, a familiar round figure waddled at their head, advancing with purpose on the ghostly door. T. R. Tobias, the God of Banking, stopped before the door and gestured for one of his Brokers to bang on it.

"Lady, I request your presence!" Tobias called out, and Rory jumped to hear his voice so clear. "I have come to collect on what you owe!"

At first nothing happened, and the Broker continued to bang steadily like a clockwork soldier wound all the way up. At last, a voice drifted through the door, female and scathing.

"I owe you nothing, Tobias," it said. "Now get out of here!"

"What I paid you was more than sufficient," Tobias insisted. "You are the one who refused to give service once I had paid. If your debt is not satisfied, I will be forced to have my employees do everything in their power to collect."

At last, the door creaked open to reveal a huge, hulking woman with an evil, glowing cigar hanging out of the side of her mouth. "I didn't refuse you, foolish man," she said, her voice deep and gritty, as if her vocal cords were coated in sand. "I asked for *proper* payment, and you would not give me what I required. So I owed you no answers to your questions. And once you left in a huff, you forfeited the right to reenter by this door. It seems pretty simple to me. You blew it. Now get out of here and take your little pets with you."

"What I gave you was more than—" Tobias began again, but the Fortune Teller cut him off, pointing at his neck.

"*There* is my fee," the Fortune Teller declared. "Still hanging around your neck. You know what? I am feeling forgiving. Give me that trinket and I will answer the question that you feel is so important that you come down here to threaten me with your big green monkeys."

"You cannot have that," Tobias said, eyes flashing with anger. His ghostly form turned away. "You leave me no choice. If you will not answer me, then perhaps you will answer my friend."

A tendril of blue mist shot out around the corner, returning in the form of a little-girl spirit. The girl walked stiffly, as if her limbs weren't controlled by her own will. And once Rory saw her wild, terrified eyes, he realized that, in fact, they weren't. Willem Kieft had taken her over.

The Fortune Teller pulled back in her doorway, disgust flashing across her fleshy face.

"That is forbidden, you know this," she spat.

"She has not passed through your door," Tobias said innocently. "She has asked no questions of you. She brings items of great value which I'm sure you would be more than happy to take from her. I fail to see the problem."

"You and your master have gone too far," the Fortune Teller said, pulling herself up to her full height as she filled the doorway. "You have bent the rules to your liking for too long. This door is closed to you!"

"You cannot stop her from passing over your doorstep," Tobias said, sounding as bored as if he were talking about the weather. "Those are the rules."

"I know what you are doing," the Fortune Teller informed him. "I will not be used. This door is closed . . . forever."

The ground began to rumble, and Tobias's ghostly face blanched. The soft glow emanating from the open doorway began to intensify, until it became as bright as a burning sun. Rory had to cover his eyes to protect them from blindness, even as the rumbling in the earth threatened to deafen him. Through his fingers, he spied ghostly Tobias turning tail and running, disappearing around the corner. The Brokers followed on his heels, but most of them moved too slowly. The burning light blew outward in a blaze of fire, burning through the Brokers closest to the door. A few staggered around the corner, their green metal skin bubbling up and melting like butter on a hot pan. The rest were incinerated by the flames, vaporized by the hot flash.

In the center of the light, the Fortune Teller was still visible. She turned to stare directly at Rory, her eyes boring into him.

"I am waiting for you," she said, her voice echoing through time. "Your blood will show you the way." She turned toward the alley. "I know you're there, Mr. Russ. I have a job for you . . ."

With that, the light faded, as did the large figure of the Fortune Teller, and when it was gone, only the rubble remained. The mist has dissipated, its duty performed, leaving them all drained and astonished. Tucket padded up to the ground, sniffing suspiciously at a pebble. Simon snorted, though the look on his face was one of awe.

"Talk about overkill. What's wrong with sending you a letter?"

Rory didn't answer. He had the sinking sensation that even though he'd done his duty as a Light by opening the Trap, Mannahatta was not yet through with him.

A Shape in the Night

William Randolph Hearst sat in his opulent office hidden in a decrepit old building deep in the Lower East Side. During his mortal days, he'd run his newspaper, the *New York Journal American*, from this old building, and the paper had been a hit. Mostly because Hearst was not afraid to sensationalize, using eye-popping headlines and lurid stories of murder and sordid crime to boost circulation. And if he had to bend the truth a bit to sell papers? Well, that was just part of the business. His proudest moment had been right before the Spanish-American War in the 1890s, when he'd used half-truths and explosive headlines to inflame the public into demanding that the United States declare war on Spain. Hearst always smiled when he thought of that war—it certainly had helped him sell a lot of papers.

Now Kieft was promising another war, a big one. Countless lives would be lost and futures destroyed in the battles ahead. And Hearst would do anything he could to get the fighting started.

He leaned back in his chair, savoring the soft buzz that always surrounded him. To some it might look strange, even a little disgusting, that so many flies hovered about his head. But information was the most important currency he could hold, and his flies went everywhere, saw everything. He sent his little beauties out into the world, into the nooks and crannies, the basements and the back alleys of the city, and they came back to him bursting with new gossip he could use to help his friends, crush his enemies, and sell a lot of papers.

At that moment a little black beauty hummed through his open window, lighting upon his outstretched finger.

"What do you have for me, darling?" Hearst asked the little insect, softly stroking its tiny feelers. The fly began to buzz, and as he listened, Hearst raised an eyebrow. The Fortune Teller, leaving a message for the famous Rory Hennessy, and more importantly, taking sides? The Fortune Teller never took sides! Kieft would want to know about this right away. He'd no doubt take steps to keep Rory away from the second and third doors, not that Hearst knew where they might be (though he'd kill to find out!).

More importantly, it was time for the people of Mannahatta to learn the facts behind the destruction of the Fortune Teller's door. Of course, it would not do to mention the *real* reason behind it all. That wouldn't be particularly helpful to the war effort. Instead, it would make for a better story if he led with the headline MUNSEE SAVAGES DESTROY FORTUNE TELLER DOOR, BUT NOT BEFORE SHE CURSES THEM AS EVIL! It might not be the truth, Hearst thought, smiling wickedly as he sent his flies out to find more fuel for his fire, but then again, the truth was whatever his paper said it was.

Night had fallen by the time Rory, Bridget, and their friends returned to Inwood Hill Park. Plopping down next to a tree near her mom's body, Bridget watched Rory and the Rattle Watchers discussing what the Fortune Teller's words—"Your blood will show you the way"—might mean. More importantly, she wondered why the Fortune Teller wanted to talk to Rory at all. Everything was getting more and more complicated and it was making her head hurt.

She glanced over at her flesh-and-blood body, lit on one side by the flickering orange flames of the fire and on the other by the otherworldly white light of the shell pit. The minute they'd returned, she'd tried to blow her soul back into her real self again—and again, she couldn't make it happen. She followed all the steps that used to work when she was taking her paper body out for joyrides over the summer. She leaned over her own mouth, closed her eyes, and blew as hard as she could. But instead of finding herself back in her real body, she remained stuck in paper. Something was holding her back, like when she got her jacket caught on the doorknob. And the scary bit, the little secret she wouldn't tell anyone, was that a tiny part of her didn't mind. After all, how could she help her mother back in her little-girl body? She needed to be strong, and her paper-and-wood body was almost invulnerable. She'd learned to live with the pushing of her soul, the feeling that she was about to explode at any minute. She could hold herself together and be Malibu Death Barbie a little longer—she'd do it for her mom.

What she really needed was a sword. She'd lost her last one, the fabled Buttkicker, under Tobias's bank. Maybe now was the time to make herself a new one. Liking the idea, Bridget pushed herself to her feet and walked into the trees, Tucket padding along behind her. She scoured the forest floor for a suitable piece of wood. Though the last Buttkicker had been made out of cardboard, this one needed to be stronger. Starlight shone dimly through the trees onto the ground before her, making it hard for her to pick out good specimens. But finally she happened upon the perfect branch. Leaning over to pick it up, she suddenly tensed as voices drifted past her on the wind.

Deciding to investigate, Bridget crept through the trees toward the voices, with Tucket by her side. Reaching the source, she realized she was listening to the hushed words of her own brother and Soka. Glancing through the trees, she spied them in a little hollow, talking in quiet tones. She knew she shouldn't eavesdrop, but curiosity got the better of her.

"Don't tell on me," she whispered to Tucket, and leaned in to hear what her brother and Soka were saying.

"You've been a little . . . distant," Rory was saying. "And I don't understand why. I like you, you know? And I thought you kinda liked me, too. And you're not feeling well, so I, uh, thought I could, I don't know, be there for you or something . . ." Rory trailed off, kicking at the ground in embarrassment. Bridget wanted to clap. Her idiot brother was finally telling Soka how he really felt! This was awesome!

"I do . . . I do like you," Soka replied. She stared miserably at her feet. "It is just . . . there was this boy in the park . . ." Bridget's heart sank. *No! Don't mention him!*

"What boy?" Rory asked, his eyes flashing.

"No, it wasn't like that," Soka reassured him. "His name

was Finn and he was our guide. He . . . he died protecting me. I didn't ask him to, but he did it anyway. And it hurts me to think about it. And if I get too close to you and something happened to you . . . I couldn't bear it."

"So what are you saying?" Rory asked, looking so sad Bridget wanted to burst out of the trees and give him a hug.

"Can we just be friends?" Soka asked, finally looking up at him. "That is all I can give you right now. I'm sorry."

Bridget's heart sank again. "Of course," Rory said, too casually, trying to save face. He reached out and shook Soka's unresisting hand. "Friends. You got it." With that, he strode away, quickly, eyes blinking away the tears. Bridget wanted to kick Soka with her steel-tipped boots. Even she knew that you couldn't protect yourself from love. Either you loved or you didn't. And as Soka leaned against a tree, tears running down her face, Bridget knew that the Indian princess loved him. She thought about giving her comfort, but she didn't think Soka would welcome it right now. Instead she headed back to camp, leaving Soka behind to grieve for her lost love.

In his dream, Rory was floating high above the city. The cloudy night sky shone with the reflected glow of the millions of glittering lights spread out beneath him. The city was a bonfire, the buildings ablaze in a fire that never flickered out. He had seen it many times before, but still the beauty took his breath away.

He suddenly realized that he wasn't floating at all; his feet stood upon something solid, even though he could see right through to the streets far below. A memory tugged at him: he had been in this place before. Turning, he saw the huge mirrored spire of the Chrysler Building right behind him. He *had* been here before, with Hex and Bridget, only then it had been day. It felt like a lifetime ago. He gazed uptown, toward the park. Whereas before it had been covered in an impenetrable blue glow, now he could see through to the darkened trees and faint lamplights that lined the winding paths. A feeling of accomplishment washed over him. At least he had succeeded at something.

"Enjoying the view?" a dry voice said behind him. Rory spun to see the man with the black eyes sitting atop the spire. He looked like a dark angel watching over the city; it made Rory's spine shiver.

"Why are you here?" Rory asked, taking a step back. "Did you bring me here?"

"Watch your step!" the man with the black eyes warned him. "It's quite a drop."

"This is a dream," Rory shot back, though he stopped in his tracks. "I can't get hurt in a dream."

"So you know everything about dreams, do you?" The man with the black eyes looked amused. He leaned forward. "I've met people like you before, who knew everything about what can and can't happen in dreams. They soon discovered how little they really understood. For many, it was the last lesson they learned."

Rory remained still, refusing to let the man see him flinch. "Are you trying to frighten me? Is that how you get your kicks? You're just a bully."

"Aaron Burr took you up here, did he not?" The man with

the black eyes gazed out at the glowing city. "He never knew where this little lookout sprang from. It never occurred to him that I created it. He would have been too frightened to step foot out here if he had known that. He should have guessed. This is *my* city. Most if its wonders stem from me. Avoiding my touch here is as futile as trying to swim without getting wet. I am everywhere, everything."

"Then why are you bothering with me?" Rory asked.

"Even gods enjoy having their work appreciated," the man said. He waved out at the city. "Is it not grand?"

"You didn't create any of this," Rory shot back. "It's not yours. It's ours. We created you! You answer to us!"

"Do I?" the man with the black eyes asked. "Then why are you afraid to move?"

"What do you want?" Rory replied, trying not to shake. The man's deep, dark eyes were burning into him, making him want to step away, which he dared not do.

"See all the little lights!" The man with the black eyes pointed toward the East River. Rory could see hundreds of what appeared to be tiny torches moving toward the water. They were crossing a small bridge, which led to Queens, but instead of going the entire way, the torches were leaving the bridge halfway across, exiting onto a long, thin island that lay between the two boroughs. The man with the black eyes sounded almost gleeful. "Those are my people. My spirits. My gods. I have called and they have answered. They go to join me on Roosevelt Island, where I am readying my army. I've set up a war camp in the remains of the old smallpox hospital. Fitting, isn't it? People believe that decrepit old place is haunted, and now it truly is! That cursed place will soon overflow with my faithful warriors. It is not long before my war will begin. Look at all of them. You can't hope to stop such an army."

"It's very impressive," Rory admitted. He didn't know what else to say; the sight of all those torches turned his stomach. The man with the black eyes sprang to his feet, hopping down onto Rory's invisible walkway. He looked almost angry.

"Why does she want to see you?" he demanded, striding toward Rory. Rory wanted to back away, but he was afraid to fall. The man stopped a few feet away. "The Fortune Teller never takes sides. That is not her function. Why would she call for you?"

"I don't know," Rory admitted.

"You will never find her," the man with the black eyes spat. "My army is forming as we speak and soon my dream city will be a reality. You can't stop that. You never could."

"But you're here, trying to scare me again," Rory replied, working up his courage. "So I must be able to do something."

"You're nothing, you hear me!" The man covered the rest of the ground between them in a heartbeat, his eyes boring into Rory as his hot, rank breath threatened to suffocate him. Under the onslaught, Rory took an involuntary step back, and his foot passed through nothingness. Helpless, he stumbled backward and then he was falling, watching the man with the black eyes float away as he plummeted to his death on the busy streets below—

Rory, wake up!"

Rory slowly opened his eyes to the sight of Bridget's paper

face leaning over him. He knew he had dreamed again, and he knew it was important to remember the dream, but try as he might, it slipped through his fingers. Frustrated, he focused on his sister, who looked worried. He soon found out why.

"There's someone in the bushes!" She was clutching her new sword, which had the words BUTTKICKER 2 written on the side in charcoal.

"Since when are you afraid of people in bushes?" Rory said, yawning.

"I'm not kidding! We need to make sure it's not a spy or something!"

Sighing, Rory sat up. Glancing around, he could see that the Munsees were sleeping over by the cave, and the Rattle Watchers and Fritz were bunked down by the tree line. Rory knew he should wake someone up, but a suspicion had popped up in the back of his head. The bodies of his mother and Bridget lay on the other side of the shell pit. Bridget pointed past them into the trees.

"I saw it over there."

Nodding, Rory slipped into the trees, deciding to stay in the forest as he moved around to the other side of the pit. Bridget followed close behind. As he came around to the other side, he peered into the darkness at the tree line. By the light of the shell pit, he could just make out a shadow crouched down at the base of an elm tree, gazing out at the bodies lying prone before the pit. Moving very carefully, Rory sneaked forward, Bridget right behind. He accidentally stepped on a twig, sending out a snap that sounded like a gunshot in his ears. The shape heard, looking over in their direction. The light fell on its face and Rory's heart began to pound. It was just as he suspected. The figure waited a moment, then, satisfied it was alone, returned to its silent vigil.

Rory pulled Bridget back out of earshot of their visitor.

"What's he doing here?" he asked. Bridget's face was suddenly pale.

"He looks just like his picture . . ." she muttered.

"I guess we should go talk to him," Rory said, but was surprised when Bridget backed away.

"I don't wanna!" she whispered. "Look at me! I'm not even human. I don't want him to meet me like this."

"We're going," Rory said. "Come on."

"No!" Bridget held back. "You go talk to him. Please?"

"Okay. But I think you're being ridiculous."

"Don't care," Bridget muttered. Rory felt a wave of pity for his sister. She didn't even know if she could ever go back to her normal body again, and now this. He'd hide behind a tree, too.

Taking a deep breath, Rory left his sister in the trees and approached the shadow. Once he came within earshot, he purposefully stepped on some more twigs. The shape turned, stiffened, then relaxed.

"I won't be here long," it said.

"You don't have to go, Dad," Rory said softly. "No one's coming to get you."

"They will, soon enough," Peter Hennessy said, his eyes fearful. "I just wanted to see for myself . . ." A tear ran down his cheek as he glanced at his wife's body. "I did this. This is my fault. I never should have entered her life."

"It's my fault, Dad," Rory told him. "I was the one they were looking for. And she paid the price."

"This started long before you were ever thought of, son," Mr. Hennessy admonished him. "I started it when I married her. I started it when I caught a glimpse of her reading down by the river. I started it the minute I crossed Kieft and didn't kill Buckongahelas like I was told. Actually, it was way before that, to tell the truth."

"How old *are* you, Dad?" Rory asked, risking the question that wouldn't leave him alone. Mr. Hennessy glanced away, staring back out at his wife as he avoided the question.

"Has Sooleawa figured out a way to heal them?"

With a start, Rory realized that his father thought Bridget was also at death's doorstep. He knew he should tell him the truth, but a perverse piece of him, the part that was still angry, decided not to. He shook his head. "She doesn't know the magic, she said. Her mother used to know, I guess, but she's long gone."

Mr. Hennessy nodded absently, even as his shoulders slumped at the news. "Alsoomse was very powerful. She saw right through me."

"Why won't you tell me anything about you?" Rory asked.

"There are things in my past." Mr. Hennessy couldn't look Rory in the eye. "Things were . . . done to me. They broke me, pure and simple. I am broken. I can't go through it again. And I won't let you go through it, either! You have to stay safe. You're all I have left now."

Rory couldn't believe his father would give up on his mom so easily. He could barely think, he was getting so angry. "Well, I'm going to see the Fortune Teller to find out what I can do to help them. The first door in the Tenements was destroyed, but there are two more and we're going to find one."

"No!" Rory was shocked to see that his father's face had turned white. "The Tenements door was the first door, the easiest to find. And her price there was high enough. But the price of the other doors is even higher. You don't understand what she'll require of you. It's too steep! You can't do it!"

"How do you know so much about it?" Rory asked.

"Promise me you won't go looking for the Fortune Teller," his father begged him.

"I can't just stand aside and let Mom die!" Rory hissed. "Do you know where the other doors are? You've got to tell me if you do."

"Rory, you have to listen to me. You can't risk it. We'll find another way to help your mother . . ."

Rory was so angry at all the cryptic hints and hidden meanings. Why couldn't someone just tell him the truth? His stomach started to hurt the more he thought about it. Soon it was burning, and he almost doubled over with the pain. It was as if the copper spear Caesar Prince had thrown into the Sachem's Belt had pierced his stomach after all.

Mr. Hennessy noticed something was wrong. "Are you all right, Rory?" he asked.

Rory felt the burning flow through his body. He tried to ignore it, wiping the sweat from his brow. Refusing to be distracted, he tried his question one more time. "Dad, you've got to tell me if you know. Where is the Fortune Teller's door?"

The burning intensified as his father opened his mouth, undoubtedly to refuse again. But something completely unexpected popped out.

"The Little Red Lighthouse," Mr. Hennessy said, then blinked, shocked. A look of horror spilled across his face.

"Why did I say that? I didn't want to say that!" He began to back away.

Rory was lost. "Are you serious?"

Mr. Hennessy stood still for a moment, a deer caught in headlights, and then, without saying another word, he turned and ran into the woods. Still shocked, Rory let him go.

Bridget ran up behind him.

"Where is he going? What did you say to him?"

"I don't know," Rory replied, dazed. "But I think, for the first time, he just told me the truth."

THE LITTLE RED
LIGHTHOUSE

skook slithered through the underbrush in the early morning light, taking care to stay as quiet as possible. Before Kieft sent him north, he'd been keeping watch from afar on his people in the park. He knew he'd been cast out for the games he'd played, but it did not bother him. He did not feel lonely. He felt mysterious—he knew secrets no one else did, deep secrets most would never dare to unearth. One day he would be the last of his people—Kieft had promised him. He wished every moment for that blessed day to come; he would then hold the secrets of an entire race. That thought made him shiver with pleasure.

Shorakapkok—that was what his people had called these woods hundreds of years ago. Askook could remember coming to this trading camp as a young boy, collecting wampum and other fine things in exchange for the copper his father had amassed from the southern Lenape tribes. Few Munsees had actually lived on the island back then. It was far too hilly to easily grow crops. Instead, they all came together on Mannahatta to trade. Askook remembered watching his father with pride as he skillfully bartered with the men of other tribes. And when the newcomers came, even better opportunities arose. But Askook's father refused to trade with the newcomers, mistrusting their insatiable need for fur and land. It didn't matter. In the end, his father had everything taken from him—a Dutch soldier shot him for his wampum, simply grabbing for himself what the old man had refused to sell. And Askook could not blame the soldier. His father had been foolish and stubborn. Askook did not make the same mistake. He'd traded and sold everything he could—land, fur, slaves, everything. He became famous among his people for his underhanded deals. They changed his name to Askook, and though they meant it as a slur, he took the name with pride. You did not tread upon a snake. A snake had the power to make you watch your step. And the notoriety of his name grew, as did his stature. So what if they did not trust him? They still came to him when they were in need. Just as Kieft had come.

Askook moved through the trees of a Shorakapkok much changed from those early days. Now they called it Inwood, a name with very little power. But these trees still trembled with memory. This was where Wampage had spent the past century and a half, Askook was sure of it. He fingered his knife—already imagining what taking Wampage's life would feel like. Goose bumps rose upon his skin as he moved farther into the forest. Something powerful waited up ahead, he could feel it

Then he spied movement through the trees. Askook slid behind a tree before he could be seen, glancing around the trunk at the source of the disturbance. It was the figure of a man sitting alone in the shade of a giant rock, sniffling to himself. He looked familiar . . . Askook crept closer, trying to catch a glimpse. The man turned slightly, and the early morning light fell upon his face. Askook repressed a gasp. *Him! Here?* All his plans flew away as he quickly turned to run back to his master. Everything was different now that the traitor had returned . . .

Rory and his friends left the shell pit at first light, though not everyone would be making the journey to the lighthouse. Wampage had gathered up his dogs, sadly informing Rory that he could put it off no longer—he had to return to his people in the park. Both Rory and Bridget were frantic at the idea of leaving their mother unprotected, but Wampage suggested they ask Tucket to stand guard. The large dog now happily sat at Mrs. Hennessy's feet, ready to fight off anyone who might try to hurt his masters' mother.

So it was without Tucket that Rory, Bridget, Fritz, and the Rattle Watchers made their way south along the Hudson River toward the George Washington Bridge, in whose shadow lay the Little Red Lighthouse. The morning sun shone brightly over their heads, peeking through the trees that lined the path. The beauty of the day, along with the hope that they were about to find a cure for his mom's illness, lifted Rory's spirits. Bridget skipped along at his side, throwing leaves at her brother when he wasn't looking. Alexa laughed, taking the opportunity to tickle Simon's ear with a twig, almost forcing the newly minted god to drop his tea set. Lincoln practiced his boxing moves on the arm of a patient Nicholas while Fritz rode at their feet, a serene look on his face. Even Soka, who still had not shaken her ill look, seemed peaceful as they walked beneath the tall trees.

They reached the top of the hill near the bridge, and finally caught sight of their destination below. The Little Red Lighthouse seemed almost doll-like—a tiny, fire-engine-red tower nestled beneath the soaring steel girders of the giant George Washington Bridge. The lighthouse had a long history on Manhattan. The brightly painted tower had been built in 1880 on Sandy Hook, a small piece of New Jersey that "hooked" out between the ocean and New York Bay. Moved in 1921 to the spot where the majestic GW Bridge would soon be erected, the valiant little light warned ships away from the shore until it was decommissioned after World War II. Rory and Bridget, like many kids, had been introduced to the lighthouse by the children's book written about it, and their mother had taken them to visit the old building when they were younger. Rory would never have dreamed that such a beloved, whimsical structure could house someone like the Fortune Teller. Even now, part of him doubted it. A small green park nearby led right up to the river's edge, and the path that cut through it branched off, leading past the lighthouse door like a circular driveway. They stood atop the hill for a moment, making certain there were no nasty surprises waiting for them.

"Looks all clear," Nicholas announced. But as they made their descent, Rory felt his good mood begin to melt away. Even though the lighthouse was so bright and cheery, something about it made him uneasy. Glancing at his friends, he noticed the same worry on their faces.

"Why do I feel like running away?" Bridget asked nervously. "It's just a silly little red building!"

"It is a place of power," Soka replied, her face solemn. "This is no tower of whimsy."

They were closer now, and the shadow of the bridge fell upon them, blocking out the sun. Rory shivered, though he wasn't cold. A cast-iron fence surrounded the lighthouse, as if it needed to be contained. The air grew dense and oppressive as they drew near, as if someone or something were trying to warn them away. The bright red lighthouse now seemed less like a toy and more like a trap—a gingerbread house in the forest with a witch inside waiting to gobble them up.

They stopped in the shadow of the lighthouse, pulling in close to decide what to do.

"I don't think we should all go," Alexa said. "Some of us need to keep watch for enemies, in case Kieft discovers where we are. I'll stay out here."

"Me, too!" Simon jumped in. "That fat lady didn't tell me I had to visit."

"I should go in alone," Rory suggested. "If the price is as high as my dad said, I don't think any of you would want to pay anyway."

"I'm coming," Soka said firmly. Rory glanced at her then looked away. Though he refused to dwell on it, her rejection still stung. "I will pay any price."

"You can't leave me behind!" Bridget piped up. "Someone has to watch your back!"

"I'm coming," Fritz said, in a tone that brooked no argument.

"And I'll represent the rest of us," Nicholas said. Lincoln looked like he wanted to protest, but one look from Nicholas made him close his mouth. "There's no use risking more than we have to. Bang on the door if there is trouble. Or come in after us, if you have to."

"We will," Alexa said. She walked over to the cast-iron fence and fiddled with the padlock. After a moment the lock sprang open and the fence swung out. "Good luck."

His stomach rolling, Rory strode through the open fence and up to the lighthouse door. Bridget stepped up on one side and Soka on the other, while Fritz rode Clarence at his feet. Taking a deep breath, Rory reached out and pulled the door open. Pitch black waited on the other side. Pushing down his fear, Rory took a big step forward, into the darkness . . .

And immediately began to cough as smoke filled his lungs. Was something on fire? Waving his hand in front of his tearing eyes, he struggled to clear the air around him.

"Who are you!" a voice demanded. Finally able to see, Rory was shocked to find himself in a dark room dominated by a round table with a mound of brightly colored chips piled up in the center, lit only by a single lightbulb hanging above. The room was far too wide to be part of the little lighthouse, so where were they? The smoke, he discovered, came from the smoldering cigars sticking out of the mouths of the five men sitting around the table. Each held cards in one of their hands. Unfortunately, in their other hands each brandished a gun, pointed Rory's way.

"I said, who are you!" One of the men, dressed in a silk suit with a black tie, stood up, his gun trained on Rory. "Did the Gambinis send you? How did you get down here?"

"It's just a bunch of kids!" One of the other guys spoke up, grinning. He pushed back his newspaper-boy cap. "You come by to learn poker from the masters? It's a thousand just to sit in, you know. You got that kinda money?"

"I popped my first cop when I was only a little squirt," the first man said, his gun never wavering. "You can't trust 'em just 'cause they're kids."

"Then waste 'em so we can get back to our game already," a third man said, his eyes wandering over toward his neighbor's cards.

"Hey, don't waste us!" Bridget cried by Rory's side. "I love poker! The pretty black flowers are my favorites!"

"Enough of this," the first man said, his finger curling around the trigger. Rory flinched, waiting for the crack of the gun.

"Hold on, Tony," a female voice called out. Into the dim circle of light strode a tall, graceful woman in a long, slinky red dress. She held a long cigar in one hand and a pack of cards in the other. She was very beautiful, in a dangerous way. As she came closer, Rory realized he recognized her. Though she was thin and lithe where the other had been fat and lumbering, this woman was the spitting image of the Fortune Teller. She nodded toward him, turning to the men. "I've been waiting for this one. Be a dear and give us a minute, will you? That means all of you. We can finish the game in a bit. Don't worry, no one will peek at your cards, I promise!"

To Rory's surprise, all five men put away their guns without protest and marched up a concrete staircase in the back, disappearing through a door at the top. The Fortune Teller didn't even bother to watch them go.

"Rory Hennessy," she purred. "So lovely to see you."

"Where are we?" Bridget demanded. "This doesn't look like the inside of a lighthouse!"

"This is my spot," the Fortune Teller said, waving a languid hand to encompass the smoky room. "My little slice of heaven.

Come in through the door at the top of the stairs, and you sit in on the hottest high-stakes poker game in town. But enter by the door you five just stepped through . . . well, the stakes get even higher. There's no limit to what you can gamble away."

"Is that what we have to do?" Fritz asked. "Gamble?"

"You're no stranger to gambling, are you, Mr. M'Garoth." The Fortune Teller winked at him. "Now, winning, that's another matter entirely."

"I don't understand," Rory said. "Why did you call me here?"

"Well, that's a different story," the Fortune Teller replied. She reached over and picked up a box from the table. "Cigar?"

"That's disgusting!" Bridget declared. "Smoking is for losers!"

"Very true." The Fortune Teller smirked, setting the box back down. "That's why these are so popular among my clientele." She took a long puff of her cigar. "So why have I called you here, Rory Hennessy? Well, you have a question to ask, don't you? Of course you do. Normally, when someone enters through the lighthouse door, wishing to ask me something, they have to play one of my games of chance. The more random the game, the higher the stakes. Your father, for example, played me in a game of blackjack. He beat me, but only barely."

"What did he want to know?" Bridget asked excitedly.

"You will have to ask him that," the Fortune Teller replied.

"What would he have lost if you'd won instead?" Nicholas asked.

"His firstborn child." The Fortune Teller pointed a long

finger right at Rory. "Which would have been you." Bridget gasped, grabbing her brother tightly by the waist as the others gave him a shocked look.

"No wonder he was against you coming here!" Fritz declared, shaken. "So if we have questions . . ."

"You will have to make a wager and win," the Fortune Teller finished for him. She shrugged. "I'm told it's a worthwhile bet, at least by the winners. The losers . . . well, they are not so enthusiastic."

"So I have to beat you in a game?" Rory asked, confused.

"Well, you are a special case," the Fortune Teller admitted. "Your way has been paid in advance."

"By who?" Rory asked, taken aback.

"By a Dutch gentleman with a very keen eye for cards," the Fortune Teller replied ruefully. "He was a God of Justice, I believe."

"Adriaen!" Nicholas guessed and the Fortune Teller nodded. "Adriaen van der Donck beat you for Rory's question?"

"So he said. Not Rory, specifically, but rather the next Light to ask for my help. It was a little while ago, you see, and he did not know how much time would pass."

The others marveled over Adriaen's prescience, but something about this didn't sit quite right with Rory. He spoke up. "But you called for me specifically down in the Tenements. How did you know that *I* was Adriaen's Light?"

"The time had arrived, that's all," the Fortune Teller said, but her eyes glanced away and Rory could tell she was hiding something. Before he could ask what, Soka stepped forward.

"What must I wager to have my question answered?" she asked.

"Soka, no!" Rory blurted out. "Who knows what she'll demand if you lose!"

"That is not your concern, Rory," Soka said, not looking at him. She focused on the Fortune Teller. "My magic has become hard to control and I need to know what I can do. My people need a strong *pau wau* to stand beside my mother in the days ahead and I will risk anything for that."

"I need to know how to save my city," Nicholas announced, stepping forward as well. "No price is too great for that."

"What can I do to help both Rory and my home?" Fritz spoke up. "I know how to play gin rummy, by the way."

Rory watched the Fortune Teller's eyes light up as his friends offered to play her games. He didn't trust her, not one bit. It wasn't fair that he would get a free answer to his question while his friends risked so much for theirs. He felt like there was a larger game being played here and he couldn't just blindly go along with it. When the Fortune Teller looked at his friends, he saw greed and hunger in her eyes. But when she looked at him . . . he caught a glimpse of hope. He realized the Fortune Teller wasn't quite as impartial as she seemed. And that gave him an idea.

"You said the more random the game the higher the stakes, right?" Rory asked. "So what is the most random game?"

"There is no need for your friends to take such chances," the Fortune Teller answered, her tone light but her eyes sharp. "I have plenty of games. I believe I even have Boggle lying around here somewhere."

"How about flipping a coin?" Rory asked, pulling a quarter out of his pocket. "It doesn't get any more random than that, does it?"

"No, it doesn't," the Fortune Teller replied warily.

"What would I lose if I called for heads and it came up tails?" Rory asked, tossing the coin in the air and catching it.

"Your life," the Fortune Teller whispered, worry crossing her face.

"Those are pretty high stakes," Rory said nonchalantly. "So you would have to wager a lot on your end as well, am I right? Say an answer to each of our questions? That seems fair if I win the coin toss, doesn't it?"

"Rory!" Fritz cut in, nervous. "There is no need to be foolish."

"*I* will flip the coin!" Soka cried. "You won't do it for me!"

"Rory, don't you do it!" Bridget yelled at him, reaching for his arm. He pulled away, his eyes on the woman in red.

"You don't have to flip it at all," the Fortune Teller said, frowning. "Your way has been paid. Let the others play their games and earn their answers on their own."

"No, I think this is the best wager I can make," Rory said, ignoring the cries of his friends. He tossed the coin into the air and caught it, slapping it against his wrist but not revealing which side was up. "Shall I call it? Or will you?"

A hush fell over the room as the Fortune Teller stared at him. A low moan slipped out of Bridget's lips as she looked up at her brother in anguish. The tension crackled as everyone waited on the woman in red. Finally, a rueful smile flashed across her face. "All right, Rory Hennessy. You win. Put away the coin. I will answer their questions."

"What?" Bridget asked, confused. "But nobody called it."

"Rory was too valuable to risk," Fritz said, snapping his fingers as the truth dawned. "He bet that you wouldn't *let* him bet his own life!"

"And he was right," the Fortune Teller replied, a bit testily.

"But why?" Bridget asked, still lost.

"Because someone else is interested in Rory's mission," the Fortune Teller said. She held up her hand before Rory could speak. "There is no wager that can get me to reveal who that is. You will have to discover their identity on your own. But they need you to finish what you've started."

"So you'll answer each of our questions?" Rory asked, trying not to sound too proud of himself.

"I will answer them all together, because they are linked," the Fortune Teller said, taking a long puff of her cigar. "You want to know how to save your mother. You also want to save the city from destruction. The way to both of these lies with the treasure of Willem Kieft."

"I knew it!" Bridget exclaimed. "But it's gone! We were in the cave where he'd hidden it and there was nothing there anymore!"

"It's only been moved," the Fortune Teller replied. "Kieft has good reason to keep it hidden and his Munsee ally has been instrumental in making certain no one stumbles upon it. Soon after the Trap fell, the two of them moved the treasure to a secret, ancient place, where Kieft hoped no one would ever find it."

"Where?" Rory asked. The Fortune Teller smiled.

"If I sent you directly there, you would surely die. No, you must follow a path laid out for you by your Dutch benefactor, Mr. van der Donck. He did not realize it would lead to Kieft's treasure—he left this trail behind for a different purpose—but if you follow his path, you will find what you seek."

"What path?" Nicholas asked.

The Fortune Teller rose to her full height. "Van der Donck's trail leads through all five boroughs: Bronck's Land, which is now the Bronx, Queens, Breuckelen, which you know as Brooklyn, Staaten Eylandt, which is Staten Island, and, of course, Mannahatta. In each borough you will find a legacy, left behind by your erstwhile God of Justice. You must gather together the pieces of this trust and it will lead you to the root of everything, where Kieft's treasure waits. And his treasure is the key to his downfall."

"And my mom will be saved?" Rory asked.

"Follow this path to the end and your mother will live," the Fortune Teller said. "Her salvation lies in your actions."

"Can't you tell me anything more specific?" Rory asked, but she would say no more. Rory took a deep breath, trying not to become overwhelmed. "So how do I find these legacies?" he asked. "Am I supposed to talk to everyone in the five boroughs?"

"There are signposts, of a sort," the Fortune Teller continued. "In Queens, you must look in the belly of the royal steed. In Breuckelen, you must speak to the Fair Engineer. On Bronck's Land, you must look behind the Beloved. On Staaten Eylandt, you must seek out the Unlucky Patroon. And in Mannahatta, you must find the home of the Swindler. Make certain that the Swindler's home is the last you visit, or you will surely fail."

"What are you talking about, lady?" Fritz demanded. "That

doesn't make any sense! Why would he hide these all over the place?"

"Van der Donck had many enemies," the Fortune Teller told them. "These are powerful secrets he left behind, and such things must be protected."

"So we're supposed to go wandering around all five boroughs looking for these things?" Nicholas asked, incredulous. "The Fair Engineer? The belly of the royal steed? What does that even mean?"

"You have a different task ahead of you, Nicholas," the Fortune Teller told him. "The only way to protect your city is to bring everyone together, including the Munsees and even your brethren, the children of the gods. They need someone to inspire them. It is your job to find that person."

Nicholas nodded. Soka spoke up.

"What about me? What about my magic?"

"Your path lies with Rory, at least for a while," the Fortune Teller told her. "You will find your answers on the way. As will you, Bridget. Fritz, your path will go in many directions, but by the end, if you listen to your heart, you will know where you are needed most."

For a moment there was silence, and then they all began to speak at once, demanding more answers. The Fortune Teller put up one well-manicured hand to silence them. "That's all I have for you. Now, I've got a game to finish. So you're gonna have to get going. Good luck! You're gonna need it . . ."

BEHIND THE BELOVED

The man didn't know where he was. All he could see was black. Was there a bag over his head? He could smell . . . medicine? Decay? He was terrified, but not surprised. He knew his old master would catch up with him eventually. He'd grown careless since his family became ill. He knew he should have stayed away from them, especially after Rory somehow pulled the location of that wretched Fortune Teller door out of him, but even then, he couldn't bring himself to leave. And so he'd allowed himself to be caught by someone he never saw, waking up here in the dark.

Suddenly light flooded in as the bag over his head was pulled away. He was sitting in a grim, dank cell, tied to a chair. Askook stood before him, flicking his knife with his fingernail as he stared down at him. The man began to struggle, trying to break free of his bonds. But then another man stepped into view and the fight drained right out of him.

"I really should have seen the resemblance," the man with the black eyes said, staring down at him intently. "He looks just like you." The man's hands began to shake uncontrollably.

"Please," he whispered, ashamed at his weakness but unable to stop. "Please, don't hurt me."

"I *can* hurt you, you know," the man with the black eyes mused, leaning in to regard him thoughtfully. "I cannot kill you, of course. But I certainly can hurt you. As I'm sure you remember. Do you remember?" The First Adviser pointed a finger at him and waved it.

Suddenly the man began to heave as nausea and sickness washed over him. He leaned forward, vomiting on the cell floor. When he was done, he fell back, exhausted, as tears streamed from his eyes.

"And that was nothing at all," the man with the black eyes said, smiling absently. Askook peered in at the prisoner, fascinated, no doubt wondering how this magic was accomplished. The man with the black eyes leaned in again. "What fun we will soon be having, you and I. I was always able to make you dance, because of our . . . connection."

"I will die first," the man said defiantly.

The First Adviser snorted. "Well, we both know that won't be happening anytime soon," he said. "Though I did assume you'd never come back to Mannahatta, not after you ran off with Buckongahelas. Yes, I knew what you did—such a meaningless gesture, saving that savage's life. It gave me pleasure to know you were out at sea, and working as a lowly sailor, no less. And when I heard you were aboard the *Half Moon*! I almost died laughing. I thought for sure you would stay away. But instead, you snuck ashore and made yourself a little family right under my very nose. And lo and behold, your son turns out to be a Light! Young Rory Hennessy. Oh yes, I've met him. What does he think his father's name is, if I may ask?"

"*Peter,*" the man whispered, staring down.

"Peter Hennessy." The man with the black eyes rolled the words on his tongue. "Very Irish. So unlike you. Well, here we are. Your wife and daughter's bodies lie in Shorakapkok by the wampum pit, sick and dying. Your son is causing no end of trouble. He hasn't learned the lessons I taught you, *Peter.* Perhaps he should take a class with me."

"No," the man moaned. "Leave my family alone!"

"I wish I could," the First Adviser replied, mock sighing. "But somehow your son discovered the second door to the Fortune Teller. I don't know who could have told him *that.*" The First Adviser glared. "I wonder what he learned there? I don't like being in the dark, *Peter.* I need your help. I want to know what your little brat is up to."

"I'd never do anything to hurt him," the man insisted, feeling the fire of defiance flicker in his belly. He braced for the black-eyed man's punishment, but it never came. Instead, the First Adviser shrugged.

"But I have no such qualms," he said. "I could march over to your wife right now and step on her neck without hesitation. The little hound that protects them is nothing to me. Then I'd put my hand over your daughter's nose and mouth until her lungs explode. And when I catch up with your son, I will take great pleasure in burying him in pain. I will destroy every last vestige of humanity in him, until he is my dog, just like you. And you will watch it all."

"Please!" the man cried, disgusted with how quickly he'd fallen apart. "You can't . . ."

"You know I can," the First Adviser said, bending over to

stare at him with those impenetrable eyes. "But I won't. I won't if you help me."

"If I do what you want, I want your word you won't hurt any of my family," the man said, his voice sounding pathetic to his own ears.

"I promise," the man with the black eyes said.

"Promise on the Lady's name," the man insisted. A flash of irritation crossed the First Adviser's face.

"You know I won't be doing that. But you have my word, they won't come to harm as long as you help me. But if you fail me, they will pay dearly for it. Remember that. Now here's what I want you to do . . ."

After emerging from the lighthouse, Rory filled in the other Rattle Watchers on his mission.

"We'll help whenever we can," Alexa promised. "I have Bronx blood, so I can guide you there. Simon has Queens blood—"

"Wait, I'd be guiding them by myself?" Simon asked, his face draining of color. "That sounds a bit risky . . ."

"Don't be such a baby!" Lincoln punched him in the arm so hard Simon staggered. "I wish I could help, but I only have Manhattan blood."

"We'll make sure that there are friends to help you in Brooklyn and Staten Island," Nicholas promised. "And don't worry, Lincoln. We've got plenty to do right here."

"Should we tell the council?" Alexa asked. "This is an important task, after all."

"They'd want to get involved and that could be disaster," Nicholas replied. "We don't even know who can be trusted. No, if we don't want Kieft to hear about Rory's task, we need to keep a low profile. Whitman, my father, maybe a few others. The rest need to be kept in the dark."

"And you need to figure out who should bring us all together," Lincoln told Nicholas. "Maybe Hamilton? Tackapausha?"

"Maybe my dad," Nicholas mused.

"I don't know about your father, Nicky," Simon said. "He's not exactly a diplomatic genius."

"He's getting better," Nicholas protested.

"He called the God of Open-Air Concerts a damned hippie and tried to have him thrown into the Tombs for wearing a poncho," Alexa reminded him.

"So he's a little high-strung," Nicholas admitted. "I'll keep looking. Fritz, we need your help, too. Can you go to your battle-roach brethren and see if they will join our cause? We don't want to lose them to Kieft."

Fritz glanced at Rory, clearly torn, but then he nodded. "The Fortune Teller did say my path would lead me in different directions. But don't worry, Rory. I'll catch up."

Nicholas, Simon, Lincoln, and Fritz took their leave, heading south. Simon called out, "See you in Queens, kiddies!" before they disappeared into the trees. Alexa remained behind, deciding that her father's farm in the Bronx would be the best place for them to start their search. After all, there was a chance he'd left some clues behind.

They traveled north, crossing the Broadway Bridge into the Bronx. As they moved deeper into the borough, Soka fell in beside Rory.

"I've been thinking," she said. "I've got an idea how Kieft's treasure might help your mother."

"How?" Rory asked.

"You remember how Abigail Hamilton found those Munsee spells written on parchment when she stumbled upon Kieft's hiding place in the park? Kieft had been stealing our magic, writing it down for himself. My people have lost much of that magic over the years, but Kieft still has it. Which means there is a good chance that the healing magic of my grandmother, Alsoomse, survives on those pieces of parchment. The spell to save your mother is somewhere in those pages, I bet."

Rory nodded excitedly. "Of course! You can use that spell to save her!"

"Or my mother can," Soka replied, looking away. "If I can't manage it."

"We'll fix you, I promise," Rory said, then regretted his words as Soka's eyes flashed.

"I can look after myself. And I certainly don't need you to risk your life for me, so please stop doing it."

"What are you talking about?"

"You risked your life for me in the lighthouse with your coin-flip game. I didn't ask you to."

"I knew she wouldn't let me bet my life," Rory reminded her, wondering why she was suddenly so irritable. "So it wasn't really a gamble."

"Just . . . don't do it again, okay?" Soka said. She quickened her pace, catching up to Alexa. Rory sighed. He'd never understand women.

They traveled down a busy Bronx street until at last they turned into a small alley. Though the sun was high in the sky, the buildings on both sides left the alley half shrouded in darkness. Alexa turned to face them.

"I better go on alone from here."

"What?" Rory exclaimed. "No! We're going with you!"

"I don't know if Kieft is watching my father's farm, but he probably has somebody out here spying," Alexa explained. "I won't risk it. Please, just wait here in the alley until I get back."

With that, she raced down the alley and disappeared. After a moment Rory sneaked a peek around the corner and gasped. Halfway down the alley, the concrete turned to dirt, the walls melted into trees, and the buildings just faded away into stalks of corn. In the distance, he could see a large manor house set back behind a grove of flowering trees. It was beautiful.

"What now?" Bridget was asking Soka behind him.

"Now," the Munsee girl answered, leaning against the wall, "we wait."

Alexa hurried through the cornfield toward the old manor house, taking care to stay hidden among the stalks. She'd grown up on this land, helping her father with anything he needed, from harvesting the crops to researching the law. It had been a happy home, though a sense of sadness and loss never quite faded. The specter of Marta van der Donck floated above them all and Alexa had never felt as if her mother was far from her, even though she barely remembered her.

Alexa stepped out from the corn into the open to run up to the front door, when the sound of hooves on gravel made her jump. A dozen or so riders on horseback were trotting up the long driveway, led by a handsome young man in a long coat wearing a tricornered hat, out the back of which hung a thin, rakish ponytail. He guided his men up to Alexa, towering over her from atop his well-muscled steed.

"What are you doing here, Van der Donck?" he asked her, his thin voice imperious.

"This is my house," Alexa replied stiffly, strong dislike bubbling up alongside the fear. "And you and your little friends are trespassing, DeLancey."

James DeLancey smirked. "We're merely keeping the peace. In case you haven't heard, more gods have been dying. My Cowboys and I are riding around, making certain no villains are given free rein in *our* borough."

"You and your Cowboys are more likely to be the problem than the solution, James," Alexa informed him. It was true: during the Revolution, the native-born Cowboys, led by DeLancey, had taken great delight in terrorizing the Bronx on behalf of the British. After their deaths, they'd continued their marauding ways in the spirit realm, which often had put them at odds with Alexa's father. She had no doubt who they were working for now, or why they were here.

"Anyone with you?" DeLancey was asking, looking around. Yes, he was definitely searching for someone in particular. "Why are you here, anyway?"

"This is my home," she repeated, trying to keep her cool. "And you are not allowed on my property. Get out before I call the militia. You know Stephanus van Cortlandt would love an excuse to put a bullet in your chest." He gave her a murderous look but she stood her ground, staring him down while his men shifted restlessly. Finally, DeLancey's frown slipped into a mocking grin.

"Fine." DeLancey smirked, turning his horse around. "But I will be back. We're in Kieft's army, you know. We'll protect you from the Munsees whether you like it or not."

With that, he flicked the reins, galloping off down the path, followed closely by the horses of his fellows. Alexa watched them go—her fear only showing in her shaking hands—before turning to race inside the only home she'd ever known.

Alexa ran up to her father's study, heading right for his desk to tear through his papers as fast as she could. But she couldn't find any reference to Swindlers or Fair Engineers or any of it. She didn't understand what any of the clues meant. This was just like her father, she thought ruefully. He loved puzzles and riddles and had no problem solving them in record time. But he was gone, leaving her in charge of the game. And she didn't know how to play.

What had the Fortune Teller said about the Bronx? *Look behind the Beloved*; that was the clue. Alexa had no idea what it could mean. And nothing in her father's papers gave her a hint. She sighed as her hopes deflated: the whole house was a dead end.

Discouraged, Alexa made her way toward the door. But before she could walk out of the study, a portrait caught her eye, hanging next to her father's old easy chair. In the portrait, Alexa's mother was standing in this very room in front of her husband's desk, wearing a beautiful blue dress with a white shawl, and her bright blue eyes seemed to be laughing at some unknown joke. This was the Marta van der Donck Alexa pictured in her head, since her mother had died soon after Alexa was born. Growing up, she'd spent many long hours staring at the portrait, wondering what advice her mother would have given her about whatever problem plagued her that day. She would sometimes walk in on her father sitting behind that huge mahogany desk and just staring at the portrait of his dead wife, tears in his eyes. He'd loved Marta so much . . .

A thought occurred to Alexa. *Look behind the Beloved.* Could it be that easy? Barely able to breathe, Alexa gingerly reached out and lifted up the picture.

Nothing. Not even a small note taped to the back. Just the cold, hard wall. Alexa carefully let the portrait fall back into place. She should have known her father would never be so obvious. Oh well, another dead end.

She kissed the air in front of the portrait and turned to go . . .

Something held her up. She glanced back at the portrait. What was that? Something behind her mother she'd never noticed before, sitting on her father's desk.

"That's impossible," she muttered to the portrait. But still, there it was. A small brown package sitting on the desk in the background. Alexa had spent the past three hundred years staring at this portrait and she'd never noticed it before.

Because it had never been there before . . .

But what did it mean? She'd already searched the desk and found nothing. So where . . . her eyes widened as a thought occurred to her.

"You sneaky bastard," Alexa told her dad, wishing the old

man were around to hear it. "It's *in* the painting! But how can I reach it?"

She had only one option, crazy as it seemed. She reached out tentatively to touch the surface of the painting . . . and her finger sank in up to a knuckle. She shook her head in admiration. The package was *behind* the Beloved, all right. Feeling decidedly strange, she reached farther into the painting, first sinking her fingers, than her hand, then her arm into the art. She took great pains not to touch her mother (that would probably give her a heart attack), but instead reached around her toward the desk. She groped forward and forward, until she was practically half in and half out of the painting, her nose an inch from passing through. For a moment she was afraid she was going to fall in completely, but finally she got a grip on the package. With a quick yank, she pulled it free of the portrait, her heart jumping as she almost brushed against her mother's shawl.

Triumphant, Alexa gazed down at the package in wonder. Tearing it open, she felt a wash of understanding flow over her.

"Hello," she whispered as a smile crept across her face. "I've been looking all over for you."

Bridget was getting bored, sitting around waiting for Alexa to return. And now that the excitement of going on a quest had faded somewhat, she found her mind slipping against her will to thoughts of her dad. She'd spent her entire life daydreaming about the day her father would show up. And then when he does, she's too scared to say hello? What was wrong with her? When her dad ran off like that . . . she was disappointed. She'd thought her father would be more like . . . well, more like Rory. Instead, he was the Road Runner, always on the move. She knew it should make her feel better to know that it wasn't because of her that Dad left, that he seemed to leave everyone sooner or later. But it really didn't.

"I wanna take a look at Alexa's house!" she announced, not wanting to think about her dad anymore. She hopped to her feet, making sure her new sword stayed in her belt. The thing was a lot heavier than its cardboard predecessor, and it kept tripping her up. But it sure looked dangerous on her hip.

"No, Bridget," Rory told her. "You heard what Alexa said. No going anywhere!"

"Don't worry, poopy pants!" she answered brightly, tiptoeing to the end of the alley. "See how careful I'm being? I just want to peek! I won't go skipping down the driveway or anything."

She reached the corner of the last building and stuck her head out to see. Her heart leaped to see the walls fade away into swaying corn. She never thought she'd see anything as pretty as the flowering trees surrounding the stately manor house on the hill. She sneaked around the corner, keeping close to the wall. She'd step into the corn, just for a moment, to see what it was like. Then she'd go back to the others.

She walked right up to the towering stalks, staring up at the tips framed against the blue sky. But before she could take another step, a hand shot out from within the corn and pulled her into the stalks.

"Wha-" she began, before a hand clamped over her mouth.

"*Shh,*" a voice whispered. "There are enemies near. Can you stay silent? Nod if you can." Terrified, she nodded. The hand released her and she spun around to face her assailant.

"You're surprisingly active for such a sick girl, Bridget," Peter Hennessy said, smiling wryly.

"Dad . . . ?" Bridget couldn't have described the avalanche of emotions crashing over her if she tried. Instead, she began to babble in a whisper. "I'm sorry I didn't say hello back at the shell pit. You look a lot like Rory. I'm not really sick, I'm just stuck in this paper body. I'm really good at hopscotch. Are you here to help us? My favorite ice cream is all of them mashed together. Do you have a sword? I just made myself a new one. It's called Buttkicker 2. I like sports, do you like sports? Are you going to leave again?"

"Bridget, please, slow down," her father said. The look on his face made her want to cry. "I'm just happy to see you."

"Me too," she said, hopping in place. "I knew you'd come back, someday. I knew it!"

"Yes, well." Her father looked away. "Thank you for believing in me."

"Why did you grab me like that?"

"Because your friend Alexa is about to have an unpleasant confrontation, and I don't want you to get caught up in it."

"But we've got to save her!"

"Bridget?" Her brother's voice whispered from outside the corn. "Are you in there?"

Her father stepped out of the corn and quickly pulled in Rory and Soka. "Keep quiet!"

"Dad?" Rory looked thunderstruck. "What are you doing here?"

"Alexa's in trouble!" Bridget announced. "And we've got to save her." Pulling out her sword from under her belt, she began marching through the corn toward the house. Her father ran up alongside her.

"No! Those are dangerous men. We need to get away while we can."

"That's not what heroes do, Dad," Bridget informed him. "You should know that by now." They reached the far edge of the corn and peered out. Alexa was stepping out of her house just as a group of riders came galloping down the drive.

"Hey!" Alexa exclaimed. "I told you to get off my property!"

"What were you doing in there, Alexa?" the head rider asked her, pulling up his stallion in front of the house. "You went in and out awful fast."

"None of your business, DeLancey," Alexa retorted, though she was backing up to the door. The one she called DeLancey urged his horse closer as his men fanned out beside him

"I think that it is," he said. "Mine and Mr. Kieft's."

"We've got to do something," Bridget whispered.

"It's too dangerous," both Rory and her father said at the same time. Rory gave their dad a look that bordered on horror. Ignoring them, Bridget stepped out of the cornfield.

"Hey, bozos!" she yelled, and the horsemen all turned. She waved her sword in the air. "Why don't you pick on someone your own size!"

The minute DeLancey's head was turned, Alexa ran forward and swung her arm around, knocking the rider clear off his horse. In a flash, she leaped atop the horse and flicked the reins, riding for the center of the horsemen. She pulled the musket from the saddle and fired it in the air, causing the other horses to rear back and sending their riders tumbling to the ground. She grabbed a suddenly riderless horse's reins, guiding it toward the field where Bridget and her friends were waiting.

As Alexa reached the corn, the horsemen finally regained their feet and reached for their muskets. White smoke erupted as musketballs whistled around them, sending chunks of cornstalk flying into the air. Bridget was thrown back as one hit her in the shoulder, sending her stumbling into the stalks.

"Are you all right?" her father shouted, catching her.

"No problem!" she yelled back. "Just a paper cut!"

"What is *he* doing here?" Alexa demanded, spotting Mr. Hennessy. "Never mind. I've got the first package. It's what I was hoping for. Soka, can you ride a horse?" The Munsee girl nodded and Alexa tossed her the reins of the other horse. "We've got to get out of here, and fast, before they reload and mount up."

She pulled Bridget up behind her as Soka helped Rory up onto the other horse. The sound of galloping hooves grew louder as Mr. Hennessy stood helpless on the ground. Bridget reached down and grabbed his hand.

"I won't leave you behind, Dad!" she yelled. "You can ride with us." Alexa looked like she wanted to argue, but there was no time as Bridget helped pull her dad onto the horse. They barely had time to urge their horse into motion before their pursuers were upon them.

"Where are we going?" Bridget yelled as they struggled to outrace their pursuers.

"The river!" Alexa called back over her shoulder. "There's a small marina down there where we can borrow a boat."

Alexa raced the horse back through the alley and down the side streets of the Bronx, trying to go as fast as they could without tossing someone from the saddle. DeLancey's Cowboys were gaining, and soon musket fire was erupting behind them. Musketballs whizzed by as Alexa and Soka weaved their horses back and forth around the parked cars along the sidewalk. Finally, they turned a corner and galloped into the parking lot of a small marina. A few sailboats sat bobbing at a dock next to a brick boathouse.

They rode right up onto the dock next to the boathouse, where Alexa slipped down off her horse with a grunt. The rest of them followed suit as she handed her gun to Rory.

"Hide behind the boathouse and shoot at anyone who comes into the parking lot."

Mr. Hennessy took the gun away from Rory. "I'll do it. I don't want my son to get shot."

"Fine," Alexa said, giving him a hard look, as if warning him to watch his step. "Then, Rory: you, Soka, and Bridget can help me with this boat!"

Alexa pointed to the nearest sailboat, a small vessel with a single sail. Alexa dropped into the seating area, untying the ropes and hoisting the sail, as Soka, Rory, and Bridget worked on freeing the lines from the dock. A shout alerted them to their pursuers, who, led by a bloodied and angry DeLancey, were galloping into the parking lot with guns held high. Mr. Hennessy immediately opened fire on them, causing them to scatter.

"You're not going anywhere!" DeLancey called out, his handsome face twisted into a bloody sneer. "You're surrounded!"

Alexa climbed back out of the boat. "Do any of you know how to sail?" Mr. Hennessy piped up from his spot by the boathouse. "I do."

Alexa hesitated, then ran over to Mr. Hennessy. "Take the boat and sail them to the north shore of Queens, just south of Rikers Island. I'll make sure that Simon Astor will meet them there." She grabbed the gun from him and quickly reloaded it.

"Aren't you coming with us?" Bridget asked as her father quickly hopped into the boat and sat down by the tiller.

"I don't have the blood to enter Queens," Alexa called back. "So I'm going to draw away as many of them as I can. Rory!" She tossed a package to Rory, who fumbled as he caught it from inside the boat. "I found that behind the Beloved. It's from my father's lost journals. I knew they existed somewhere! But it's not complete—it stops midstory. I think you're trying to find the rest of the pages. When we meet up again, you'll have to tell me what the rest of them say. Now go!"

She ran over to one of the horses, pulling herself up as the Cowboys began to fire on her. Miraculously unhit, she galloped away, firing at the horsemen as she made her break out of the marina and down a side street.

Bridget watched her go as Rory threw the last line into the little boat and pushed it off the dock. She noticed some of the horsemen riding after Alexa, but DeLancey seemed to sense that the more important prize was escaping in the boat.

"Forget Van der Donck and stop that boat!" he cried, leading his men toward the dock.

"Get down!" Mr. Hennessy cried, ducking himself as he guided the boat out of the marina. The Cowboys lifted their guns and fired, their bullets cutting into the sail and digging into the side of the boat. But soon their target was out of range as the small boat floated away, leaving behind the smoke of battle as they sailed on down the river.

INTO HELL GATE

Nicholas sat on the grass, staring out at the park he'd never seen before. It was beautiful—and he hoped it would stay that way. He was in the wilderness known as the Ramble, in the center of Central Park not far from the Munsee village. He sighed. He wasn't feeling hopeful, not after the meeting he'd just witnessed.

Tackapausha had refused to speak to Alexander Hamilton— he still hadn't forgiven his former friend for his betrayal. So the Mayor sent Peter Stuyvesant to negotiate an alliance against Kieft. Nicholas loved his father, but negotiating was not his strong suit. The minute he had sat down with the Munsees, the old man started stepping on toes. He insulted the food, he disparaged their courage, he made it sound like they needed protection. If it wasn't for Abigail reassuring Tackapausha that Stuyvesant was only ignorant, not malicious, any hope for a Munsee-god alliance would have ended there. Peter Stuyvesant seemed to think that he was doing the Munsees a favor by of-fering his help. He didn't seem to understand that Kieft would never stop with the Munsees. They were just the first domino to fall. The black-eyed god was picking up speed now, and who knew how far he'd go.

"Quite a meeting." Buckongahelas stepped out of the trees. Nicholas didn't know Tackapausha's son very well, but what he'd seen he liked.

"Yeah, well, my dad knows as much about diplomacy as he does about dancing. Which is to say, the old man is not graceful."

Buckongahelas smiled. "My father is not much better. I think the two of them will be growling at each other for the next few days. But we don't have days. Would you mind walking with me?"

Nicholas pushed himself to his feet and fell in beside the lithe Munsee. They made their way through the trees, and Nicholas marveled at how easily the sachem's son moved through the foliage. The branches kept whacking Nicholas in the face, but Buckongahelas just flowed past them untouched.

"I wish you could teach me that trick," Nicholas muttered as another branch smacked him in the cheek. "I'm getting banged up back here."

"It comes from belonging," Buckongahelas replied with a slight smile. "I feel the way you do now when I walk through your city streets. That was why I took to the ocean. I didn't feel as battered there. Here we are!"

They stepped out of the trees into a small clearing. To Nicholas's surprise, the space was filled with Munsee Indians, both young and old. Buckongahelas's wife, Abigail, stood at the back, and by her side, to Nicholas's further surprise, were

Wampage and Sooleawa. Nicholas glanced at Buckongahelas in confusion.

"What is this?" he asked.

"My people are worried," Buckongahelas told him. "Soon Tackapausha will come to us with a plan of action, but it is not our way to blindly follow our leaders. We want to know why we should ally ourselves with those who so recently wished for our destruction."

"Should I go get my father?" Nicholas asked, turning. Buckongahelas grabbed his arm.

"No," he said. "There is too much bad history there for my people to listen to his words. We don't trust your people. But you worked to bring down the Trap and Wampage says you are a good man. You are no god, so you have nothing to gain by our extinction. So tell us . . . why should we risk any alliance with your people?"

Nicholas looked out at the crowd. It wasn't his place to speak to them. He was no god. But someone had to step up. "You cannot afford not to," he said, turning to the crowd. "And neither can we." He began to explain about Kieft and his army and what needed to be done to stop him. As Nicholas spoke, he heard murmurs of agreement run through the crowd. At one point he thought he saw Sooleawa smile, though Wampage stared at him as inscrutably as ever. He hoped the Munsees would listen, because he needed them. They needed one another. That was the only way they would survive.

Rory, Soka, and Bridget sat silently watching Mr. Hennessy guide the boat down the Harlem River. Rory didn't know what to say to his dad, who had suddenly shown up out of nowhere. He thought the dark mood in the air was due to the chill between him and his father, but then Soka spoke up.

"I don't know what is going wrong," she said miserably. "I tried to cast a spell back there . . . it was supposed to create a black cloud that would blind those riders and help us escape. I have seen my mother do it a thousand times. But it would not work for me at all . . ." She looked miserable.

"It's okay," Bridget said, reaching behind her to pull a small musketball from her back. "We made it, right? You've saved me plenty of times!" She began to hiccup. "You . . . *hic* . . . you just need to . . . *hic* . . . believe in yourself!" She gave one last hiccup, which turned into a dry heave, and then quickly leaned forward. A few small musketballs flew out of her mouth and landed on the floor of the boat with a clatter. She made a face. "Well . . . that's gross."

Rory couldn't keep quiet any longer. "Why did you come back, Dad?"

His father sighed, lightly steering the boat to the center of the river. "I owe you. You're in a lot of danger and I don't want you to get hurt. I couldn't stop you from seeing the Fortune Teller, but maybe I can protect you from whatever you're trying to do now."

"You don't know the half of it!" Bridget exclaimed. "Rory saw the Fortune Teller and guess what she told us—"

"Bridget!" Rory cut her off. "I'm sorry, Dad, but some trust has to be earned."

"Rory, don't be mean," Bridget told him, shocked, but their dad only nodded.

"I understand," he said. "I won't pry."

"We're trying to find Willem Kieft's treasure so we can save Mom and the whole city!" Bridget yelled. Rory gave her a furious look, but she only shrugged. "I don't want to lie to my father! He's helping us and he deserves to know."

Mr. Hennessy looked away, toward the shore, and Rory thought he saw the sunlight glisten off a tear on his cheek. Rory sighed. "Alexa said this was a piece of Adriaen's lost journal. So let's see what it says." He pulled out the package Alexa had given him and opened it up. On the cover he read the word *one*.

"I wonder what that means," Bridget asked.

"Alexa said something about this being incomplete, so maybe it's the first section," Rory guessed. He turned the page and began to read aloud.

I stare out my window on the second floor of my farmhouse, watching Kieft disappear into the corn. I cannot trust him, I know this. He was evil in life and remains evil in afterlife. But I cannot deny the truth of what he says. We are fading, we newcomers, even as the Munsees remain strong. The land is rejecting us, dwindling us, and our mortals are suffering for it. The Munsees belong here, and have always belonged, but we . . . it pains me to say it, but Kieft is right. We must find a way for the land to accept us or we will be but memories of ghosts, soon to be forgotten.

I was surprised to hear Marta urge me to listen to Kieft.

She hates him as much as anyone. But my wife is shaken by how weak we are becoming, even the old ones like Verrazano. Peter Minuit has disappeared, and we fear he is gone forever. Anyone could be next. We float along atop Mannahatta like a ship on a current. We need an anchor to hold us fast. Kieft believes he has found that anchor. His suggestions do not sound like him—he speaks of rules we must all follow. No god can go where he or she was not remembered to be. No god can kill another god, even by proxy. Any god abandoning the responsibilities that the mortals have given him will be stripped of his power. As rules go, these are not too onerous. Restricting where a god can go binds that god closer to the place where he dwells. Preventing gods from killing one another shows respect for the mortals who created us. They are rules meant to show the land that we honor it. But Kieft never cared for rules, at least not ones he must follow. I worry there is some loophole he will slip through. But his ideas . . . they are sound. If I can but trust the mind that offered them up.

Marta waits downstairs to argue for the plan. She approves of these new rules and sees no other option. Perhaps she is right. But something in the back of my mind is screaming "Do not trust him!" What shall I do? Time runs short and I grow weak. What will become of us? We must decide quickly before we all drift away into nothing . . .

Rory finished reading and looked around in confusion. "What is this?"

"I don't believe it . . ." Mr. Hennessy began, looking shaken.

"What?" Rory asked, leaning in. "Do you know what this is?"

Mr. Hennessy hesitated. "It sounds like the story behind the Agreement."

"What agreement?" Soka asked, her face dark. "An agreement to oppress my people?"

"Not really, though that was sort of how it turned out. It was more of a pact between the land and the newcomers, to help the land to accept them."

"Accept them?" Soka sounded incredulous. "But they were invaders!"

"Everyone is an invader," Mr. Hennessy replied, his voice weary. "The Munsees didn't spring to life on Mannahatta. They traveled here from far off, finally settling here a thousand years ago. We're all newcomers in some respect. But to stay, everyone has to play by the house rules. Even the Munsees made their own agreement, centuries upon centuries ago. It was that pact that they called upon to survive when their own people were driven away. And when the newcomers arrived, they had to negotiate their own contract."

"So those rules, like the blood and the fact that no god can kill another god, those aren't natural laws?" Rory asked. "They were negotiated?"

"Sacrifice," Mr. Hennessy said. "Everyone has to sacrifice something. No one is immune, not even the gods. Of course, the Agreement is a big secret among the gods, now. None but the oldest who were there even know of its existence, and they have pushed the memory out of their heads. It is much more comfortable to think of these rules as natural laws, rather than a burden that is accepted for being allowed to exist. I doubt if you asked even Peter Stuyvesant that he would admit to it."

"Who is this agreement with?" Rory asked.

"With the land itself. Think of it as rent that must be paid."

"The gods made an agreement with some dirt?" Bridget asked, incredulous.

"Even the trees and the grass and the mud have a protector," Mr. Hennesy replied, his eyes pained. "We humans aren't the only things that matter, after all."

Rory's eyes narrowed. "How do you know so much about all of this, anyway?"

Mr. Hennessy opened his mouth to speak, but then he spied something in the distance. "Hell Gate!"

"What?" Bridget asked, craning her head to stare down river. "There's an actual gate to hell? Awesome!"

"No, it's that stretch of water up ahead between Wards Island and Queens, where the Harlem River and the East River meet. It's an extremely dangerous passage—thousands of ships have been sunk trying to sail through. If you try to make the passage at the wrong time, the rapids will toss you around like a toy. We need to skirt around it to land in Queens. Hopefully we won't get too close."

Rory could see the turbulent waters now, with swirling whirlpools and angry whitecaps churning in the distance. Mr. Hennessy began to look worried, pulling hard on the tiller to guide the little boat away from the rapids, but they only floated nearer and nearer to the rough water.

"So the tides are not in our favor," he admitted, his voice tight. "It's all right. I'll hold her steady and we'll slip around the edge. I just wish we had a bigger boat." He struggled to hold the tiller still as the turbulent water pulled at them. Suddenly he cried out as the tiller slipped from his hands and the boat swung around crazily, heading directly for the rapids. Rory lunged for the tiller, pushing it back toward his dad, and together they struggled to hold it on course.

"I think we're going to make it!" Mr. Hennessy cried. And for a moment Rory believed him. But then the unthinkable happened—the tiller snapped in two.

The boat spun out of control, sending its passengers flying to the floor. Rory looked down at the broken piece of wood in his hands—he noticed that the base of the handle was riddled with bullet holes. The bullets must have chopped off half the tiller, so it didn't need much more than a push to snap in half.

"Hold on to the boat!" his dad screamed as the sounds of the rushing water grew louder. "No matter what you do, don't let go!"

And with that, the waters swept them into Hell Gate.

Rory clung desperately to the side of the boat as the rapids spun them around like the teacup ride at Disney World. The screams of his fellow shipmates mixed with the pounding roar of the rapids as they all struggled to hold on. Water gushed over the edge of the boat, dousing them in salty spray until they were soaked to the bone. They were at the complete mercy of the waves as they were swept farther into the bowels of Hell Gate.

A large rock suddenly loomed ahead of them, directly in their path. Rory barely had time to scream before the rapids rammed them, sideways, into the jutting stone. Miraculously, the boat's frame held, but the mast didn't fare so well—it splintered on impact.

"Quick, cut the lines or we'll capsize!" his dad cried as the mast began to fall over the side, tipping the little boat. Soka pulled out a knife from her tunic and handed it to Rory before pulling out a second one for herself. Together they sawed frantically at the lines while Bridget hacked at the ropes nearest her with her sword, Buttkicker 2. The mast was quickly swept away once it touched the roaring waters, and soon the lines started to run out. The boat began to dip, still attached by one last rope. Rory had visions of the small sailboat capsizing, trapping them under the waves, where the turbulent current would pull them down to the river bottom to lie forever among all those broken ships. But his dad finally managed to crawl over and cut the last line, freeing the ship from the mast, which had been completely swallowed by the rapids. Rory sighed, but the close calls weren't over yet.

As the rapids tossed them around, they slammed into another rock. Water began to leak into the boat as the sides were breached, and Rory couldn't see how they'd survive. But finally his dad was able to grab hold of the stub of a tiller. He pulled it around with both hands as he tried to guide them past the rest of the rocks and through the rapids. Suddenly they seemed to be hitting fewer rocks. Over and over they seemed to be rushing toward destruction only to have Mr. Hennessy somehow nudge the boat just enough to get them through. For the first time, Rory was actually impressed by his dad. And then, finally, after one last violent dip and spin, they sprang free of the rapids, bursting out the other side of Hell Gate into the calmer waters of the upper reaches of the East River.

Mr. Hennessy, by now knee-deep in the water that was slowly

filling the boat, collapsed back as the boat drifted toward the far shore. Rory was so exhausted he couldn't even remember what they had been talking about before their brush with death. He just lay against the side of the boat as it floated onward to Queens.

THE ROYAL STEED

Nicholas sat in the back of the council room, trying not to worry. As Alexa finished her report on DeLancey's Cowboys' running amok in the Bronx, which duplicated reports from other boroughs, the shell-shocked looks in the faces of the councillors did not inspire confidence. Even his bulldozer of a father seemed uncertain. Nicholas caught Alexa's eye and she shook her head; she could see it, too.

"They look like a bunch of kicked dogs," Lincoln muttered to Nicholas. "They're gods, for goodness' sake. You'd think they'd be a little less wussy."

"They're used to petty little struggles among themselves," Nicholas whispered back. "But half of Mannahatta has followed Kieft to Roosevelt Island. This war will be bigger than even the old battles with the Munsees. So no matter what, they're looking at the end of *something*. And no god wants to see anything end."

"Spirits are rising up on our side as well, don't forget!" Whitman was saying, his characteristic exclamation points ringing out. "And there are many, the silent majority you could call them, who are simply hiding, hoping everything turns out all right. When the real struggle begins, they will join our side!"

"Not when they see these," Peter Stuyvesant said, nodding toward the door. One of his farmhands, Diedrich, strode into the room, dropping three knives into the middle of the council table with a clatter. Nicholas's heart sank as he recognized the evil metal blades—he'd almost been sliced open by one such weapon not long ago. The councillors' faces turned ashen.

"Where did he get these?" Hamilton asked, his voice shaking.

"We pulled them off a group of mobster spirits that were cavorting downtown," Peter said. "Thankfully, they were too drunk to put up much of a fight."

"But I thought there was only one knife and we still have it!" Babe Ruth announced, his round face confused.

"Well, darling, someone has managed to make a couple more," Mrs. Parker said drily.

"Are we sure these are really god-killing knives?" James Bennett asked.

"More certain than I would ever want to be," Peter replied. "The mobsters were boasting about a murder they'd committed earlier that day. I pulled a locket off of them, myself. I destroyed it, of course; we're lucky no one thinks to put the lockets on. At least not yet. But it's coming if we don't do something soon."

"Three valuable knives given to a couple of small-time crooks?" Mrs. Parker mused. "What is Kieft doing?"

"He's making certain that chaos reigns," Hamilton said. "He must be passing these out to every spirit who wants one. The fear alone will drive people to his side."

"But he could destroy Mannahatta forever!" Whitman said. "Why would he want that?"

The councillors erupted in frightened chatter as they tried to come up with some reason for this wanton destruction. Nicholas felt his spirits sag. He'd been trying to find the one who would inspire them. He'd thought he might have found him among the Munsees, but Buckongahelas had no desire to lead any gods into battle. Then he'd hoped he discover the leader among the council members. But as he glanced around the roomful of frightened councillors, he knew that wouldn't be happening, either. He'd have to continue his search. His eyes rested on the evil knives in the center of the table. He'd better find this guy soon. Because time was running out.

Rory, Bridget, their father, and Soka landed in an industrial yard in the north of Queens, the boat coasting onto shore just before it could sink completely. Simon was waiting for them, grinning.

"Nice ride," he said impishly as he kicked at the ruined boat. He glanced over at Peter Hennessy. "Where did he come from?"

"He showed up to help us!" Bridget exclaimed proudly, and Rory shook his head at the pride in her voice. He couldn't shake the feeling that they would both soon be disappointed by their old man. Simon shook Mr. Hennessy's hand warmly, however, and welcomed him to the hunt.

Simon led them to a group of horses he had tethered to a warehouse door. Heavy bags hung from one horse, and when the stallion shifted, Rory thought he heard the sound of china clinking. Simon was now the God of the Good China, and he couldn't go anywhere without his crockery. The new god untethered their steeds, helping Rory up behind him as Mr. Hennessy and Bridget shared a horse, his sister chatting away excitedly to her father the whole time. Soka took the third horse, looking lonely. Rory caught her eye, but she glanced away; he guessed she was still mad about his stunt at the lighthouse. Even though it had probably saved her from gambling away something important to her. It made no sense to him. He didn't care, he told himself, so emphatically that he almost believed it.

"So, where to?" Simon asked.

"The Fortune Teller told Rory to look in the belly of the royal steed," Soka said. "So I gather we're looking for a horse of some kind."

"But there aren't any kings in Queens!" Bridget exclaimed, then giggled at what she'd just said.

"Maybe a breed of horse?" Simon conjectured. "Royal horses?"

Mr. Hennessy suddenly snapped his fingers. "There is one king in Queens, you know. *Rufus* King."

Simon slapped his forehead. "Of course!"

"Who's Rufus King?" Rory asked.

"He was a bigwig during the Revolution," Simon explained. "Helped write the Constitution and I think he was a senator for a while. But beyond that, the guy never won at anything. He ran for governor, he ran for vice president, he ran for president, and he never won! He had the worst luck. That's why he's the God of Also-Rans."

"He was a pretty bad gambler, too, as I remember," Mr. Hennessy added. "He couldn't come in first at *anything*. Not the guy you want betting on you to win."

"Well, he's probably betting on someone right now, 'cause today is racing day, and he *never* misses racing day." Simon's face brightened. "I love racing day!"

"What's racing day?" Bridget asked.

"You'll see," Simon told her cryptically. "Come on. We've got some ground to cover if we want to beat the starting gun!" He flipped his reins and soon they were galloping away from the river and into the heart of Queens. And what a ride it was!

Back and forth they rode from the mortal world to the spirit world of Queens, weaving in and out of the past. They galloped from the crowded present-day city streets to tranquil open farms with wheat swaying in the fields, through bustling nineteenth-century open-air markets, where peddlers cried their wares while pulling heavily laden pushcarts, and down shadowy back alleys lined with what appeared to be opium dens, with dangerously fragrant smoke drifting from the dark doorways. On and on Rory and his companions rode, threading in and out of the rich tapestry of history, until finally they emerged into a festive sight.

A huge crowd of spirits and gods milled about an open fairgrounds, filling a large grandstand decorated with red, white, and blue bunting. More spirits lined a long dirt road that stretched into the distance. A brass band played old marching songs while vendors selling peanuts and hot dogs worked the crowd. Simon slowed his horse, leading them over to a hitching post behind the stands.

"What is all this?" Rory asked, gazing around.

"The greatest sporting event ever devised by mankind!" Simon enthused, his eyes bright. "The Vanderbilt Cup Race!"

"What do they race, exactly?" Rory asked. "Horses?" Simon gave him an incredulous look.

"Are you joking? Do those look like horses to you?" He pointed across the crowd of people to a cleared-out area on the other side of the track, where Rory saw a group of funny-looking machines.

"Are those go-karts or something?" he asked doubtfully. Simon narrowed his eyes, not pleased with Rory's lack of enthusiasm.

"Those are cars!" he exclaimed. "The greatest cars ever made."

Rory wasn't so sure about that. They certainly didn't look like any cars he'd ever seen. Their chassis were long, rickety, metal cigars with the back third scooped for a riding bench and steering wheel. Each unwieldy body rested on tall, thin, fragile wheels, which resembled bicycle tires. Smoke billowed out from under many of their long hoods. Rory had seen faster-looking vehicles in the Boy Scouts' pinewood derby, where none of the cars were bigger than his hand. But Simon was fanatical in his enthusiasm.

"The Vanderbilt Cup Race was the first—and the greatest—race in the history of racing! Starting in 1904, they invited all the greatest racers in the world to compete. Chevrolet! Mercedes! Fiat! Hotchkiss! They all started here!"

"That's what cars were like in 1904?" Bridget asked, looking askance at the smoky vehicles. "How did anyone live to see 1905?"

"They're built for speed, not beauty," Simon answered, peeved that no one shared his enthusiasm. "Anyway, the race was shut down after a few years because too many spectators died. Hey, they knew what they were getting into when they lined the track, that's what I say! But the race lives on here, and instead of once a year, it's every week!"

"Have you ever raced in it?" Rory asked. Simon looked away, his face pained.

"No," he said. "You have to either be a god or be sponsored by one. And no one would sponsor me. I even built a car of my own–" He cut off, as if he had said too much. "Anyway, I've always wanted to race, if only to show that stupid Willy Vanderbilt that I'm better than he is! 'Cause I am!"

"Are you sure Rufus is here?" Mr. Hennessy asked, putting the focus back on their mission.

"Of course," Simon answered, hopping down off his horse. "I told you, he never misses a race. Come on."

The others dismounted, following Simon into the crowd. Rory began to feel a bit uncomfortable surrounded by so many gods. Mortals were not meant to be around so much concentrated divinity. But he gritted his teeth and said nothing.

"There he is!" Simon shouted, pointing. They pushed their way past the excited spirits, making a beeline for a fat, balding man who was gesturing wildly at another man holding a small pistol. Simon stepped up to him and tapped him on the shoulder.

"Rufus? Busy?"

"Of course I'm busy!" Rufus King shouted back without turning. "I'm trying to prevent that damned Vanderbilt menace from racing in my car! He'll probably crash it! It doesn't belong to him!"

"But he won it from you fair and square at the last race," the man with the starter pistol explained, his weary voice betraying his impatience. "You know the rules: the winner of the race gets to take the car of one of the losers. He chose yours. If you want it, you'll have to win it back. You have another car, right? You lose every race, after all, and you never seem to run out of cars."

"Number fourteen wasn't supposed to be in the last race!" Rufus yelled. "She's never supposed to be in *any* race! I'm saving her for my victory parade once I win the Cup! But my latest driver grabbed the wrong car and it cost me my baby! She is my pride and joy! My steed! She belongs to me!" Rory exchanged an excited glance with his friends at the mention of the word *steed*. He pushed forward.

"Sir, this number fourteen car is your steed? Can we see it?"

"Who are you?" Rufus said, noticing him. "Of course you can't see it. It's mine! Or it will be, again. Hey, come back here!" This last exclamation was directed at the man with the starter pistol, who'd seized Rufus's momentary distraction to make himself scarce. "Now you did it! He got away!"

"Rufus, we need to talk to you," Simon said.

"Young Simon Astor," Rufus exclaimed, noticing the Rattle Watcher for the first time. "Come to ask me to sponsor you again? I may have fired my driver and lost my best car, but I'm not *that* desperate."

"We're not here to race, sir," Rory said. "We just need to look in your car."

"Who *are* you people?" Rufus asked, confused. He blinked, looking closer at Soka. "Aren't you a Munsee, girl?"

"Just talk to us for one moment under the grandstand," Simon said. "We'll explain everything."

Rufus agreed to follow them as they pushed their way through the crowd. Rory was becoming more and more uncomfortable, sweating under the power of all these gods of Queens. Bridget looked fine, however. She must be protected by her paper body, he surmised. If only he were so lucky.

As they pushed past a small group of gods, Rory overheard one of them talking in low tones. "The Munsees are the true menace. They've been killing gods all over Mannahatta. It's only a matter of time before they come to Queens. We need to make a stand now. You bunch have the blood to cross the river. Are you with me, fellas? Or will you let them slaughter our families in their sleep?" Rory burned to hear these lies. He ran up to Simon, who was walking by Rufus.

"There's a guy back there lying about the Munsees," he whispered, pointing. Rufus overheard and grimaced.

"That's Robert Moses, one of Kieft's men. He's been recruiting all over the borough. I don't believe much of what he says, but others do. I'm a staunch supporter of the Munsees, myself. They have as much right to live their lives as anyone, I figure. Well, here we are under the grandstand. What do you want to tell me?"

"Did you know Adriaen van der Donck?" Simon asked. A look of recognition passed over Rufus's face as Simon continued. "Did he give you anything?"

"So you're the ones, huh?" Rufus said, looking uncomfortable. "Yes, he gave me a package, and told me to keep it safe. And I thought I did."

"What do you mean you *thought* you did?" Mr. Hennessy asked.

"It was only meant for my victory lap! So I figured it was the best place to hide it. In plain sight, if you will."

Rory sighed. It was just as he thought. "So it *is* in the car?"

"I hid it under the floor," Rufus said, eyes wide with innocence. "And then that cheat Vanderbilt went and beat me, taking the car as his prize. I just need to win it back."

"Are you a good driver?" Bridget asked.

"Yes," Rufus said, then shrugged. "I mean, I'm okay. And by okay, I mean I'm pretty awful. I usually have a driver, but I had to fire him. Plus he quit. Said I was cursed, since none of my cars ever won. So shortsighted."

"So what do we do?" Soka asked.

"We win the car back!" Simon exclaimed. "And I'll drive!"

"Why don't we just ask to see the car," Rory suggested.

"I know Willy Vanderbilt," Simon told him. "He won't go for it. He's just awful."

"We've got to try," Rory answered, and took off through the crowd toward the cars, leaving his friends to hurry after him. Robert Moses was still telling lies and recruiting as Rory passed him; Rory wanted to do something to expose Kieft's man, but he had no time to dawdle.

Reaching the area holding the racing cars, he marched right up to car number 14. A tall, handsome man in a bomber jacket and jaunty cap was leaning against the hood, laughing with some collegiate-looking friends.

"Mr. Vanderbilt?" Rory said, and the tall man turned to him. "Would you mind if we took a look at your car? It's vitally important."

Vanderbilt didn't even glance at him. Instead, he smiled insolently at Simon, who was running up behind Rory. "Hello, Astor. Come to watch real drivers race?"

"I could mop the road up with you," Simon spat. "If they let me race."

"I wish they *would* let you race, so I could humiliate you in public, rather than just in private like I usually do." Vanderbilt's friends burst out in mocking laughter.

"Shut up, meanie!" Bridget said, her hands on her hips. Rory sighed, not liking where this was going.

"Look, it's a talking doll!" Vanderbilt declared, snorting with laughter. "Where's the string?"

"You shut up and let us look at the car."

"Get out of here, kids," Vanderbilt said, shooing them with his hand. "Go play with your little toys. The big boys are getting ready to race."

With that, he turned his back on them. Rufus and Simon shrugged as if to say, *See?*

Rory sighed. "What if we beat you?" he asked Vanderbilt. The insolent young god turned around, a disbelieving look on his face.

"Excuse me? That could never happen."

"But if it did," Rory continued, "we'd get your car, right?"

"Of course," Vanderbilt replied. "But it's never going to happen."

And he went back to ignoring them. They moved away and

Rory whispered fiercely to Rufus, "Can I drive your car?"

Before Rufus could respond, Mr. Hennessy cut in. "You are not driving that car. You're thirteen years old. You've never driven a day in your life, I bet."

"I'll drive it!" Simon offered. Rufus shook his head firmly.

"I've seen what you've done in practice races," he said. "You are not setting foot inside any of my cars. You're worse luck than I am."

"I'll do it," Mr. Hennessy said. "I've raced my fair share of cars. That's pretty much all I did during the fifties when I was on shore leave." Rufus looked torn, but then gave him a nod, pointing to a car on the outskirts of the clearing. It was painted bright red, with the number 13 on the hood. Simon gave Rufus a look of disbelief.

"*Thirteen?* Could you *make* it any harder on us?" he asked, shaking his head.

"Who's your mechanic?" Rufus asked Mr. Hennessy, ignoring Simon. "Every car needs a mechanic to ride alongside."

"I'll do it," Rory offered, but his father shook his head.

"It's too dangerous. You'll get hurt." He turned to Bridget. "Would you like to ride with me?"

Bridget practically vibrated with excitement. "Really? Can I? Really? Okay!"

Rory couldn't fault his dad for going with the child with invulnerable skin. But he felt disappointed all the same. His father patted his shoulder before walking over to the car with Bridget at his side. Simon walked with them, explaining the nuances of the track to them, leaving Rufus, Soka, and Rory standing off to the side.

"I need to let the scorers know who my driver is," Rufus said, excusing himself to head to the main grandstand. Rory glanced at Soka, who gave him a small smile.

"Those things look pretty dangerous," she said. "I think it's better if you stay right here, where you won't crash and burn to death."

"Nice to know you care," Rory replied, and Soka's smile faltered as she remembered to be angry. Shaking his head, Rory turned to follow after Rufus and grab a seat in the stands to watch the race. Soka followed close behind.

They passed near Robert Moses again, who was busy making his pitch to a new group of gods. Rory began to get angrier. How dare that Moses fellow lie like that, as if it was nothing to distort the facts. His belly began to burn as he thought about it. Why didn't he just tell the truth?

Suddenly the burning in his belly intensified, and he bent over double with the pain. That's when things started to get a little weird.

"I want to use you to curry favor with Kieft so he will give me more power," Robert Moses was saying. His face changed as he heard himself speak, his eyes going wild as his words came out differently than he intended. "I don't really care if the Munsees are a threat, and it's highly unlikely they'll ever leave Central Park, to be honest, but if you show up to fight, then maybe we can kill them once and for all and steal their power." The crowd around Moses began to murmur, not sure what was going on. The burning in Rory's stomach worsened as the press of divinities all around him seemed to feed the fire within. Suddenly other gods began to speak, unprompted.

"I pulled a spark plug in number eleven and then bet against it," one short little god said, looking horrified with what he was saying.

"I kissed a goddess who wasn't my wife!" another god said unwillingly.

"I'm afraid of children!" a tall goddess announced. "They're short and scary!"

"I'm not wearing any underwear!" another god cried, looking mortified even as he said it.

"I'd just as well stab you in the back as help you," Moses said, and then backed away, like a cornered rat. He spotted Rory, and suddenly his eyes narrowed with recognition. Rory was too overcome to react, until Soka grabbed his arm and dragged him away from the circle of truth-telling gods. She pulled him under the grandstand. Rory noticed that she seemed to be holding her mouth shut with her hand.

Rory bent over, breathing deep, until the burning in his stomach dissipated. He nodded to Soka. "It's gone." Soka opened her mouth in relief.

"What were you doing?" she asked.

"I don't know."

"Everyone suddenly decided to tell the truth," Soka pointed out. "Did you make that happen?"

"Well, my belly started to hurt, and I was angry with that hypocrite lying about the Munsees, and the next thing I knew, everyone was telling the truth."

"Have you always been able to do this?" Soka asked. "Or is it recent?"

"It's been happening ever since I wore the Sachem's Belt

when I opened the Trap!" Rory said, the truth dawning. "Maybe it melted into my skin or something when Caesar Prince destroyed it. Did the belt make people tell the truth?"

"It did in the hands of a Light," Soka said. "But never like this. You even do it to gods!"

"I wonder if Prince knew this would happen," Rory mused.

"What did you do?" Simon poked his head around the corner of the grandstand. "I overheard Robert Moses tell some men to nab you the minute the race is under way! And not only that, he's put two and two together and recognized Bridget as well! Look!"

Moses was standing near the track, leaning over the rope near two unsavory-looking drivers in identical black cars, whispering to them and pointing to Rory's dad and sister, who were preparing their car for the race.

"Those are the Lamborghini twins!" Simon said. "They're the dirtiest drivers in the borough. Your dad doesn't stand a chance!"

"We have to do something!" Rory cried.

"I've got it!" Simon snapped his fingers. He ran off. "Simon!" Rory called after him, but to no avail. The officials called for the drivers to make their way to the starting line and Rory began to walk toward the track. "I've got to warn them," he told Soka, heading toward his dad's car, even as a group of tough-looking spirits spied him, forcing their way through the crowd in his direction. Fear shot through him as he realized he wouldn't be able to make the track before the toughs reached him. But then a loud explosion made him jump. Spinning, he came face-to-face with the most dangerous-looking, poorly constructed car he'd ever seen. The rivets were uneven, the tires were wobbly, and smoke poured incessantly from under the hood. And behind the wheel, smiling like an idiot in his hat and goggles, sat Simon.

"This is my baby!" he declared. "I built her myself and keep her here at the track, just in case! Hop in, we're going to race!"

"You're crazy," Soka said, backing away. "That looks like a death machine."

"I'm a great driver!" Simon assured her. "This is the best way to make sure your dad and sister are all right, Rory. If we race, those goons over there can't touch you, and we can draw the twins away so your dad can win. Or maybe we'll win, ourselves! Never know!" He grinned again. Rory glanced back through the thick crowd at Moses's men, who were getting closer and closer. Out of options, he climbed up next to Simon, who waved at Soka to join them. She sighed and hopped in next to them, forcing Rory to squish into the middle so she could fit.

"You better not kill us," she told Simon, and he gave her a mocking salute before putting the car into gear. It lurched forward, sending a belch of smoke into the air before stalling.

"Whoops! Gotta pop the clutch!" Simon yelled, and he fooled around under the wheel. Finally, he restarted and the car began to move forward, pushing its way through the crowd toward the starting line.

They pulled in behind the first line of cars. Mr. Hennessy and Bridget saw them, and while Bridget waved, Mr. Hennessy looked furious. Rory pointed to the Lamborghini twins, making fierce faces. His father seemed confused, not understanding.

"Hey!" William Vanderbilt was standing in his car, pointing at Simon. "They can't race! They don't have a sponsor!"

"I'm their sponsor!" Rufus King announced, running up.

"You are already sponsoring a car," the official ruled. "You can't have two in a race."

"Wait!" Simon called out. "I'm my own sponsor."

"You have to be a god, idiot." Vanderbilt sneered, sending a ripple of laughter through the crowd. Simon hesitated for a moment, listening to the mocking snickers, and then stood up in his seat.

"I *am* a god," he announced. A hush fell over the crowd. Even Rufus's jaw dropped.

"That's impossible," Vanderbilt scoffed. "You weren't a god last week." He nudged his mechanic, smiling slyly.

"Well, I'm a god today," Simon replied, and pulled out his locket. A shock ran through the crowd. Rory worried that Simon's revelation was a mistake. But it was too late now. The official leaned in to take a good look at the locket, frowning. He shot an arm in the air.

"He is qualified," he shouted, then backed away, disturbed. Simon sank back down in his seat, staring belligerently at a flabbergasted Vanderbilt. But then the countdown began and Vanderbilt returned to his own seat, revving his engine. There was no time to ponder the wisdom of Simon's declaration. They had a race to win.

"Three! Two! One! Go!" The pistol rang out and twenty cars roared to life, exploding across the starting line and down the dirt road.

"Here we go!" Simon screamed, and put his foot on the gas. Soka screamed as Rory held on for dear life.

Five seconds later, they were sputtering down the road at a comfortable fifteen miles an hour, and all the other cars were out of sight.

"Don't worry," Simon said, bent over the wheel of his automobile, lazily ambling down the road. "We'll catch up."

A Tight Race

There is a tunnel that only the roaches know. It leads deep down, beneath the subways and pipes, and ends in a large, hollowed-out cavern. The walls of this cavern are lined with the white bones of a giant rib cage, the remnants of some forgotten ancient creature who burrowed its way into the depths to die. It is here that the battle roaches of Mannahatta come to hold council.

Lanterns hung from the bones on the wall, the flickering light reflected in the armor of the thousands of battle roaches filling the cavern. Every clan had come at Fritz's call, even the M'Bairds, who had sided with Kieft in the past. Only Fritz's own people, the exiled M'Garoths, were absent. They refused to concern themselves with the world above, practically ostracizing him for his involvement with Mannahatta. Fritz had barely seen his wife, Liv, in months, which hurt more than he would admit. But he could not dwell on the past. He had a future to save.

Fritz stood on the stone dais, Hans and Sergeant Kiffer by his side, looking out at his brethren. The clans had come partly from curiosity, partly out of fear for their beloved city. Battle roaches took their duties as protectors very seriously. The problem, Fritz discovered, was that they didn't know who needed protecting.

"We're at a crossroads, friends," Fritz began, and the room quieted. "War is coming. Now, I'm not afraid of battle. What I am afraid of is injustice. And Willem Kieft is the very definition of that word."

"He says it's not his fault that war is upon us," one of the M'Baird clan elders shouted. "It's the Munsees who are to blame. They want revenge!" The crowd began to murmur at this, forcing Fritz to raise his voice.

"If they'd wanted revenge, they would have taken it the moment the Trap fell," he shouted, quieting the room once more. "We almost did fight, but the Munsees backed down. It was Kieft who wanted to fan the flames, not the Munsees. We need to be on the right side of this!"

"Why should we listen to you?" another roach called out. "Where is your clan? I don't see them here. I even heard that they exiled you for stirring up trouble." Fritz had heard this, too. Some of the elders of his clan only wanted to hide from their troubles. Apparently they'd had a vote to shun him, and Liv was the only dissenting vote. She cared about the clan the way he cared about the city, so he didn't expect her to break their law. He'd just have to find a way to go on without her, no matter how much it hurt.

"Maybe someone else should be speaking with us, then," another roach exclaimed. "Why would we follow an exile?"

"Because he is right!" a new voice called out. Fritz's heart almost stopped as a large group of roaches entered the cavern, led by the beautiful rat rider he feared he would never see again. "My husband has sacrificed everything for this city," Liv said, her voice ringing with pride. "He has given up family and friends in order to do what was right. Can we do no less? I care about my clan above myself, as does each of us, but the time has come to stop being M'Garoth or M'Korenth or M'Baird. The time has come to be a battle roach of Mannahatta! And that means protecting this city from those who wish to do it harm. The M'Garoth elders don't understand this, so we left them behind to hide in their hole. Will you hide as well? Will you let the liars and thieves take this city from us?"

A resounding "NO!" rang through the cavern as the battle roaches, caught up in Liv's rousing words, rattled their swords.

"Then listen to what my husband has to say! For no one cares more about this city than he does."

Liv looked to Fritz and his heart almost burst. For a moment it felt as if just the two of them were standing alone in the giant cavern, and the months apart meant nothing. Then he began to speak and he could feel the roaches responding, even the M'Bairds. Nicholas would have this army at least. Out of the corner of his eye, he saw Liv smile, and he knew he could not fail.

⁓⁓⁓⁓

Can't you get this thing to go faster?" Rory cried. They'd been puttering along for a half hour and the other cars were long gone. They could hear some of the spectators heckling them. "I can get out and walk quicker than this!"

"It just needs to warm up," Simon assured him. "I'll hit the next gear then. Change gears too soon and who knows what could happen!"

"If we don't go faster soon," Soka said, "we will never catch up."

"Fine," Simon said, gritting his teeth. "But if this beautiful work of art of a car falls apart, you are buying me a new one!"

"Come on!" Rory screamed, frustrated. Simon reached down and fiddled with a knob.

"Remember, I warned you," he said, and gave it a turn. The car suddenly lurched forward and took off like a rocket, shooting down the dirt path while veering left and right. The spectators who lined the track scattered in all directions. Rory very quickly realized that Simon was not a good driver, an unsettling thought when racing down a dirt road at eighty miles an hour in a death trap of a car.

They made a turn, two wheels rising off the road. Rory was certain they were going to crash if they kept swerving around like this, but they couldn't slow down. If they wanted to catch up and protect his family, they'd have to take some chances. He only hoped they weren't too late.

Bridget screamed with excitement as her dad wrenched their car around another hairpin turn. With the wind in her face, she felt like she was flying, which, in a way, she was, since the only thing holding her in her seat was her fingertips. She was glad for the goggles her dad had handed her, as the dirt came flying at her, and even worse, yucky bugs splattered her eyewear.

If those things hit her paper eyeballs, she'd never get the stain out.

Her dad was a pretty good driver, swerving from side to side as he urged number 13 to gain ground on Vanderbilt's number 14. She couldn't help smiling—this was what she'd always wanted: to go on an adventure with her dad. And this roller coaster of a race definitely qualified.

The spectators had thinned along this part of the track, and they now seemed to be driving through an old, ramshackle neighborhood lined with ancient clapboard houses. With a shock, Bridget realized that real cars, present-day mortal cars, were driving up ahead. They were on a real road! And they were going to crash!

But Vanderbilt deftly swerved to the right, just whispering by a large pickup truck rattling down the street, its driver completely unaware of the crazed road race that was occurring around him. Her dad followed suit, but on the other side, sliding between the pickup and an old Toyota, before slotting right back in on Vanderbilt's tail. Bridget could almost hear the cocky Vanderbilt cursing when he realized he couldn't shake the Hennessys. Maybe they could win this after all.

She glanced over her shoulder to check if Rory's car was anywhere behind them. She couldn't see it, but she did spy two black torpedo-looking cars, driven by dark men in black goggles, and she didn't like the look of them one bit. They came up fast behind number 13, and before Bridget could say a word, the lead car clipped their back wheel.

A loud screech sounded as Mr. Hennessy struggled to hold on to the wheel. The entire car slid sideways, sparks flying, and Bridget feared they'd flip over like cars in the movies, only worse since this would be for real. But her dad forced the wheel back around, regaining control.

"Who are they?" he yelled.

Bridget threw up her hands. "I'm guessing bad guys!" The two black cars were pulling up alongside them now. "Twin bad guys! They're right next to us!"

"Hold on!" her dad screamed, and gunned it, shooting up onto the sidewalk just as an old Pontiac in front of them slowed to make a turn. They just made it past the car, shooting out into an intersection like a bullet from a gun. Bridget let out a whoop and glanced back. One of the black cars had spun around, falling over on its side. The other, however, deftly avoided the crash and continued on their trail.

Her dad slid them back onto the road proper, and she noticed that they'd nearly caught up to Vanderbilt, who was looking over his shoulder, checking their progress. A burst of exhaust washed over Bridget as the remaining black car shot right past them and then braked suddenly, trying to cut them off. Dad spun the wheel, just maneuvering around in the nick of time. Vanderbilt glanced back again, this time yelling something to the black car. Bridget thought it was something like "Play fair!" She shook her head. These guys would never play fair, not in a thousand years.

As they sped up toward Vanderbilt's car, Vanderbilt was looking behind more frequently, obviously confused. The black car pulled up alongside Bridget's car, and the driver smirked before flooring it, pulling ahead. Bridget had no idea what he was doing. Vanderbilt screamed at the car as it passed him, calling the driver a maniac.

As if in response, the black car suddenly swerved in front of Vanderbilt's car, causing him to turn his vehicle wildly. The rear wheel clipped the Hennessy car, and this time Mr. Hennessy couldn't keep control. Their car spun crazily. Bridget screamed as she was flung from the car, landing heavily on the ground, where she skidded for a good twenty feet before hitting a parking meter. She scrambled to her feet just in time to see her car and Vanderbilt's car push the black car, which could not escape the carnage it had instigated, right into the side of a little grocery store. The black car was crushed into scrap metal and Vanderbilt's car immediately burst into flame.

"No!" Bridget cried, running over to beat at the flames. She spied Vanderbilt lying on the ground, legs pinned beneath the front hood. He was barely conscious, and kept muttering "Not fair" under his breath.

"Get the journal!" Mr. Hennessy screamed. He was pulling himself from the wreckage of their car, and he appeared unharmed. "It's going to burn up!"

"But, Vanderbilt!" Bridget stood frozen, before making a decision. She ran up to Vanderbilt, putting her weight against the fallen engine. The flames licked her hair, setting one or two strands aflame, but she did not pay attention. She pushed and pushed, with everything she had, until she'd lifted the car off the pinned-down driver. Vanderbilt weakly pulled his legs free and then collapsed. She dropped the engine back to the ground with a crash and grabbed Vanderbilt around the waist, pulling him across the street to safety.

"Thank you," he whispered. "You're a good egg." Then he passed out.

Bridget turned to run back to the car to grab the package

when the entire vehicle suddenly exploded into flames. *"No!"* she screamed, but it was too late. She ran across the street to the burning car, ready to leap into the center of the flames.

"Bridget! Stop!" Her dad rushed to her side, grabbing her shoulders. "It's over."

"But it's all burned up!" she cried, collapsing in his arms.

"It's okay. Do you think I'd let you down?" With that, Mr. Hennessy handed her a slightly chárred, but completely readable journal and smiled. "I pulled it out from under the floorboards just before she blew."

Bridget opened her mouth to say thank you, but instead she just collapsed into dry sobs, clutching at her dad as if she never wanted to let him go.

"Honey, we've got to move!" Mr. Hennessy suddenly screamed. Looking up, Bridget saw the other black car, which she'd thought was out of the race when it fell over, roaring down the street, gunning right for them. Her dad started to pull her to the side, out of the car's path, but there was no time. Bridget pushed her dad behind her, bracing for impact.

"GERONIMO!" a familiar voice screamed as a loud car horn blared. From out of nowhere, Simon Astor's car appeared from a side street, barely holding itself together. Simon was bent over the wheel, honking the horn and yelling at the top of his lungs. Her brother and Soka were holding on for dear life, terrified, as Simon drove his car directly into the oncoming vehicle, smashing into the black car's hood from the side right before it could hit Bridget, sending both automobiles careening into a nearby store.

Bridget and her dad ran up to Simon's car to see if they were all right. To their surprise, not only were Simon, Soka, and

Rory unharmed, though a little dazed, but Simon's car was still running. The black car, on the other hand, was totaled. Simon looked at the wrecked vehicles all around him.

"Told you my car was the best," he said in a sprightly tone as he hopped out. Right on his heels, Rory ran over to the burning shell of number 14, muttering "no" to himself. Bridget ran up to him.

"It's okay!" she told him. "We grabbed the package before it could get burned. We got it!"

"What about Vanderbilt?" Simon asked sourly. "I hope you let him fry."

"He's fine." Bridget pointed across the street to where Vanderbilt lay, unconscious. "We pulled him to safety."

"Bridget saved him," Mr. Hennessy said. "It was amazing." Bridget blushed.

"I couldn't let him burn up," she said. "That would have been gross. But it was Dad who made sure to pull the journal from the burning car!"

"Wow," Rory said, looking surprised.

"Did I just impress my son?" Mr. Hennessy said drily. "What a day it is for me!" He sounded flippant, but his eyes shone as he said it.

"Well, let's see what you've got there," Rory said, taking a step forward. Suddenly he crumpled to the ground.

"Rory!" Soka cried, dropping down to his side. Bridget quickly knelt down and instantly noticed the blood in his hair.

"He must have hit his head on impact," Mr. Hennessy said, brushing by her to examine Rory's wound. He looked shaken. "He's out cold. We need to get him away from here."

The sound of revving engines floated in and Mr. Hennessy

glanced up the street. "Robert Moses will be along soon, as will others of Kieft's allies," he said. He stood up. "I'll take care of them. You need to get Rory to Brooklyn. I'll stay behind."

"No!" Bridget cried. "You have to come with us."

"I can delay Moses long enough to give you time to cross the borough line," Mr. Hennessy said, looking over Bridget's head at Simon. "Can you get them there?"

"You can count on me, sir," Simon answered. Together, Mr. Hennessy and Simon lifted Rory and placed him in the back of Simon's car. Ashen, Soka climbed in next to Rory, cradling his head in her arms. Simon hopped into the driver's seat and gestured to Bridget. "Come on, girl!"

The sound of engines was getting closer. Bridget grabbed her father's waist, hugging him for all she was worth. "You have to come!" she cried. "I just found you!"

"I'll see you again, I promise," her dad told her, kissing the top of her head. "I won't let anyone hurt you." He lifted her up and placed her in the seat next to Simon. "Go!"

Simon guided the car around the wrecks, taking care not to get too close to the burning vehicles. Then he gunned it, picking up speed as they raced away from the scene. Bridget spun around to watch her father as they sped off. Mr. Hennessy waved, once, before turning to face their pursuers. Then Simon made a hard left and her father was gone.

9

THE OLD STONE HOUSE

In his dream, Rory was standing in a circular room, with a roaring fire burning in the middle. The smoke drifted up toward a hole in the ceiling. Glancing around, he realized he was in some kind of tepee. Strange, crude paintings covered the curved walls, the colors disquieting and ominous. The pictures depicted demons wearing feathers and holding knives, bending over the screaming forms of women and children. The hints of red in the paint made Rory shudder. On the other side of the fire hung clumps of what appeared to be wigs. Looking closer, he realized that they were scalps. He felt sick.

"This room always soothes me," a voice said. Jumping back, Rory spun to find the man with the black eyes stepping into the tepee. A cloth bag was slung over his shoulder. He dropped the bag to the dirt floor, where it landed with a clatter. "It reminds me of who I fight."

"This isn't right," Rory told him. "This isn't a Munsee place. They don't even have tepees, they have wigwams, which aren't round."

The man with the black eyes shrugged. "A small detail. The

god whose room this was didn't cater to such literal truths. He was the God of the Savages, and epitomized every fear the Europeans had about the natives. He was the one they prayed to when they went out into the wilderness, afraid of the dark forests and the dark people who inhabited them. He did not need to be true, for those who worshipped him didn't care to know the truth themselves. I always liked him. I felt a twinge when the mortals no longer needed his particular brand of slanderous terror, which is why I like to frequent his room now that he is gone. I like to think I keep his memory alive."

"I think it's disgusting," Rory said. "Why would you want to live in some dead guy's room anyway?"

"Because it is the perfect place to do dark deeds," the man with the black eyes said. He bent over and upended his bag. Knives fell out with a clang, landing in a big heap on the ground. He picked one up, running his finger lightly along the blade with a smile. "Do you have any idea how long it took me to perfect these? Centuries! First, I had to learn the Munsee magical arts, which was not easy. I had a devil of a time finding a savage who would teach me! Thankfully, I am not without powers of my own and I finally captured a medicine woman to be my tutor. She did not last long under my care, but I learned much before she died. I still miss her . . . she was a feisty one."

"You're a monster," Rory snarled.

The man with the black eyes shrugged again. "Perhaps. I don't really care. It is exhilarating to finally be able to share a little of my story! Of course, you won't remember this, and even if you did, you will not survive the week, so I am free to brag a bit."

"You keep threatening to kill me, but you haven't been able

to yet," Rory answered, refusing to show fear. "Isn't that a little cocky of you?"

"I knew I needed a weapon if I wanted to kill gods," the man with the black eyes continued, ignoring Rory's question. "Munsees could kill gods, so I had to somehow instill the essence of a Munsee into a weapon of some kind. I picked a knife, since those were the easiest to both fashion and wield. The hardest part was finding the right mix of metal to blood during the forging, which I did right here, over that fire. I 'borrowed' some Munsees and experimented with them. A few of them lasted until well after the Trap was sprung. The last one, the one who finally helped me forge my first blade, lived until last year, when I buried my first finished knife, the fruit of his suffering, into his heart. A clean death—I like to think of it as my way of saying thank you."

Rory tried not to picture those poor prisoners being experimented on by the First Adviser. He could almost hear their screams. A wave of dizziness washed over him, suddenly, and he staggered back. In a moment the feeling passed, but when he turned back to the First Adviser, the black-eyed man was staring at him with a sharp look in his eye. He began to spin the knife in his hand.

"There's something different about you today, boy," he said, taking a step forward. "You seem especially . . . vulnerable. Are you injured? The way you sway where you stand . . . is it a head injury? I *was* able to find your dreams so easily this last time. Your defenses are weak. I wonder . . . could it be this easy? Could I just do *this*?"

Suddenly the man with the black eyes seemed to grow, blocking out the room as he towered over Rory. His body began to change, stretching out in all directions as if to swallow Rory whole. His eyes burned, pressing into Rory with the force of their hate, making him cry out. And then the knife, the glittering instrument of death, plunged down toward Rory's heart.

But before the knife could end him, the air before Rory erupted in fire. The man with the black eyes was driven back, cursing, as Rory heard a woman's voice in the flames.

"HE IS MINE!"

Rory fell back, into darkness, the thunderous sound of the woman's voice filling him with both hope and terrible fear . . .

Rory woke up to a pounding headache. He was lying on his back, staring up at the sky. The late afternoon sun shone overhead, occasionally darting behind a cloud. He felt like the world was spinning, and at first he thought it was his head. But then he realized that whatever he was lying on was moving and he tried to sit up to see what was going on.

"You stay where you are!" Soka's voice said, and her head appeared hovering over him as she gently forced him back down. But not before he saw that he was stretched out in the back of some kind of wagon and Soka was sitting next to him. She turned behind her. "He's awake!"

"You scared the crap out of me, Rory Hennessy!" Bridget's voice said. "If you do that again, I will kill you myself!"

"Where am I?" Rory asked.

"You're safe, my boy!" Rory glanced to the front of the wagon, where a familiar man sat next to Bridget, guiding a pair of horses. It was Walt Whitman, the God of Optimism. He must have picked them up at the border. The eternal optimist glanced back to give him a smile. "We're taking you to the Old Stone House, where a friend is going to check on your head. Then you can plan your next move."

"Where's Dad?" Rory asked, wincing as he forced himself to sit up. Soka looked like she wanted to protest, but he waved her off. She sat back; to his surprise, she looked like she'd been crying.

"He stayed behind to keep that Moses guy off our backs," Bridget said. "He was very brave. I hope he's okay."

"Well, he's lived this long, so he's probably fine," Rory said, not wanting to worry about his old man but not able to help it.

"What about you?" Soka asked, her eyes concerned. "Do you feel all right?"

"A little woozy," he replied. "But I think I'll live. Where are we going again?"

"That's it up ahead!" Whitman said. Their wagon was rolling along a side street surrounded by elegant brownstones toward a small park. In the middle of the park sat a simple two-story stone building. Whitman explained its importance as they approached it.

"The Old Stone House has been around for three hundred years," he told them. "It's been torn down and built up a few times, but the foundation remained. It's a place of sacrifice, one of the holiest spots in New York! During the Revolutionary War, the British attacked General George Washington's men here in Brooklyn, trying to kill the Revolution before it really began. But the American people would not be beaten down! A group of brave soldiers from down south, Colonel Smallwood's

Marylanders, made their stand here, taking the house from the British, then losing it, then taking it again, then losing it again. So many of them died here for their country!"

"Did they finally beat the British into a bloody pulp?" Bridget asked, caught up in the story.

"Not quite, though it was a noble effort! America lost the Battle of Brooklyn, and New York suffered under British rule for the rest of the war. But more importantly, if not for the Marylanders' refusal to give in, George Washington would never have escaped with the Continental Army. The Marylanders held off the British until the Americans were able to retreat to safety. You don't always have to win the battle to be a hero, you know. Sometimes it is heroic enough just to survive to keep fighting."

They rode up to the door. The elegant structure was two stories of flagstone and mortar, a simple stone house just like its name suggested. But something about it seemed *strong* to Bridget. This was a house that survived.

Halting the horses, Whitman hopped out of the wagon to help Rory out of the back. Rory still swayed on his feet, so he needed both Soka and Whitman's help making it through the door, where a surprise waited for them in the main room of the house.

"Fritz!" Bridget cried, running forward to greet the battle roach, who stood on an old pitted table with Clarence by his side. Fritz seemed both delighted and concerned to see them.

"I can't leave you alone for five minutes!" he told them.

As Whitman and Soka helped him sit down in an overstuffed chair by the fireplace, Rory glanced around. The main room of the house sported worn stone walls and a big fireplace, with wooden beams crisscrossing along a hard wooden ceiling. It felt like a cozy safe place. "Is he okay?" Fritz was asking Whitman.

"I'm right here," Rory said peevishly. "And I'm fine. How did your recruiting go?"

"Very well," Fritz said, smiling. "The battle roaches know which side is just. Even my own clan finally came to my side."

"Did Liv come, too?" Bridget asked.

"Yes, in fact, she did," Fritz replied, trying not to grin but failing. "I left her in charge of the roach armies so I could come help you."

"I knew you crazy kids would be reunited!" Bridget announced, and Fritz shook his head at her enthusiasm.

"Thank you for your belief." He turned to Rory. "Did you find anything in Queens?"

"The second package!" Rory exclaimed, looking around in fear as he realized he didn't know where it had gone. He sighed with relief when Soka pulled it out of her pouch. "Can you read it out loud?" he asked reluctantly. "I can't focus that well, right now."

"I'll read it," Whitman offered, taking the pages. "Soka told me about this agreement your father mentioned, about the rules all gods must follow. I'd never heard of it! We'd always assumed our restrictions were part of the natural order of things. But if this is true, it will change everything we believe we know about ourselves. We must ask the old-timers what they have been hiding. I am curious to see what else is in these pages." He opened to the top page. "Three," he read.

"I hate skipping ahead!" Bridget pouted. Whitman snorted and began to read:

*I found it difficult to keep Kieft's manservant's secret, espe-
cially since Kieft demanded that Henry accompany us on our
journey. But I had promised, so I said nothing. Marta warned
me before we left not to trust Kieft. She was certain he would
betray me. I assured her that the stakes were too high for such
games. Even Kieft knew that. As I took my leave, I could see
the worry on her face, but what could I do? Survival was at
stake, and that made for strange bedfellows.*

*Before we left, I asked Kieft why we needed to make our
pact with the land in such a remote spot. Couldn't we do it
from the safety of home? He simply smiled and told me there
was no other way, but not to worry. It would be a painless
journey, he said. I should have known better. That journey
would bring me nothing but pain—pain and sorrow. But even
if I had known, how could I have turned away?*

Rory glanced around in confusion. "What does this mean?"

"Who is Henry?" Bridget asked.

"This doesn't tell us anything!" Rory said, annoyed.

"Perhaps it does," Soka said thoughtfully. "He would not
write about this man Henry's secret, whatever it was, unless he
thought it was important. He must be part of what Adriaen is
trying to tell us."

"But we don't even know who this guy could be!" Rory said.
"Who can keep track of Kieft's servants, especially one from
three hundred years ago!"

"Well, we know one thing," Fritz said. The others looked at
him. "Wherever they made this pact with the land, that's where
we're going. It's the only thing that makes sense. This is a treasure map, of sorts. And we have to follow it to the end."

They stared at one another, mulling this over, until a loud knock on the door made them jump.

"There they are!" Whitman said, striding over to the door. "I asked some friends to bring us someone to take a look at your head, Rory." After glancing through a peephole to make sure he knew his visitors, he threw open the door to reveal two men, who strode into the room like soldiers, escorting a small woman in a nun's habit. Rory immediately recognized her as she hurried to his side.

"You are one of the nuns, aren't you?" Rory asked as the nun bent over him to check his wound. "From the Abbey?"

"I am Sister Charity," the nun said. "The Abbess sent nuns to the different boroughs to assist with the wounded in your struggle. I was traveling with these soldiers' regiments when Whitman's request for medical help came. And when I heard it was you . . . the Abbess told us to keep an eye out for you. She's taken a liking to you, I think." Sister Charity inspected his wound. "This was quite a crack you received. Normally, you would have to rest for weeks to recover. But I know you don't have that much time. Luckily, in your case, I am allowed to call on some extreme measures." She muttered strange words to herself as she placed her hand over his wound. Rory began to feel warmth spread through his head. The feeling was familiar; he'd experienced this touch before. *Her touch,* he thought, and then wondered where that thought came from.

"Is that the Abbess?" Rory asked, his voice weak as the healing power flowed through him. "That touch I feel?"

The nun paused in her chanting, though her hand still covered his wound. "Not exactly. We nuns serve man, but not only man, and this power comes from she whom we also serve."

"Who?"

The nun said nothing, returning to her chanting. Rory felt another wave flow through him and he had no strength to ask more.

Meanwhile, Whitman was introducing the soldiers as Colonel Wood and Colonel Smallwood.

"The same Colonel Smallwood from that story you told me about the heroic Marylanders?" Bridget asked, popping up to say hello. The shorter, fatter of the two colonels gave her a slight bow, his round red cheeks flushed with pleasure. He wore a blue overcoat with gold tassels on the shoulders, and his hair was powdered white.

"So you've heard of my brave men and their valiant stand?" Smallwood said, his voice booming as he waved his arms about energetically. "What a day that was, let me tell you! The British surprised us, but my men had blood of pure ice water. You should have heard the muskets fire. *Boom! Crack!* The smoke from the gunfire covered us all in a fog, turning the damned red-coated foe into demons in the mist. It was enough to scare the pants off of a Hessian! But we would not break! That's where you learn who you really are. Out in the thick of it!"

"Wow!" Bridget was impressed. "You're hard-core! And was your friend in your brigade?" She nodded at the taller colonel.

"Oh no," Colonel Wood said, smiling. He sported a long blue coat with two rows of big gold buttons that hung down over a pair of bright red trousers, which were tucked into a pair of big black boots. He had the coolest mustache Bridget had ever seen—it ran down from his ears along his jaw until it leaped up above his lip, leaving his chin completely bare.

"Colonel Wood was the leader of the famous Red Legged Devils," Whitman explained. "They were the fiercest fighters in the Civil War. I remember them vividly—I was mortal during the war, and I wanted nothing more than to be a solider in Brooklyn's Fourteenth regiment. Lincoln's favorite, you know. He often asked them to attend public functions with him."

"President Lincoln appreciated our backbone," Colonel Wood said modestly. He was less effusive than Colonel Smallwood, but he seemed just as brave.

"So will both your regiments join the fight against Kieft?" Whitman asked them.

"How can I fight for one oppressed people and not another?" Wood asked. "The Red Legged Devils will answer the call."

"I always did like my tragic last stands," Colonel Smallwood said. "It's no fun if it isn't hopeless."

"That's heartening," Fritz said wryly.

"What are you lot doing here, anyway?" Smallwood asked the roach. "Recruiting?"

"Actually, they've got another mission," Whitman told the colonels.

"It's nothing really," Fritz cut in quickly. Bridget could tell that he didn't quite trust the two soldiers. "Just a little task we have to finish."

"Spies, eh?" Wood said, nodding knowingly.

"I hate spies," Smallwood cut in. "Either fight or go home. None of this lurking around—that's not true soldiering."

"We're not spies!" Bridget retorted, stung. Fritz gave her a warning look, but she ignored it. "We're looking for the Fair Engineer!"

"Is that ironic?" Smallwood asked. "There's only one engineer around here, but I don't think anyone would call him fair."

"I thought of him," Whitman said. "But it didn't make sense. He's the opposite of fair."

"Maybe they mean fair-minded," Colonel Wood mused. "Of course, I don't know if we'd call him that, either . . ." Bridget couldn't take it anymore. She hopped right in the middle of the room.

"Who are you talking about!" she cried. "Do you know who we're supposed to meet?"

"Maybe," Whitman said slowly. "He doesn't quite match the description, but the colonels are right. Maybe the word *fair* doesn't mean what we think it does."

"There you go," Sister Charity told Rory, standing up. "You should be fine now. Just try to protect the area."

Rory pushed himself to his feet. He felt much better. "Then let's go see this guy, fair or not. Before we run out of time."

Peter Hennessy sat in his chair, stone-faced, as Kieft stared down at him. The First Adviser did not look pleased at what he was hearing.

"Where has this unexpected backbone come from?" the man with the black eyes asked, his eyebrow raised.

"I won't do it," Mr. Hennessy said, as he'd been saying for the past half hour. "I've broken too many promises in my life. I won't betray my children."

"Was that why you led Moses on a wild-goose chase?" Kieft

asked. "He told me that you must have circled Queens three times before he realized what you were doing."

"They're my children," Mr. Hennessy repeated, his arms crossed protectively across his chest.

"What about your wife?" Kieft asked. "Aren't you afraid of what I'll do to her?"

"I realized that you won't dare do anything to her," Peter said. "She's not just leverage against me, but also Rory. And Rory is more important than I am. So you wouldn't harm her or Bridget's body."

"How . . . calculating of you," Kieft said. "But you are not the only one who can hedge his bets." He held out his hand and a small fly buzzed down to land on his palm. "Have you met any of Hearst's little pets? Very useful for overhearing secrets. This little one spent the past day nestled in your shirt collar. She listened in on everything and then she relayed it all to me. So I know all about Van der Donck's journal and his account of the Agreement."

Mr. Hennessy's face fell as he realized that he'd betrayed his children just by being in their presence. Kieft leaned in. "You can imagine my delight at learning that they are following such a doomed path. You well know how difficult it is to travel. Still, it is time to stop this charade. You not only carried this little fly with you, you also transported a few of her siblings, who are even now nestled in the clothing of your progeny. Once they have gathered enough intelligence, they will return to me and then I will find your son and finish this. Your son has proven quite adept at slipping from my grasp, a skill I salute him for, by the way. But I am done playing games."

Mr. Hennessy let out a moan. Kieft smiled. "Don't worry. Your son is mine, but that doesn't mean I will kill him. He is much more valuable by my side than he is under the ground. So you still have a role to play. He doesn't have to know your part in this. Help me one more time, and he will go the rest of his days remembering his daddy the hero, not his father the turncoat. How does that sound?"

Mr. Hennessy stared back in horror, unable to face this choice. No matter what he did, he always ended up hurting the ones he loved.

THE FAIR ENGINEER

Nicholas, Alexa, and Lincoln heard the strains of the jazz band playing down the hall as they approached the unmarked door in the back of an unremarkable building in Greenwich Village. They reached the door, knocking once, then three times, then once again. A small panel slid back in the middle of the door.

"Password?" a voice demanded.

"Salamander salad," Lincoln replied, having picked up the password from a friend. The music washed over them as the door opened to reveal a dour-looking mobster in a pin-striped suit.

"Welcome to Chumleys," the man said, and the Rattle Watchers pushed past him into the memory of one of New York's most famous speakeasies. During Prohibition in the late twenties and early thirties, the government made it illegal for anyone to drink alcohol. So secret bars, called speakeasies, popped up in cities all over the country, where if you knew the password you could dance to the hottest music, rub shoulders with celebrities and criminals, and, most importantly, have a drink.

Nicholas, Alexa, and Lincoln were interested in none of these things as they pushed their way through the crowded room. The little place was packed. Tables were set up all around, with a bar in the corner and a lively five-piece jazz combo playing on a small stage. Brightly dressed spirits danced the Charleston in the middle of the room, laughing and spinning. Some were mobsters, some were thrill seekers out on the town. But most were children of the gods. Which was why the Rattle Watch was here.

"Don't they know there's war coming?" Lincoln muttered, glaring at the dancers.

"Of course they do," Alexa replied. "That's why they're dancing."

They made the rounds, speaking in low tones with various groups of children of the gods, trying to recruit. But no one seemed to care. And then a voice rang out.

"Well, look who it is! Mr. and Mrs. Goody Two-shoes!"

In the corner, squeezed around a small table, sat Nicholas's old gang: Teddy Twiller, Randolph Morris, a very drunk Robert de Vries, an embarrassed Jane van Cortlandt, and their ringleader, the one who'd called out with a sneer in her voice, Martha Jay.

"No surprise to see you here," Nicholas said as they approached the table.

"No luck getting idiots to join your little army?" Martha asked, waving a drink in her hand.

"It's weird how no one wants to go get killed!" Teddy Twiller said mockingly.

"You won't be laughing if Kieft wins!" Lincoln announced, his eyes burning.

"Why are you so sure Kieft is such a bad guy?" Randolph slurred. "He gave us such pretty knives!"

"So it's true!" Alexa leaned in. "Tell me you are not dumb enough to go running around with those evil knives! What are you thinking!"

"Haven't you heard?" Martha asked. "Anyone can be a god now. Isn't our old friend Simon now the God of Plates, or something like that? Why should he have all the fun?"

"You don't understand what you're messing with, Martha," Nicholas said.

"Don't you always say we need to have a goal, a purpose?" Martha asked. "Well, my goal is to be a god. I can have a purpose, now. I can matter. All it takes is one little stab with this!" She pulled out a familiar knife, and the Rattle Watch stepped back in alarm. Nicholas noticed that not all of Martha's companions seemed happy at the sight of the knife. Robert de Vries looked green and Jane van Cortlandt glanced away unhappily.

"This will end badly," Alexa warned. "Kieft didn't give you that knife so you could become a god. He did it to sow chaos and fear. You can't murder your way to the top."

"If you want to be a part of something noble and just," Nicholas said to the others, realizing that there was nothing more they could say to Martha, "then join us. We hope you do." With that, he led a disheartened Alexa and Lincoln back the way they came, leaving Martha Jay and her friends playing with the knife like the children Nicholas feared they'd always be.

After taking leave of the colonels and Sister Charity, Whitman bundled up Bridget and her companions in his wagon and quickly drove them west across Brooklyn toward the river. The light was beginning to fail as they trotted into Brooklyn Heights, the upscale neighborhood of old brownstones and quiet, tree-lined streets hugging the river directly opposite the soaring skyscrapers of downtown Manhattan. They pulled up outside an unassuming brick building, poured out of the wagon, and followed Whitman up to the front door.

"Who are we here to see?" Fritz asked at Whitman's feet as the god knocked heavily on the thick wooden door.

"His name is Washington Roebling, and he is the God of Dangerous Projects. He built the Brooklyn Bridge."

"Well, that sounds like an engineer, all right!" Bridget said. "So why didn't we come here in the first place?"

"Because he didn't fit the description. *Fair* is not a word I would attach to him, in any definition of the term."

"Because he's ugly?" Bridget asked innocently.

"You'll see . . ." Whitman replied cryptically, and the door creaked open before Bridget could press him further. A young maid stood in the doorway, dressed in an old-fashioned frock and apron.

"Are you here to see the master?" she asked, not looking any of them in the face.

"Yes, is he in?" Whitman asked.

"He is, sir, but the Mrs. is not home. That might make it hard . . ." She trailed off. Bridget was dying of curiosity to learn about what was going on with this mysterious engineer.

"We can't afford to wait," Whitman told her, and the maid nodded meekly, turning to lead them into the house.

As they walked up the stairs, Bridget glanced at her brother, worried. He seemed to be all better, but she couldn't be sure. Soka walked by his side, watching him as if he would fall apart at any moment. His injury seemed to have woken her up, Bridget noticed. Maybe now she'd admit that she and Rory were destined to get married. Bridget would be maid of honor (of course!) and she'd catch the bouquet and everything. She could hardly wait.

When they reached the top of the stairs, Whitman turned to the rest of the party.

"All I ask is that you try not to stare," he said, and then nodded to the maid to take them to Roebling's room. Bridget was bursting to know what was going on. The maid opened the door.

"Mr. Roebling, visitors!" she called. A man's voice drifted out, too weak to be understood. The maid turned back to them. "The master will see you."

Whitman led them into the room. At the sight of the god, Bridget gasped, her heart going out to him.

Washington Roebling sat in a wheelchair, his limbs twisted beneath him like gnarled old tree branches. His face was locked in a rictus of pain, and his eyes darted to and fro as if he couldn't quite see his visitors. When he spoke, his voice slipped out of him soft and slow, as if every syllable were an exhausting battle.

"Do not worry, child, whoever you are," he said, and Bridget had to force herself to remain patient with the slow trickle of his words. "I may look a fright, but I am no monster."

"Why do you look like that?" Bridget asked. "It's horrible!"

"Bridget!" Rory whispered, mortified.

"No, it is fine," Roebling said softly, and they had to strain to hear him. "The city remembers me this way, so this is how I remain. It is not all bad. My wife, Emily, keeps me abreast of the world outside. Even now she is meeting with some of your friends, Mr. Whitman, to convey my support for you in your fight against Kieft. And when she is not home, I can see the world from my window with my telescope. If only the world close up were as easy to see." Roebling stopped, breathing heavily from the effort of making his little speech.

"If I may ask, why are you remembered like this?" Soka asked carefully. Roebling glanced up at Whitman, imploring him with his squinting eyes.

"The building of the Brooklyn Bridge took a heavy toll on Washington's family," Whitman said, speaking for Roebling. "His father, John, designed it, but he had his foot crushed during an early accident on the site and died a month later. Washington took up the task, which he fulfilled brilliantly until he had his own horrible accident."

"What kind of accident?" Bridget asked, riveted.

"I was too impatient," Roebling breathed, then looked to Whitman.

"I don't have a thorough knowledge of the incident," Whitman apologized. "But this is what I do know. In order to build the bridge, Mr. Roebling and his workmen had to sink the base of the great towers deep into the riverbed. To do that, they had to find a way to dig underwater. So they built something called a caisson. A caisson is a large underwater room, which is sunk into the river all the way to the bottom so the workmen can dig underwater without getting wet. When the digging was done, the caissons were filled, forming the base of the towers that hold up the bridge."

"So did the room collapse on you or something?" Bridget asked the crippled god, who shook his head.

"Worse," he whispered. He glanced at Whitman, who continued the story.

"The hardest part about digging underwater is keeping the water out of your caisson. To do that, Washington would fill the entire caisson with air compressed at a much higher pressure than the water outside. Sort of like when you turn a glass upside down in the sink and push it underwater. The water doesn't flow into the glass because the air inside keeps it out. There was one problem, however. The caisson needed extremely high air pressure to keep the Hudson River from flooding in. And people aren't meant to live under such pressure. Working in the caisson was extremely dangerous because of it."

"Time moved differently down in the caisson," Roebling said, his voice weak and slow. "Men would hallucinate and lose themselves. They'd be overcome by a ravenous hunger and you'd have to stop them from gorging themselves. Only the strongest could work under such conditions, and many suffered and even died. Because worse than working in the caisson was coming out of the caisson, back into the world above."

"I'd think they'd be lucky to come back out again," Soka said, confused.

"Have you ever heard of the bends?" Whitman asked them.

"It's the diving disease," Rory said. "When deep-sea divers swim to the surface too fast, they get sick."

"Yes," Whitman said, nodding with approval. "The change in air pressure does bad things to their blood, twisting their joints and crippling them. That's what happened to Mr. Roebling and hundreds of his workers. They didn't completely understand about the bends back then, so even though they had an air lock to help decompress the workers when they returned to the surface, they didn't know how to use it. You're supposed to wait in an air lock for twenty minutes."

"I was impatient and emerged after only two minutes," Roebling whispered. "And it crippled me for the rest of my life. My wife, Emily, had to be my face on the project, helping me complete the bridge while I could only sit here in my room, watching through the window with my telescope. The great bridge took much from my family. But it was worth it. For it is bigger than myself. I would suffer a thousand times more if given the choice again."

He lapsed into silence, drained. Bridget could feel the great pride that came with sacrificing oneself for something so monumental. She glanced down at her paper fingers. She was not so different.

"Mr. Roebling," Fritz said, breaking the silence. "We came to see you because we were told to find someone called the Fair Engineer. Is that you? Did Adriaen van der Donck ever give you something to hold for him, something to keep safe?"

In a flash, Roebling's entire demeanor changed. He grew agitated, rocking in his wheelchair with such force that Bridget was scared he'd fall over. He began to shout, as loudly as he could manage.

"Do not mention that man's name here, in my home!"

"I'm sorry?" Whitman said, stepping back in confusion. "I don't understand."

"His name is not to be spoken here!"

"Sir, we have reason to believe he left something behind for us, and we need to find it—" Fritz began, but Roebling was having none of it.

"If you are here on his behalf, then you can leave right now! Go! Get out of my house!"

"But, we only want to help!" Bridget assured him. Roebling, however, could no longer speak, though he continued to twitch in his wheelchair. The maid stepped up to them, ushering them gently out of the room, closing the door on the sight of the angry god.

"I think you should leave now," she said. "That is enough for today."

"But—" Whitman began.

"That is enough!" The deferential act had disappeared, and now the maid was all business. She pushed them down the stairs and out onto the front stoop. "You may try again tomorrow, once the master has calmed down. Good day." With that, she closed the door firmly in their faces.

They were still standing around on Roebling's front stoop debating what to do when a tall, graceful woman in a nineteenth-century-style hoopskirt came striding purposefully around the corner. She immediately spotted them, her eyes widening.

"Mr. Whitman! What are you doing here? The Breuckelen council has been looking all over for you! I stopped by to pledge our support to your cause, but you weren't there to receive it, though the colonels showed up to speak for you. The borough is split into three camps and they need your steady hand to pull the undecideds onto our side."

"I will head over there directly, Emily," Whitman said apologetically. "I was optimistic I could help my friends here and still attend to my duties, but it appears my time has run out."

"What task brought you to my door?" Emily asked. "And who are your friends?" As they were introduced to the wife of Washington Roebling, Bridget was impressed by the older woman's grace and poise. Emily shook all their hands in turn, wonder crossing her face when she shook Rory's.

"So you are the one we all have to thank for ridding us of that horrid Trap," she said warmly. Rory simply blushed and glanced away. Bridget noticed Soka glaring at the older woman, which made her giggle a little.

Fritz spoke up from the vicinity of Emily's left foot. "We came to ask your husband a question about Adriaen van der Donck, but then he flew off the handle and kicked us out."

Emily sighed. "I'm not surprised. Adriaen and I became friends long ago when I came to Mannahatta to speak on my husband's behalf about the importance, from an engineering perspective, of taking down the Trap. We were only friends, of course. Adriaen had loved his wife completely and never got over her passing, while I love my husband. But Washington cannot leave his room, and his imagination runs wild. We often had the same problems when we were mortal. He watched the progress of the bridge being built from our window, but I was the one who had to go out among the workmen and investors and city councilmen and make it happen."

"Some say you were as much the builder of that bridge as your husband," Whitman told her, but she waved this off.

"I did what I had to. Washington was usually fine, but sometimes he grew jealous of my time away. Men like Adriaen made it worse. If he kicked you out, it will be a day or so before he's calmed down enough to receive visitors. Is there something I could do to help?"

"So it's safe to say Adriaen never had any dealings with your husband?" Whitman asked.

"None, sorry," Emily replied. She glanced up at the window at the top of her brownstone. "I should go inside. He's probably watching us now with his telescope and I don't want him to get agitated again. Good day to you." She nodded pleasantly and climbed the steps to her front door.

Bridget glanced around at her friends, waiting for someone to say the obvious, but they all seemed ready to let Emily go. They were so stupid, she thought. It was right in front of their noses.

"Mrs. Roebling!" she called out, stopping Emily halfway through her front door.

"Yes?" Emily replied, glancing back down at them.

"We came by because we thought your hubby might be the Fair Engineer, who we were supposed to find. But I don't think it's him. I think you're the Fair Engineer."

"Oh, do you?" Emily said, looking confused. Bridget could see the truth dawning on her friends' faces, and she had to resist the urge to stick her tongue out.

"You were friends with Adriaen, right?" Bridget asked. "Did he give you something to hold, something special? A package?"

Emily's eyes widened and she quickly ran down the stairs to them. "You are the ones, then? He never said."

"It's us all right," Bridget replied.

"So you have the package?" Rory asked.

"I hid it, long ago," Emily replied. "It won't be easy to retrieve."

Just then, the front door flew open to reveal the maid. "Madam! Madam, the master is calling for you. He requires your presence right away!"

Emily turned to the children, her face apologetic. "I have to go. He has already associated you with Adriaen. I can't escort you to my hiding place now; it will hurt him deeply."

"Tell us where to go," Rory said urgently. "We'll go get the package ourselves."

"All right, but you must be careful. Walt, are you going with them?"

"I can't right now," Whitman said, throwing up his hands. "I have to return to steady the council. Can you wait until I return, Rory?"

"We don't have time," Rory said. "I'm sorry, we need to go now."

"You have to be careful, then, and follow my instructions exactly," Emily told them sternly.

"We will," Bridget reassured her. "Where did you put it?"

Emily turned toward the great bridge that spanned the river and pointed at the base of the tower on the Brooklyn side.

"I hid it in the bottom of the caisson."

INTO THE CAISSON

Nicholas and Buckongahelas stood on a small hill in the Ramble, watching over the military exercises in the corn-field below. Rows of Munsees were taking turns running through the stalks, firing arrows at the surrounding trees, while nearby, pairs of warriors sparred with their copper spears. On the opposite end of the field, a group of gods and spirits prac-ticed hand-to-hand combat, deflecting fake knives with cudgels and steel armor attached to their forearms. Nearby, squads of battle roaches, led by Liv M'Garoth atop her rat, were practic-ing their maneuvers. In another corner of the field, Lincoln led a group of children of the gods in mock sword fights. More children had shown up than Nicholas expected, which gave him hope, including, to his surprise, Jane van Cortlandt and Robert de Vries. Jane had confided that the knives scared her. She didn't want to be a murderer; it was time to do what was right. Hearing this, Alexa had hugged her so tight that Nicholas was frightened the poor girl would suffocate.

"I wish there were more," Buckongahelas muttered at Nich-olas's side as he looked over the troops.

"There will be," Nicholas replied. "More gods and spirits are joining every day. Especially the gods, now that there are disgruntled spirits roaming about with knives. I think that plan is backfiring a bit on Kieft."

"I'm not so sure," the Munsee war leader mused. "He was never a foolish man."

"I just wish our leaders could decide on what to do with this army," Nicholas said. "My father and your father, Hamilton and the rest—they can't seem to come to any kind of agreement."

"Well, Kieft's army hasn't done anything yet," Buckongahelas said. "Which means our army can't do anything. Something tells me the decision will be made for us, and soon."

Nicholas continued watching the action in the field, trepidation gnawing at his heart. He could only hope he found the leader he was searching for before Kieft made his move.

Soka stood at the edge of the little plaza that surrounded one of the double-arched towers that held up the Brooklyn Bridge, leaning carelessly against the guardrail as she stared across the river at Manhattan lighting up at the onset of evening. Tears rose unbidden as she took in the bold, bright city before her. She'd been up and down New York since the Trap fell, but it had never before hit her just how wonderfully strange was this new world outside her park. As she stood far above the water rushing to the sea, the wind whipping through her hair, she felt like an eagle perched on a mountain ledge, privileged to see the world from such rarefied air. The setting sun sent stabs of golden light glinting off of the towering metal buildings across the river, each skyscraper fighting the rest to be the closest to heaven. She'd never dreamed such a world existed, and all the while it lay just outside her little village in the Ramble. Staring at the twinkling city before her, Soka forgot for a moment about her worries and just gloried in her freedom.

She heard a shout from behind her and reluctantly turned, the euphoria already fading. Rory had found the door in the giant, brick-lined pillar that held up the east end of the suspension bridge. In his mortal world, this door did not exist, but here in the spirit realm it was the entrance to the past, where the old caissons were still in use deep underwater, keeping out the river while trapping inside the souls of those who had died during those dangerous days of the bridge's construction. According to the Fair Engineer, those damned souls still worked in the high-pressured air of the caisson, eternally digging into the riverbed, chained to the bridge for all time.

"Do not let them know you are mortals," Emily had warned them. "They hate mortals for being able to breathe the free air. They'd try to trap you down there with them. So get in and get out—if you follow my instructions exactly, they shouldn't bother you."

They'd agreed. The last thing anyone wanted was to die in that caisson.

Now it was time to pass through the door, and Bridget and Fritz moved in front of Rory, who was about to enter.

"Remember to be careful in there, Rory," Fritz told him. "You're still healing."

"I'm fine!" Rory protested. Soka sighed, still feeling a twinge as she recalled him lying in her lap on the floor Simon's car, unconscious and bleeding. She thought she'd lost him and it had hurt even worse than she'd feared.

"I'll look after him," she promised, stepping to Rory's side. "If he staggers, I will see."

"I can look after myself," Rory said.

"So I've noticed," Soka replied, then turned to step through the door into the Brooklyn Bridge.

They stood at the top of an old set of stairs. Fritz trotted toward them atop Clarence, and together the two began hopping down one step at a time. Bridget followed and then Rory, with Soka last. Soon they left the light of the open doorway behind as they descended into the dark.

They reached the first landing, which was dimly lit by a flickering lantern on the wall. Bridget tried to take it off its hook so they could have light on the stairs, but the lantern wouldn't budge. They'd have to rely on these little way posts to guide them—there was no other light. The stairs continued down from the landing, and they followed them deeper into the tower.

Soka could just make out Rory's jacket in the near darkness. She'd been so scared that he would be hurt the way Finn had been, that she'd pushed him away. And then he got hurt anyway, and it had nothing to do with her. In the end, people were hurt no matter what she did. Maybe the time had come to stop being afraid.

The soft light grew stronger as they approached the bottom of the stairs. Soka could hear the loud drip of water sliding down the old stones, each drop sounding like a gunshot in the quiet stairwell. They reached the bottom of the stairs, where a trapdoor waited in the middle of the floor.

"This must be the air lock," Fritz said. He hopped down off Clarence and gave the rat a pat. "You wait here, old boy. The ladder's a killer. We'll be back soon enough."

"Let's go spelunking!" Bridget said brightly, leaning over to lift the trapdoor. A sickly yellow glow rose up out of the hole in the floor, but Rory didn't hesitate before climbing down through the hole, with Fritz riding on his shoulder. Bridget followed and Soka went last, pulling the trapdoor shut after her.

The room they descended into was just large enough to hold them. An old lantern lit the space from one high corner, though it barely beat back the shadows. A round wheel poked out of the wall, and a second wheel rose out of the floor next to another trapdoor. Soka guessed it led down to the caisson. On the wall near the ladder hung a strange-looking clock, with a single arrow pointing up to the number 0.

"That's the pressure gauge," Fritz told her, noticing her confusion. "That tells us when it's safe to go down, and later, when it's safe to go up."

"So now what?" Bridget asked.

"Now we pressurize," Fritz said. "Soka, could you turn that wheel by you on the floor?"

Soka leaned over and gave the wheel a big turn. The sound of air hissing into the room cut through the silence, and the arrow on the pressure gauge began to move, sliding past number after number as the air pressure rose to match the pressure down in the caisson. Finally, the hissing stopped, as did the gauge.

"Can I open it now?" Rory asked, kneeling by the trap-door.

"Yes," Fritz answered. "But remember, this is the easy part. The hard part will be when we come back. Then we'll have to reduce the air pressure and wait twenty minutes before opening the trapdoor above us. Any sooner and Rory and I run the risk of being crippled or even dying. Soka is a spirit, so she should be safe. I don't know what would happen to you, Bridget."

"I don't want to find out!" Bridget said. "I'm already feeling a little weird."

"Emily said the air pressure can play tricks on your mind," Fritz warned them. "Some of the men reported hallucinating while they worked. So stay focused, find the package, and then we get out! Okay? Rory, I said, okay?"

"Okay," Rory answered impatiently, his hand on the trap-door. "Can I open it now?"

"Yes." Fritz lifted his helmet over his head and nodded. Rory pulled up the trapdoor and it fell over with a thump, making them all flinch.

"Careful!" Fritz warned. "We don't want to attract any at-tention."

But Rory was already disappearing down the ladder, taking Fritz with him. Bridget followed and finally Soka climbed be-hind them into the depths of the caisson.

They climbed straight down through a cramped shaft barely wide enough for their bodies. Even Soka could tell the air was strange down here—she felt it pushing on her like an invisible hand trying to suffocate her. The shaft was pitch-black, with only the dim light coming from the air lock to cut through the darkness. Soka felt like she was descending into hell. Eventually, flickering red light began to rise up around them, and then suddenly they passed out of the shaft and into the caisson proper.

The ladder led down to the rocky ground, where they carefully stepped off the final rung and gathered in a small group. Gazing around, Soka felt a shudder run through her. This truly was a hellish place. The caisson looked more like an ancient underwater cave than a man-made room. Rocky walls rose up on all sides, though wooden walls separated various sections of the caisson from one another. Wooden supports rose up along the rock wall every few feet, keeping the ceiling, and the entire bridge, from falling down on top of them. Red light from various lanterns cast devilish black shapes onto the walls.

Everywhere they looked they saw the shadows of men, swinging pickaxes into the stony ground or lugging wheelbarrows filled with rocks toward larger shafts, where they dumped their cargo into large containers at the base. One such container, completely filled, began to rise up its shaft, disappearing into the ceiling. That must have been how they cleared all the rubble from the site, Soka guessed. The men spoke to one another in low tones, but Soka could not pick out any words. It sounded like meaningless rumbling. The only other sounds were the bite of the pick into the stone and the grunts of the men. Soka swallowed—she prayed none of the shadow men looked in her direction. She clutched her bow, which hung from her shoulder as always, but she didn't know if an arrow would do any good down here.

"Quick, let's find it and get out of here," Fritz whispered. Soka

remembered Emily's instructions. She'd hid the package beneath an overturned wheelbarrow near one of the wooden walls. Soka gulped as she looked around—the caisson stretched on in every direction, seemingly without end. Which wall did she mean?

"I'll go this way," Rory said, and started to walk off in one direction. Soka grabbed his arm, holding him fast.

"We stick together," she hissed. "Otherwise we'll never find each other again."

Rory started to argue, but then he reluctantly nodded. They picked a direction and began to walk toward the nearest dividing wall.

That particular wall didn't have any wheelbarrows nearby, and neither did the one after that. Soka's heart was in her mouth as she glanced around—with every second that passed she grew more fearful that one of the shadow workers would notice them. But so far, they stayed away, keeping to their work. As they searched, however, a new worry cropped up. The first sign came from Rory, who kept glaring at the walls.

"Someone's watching me," he muttered. "I can feel his black eyes on me." In his fear, his voice grew louder. "Where is he? I can feel him!" Soka placed a hand over Rory's mouth to shut him up, furtively looking around to make certain no one heard them. They checked the next wall—no wheelbarrow. Now Bridget was starting to look uncomfortable.

"Soka, I don't want to freak you out," the paper girl said quietly, pulling out her little wooden sword. "But I think my sword is whistling. Do you think the shadow guys can hear? What song is that? It's on the tip of my brain! Man, it's killing me!"

"It's the air," Soka whispered. "It's making you hear things. We've got to find this package quickly before we all go crazy."

"Too late," Fritz said from his place on Rory's shoulder. He started to talk louder, as if struggling to be heard. "I feel like I'm inside a seashell!"

"It's 'Jingle Bell Rock!'" Bridget exclaimed. "I love Christmas!"

"Be quiet!" Soka hissed. "It's all in your head!" Some of the shadow men had started to glance in their direction. It was only a matter of time before they realized they had strangers in their midst. At the next wall there was a pile of stones, but no wheelbarrow.

"Maybe somebody is using the wheelbarrow," Bridget suggested. "Man, I could use some eggnog right about now."

"Emily swore that the wheelbarrow hadn't been used in a century," Soka reminded her. "These men are locked in a hellish routine. They've got no reason to change it."

"We better find it soon," Rory said through gritted teeth. Soka was alarmed to see how haggard he looked. "I can't take much more of this demon's voice in my head. Wait, what's that!"

The next wall had come into view, and there was a wheelbarrow, overturned near the rock wall. Before anyone could react, Rory bolted forward, staggering as he pushed through the heavy air to reach Emily's hiding place. He righted the wheelbarrow in one smooth motion, sending it clattering against the wall. The shadow men had really started to notice them now; some were leaning against their pickaxes and watching them with great interest. Even their mumbling had started to hum a little louder, though Soka still couldn't make out the words. She had a bad feeling about this.

Rory was oblivious, however, desperate to escape whatever voice he was hearing in his head, and he dug through the dirt where the wheelbarrow had been with his bare hands. Bridget knelt down next to him and began to dig as well; her paper-and-wood hand cut through the dirt more easily than Rory's flesh ones. But Rory dug with such abandon that Soka worried he'd hurt himself. She glanced around—the shadow men were still watching. She tried to gauge the distance from their spot to the ladder—it seemed a mile away.

"I found it!" Rory shouted, the compressed air making him completely heedless of the shadow men. He lifted a brown-wrapped package into the air, dirt still falling in clumps from his prize. In his elation at finding the treasure, he didn't watch what he was doing, and his other hand grazed a sharp rock by his knees. A red line appeared along the back of his hand, and a single drop of blood landed on the ground.

A hush fell over the caisson as all work ceased and the mumbling dried up in an instant. Rory didn't seem to notice, but Bridget was looking around with worry on her face and Soka could feel her stomach turn as she realized that every single shadow man was staring at that drop of blood. The murmuring picked up again, growing louder and louder, but this time Soka could make out a word being repeated over and over again.

"Mortal. Mortal. Mortal. Mortal. MORTAL!"

"Rory!" she called. Rory looked up, his eyes widening as he saw the spirits all around. "Rory, we've got to run. Are you ready?"

"Wait!" Fritz ordered them. He pulled something out of his armor. "Go on my signal." He tossed something through the air, which landed at the feet of the nearest men. A loud crack sounded, making the shadow men leap back in confusion.

"RUN!" Fritz screamed, and Soka took off, Bridget and Rory behind her. The shadow men's confusion didn't last long, and soon they were giving chase. Fritz threw firecracker after firecracker at the men up ahead, clearing a path to the ladder. But it looked so far away.

It didn't help that Soka felt like she was running through mud, forcing herself to push forward. Rory passed her, his face in agony as he pushed himself to move faster. A group of shadow men reached out to grab him and he kicked them away, reaching down to grab an ax on the fly. The package still tucked under his arm, he flailed the ax around one-handed, trying to clear a path.

"He's like the Terminator!" Bridget gasped at Soka's side. But then a shadow man ducked, letting the ax swing wildly above his head, before reaching for Rory's throat. A *thwack* sounded through the air as an arrow appeared in the man's chest, driving him back. Soka lowered her bow.

"Even Terminators need help," she said, and ran to catch up with Rory. Soon she was firing arrows left and right as she ran, even as Fritz continued to toss firecrackers. There were just too many of them. Bridget began throwing rocks at the scores of attackers, but she couldn't keep up—for each man struck, three took his place. They reached the shaft, and Soka gasped. The ladder was completely surrounded by shadow men. How were they going to get past them all?

"We're trapped!" Fritz exclaimed.

"No!" Bridget cried. She held her sword up high. "Ready, Buttkicker 2? Time to deal some justice!"

With that, she ran toward the ladder, blindly whacking at the group of shadow men before running into them headlong and toppling them like bowling pins. The shadow men recovered quickly, trying to stop the dynamo in their midst. But Bridget was like a girl possessed, and she beat back everyone in her way, opening up a passage to the ladder.

Soka ran up to Rory, grabbing his arm even as Fritz kept the shadow men around them at bay with his firecrackers.

"Come on!" she cried. "Your sister is clearing the way!" Together, they ran for the ladder. Bridget continued her battle, smacking any shadow man who came too close. One of her fingers was bent back unnaturally and some of her hair littered the floor. But Bridget smiled proudly.

"I'm a superhero!" she cried before smacking another shadow man in the face. She looked so happy that Soka feared she'd never be satisfied as a simple mortal again. She pushed Rory to the ladder, turning to send more arrows flying into the seemingly endless army of shadow men. Even close up, she couldn't make out their faces—they were only sweaty bodies in dirt-streaked clothes. But she knew what would happen if they got too close.

"Bridget," she called out. "Time to go!" Bridget kicked at the large group of shadow men before climbing up the ladder. Soka turned to send another arrow into the mass of shadow men that now completely surrounded her.

"Come on!" Rory screamed from above her, and Soka spun,

leaping halfway up the ladder and starting to climb. A hand reached out to grab her ankle and for a horrifying moment she was certain she was about to be pulled down into the mob. But Fritz sent one more firecracker down the ladder, knocking the hand clear off and freeing her to climb.

It seemed to take forever to make her way up the shaft in the dark. But finally she spied the yellow light of the trapdoor. With a relieved sigh, she pulled herself into the air lock. But her relief was short-lived as Fritz looked down through the trapdoor.

"They're coming!" he warned them, sending another firecracker down the hole. "That didn't even faze them. We've got to close this trapdoor!"

Bridget sprang forward, yanking down the trapdoor just as hands appeared in the opening. She slammed the door down a few times until the hands fell away and she could finally close it. Before they could relax, however, the trapdoor began to shudder, as if someone were beating on it. The hinges began to rattle with each blow.

"The door won't hold for the twenty minutes it takes to decompress," Fritz said. Soka looked around at the brave battle roach, the loyal paper girl, and the determined Rory Hennessy. She reached out to touch his face.

"Good-bye, Rory," she said quietly, the fear in her stomach gone. It was time for her to do the protecting. She leaned in and kissed his cheek. "Be well."

With that, she turned to the trapdoor, pulled it open, and dropped into the hole.

She landed on top of a mass of shadow men hanging from

the ladder like mindless animals. Looking up, she reached for the trapdoor she'd just opened and grabbed it.

"Whatever happens, don't open this door!" she shouted, and then pulled it shut, leaving her in the dark with the shadow men. She kicked down, hard, driving the men away from the trapdoor. She wasn't mortal, so she knew they weren't as keen to take her, but that wouldn't stop them in their killing frenzy. She wouldn't let them pass, however. She refused to let them get to Rory. He would survive, if it took everything she had.

She began to feel warm, and then suddenly she realized she could see a little. Something was lighting her way. The warmth intensified and she was able to make out the faces of the shadow men below her. They were black as soot, eyeless, with red slits for mouths. The light grew brighter and she suddenly knew where it was coming from. It was pouring out of her. All the magic she'd been missing for the past few days flowed through her again, only this time it was tenfold as strong. The light grew blinding as the power flowed through her and she suddenly felt the earth surrounding her. She was a part of the land that gave her strength. Her mouth opened to say the words and she dropped like a burning stone into the mass of attacking shadow men, exploding like a sun melting everything in its path . . .

Rory stood frozen, staring helplessly at the trapdoor Soka had just dropped through. He felt like someone had kicked him in the gut. What was she thinking? She'd pulled the door shut before he could stop her. He fell to his knees by the door, reaching out to grab it.

"Don't touch that!" Fritz yelled. "Don't waste her sacrifice!" Fritz ordered Bridget to turn the wheel on the wall, which she did, and the air began to hiss. The gauge dipped lower and lower, but with painful slowness.

"And now we wait," Fritz said, pulling off his helmet. He looked devastated, and Bridget fell into the corner, sobbing her dry tears. Then, suddenly, the ground began to shake. Rory had to reach out to steady himself as dirt fell on them all from the ceiling. Finally, the rumbling ceased, leaving them all looking to one another in confusion.

"Was that an earthquake?" Fritz asked. He placed his hand on the trapdoor, pulling it back with a gasp. "That's hot!"

Rory held his hand above the trapdoor, which indeed radiated heat. "What did she do?" he muttered.

"I don't know," Fritz said. "But whatever it was, it sounds like the shadow men have been beaten back."

Bridget collapsed in a new wave of crying, and Rory reached out to give her a hug. She fell into him, clinging to him as she sobbed. Finally, her crying slowed, and Rory leaned back against the wall, exhausted and heartbroken.

Time passed, so slowly, and they didn't speak. They were in too much pain. Rory didn't even bother to pull out the package Soka had sacrificed herself for. It hurt too much. Finally, the gauge hit zero. Fritz crawled over to Rory and climbed into his shirt pocket. "Time's up," he said gently. "Let's go." Forcing down his tears, Rory pulled down the trapdoor and climbed up the ladder. Clarence was waiting for them, and Fritz hopped aboard his rat steed, leading the way back up the stairs. The climb up seemed much longer than the descent. Their steps were heavier with their loss. Rory kept visualizing Soka's face before she left. He could still feel her lips on his cheek. It had sent his heart racing. But then she was gone.

They reached the top of the stairs and stepped out onto the bridge. The sun had set, but the beautiful lights of New York City lit up the sky in every direction. And all Rory could think was that Soka would never see these lights again. She'd just begun to live her life outside of the Trap, and now it was over. He'd never see her again.

He walked over to the rail, where he had watched Soka gazing with wonder at the Manhattan skyline. He would remember that look on her face, so beautiful in her delight. He would remember it always.

A commotion drew his attention behind him, and to his shock a blackened figure stumbled out of the door cut into the bridge tower. At first Rory thought it was one of the shadow men, braving the world above to drag him back down to hell. But then he saw the braid, still smoldering. He took a hesitant step forward.

"Soka?" he said, wonder coloring his voice. "Is that you?"

"You're all right?" Soka croaked back. Her clothes were black, is if she'd been in a great fire. Bridget ran to her, but Soka only had eyes for Rory.

"We're fine," Rory said. Tears rose to his eyes as the dam broke inside. "I thought you were dead! I thought—"

"Shut up!" Soka said, striding up to him, wiping her face clean with the back of her hand. She grabbed the back of his head, pulled him toward her, and kissed the life out of him. His heart pounded so hard he thought it would explode, then she finally let go, the tears sending streaks through her soot-covered cheeks.

"That was awesome!" Bridget's voice cried from somewhere behind them, but Rory didn't look. He only had eyes for Soka as the pain melted away.

THE IRON SHIP

Alexa crept down the alley, keeping to the wall. Her path was filled with moaning bodies, dead or dying. The worst part was that she knew them. These were her former friends and enemies. These were the children of the gods.

She'd heard there'd been a big fight among the children, caused by a large haul of lockets one crew had obtained. Nicholas advised her not to go, but she had to see the aftermath for herself. Now she wished she hadn't.

"Alexa?" a voice moaned near her feet. Glancing down, she spied Teddy Twiller lying against the wall. His face was pale and his shirt was covered in blood. Alexa could tell right away that he wasn't going to make it.

"Teddy," she said, kneeling down by his side. "What happened?"

"We thought everything would be wonderful when we became gods," Teddy breathed, barely able to talk. "But there weren't enough lockets for everyone. So Lola Greeley stabbed Martha in the back to take her locket, and then Freddie Clinton killed her, and then everyone was killing everyone else. Randolph is dead, too. I think Hedy Barnum got him, or maybe her sister. I didn't even know who stabbed me, but he got his before he could take this beauty. Look!" He pulled a bloodstained locket from under his shirt. "I'm a god, Alexa! The God of Broken Traffic Lights. I did it. I made something of myself. Finally, I'm somebody. I'm somebody . . ." And with that, Teddy Twiller died.

Alexa knelt there for a while, head bowed, until the locket crumbled away into nothing.

Rory and Soka were still standing with their arms around each other atop the great bridge when a wagon came racing toward them from the Brooklyn side. Whitman was driving, and he stood up when he saw them.

"Quick! Get in the wagon! We've got to get you off the bridge!"

They ran over to him, leaping into the back. Rory reached down to lift up Fritz and Clarence before climbing in himself. Whitman turned and sprayed something all over them.

"What was that!" Rory said, spitting out the foul-tasting stuff.

"Bug spray," Whitman replied. "We've gotten word from a spy in Kieft's camp that they're using flies to spy. And by the looks of those dead insects at your feet, we just took care of any that might be on you. Kieft already knows you're in Breuckelen, though. He's sent some of his local goons out to nab you. And I don't know what you did down there, but we all felt it, so they're probably on their way. Colonel Smallwood and Colonel Wood are guarding the entrance to the bridge, so hopefully the way is clear. Don't worry, I have a plan to get you out of Breuckelen and on your way."

He flicked the reins, urging the horses to pull the wagon as quickly as possible across the bridge, past two regiments of vigilant soldiers headed up by a waving Smallwood and Wood and into Brooklyn. As they raced down the streets of Brooklyn, Rory felt a hand take his. Looking over, he saw Soka smiling at him. Even covered in soot, she was beautiful.

"We're going to be fine," Rory told her.

"I know," Soka replied. "She promised me."

"Who promised you?" Rory asked, but Soka wouldn't answer. She gazed out into the night, the wind sending her hair flying, and her hand still holding tight to his.

At last, they pulled into a large shipyard. Waiting at the dock was the strangest-looking boat Rory had ever seen. It resembled a long raft, made completely of iron, with a single round pilothouse poking out two-thirds of the way back. As they drew closer, Rory noticed a bump toward the bow—and the two guns sticking out of it. A man stepped out of the pilothouse as they pulled up alongside, waving.

"Get aboard, quickly!" he said. "They'll be here soon!"

Whitman helped them aboard the strange vessel, then hopped back onto his wagon. "I've got more work to do here. Lieutenant Worden, take them to Staten Island!"

"Aye aye, Mr. Whitman," Lieutenant Worden said, saluting. He turned to Rory, Bridget, Soka, and Fritz. "Welcome aboard the USS *Monitor*, the finest ironclad ever built. We'll get you to Staten Island in one piece, I promise."

Gunfire suddenly rang out, and they all ducked.

"Get belowdecks!" Worden yelled, pushing them into the pilothouse. To Rory's surprise, a ladder inside led down below. Most of the boat seemed to be below water, like a submarine. Worden was shouting, "Fire at will, man!" The boat shuddered as the gun turret rotated to aim at a group of Kieft's men who were advancing with guns blazing. They appeared to be mobsters from the twenties, judging by their tommy guns. The ironclad began to pull away from the dock as its guns locked into the oncoming men and fired. A crack split the air as one of the guns lit up, sending a shell exploding onto the docks. When the smoke cleared, Rory was dismayed to see that most of the mobsters had gotten out of the way of the shell. They fired at the retreating ship, and Rory heard the *plink* of bullets hitting the iron all around him. Lieutenant Worden turned, and started, surprised to see them all still in the pilothouse.

"Get belowdecks! That's an order!"

Rory climbed down the ladder into the bowels of the ship, followed by Bridget and Soka. He placed Fritz and Clarence on the ground and looked around. They were in an incredibly cramped hallway, where crewmen were rushing back and forth. A small table stood nearby, and Rory walked over, sitting down. Soka joined him, and Bridget sat on his other side, beaming like the Cheshire cat.

"What?" Rory asked his sister. She shrugged, still smiling.

"Nothing."

Suddenly the gunfire stopped, and Lieutenant Worden poked his head down belowdecks.

"We're away," he told them. "Don't worry, you're safe here. The Confederate army couldn't crack us, and neither will Kieft.

We'll get you to Staten Island in no time." He disappeared back into the pilothouse.

Rory let out a long breath.

"Well, that was something, wasn't it?"

"Why don't we read the journal," Soka suggested, finding his hand again. Rory pulled out the package and tore it open. Inside was a small sheaf of papers with the word Two written at the top.

"At last we'll fill in some blanks," Rory said. "Maybe we'll find out who this Henry was who Adriaen mentioned in the last—I mean next—entry." He began to read aloud.

After much discussion with Marta, I agreed to Kieft's plan. But persuading the others in Mannahatta was not so easy. Peter Minuit's disappearance helped, as did my wife's passionate arguments. She really is a remarkable woman. Only recently having given birth to our daughter, Alexa (the first of the children of the gods!), still she rushes throughout Mannahatta, persuading god after god to our way of thinking. I believe she does it for Alexa—she wants to secure this new land for her daughter. I cannot express the love I feel for this wonderful woman. I am truly blessed to have her. I do this for her—so that we may have eternity together in peace.

Once the gods came around to the plan, Kieft began to collect the blood. Each god had to squeeze a single drop into Kieft's pipe. To that end, Kieft sent around his manservant, a strange man named Henry. Henry acted like a spirit, but something about him rang false to me. He seemed too . . . real, and not without power of his own. But the man was skittish in Kieft's presence, flinching at every word the god threw in his direction. Then I accidentally discovered his secret . . .

I was walking down a side alley in New Amsterdam, enjoying a brief rainstorm that was washing over the town, when I spied Henry in the distance. He was staring up at the sky, his face peaceful as the water rained down on his face. But then we were both startled by a voice, crying out from down the street. It was one of the Rattle Watch, the mortal guards who stroll the city as protectors. The guard was staring right at Henry, demanding that he identify himself. Henry started, his hand flying up to his forehead. Obviously finding nothing there, he quickly turned tail and ran, disappearing down a side street with the guard in pursuit. I realized then why Henry bothered me so. He was mortal!

I cornered him the next day, demanding answers. He seemed so terrified I thought he was going to die of a heart attack. After I promised not to tell his secret, he confided that he was indeed mortal, but long ago he had learned to see Mannahatta and decided to live there. He had lived with the Munsees for a time, learning some of their magic. One such spell was a special concoction he wore on his forehead, which rendered him invisible to mortals, but the rain had washed it off.

He asked me not to tell anyone. Kieft knew, Henry told me, and used this knowledge to his advantage. But when I offered to intercede, Henry begged me not to. Just keep the secret, he begged me. He loved Mannahatta and never wanted to live in the mortal world again. I agreed to keep his secret, but I secretly swore that I would find some way to help that poor man before Kieft used him up and tossed him aside as he did all his tools.

We finally gained a drop of blood from every god (as well

as little Alexa, just to be safe). Kieft then informed us of the next step we must take. We must make our case to the land, in a place of great power. Only then would we see whether we would ever be accepted by the land as one of her own.

Rory finished reading, glancing through the pages to see if he'd missed anything. He sat back. "You know what I think?" he asked. "I think our dad is Henry."

"That's what I think, too!" Bridget cried, clapping.

"But if he's mortal, how is he still alive?" Fritz asked. "This was over three hundred years ago!"

"I'm tired of all these secrets!" Bridget exclaimed.

"What I don't understand is what these pages are supposed to tell us," Rory said, frustrated. "I don't understand how any of this has anything to do with Kieft's treasure."

"Remember, Adriaen didn't write this to tell you how to find Kieft's stash," Fritz reminded him. "He was documenting the origins of the Agreement. He apparently felt your father—if Henry, indeed, is your father—was an important part of it. We just don't know why, yet. Maybe the next package will tell us more."

"I hope so," Rory said. "We're running out of packages and we still don't know where this place of great power is. I bet Dad knows where this place is! Why did he have to stay behind?"

"To save our lives," Soka reminded him. "Don't worry. We will find it. I have faith."

They lapsed into silence as the ironclad chugged along the East River, moving slowly but inexorably toward its destination, the fabled land called Staten Island.

STAATEN EYLANDT

Boss Tweed sat in his chair in the back room of the tavern in Five Points, listening to the reports of the mayhem unleashed by his gangs. Gang leader after gang leader shuffled through, telling lurid tales of the gods they'd murdered, or the innocent spirits they'd maimed, all in the name of chaos. One by one, they handed over the lockets they'd stolen, and if Tweed decided to reward them, he placed that locket around his lackey's neck, turning the dirty murderers into the God of Blues Clubs, or the God of Stolen Cable, or the God of Suspicious-Looking Moles. Once they became deities, of course, they couldn't murder any more gods, as that would be breaking the rules they now had to follow. So Tweed withheld lockets from the best killers, promising them the juiciest godships at the end of the killing spree. But his men were becoming harder and harder to satisfy.

One such talented killer stood before him now, spinning a tale about some old-lady Goddess of Rent-Controlled Apartments he'd stabbed in her own bedroom. Kid Dropper, his name was, one of the mobster spirits, and the greed for a locket all his own was written on his face. But when he finished his story and asked for his reward, Tweed put up his hand.

"I can't just yet, Kid," he said. "You're too valuable to waste. The minute you put that locket on you'd be useless to the cause, you know that. And why would you want to be God of Rent-Controlled Apartments, anyway? What kind of life is that? I've got a good one set aside for you. God of Bribery. You'll have it soon, I promise."

"Why can't I have both?" Kid Dropper snarled, not happy. Tweed sighed. There was no way he was handing out more than one locket to this little murderer. He'd begun to doubt the wisdom of wearing more than one locket, anyway. He wore three, himself, making him—in addition to God of Rabble Politics— God of Old Elevators and God of Number Two Pencils. Quite frankly, the added duties were a pain in the neck. Of course, it could be worse. He could be like that idiot Jay Gould, God of Crooked Finance, who'd hoarded twenty of the lockets and then threw them all on at once. He could barely function, he had so many duties to fulfill, and soon he couldn't keep up with them all. Eventually, he ignored his tasks one time too many, and all his lockets melted away, turning him into a fallen god. That's when they all learned: fail at the duties assigned by one locket, and you lose them all.

"Two lockets are more trouble than it's worth," Tweed told the mobster. "Be patient. You know I'll take care of you."

"Maybe I'll just take care of you!" Kid Dropper cried, pulling out his god-killing knife and launching himself at Tweed. Tweed fell back, throwing himself to the ground just in time to avoid the knife thrust. Before the mobster could get in another stab, two of Tweed's men burst into the room, guns blaz-

ing, filling Kid Dropper with hot lead. The mobster fell to the
ground, dead.

"Didn't I tell you to search them before they came in here!"
Tweed screamed, throwing his overturned chair at his lackeys.
"No one brings a knife into my presence! No one! Now take
that carcass out of here!" His men quickly dragged the body
from the room, leaving Tweed to fume. This was getting out of
hand. Where was the respect? Tweed hoped Kieft knew what
he was doing. Because if they let this go on too long, no god
would be safe.

***

Rory stood on the rocky, moonlit beach watching the USS
Monitor chugging away, the odd iron ship barely a shadow on
the water against the bright lights of Manhattan at night. The-
ories about his father ran through his head, but he had no answers. He glanced at Soka standing near him. The Munsee girl
was tugging thoughtfully on her long braid as she watched the
iron boat leave. Her eyes seemed to twinkle in the moonlight.
Rory looked away quickly, before she could notice him staring.
But not before Bridget saw him, and she smiled hugely, making
little kissing noises with her mouth. He smacked her on the
shoulder.

"Ow!" she whined, though he knew she barely felt it. She
stuck her tongue out at him before looking around the bay.
"What is this place? What are all those weird shapes in the
water?"

Indeed, the bay was littered with dark shapes poking up out
of the sea. As his eyes adjusted, Rory thought they looked like
ships, or the shells of ships. Every type of seaworthy vessel

seemed to be represented: tugboats, sailboats, old tankers—all decaying in the water.

"This is a ship graveyard," Fritz told them, turning Clarence around to face them. "Listen."

At first Rory couldn't hear anything but the wind, but then he realized that the wind itself was alive. Soft voices whispered, just faint enough to be impossible to understand, but insistent, as if someone were trying to get his attention.

"What is that?" Soka asked, hearing it, too.

"The souls of the ships," Fritz replied. "No one died aboard them, so there are no human ghosts here, but the ships themselves live on. They're harmless, but they tend to keep the mortals away. So it's a good place for you to wait for me to return."

"Where are you going?" Bridget asked, hopping over to him. "I'll come!"

"No, you all should wait here," Fritz told her. "There is no one to meet us here like in the other boroughs, so I'm going to visit a friend. I've got a hunch about who this Unlucky Patroon is we're supposed to find, but I want to make certain. I'll be back!"

Before they could protest, Fritz flicked the reins, sending Clarence scampering away into the trees. Unsure what else to do, Rory and Soka sat down on a large rock near the water. Already bored, Bridget skipped down to the water's edge and picked up pebbles, sending them skipping across the bay, one by one.

"Stop that, Bridge," Rory told her. "You'll disturb the ships."

"I'm talking to them!" Bridget replied brightly, sending

another stone hopping across the water's surface. "It's Morse code for boats!"

Rory decided to ignore her. He could feel Soka sitting right next to him, as he stared across the bay toward Manhattan, which twinkled in the distance like a fairy city. After a moment he glanced at her, asking the question that had been on his mind ever since their escape.

"What happened to you down in the caisson?"

"I don't know," she answered, her eyes touching him briefly before returning to the bay. "It was as if a dam broke inside me and everything came exploding out. Even now I can feel the waters surging within me. I'm barely holding on, actually."

"Can I do anything?" he asked.

"Sit with me. I feel better when you sit with me."

And so they sat, side by side, staring out at the magical city glowing in the distance, as the paper girl danced along the shore, sending messages by pebble to all the dead ships in the bay.

An hour or so later, Fritz returned, riding out of the trees as quickly as he could. He pulled up in front of Rory and Soka as Bridget came running up.

"I found him," Fritz said breathlessly. "I found your Unlucky Patroon."

"That's fantastic," Rory said, leaping to his feet.

"Not quite." Fritz stopped him. "He's been captured by the British and no one knows where they're holding him. He really is unlucky, poor guy. Come on, my friend will explain everything."

Fritz led them through the trees into Staten Island. Rory was surprised by all the forests in the borough—it didn't really feel like a part of the city at all. They passed an area with a few well-lit suburban streets and one typical downtown area with shops and the like, but then they plunged back into the woods. Soon they found themselves walking through a field of wheat, and Rory spied a farmhouse, much like the Stuyvesant homestead, sitting at the end of a country lane. Fritz led them up to the front door, where a short Dutchman with kind eyes waited for them.

"Rory, Bridget, Soka," Fritz said. "May I introduce David de Vries, farmer, adventurer, and one of the original settlers of New Netherland."

"I've heard of you," Soka said, shaking De Vries's hand warmly. "My people speak of you as a great friend."

"It is true," De Vries said, smiling at the compliment. "Adriaen Van der Donck and I were both great admirers of your people, and we tried to champion your cause, to no great success, unfortunately. But I still do what I can. Please, come in."

De Vries led them into a warm living space with a merry fire burning in the hearth. He gestured for them to take seats on the hand-carved furniture, which was as comfortable as it was well-worn. De Vries disappeared into the kitchen, returning shortly with steaming cups of tea for all of them. He sat down by the fire and took a deep sip from his mug before speaking.

"I knew Adriaen was giving pages from his journal to various safekeepers around the boroughs. He and I were old friends, and though he never told me what was written in the journals, he let me know of their existence. I even thought of tracking them down myself, especially after his murder, but I can only travel from Staaten Eylandt to Mannahatta. My blood does not allow me to visit the other boroughs. And our Unlucky Patroon, as Fritz called him, refused to let me see his pages. Loyal fool. Ah well, it was probably for the best.

"It doesn't surprise me that he wrote about the Agreement, and that he kept his writings secret. We who were around then decided it was best to hide the origins of our unbreakable rules. After all, it does sound better to say we've always belonged here than to have to admit that we bargained our way into staying. We like to think that we own this place, when really we're still just renting. That's all any of us will ever be—renters. The land will outlast us, as it has outlasted the Munsees and the ancient, extinct creatures from the days before man. Who will remember us after our mortals are gone? We will have to throw ourselves upon the mercy of the land, as the Munsees did. As *we* did all those years ago when we sent Adriaen and Kieft to bargain for our existence."

"Who did Adriaen give his pages to?" Rory asked.

"To a man named Cornelis Melyn. He was the patroon, what the English would call a landlord, of Staaten Eylandt during the first days, and he was always a staunch opponent of Kieft's. In fact, Cornelis was the one who stood up to Kieft after his war with the Munsees and demanded he be arrested for what he'd done. Instead, the new governor, Peter Stuyvesant, banished Cornelis for causing a ruckus."

"But Peter is our friend!" Bridget cried, shocked.

"Stuyvesant was a hard man when he was alive," De Vries said. "And not always popular. I know I had my disagreements with him. But people change. Even gods. Either way, it is more a testament to Cornelis's bad luck that he got banished. That man just had the worst luck. Cornelis was always a friend to the Indians, but during Kieft's war with the Munsees, some neighboring tribes got confused by whose farm was whose and burned Cornelis's plantation to the ground by mistake. Bad luck. Then, as I said, Cornelis tried to do the right thing and have Kieft punished, and instead, he was banished by the new governor. To make things even worse, Cornelis had to travel back to Amsterdam with Kieft, who'd been recalled. What happened next? I bet you can guess—a storm blew up and sank their ship off the coast of Wales. Kieft died in the wreck, and Cornelis was washed ashore, barely alive. Somehow he made it back to the motherland, where he successfully lobbied to be allowed to return to New Amsterdam."

"That doesn't sound too unlucky," Rory said.

"Just wait," De Vries said wryly. "It gets better. He traveled all over the Netherlands, gathering people to go back with him to colonize Staaten Eylandt. They sailed here and founded a new patroonship. And it took hardly any time at all for Cornelis to push Stuyvesant over the edge again, causing Peter to arrest him for the second time."

"He doesn't sound like the brightest of men," Soka noted.

"Oh no, he's quite bright," De Vries disagreed. "He just has no sense of how things work. He thinks things should be fair, regardless of all else. And life isn't fair. To that point, while Cornelis was imprisoned the second time, another Indian uprising popped up, another group of young warriors became confused about whose homestead was whose, and Cornelis's plantation was burned down . . . again."

"Ouch!" Bridget said, wincing.

"He left soon after that, not to return until he became a

god. And his luck hasn't gotten much better. The British have been keeping an eye on me lately, since I've been stirring up some trouble to help our cause against Kieft. Last week, I was supposed to see certain friends of mine, but I didn't want to lead the British to them, so I asked Cornelis to go check on them in my stead. And that was the day the British soldiers decided to raid the woods by my plantation. They took my friends and they took Cornelis. I haven't heard one word about him since."

"Why are the British doing raids?" Fritz asked.

"Admiral Howe's orders," De Vries replied. "He's placed himself squarely on Kieft's side. His redcoats have been scouring the island, looking for dissidents."

"Who are your friends?" Rory asked. "More patroons?"

"Not quite," De Vries said, his eyes dancing. He raised his voice, calling into the next room. "Perewyn! I think you can come in now. These are allies!"

They all turned as a man walked into the room. Soka was the first to gasp.

"You are of my people!" she cried. And it was true—Perewyn was an Indian. He was much older, with white hair tied up with eagle feathers and tattoos of many animals all over his arms and face. Many pouches crisscrossed his bare chest, and he leaned against a long staff of wood as he limped into the room.

"Not quite your people, young one," Perewyn said, his voice deep and gravelly. "I am a Raritan. This was our island. Though your people and mine are close kin."

"Perewyn is the *pau wau* of the Raritans," De Vries explained. "It was the rest of his people who were captured along with Cornelis."

"Why have we never heard of your people still inhabiting this island?" Fritz asked the old medicine man.

"We had enough strife during the early days of your colony," Perewyn said. "We heard of your gods' battles with the Munsees, and we wanted no part of it. We shed enough blood during our mortal wars with the Dutch. So we kept to the trees. That is how we avoided the Trap." He looked at Soka, his face saddened by the memory. "Though I regret every day that we could do nothing for your poor people. Eventually, we made ourselves known to David, who has always been a friend to us. He agreed to keep our secret. He and Adriaen were very kind."

"Adriaen knew?" Fritz asked, astounded, turning to De Vries. The Dutchman shrugged.

"He did, and he agreed that there was no reason to involve the Raritan in any of our schemes against Kieft. They had suffered enough and deserved to live in peace. Which was what they were doing until Admiral Howe's men stumbled upon them on the day I sent Cornelis out to visit them. And now they are all prisoners."

"Did you try to find where they're being held?" Fritz asked.

"Howe is watching me," De Vries said, shaking his head. "He suspects that I was the one who was harboring the Raritan. I've been trying to figure out how to get close, but I can't sneak by them."

"We can help!" Bridget assured him. "We're good at sneaking around!"

"If Howe is working for Kieft, then I'm sure he knows who we all are," Fritz said.

"We have to try," Rory said. "Cornelis has Adriaen's journal pages."

"I wish I could work my misdirection spell without it blowing up in my face," Soka said, frustrated. "We could walk right inside."

"I am not without my own powers, you know," Perewyn said thoughtfully, his eyes narrowing. "David, I think I might have an idea. *We* could not do it because they were expecting to see us. But these three might, along with their roach friend, of course." He nodded at Fritz. "Are you certain you would risk yourselves?"

"Of course," Rory replied promptly. "What do you want to do?"

"It involves playing a little dress-up—"

"YES!" Bridget cried, hopping in place. "Who do we get to be? A French aristocrat? A gigantic puppy? Britney Spears?"

"I do not know who that is," Perewyn said, smiling at the paper girl's enthusiasm. "What you must ask yourself is: Do you look good in red?"

14

THE PERFECT DISGUISE

Peter Stuyvesant was not happy as he walked down the corridors of City Hall, the thump of his peg leg resounding through the halls. More gods were being murdered, no doubt by those knives being passed around like party favors. More and more gods were flocking to Roosevelt Island to join Kieft's army. And still the council argued and wavered over what to do next. He'd tried giving them the verbal swift kick in the short pants, but they needed more than that. They needed someone to inspire them, to lead them. And as much as it pained him to say it, that person was not him.

This unpleasant thought still curdled in his brain when a minor god stepped up to him, begging a word.

"And who are you?" he asked the god.

"J. P. Morgan, God of Dividends," the man replied, his face sour. "That's the problem."

"What are you talking about, man?" Peter asked, his patience nonexistent.

"You've never heard of me," Morgan replied, frowning. "And yet, in my day, I was the most powerful force in banking the city had ever seen. I single-handedly stopped the world from falling into a depression. For this, I become God of Dividends? How am I not the God of Banking?"

"Tobias is the God of Banking," Peter reminded him, annoyed that his time was being wasted with such frivolity. He began to clomp away, but the minor god ran after him.

"And who is he?" Morgan asked. "I have never heard of him. At first I assumed he had been a major force in the early days of the colony, but I can find no record of him. I don't know how he became the God of Banking, but he should have receded when I came along. Become the God of Deposits or something. The duties change when others with a stronger pull on the mortals' memories arrive, you know that. By all rights, I should be a major god. Something is wrong here!"

"Why are you telling me this now?" Peter asked, trying to move past the insistent god.

"You are not the first I've aired my grievance to," Morgan assured him, his face red. He ticked off his fingers, one by one. "I told the Mayor, I told Greeley, then Hearst, hoping the newspapermen would try to dig something up. They all brushed me off. Now I'm telling you, because you seem to have some power around here. It's true, I tell you. Something is not right with T. R. Tobias."

Though Peter assumed the minor god was merely suffering from delusions of grandeur, he couldn't shake the thought that maybe something *was* wrong with T. R. Tobias. He'd never heard of the man, either. No one seemed to. It was very strange. Just who was T. R. Tobias?

A buzzing drifted in through the open window nearby. It sounded liked a hummingbird. He heard shouts float up from outside and hobbled over to the window. At first, he didn't know what was going on, but then he saw the pill-shaped spot in the sky, soaring toward midtown.

Great, he thought to himself, dismay flowing through him. Just when he thought things couldn't get any worse. *He* was back.

<hr />

Soka sat with the Raritan medicine man on a bench behind the manor house, overlooking a small garden. David de Vries had ridden out at first light to scrounge up some redcoat uniforms, while Rory was taking a much-needed nap upstairs. Perewyn had asked her to join him outside for a moment, and now they sat side by side, looking out at the rows of tomato plants and peas.

"You are in training to be a *pau wau*, correct?" Perewyn asked.

"Yes," Soka admitted. "My mother is the medicine woman for my people. I thought I was the one to follow her. Now I am not so sure."

"Why? I can feel your connection to the land. It is very strong."

"I don't know about that," Soka said, sighing. "I used to think so. But ever since I left my village, I've lost control. One moment I'm working magic I never dreamed I'd manage, and the next I'm unable to do the simplest of spells. I don't know what's happening to me."

"The land's gifts are hard to predict," Perewyn told her. "My powers have been waning over the last century—when I heard about the Trap, I blamed it on that atrocity. But the

Trap is gone, now, and my powers remain weak. I had hoped to discover whether you had a similar experience, but I see now that something very different is happening to you. I am not surprised to hear that you've worked great magic. I can feel it in you. Your mother must be something to behold as well."

"She's ten times the *pau wau* I'll ever be," Soka said ruefully, kicking at the dirt. "I don't know how I will ever take her place."

"Is she going somewhere?" Perewyn asked, eyebrow raised. The question caught Soka off guard.

"Um . . . I guess not," she said. "But I always assumed . . ."

"We are not mortals," Perewyn reminded her. "Death is in our past more than in our future. We may fade one day, but who knows when that will be. Our people are long gone, and yet we remain. Do you know how many Raritan were taken by the red-coated men?"

Soka shook her head. Perewyn held up a single hand with all fingers extended.

"Five," he said. "That is all who remain of my tribe. Those five and I. And yet our people were once as numerous as the stars. From what I hear, the Munsees have many more than that. Why is that? You have been cut off from the land by the Trap, and yet your people did not dwindle, while we remained free, and now we are almost gone."

Soka shook her head, unable to answer. Perewyn smiled ruefully.

"I have thought long on it. I have come to believe it is because we retreated from our duties. We hid in the trees and ignored the call of the land. We remain, you and I and all our people, not because we have mortals who remember us. We are here for a different purpose. My people ignored that fact, and we have suffered for it. You, on the other hand . . . I think you have a clearer idea than any of us what is required of you. Your mother may be *pau wau* to your people, but you are meant for something more."

"What?" Soka asked, frustrated. "Didn't you hear me? I can't even work a simple spell. The one big spell I performed wasn't even really me—" She cut herself off, mortified that she'd said so much. Perewyn nodded to himself, glancing at her.

"That rumble I felt earlier, that was you?"

Soka looked away, not liking how the white-haired medicine man's gaze seemed to look right through her. "It wasn't really me. At least, I don't think so."

"Then who was it?"

"There was a voice in my ear," she confided, glancing around to make certain no one else heard. "It floated into me from all around. It was a woman's voice. She asked why I needed her help. I told her I had to protect my . . . my friends. And she promised to help me. That's when I exploded. It wasn't even me doing it!"

She looked back to Perewyn to see his expression—he looked thoughtful, but not as surprised as she'd expected. Finally, he patted her shoulder. "I will watch you. You are a puzzle that can be solved. You will see. Come, I hear a horse approaching. David has returned."

He stood up and walked back into the house. Soka watched him leave, more confused and frightened than ever before.

Rory stood in De Vries's living room, dressed head to toe in a pilfered British redcoat uniform, watching Fritz struggle not to laugh.

"Those were the smallest uniforms you could find?" the battle roach asked De Vries, who shrugged apologetically.

"There are some tall soldiers on this island."

Glancing at Soka and Bridget on either side of him, Rory could see that his uniform, though it was two or three sizes too large for him, at least fit him better than the others'. Soka's jacket was far too big for her, and her pants had to be rolled up over her boots. But she'd pulled the belt in tight, and the result was that she actually looked kind of cute (though a little too womanly to be taken for a male soldier, he feared). Bridget, on the other hand . . .

"This is awesome!" Bridget cried, raising her arms above her head. Since half the length of the sleeve fell down over her hands, Rory wasn't so sure he agreed. There was room in her jacket for three more Bridgets, and the gold-button-lined overcoat, which was meant to fall to a soldier's knees, was so long it bunched up around her feet like a throw rug. Underneath, her pants billowed out above her stockings so far she looked like she was wearing a hoop dress. She'd already stuck on her tricornered hat, which covered her eyes so completely she had to push it back to see, peering out from under the rim like a turtle sneaking a look from inside its shell. Rory didn't know how she could walk in that getup, let alone be taken seriously. But Bridget was practically bouncing from excitement.

"I've decided on my redcoat name!" she announced. "I'm Lieutenant Periwinkle Applebottom!"

"Are you kidding?" Rory asked De Vries and Perewyn, ignoring his sister. "There is no way we'll be mistaken for real redcoats."

"Leave that to me," Perewyn assured him. "I have a little trick that will help." The old Raritan *pau wau* pulled out a small bowl filled with a bright yellow substance. He dipped a long brush into the bowl and proceeded to paint a small symbol on each of Soka's cheeks. He stepped back, nodding in approval. Fritz didn't look so impressed.

"What did you do?" he asked the medicine man. "She looks the same to me."

"That's because you expect to see her," Perewyn told the skeptical roach. "But a British soldier will see the uniform and expect to see one of his regiment, which is what he *will* see." He turned to the three costumed kids. "He will speak to you as if he knows you and, to him, you will look and sound like one of his own. So long as no one points you out as not belonging, none of them will be the wiser. Just keep the uniforms on, no matter how poorly they fit. They trigger the assumptions that feed the magic." Perewyn proceeded to paint Rory and Bridget's cheeks while De Vries explained the plan.

"The three of you will march Perewyn and me down to the Rose and Crown tavern, where the British have their command quarters. There, you'll turn us in. They'll take us to the same place where our friends are being held, wherever that is, and you'll make certain that you're the ones accompanying us. If worse comes to worse and you can't come with us, at least Fritz can follow us secretly. So, one way or the other, we'll find our friends. And then the next step will be to figure out a way to free them."

"The old *Star Wars* trick, eh?" Bridget said, nodding her head knowingly. "We're Han Solo and Luke and you guys are the Wookiee. Works every time."

De Vries blinked in confusion, then decided to roll with it. "Exactly. I'm the cookie. Of course it works every time."

"I don't know," Fritz said. "It sounds to me like we're sending the two of you to be captured, and you're expecting us to bail you out."

"I have faith in you," Perewyn said. "This is as good a way as any."

"We'll do it," Rory said firmly. "We won't let you down."

"Of course you won't," Perewyn replied, glancing at Soka. "You have powerful friends."

Rory didn't know quite how to take that cryptic statement, but he let it pass. He was getting closer to finishing this chase and saving his mother, and nothing was going to slow him down.

Midmorning found Rory, Bridget, and Soka marching down a country lane, De Vries and Perewyn in shackles in front of them. It was a beautiful morning; the soft sun danced across the surrounding trees, which swayed slightly in a cool breeze. The world was still, with no sounds of cars or planes or any other signs of civilization to bother them—only the birds in the branches above disturbed the silence. Rory knew that right on the other side of the trees waited the mortal world, with its car horns and rumbling trucks, but here in Staaten Eylandt, it was as if the colonists had just arrived.

Bridget was having trouble walking—she'd fallen on her face

three times since they'd left De Vries's farmhouse—but she refused to acknowledge that her uniform was anything but completely awesome. Rory couldn't see how the three of them could fool anyone. As they came closer to the redcoats' headquarters, his misgivings grew, until finally he opened his mouth to suggest they go back.

"Who goes there!" a British voice called out before Rory could get the words out. It was too late, he realized, as two redcoats stepped out of the trees, striding over to them with muskets pointed straight at their hearts.

"Prisoners for Admiral Howe," Rory answered, following the script De Vries had laid out. "We found this savage on De Vries's plantation and took them both prisoner."

"Jolly good," one of the redcoats said, his beady little eyes staring at the prisoners hungrily. "We'll take it from here, soldier."

"Yeah, good job," the other said, smiling to reveal a mouth full of rotten teeth. "You can head down to the Black Horse—you've earned it."

Rory glanced into the trees, where he knew Fritz was watching them. Were they going to be turned away before they could even reach the house? Soka was having none of it.

"We are not letting you take all the glory for our arrest!" she told them sternly. Both soldiers flinched, caught out. "We are bringing these prisoners in ourselves, so the ones in charge know who caught them. Get out of our way!"

After a moment the soldiers reluctantly stepped aside. As they passed, Bridget turned to them, pushing back her oversize hat to glare at them.

"Have a smashing good day, guv'nor!" she told them, her

voice unnaturally low and gravelly, like a four-year-old's impersonation of a man. Rory flinched at her awful attempt at a British accent. One of the soldiers narrowed his eyes as he watched her pass.

"You have a cold or something, soldier?" he asked Bridget, who opened her mouth to no doubt give an equally gravelly-voiced response, but Rory kicked her on the shin.

"Ow!"

"He's been coughing all night," he said, thinking quickly.

"Haven't been eating Typhoid Mary's cooking, has he?" The other soldier laughed. "That'll put you in your grave a second time, am I right?"

Rory forced himself to laugh, though inside he was seething. Typhoid Mary was still out hurting people as she'd hurt his mother. It burned him to know about it and be so powerless to stop it.

They left the soldiers behind as they continued down the lane until they reached a low, one-story stone house picturesquely sitting beneath a gigantic flowering tree. This was the Rose and Crown; during the Revolution this small building had served as the headquarters for England's invading army. From this spot, Admiral Howe launched his attack on New York City, capturing it decisively, but failing to take General Washington, who escaped with the majority of the Continental Army. Howe had underestimated the American resolve and it eventually cost the British the war.

Soldiers were gathered outside, talking and drinking, as the children approached. Rory gulped, hoping their disguises held up as well here as they had on the road. They were noticed as they came nearer, and one of the soldiers called into the stone tavern. Presently, a paunchy man with a pasty, unhealthy-looking face stepped outside. The soldiers stood at attention, saluting; Rory followed suit, relieved to see both Soka and Bridget saluting as well (though the sight of Bridget's sleeve falling over her hand as it hit her forehead made his stomach roll). This must be Admiral Howe.

Rory and his friends marched up to the admiral, pushing De Vries and Perewyn before them. Howe's eyes lit up when he saw who had been captured, and he smiled evilly.

"I knew it was only a matter of time, De Vries," Howe spat, getting into De Vries's face. "I knew you were harboring the enemy. And now I have proof. Are there any more savages on your property?" De Vries said nothing, looking past Howe as if the admiral weren't there. Howe didn't seem offended; he turned to Perewyn with the same glint in his eye. "What say you, savage? Any more pests infesting my island? You have nothing to say? That's fine. You'll talk soon enough." He spun around, shouting at some of his men. "Take them inside and prepare them for transfer!" Two soldiers ran up, grabbing De Vries and Perewyn and dragging them roughly into the stone house. Howe then turned his attention to Rory, Soka, and Bridget, who stood at attention, feeling exposed.

"Good job, privates," Howe commended them. "This is an important step to ridding Staaten Eylandt of all who would oppose us. We will finish the job we started three hundred years ago when the colonists got lucky and somehow tricked King George into signing a peace treaty. This time we will crush them all! Am I right, men!" The redcoats let out a rousing cheer, throwing their fists into the air. Rory and his companions belatedly joined them, and Rory winced to hear Bridget's growly cry. Howe gave Rory's shoulder a pat. "That is all, men. You may return to your posts. Your contribution to the cause will not go unnoticed." He turned to go. Rory glanced at Soka and Bridget in a panic. They were being cut out! He knew Fritz could follow the prisoners, but he didn't trust that he could get inside wherever they were being held. Rory didn't like that gamble, so he decided to make a gamble of his own.

He quickly ran up to Howe's side as the admiral reached the door of the tavern. Glancing around to make certain no one else was within earshot, Rory muttered into Howe's ear.

"A certain First Adviser would like me and my fellow soldiers to accompany the prisoners."

Howe froze, turning to Rory with wide eyes. "You? You are a spy for Kieft? Is it not enough that I do what he asks? He has to look over my shoulder and infiltrate my own army? That is unacceptable! You tell your master that he cannot order me about on my own island!"

Rory pushed down the panic—Howe's nostrils were flaring as he stared daggers at Rory. He thought fast. "These are important times. Nothing can be left to chance. You know you are one of Kieft's most trusted lieutenants. I am here to make certain no one tries to topple you from power. You are focused on the big picture. I make certain no one slips through the cracks. Like De Vries."

"You could have told me," Howe said, partly mollified. Rory wondered who the admiral thought Rory was. "I don't appreciate the skulking about."

"I'm sorry, I should have come to you sooner. But my two fellows and I must accompany De Vries and the savage. They are of special importance to the First Adviser and he will have my head if I don't make certain they arrive at their destination in one piece, generally speaking, of course."

Howe stared at him, his narrow gaze trying to pierce Rory's innocent facade. Finally, he nodded, seeming to buy Rory's story. "Be ready—we leave in an hour. I will be accompanying you. I want you to report back to Kieft about how good a job I'm doing carrying out his plans. Scratch my back and someday I will scratch yours. Understood?"

"Of course, sir," Rory replied, and Howe nodded once, curtly, before disappearing into the tavern. Rory let out a long breath. That was close. But he'd done it. They were going to find Cornelis and the Raritans. He had to hope that their disguise held out long enough to free the prisoners. Otherwise things could get very hairy—Howe did not seem the forgiving type. Rory would have to do everything perfectly.

THE BEST-LAID PLANS

The dirigible floated above the city, a long, pill-shaped balloon the length of two city blocks with giant fins at the end. As it passed over the city, the spirits of Mannahatta gazed upward in awe. Some felt fear as the shadow of the dirigible passed over them. Others knew wonder, feeling a stirring inside to explore the heights of Mannahatta. And one boy in particular felt hope wash over him.

"Why didn't I think of him before?" Nicholas Stuyvesant wondered aloud, breaking into a run.

Nicholas reached the Empire State Building just as the dirigible approached the needle at the top. Lincoln, Alexa, and Simon were already there, waiting.

"Did you know he was coming back?" Alexa asked him. Nicholas shook his head.

"I thought he was gone for good, actually," he replied. "We'd become too boring for him."

"I'm so excited!" Lincoln was practically hopping up and down. "The man is a genius at war!"

"He's a genius at getting people killed," Simon snorted. "Not really the same thing."

"I think he might be the one I'm looking for," Nicholas said.

"Really?" Alexa asked, dubious. "Isn't he a little . . . flighty?" Nicholas wasn't even listening, staring up at the giant balloon.

"Come on, my father's probably already up there to greet him when he gets off the dirigible," he said, leading them into the Empire State Building, where a special elevator waited to shoot them to the top. He sighed, a thought occurring to him. "Man, my dad is *not* going to be happy. He is not a fan."

They reached the top of the Empire State Building quickly, stepping off the elevator into a waiting room. When the building was built, the very top floors had been designed to be a port for the newfangled air vehicle called the dirigible. Filled with lighter-than-air hydrogen, the dirigibles floated through the skies like giant blimps, driven by huge propellers. The architects of the building had believed that their new building would be the perfect place for this new mode of transportation to dock. The dirigible would float up to the building, anchor to the tall needle at the peak, and the passengers would disembark directly into the waiting room on the top floor, grabbing their luggage and riding the elevator down into the very middle of Manhattan. It had been a noble dream. There was only one problem: wind.

It was so windy around the Empire State Building that the one time they actually tried to dock a dirigible, it almost impaled itself on the needle. Judging this far too dangerous, the city shut down the dirigible port. But here in Mannahatta, that first dirigible sometimes returned to dock at the very top of the tallest building in New York.

The huge vessel was being anchored as the Rattle Watch ran out into the waiting room. Peter Stuyvesant was already there, looking annoyed, and the rest of the council was arrayed around him. None of them looked too excited to be there.

"Just what we need," Peter muttered to his fellow councilmen. "A big shot of foolhardiness."

"Maybe he's mellowed," Bennett said, his pad in hand as he took notes for his evening edition. "After all, he's been off exploring the skies for twenty years. Maybe he's changed."

"And maybe I'm a spider monkey," Mrs. Parker muttered to Zelda Fitzgerald, who giggled. The dirigible was stable, now, and the small, boxy passenger compartment that hung from the huge, hollow balloon had lined up with the ramp. The door flew open to spit out the whirlwind of a man that was Teddy Roosevelt. His safari hat sat rakishly atop his head, and beneath his bushy mustache he was grinning like a madman. He ran down the ramp so rambunctiously that his small glasses flew right off—thankfully the string tied to the stems prevented them from coming off completely.

"By Jove, I hear there's a war on!" he cried, bounding up to the council members and shaking each of their hands vigorously.

"Yes, Teddy," Mrs. Parker told him, her voice tired. "But we've got it under–"

"Jolly good!" Teddy cried, cutting her off. "Well, if there's one thing Teddy Roosevelt knows, it's how to wage a jolly good war! We're going to wipe the floor with that Kieft fellow." He spied Peter Stuyvesant and patted the old god on the cheek. "Perk up, pouty face! Still as dour as ever, I see. I'm here now! We're gonna win this thing, hands down! Tallyho! We've got some planning to do!"

Teddy ran past the Rattle Watch to the elevator, turning at the open doors. "I said, Tallyho! Chop Chop!" He clapped his hands and to Nicholas's amusement, the council members ran after him, joining him in the elevator. Only Peter took his time, stomping across the floor, his face a thundercloud. Nicholas heard him mutter as he passed.

"He's lucky I don't have one of those god-killing knives on me right now," Stuyvesant seethed, passing his son as if he weren't even there, he was so wrapped up in his anger. He took his time entering the elevator, and just as the doors shut, Nicholas thought he saw Teddy good-naturedly smack his father on the butt.

Nicholas turned to the rest of the Rattle Watch, who were struggling not to laugh.

"Now, that's inspiring," he said with a grin.

Admiral Howe and a small group of redcoats and Hessians marched the prisoners down to the waterline. Rory, Soka, and Bridget followed (keeping their distance from the Hessians, as they still remembered the battle at Dyckman's Farm the week before), trying to figure out where they were going. They reached the very same boatyard where the USS *Monitor* had dropped them off. The wrecks of all the old ships seemed less spooky under the bright morning sun, but Rory could still hear the whispers of the dead boats if he listened hard.

A small schooner waited for them in the bay, anchored to a rotting dock. Howe marched the prisoners onto the schooner, and they soon cast off, floating out into the bay. For a moment Rory was worried they'd left Fritz behind, but at the last minute, he spied Clarence, the battle roach clinging to his back, running down the dock and leaping onto the stern of the ship before quickly disappearing into the hull. The crew hoisted the sail and soon they were clipping along at a brisk pace, leaving Staten Island in their wake.

Rory tried to figure out where they were going, but the direction they were sailing in made no sense. They seemed to be heading around the island, away from the city and out to sea. Rory decided it was wiser to keep his mouth shut—no use arousing more suspicion with his questions. Howe was sneaking penetrating looks at him, as if trying to guess what stories Rory would be bringing back to Kieft. Rory hoped the admiral never realized he wouldn't be talking to Kieft at all.

A black dot appeared on the horizon, floating in the middle of the wide expanse of blue in sharp relief to the deep fog behind it, which marked the beginning of the mist beyond the bay. As they sailed closer, Rory realized the dot was a ship, a large vessel with dozens of guns sticking out of the side, and four bare masts rising up from the decks. He heard De Vries gasp.

"That's the *Jersey*!"

"Indeed it is," Howe replied, lips tightening into a half smile. "You know its history, then? It is quite a tale. After we routed the American rats from New York at the onset of the American Rebellion, we didn't want to keep our prisoners of war in a normal prison where they might receive help from a sympathetic populace. Thankfully, the *Jersey* was floating out in the harbor, recently converted into a hospital ship."

"Hospital ship?" De Vries spat, incredulous. "Is that what you call it? How many good men died on that boat!"

"People die in hospitals," Howe said innocently, a sneer sliding across his face.

"The *Jersey* was no hospital ship," De Vries maintained. "It was a slaughterhouse."

"We did lose more than our share of agitators, true," Howe admitted, and he seemed rather pleased at the fact. "But what is war without suffering? Fear is a powerful weapon. Stronger than guns, stronger than armies. And every dead body we dumped over the side was worth a thousand bullets in our war against the rebels."

"It was an atrocity," De Vries said. "We in the spirit realm watched in horror."

"You will be doing more than watching, now," Howe told him. "You will be rotting."

Rory's stomach felt queasy, and Soka and Bridget looked equally green. He forced down his fear—they could not afford to get caught because of a frightened mistake.

They reached the boat, passing under the bow, which had the words HMS *JERSEY* painted on the old wood, the letters cracked and yellowing. Everything about the ship felt wrong to Rory—old and decaying and full of hate. It seemed to be staring at him malevolently, as if dying to gobble him up. The schooner pulled up alongside the much-larger prison boat, hooking up with a half-rotted rope ladder hanging down the hull. Howe made De Vries and Perewyn climb up first, and then his soldiers followed. Rory, Soka, and Bridget went next, desperately holding on to the slick rope as they pulled themselves up. Howe was the last one off the schooner, climbing onto the deck directly behind Rory, which made Rory distinctly uncomfortable.

"Take a good look around," Howe told him quietly. "I think Kieft will find this all to his liking. He sends me the prisoners and asks me to dispose of them—this is the best place to keep them. Far from friends who might help them. Just floating in the middle of the ocean, waiting to die."

Rory suppressed a shudder. The deck of the prison ship didn't seem too bad. Sailors in striped shirts and colorful sashes climbed over the rigging, much like on the pirate Captain Kidd's ship, the *Adventure Galley*. But there were soldiers everywhere, and though they called it a hospital ship, Rory couldn't see any doctors. Howe's men passed De Vries and Perewyn over to a pair of ill-favored sailors.

"Take them belowdecks and put them with the others," Howe ordered them, and just like that, De Vries and Perewyn were taken away. Rory looked around at all the soldiers and sailors and realized he had no idea what to do. A glance at Soka and Bridget showed him that they were equally lost.

"Would you like to see where we keep the prisoners?" Howe asked Rory, still waiting for some clue about what Rory was looking for. But Rory gave nothing away, nodding quickly.

"We'd be happy to. Lead on!"

Howe took Rory and his friends belowdecks, and it was there in the hold that the true horror of the HMS *Jersey* was revealed to them.

Rory had never seen such human misery. The space was one huge human cage. Hundreds upon hundreds of prisoners were packed together behind a large wall of bars. Most were so covered in filth that Rory could barely recognize them as human. But upon closer inspection, he began to make out all types of spirits, from all walks of life. The only thing they had in common was that they had all spoken out against Kieft.

"You can see that we're treating our guests as well as they deserve," Howe told him. "You tell Kieft that. I don't want him to think I'm soft."

"He won't," Rory muttered. How could he find anyone in this mass of misery? What was he thinking? Their plan now seemed hopelessly naive. But then he spied a familiar face. De Vries was pushing to the front, pulling a short, balding, doughy man in a filthy coat and hose behind him. This must be the hapless Cornelis Melyn, Rory thought. There *was* something about the man that seemed accident-prone. Maybe it was in his wide, innocent eyes, or in the way he tripped over at least ten people as he tried to follow the smoother De Vries. He radiated goodwill, however, and Adriaen had trusted him, so there must be something special about the man. But how could they talk to him? Howe was watching him like a hawk.

That problem was suddenly solved when a loud crack sounded on the opposite end of the galley.

"What was that?" Howe demanded of a nearby sailor. When the spirit shrugged, as bewildered as the rest of them, Howe sighed angrily. "I must do everything myself!" He hurried over to the source of the small explosion to investigate, followed by his men.

"Well done, Fritz," Soka muttered at his side, and Rory realized that the battle roach had set off one of his firecrackers. But they had to move quickly—the diversion wouldn't last long.

They hurried up to the bars, where De Vries waited with Cornelis.

"I'm glad to see you're all right, Mr. Melyn," Rory began, but Cornelis backed away.

"Why is this blasted redcoat speaking to us, David?" he said loudly. De Vries tried to hush him, but Cornelis was having none of it. "Stop making that shush sound, it's irritating. It's bad enough that I'm in jail, I can do without the weird noises. Now let us move away from these guards before they decide to make an example of us before your friends show up."

"These *are* my friends," De Vries explained impatiently.

"You are friends with the redcoats?" Cornelis asked incredulously.

"They're not really redcoats! See! Look at the one in the lead. He's not a redcoat, he's a mortal. And the one to his left is an Indian, for heaven's sake!"

"What are you talking about?" Cornelis waved De Vries off as he peered intently at Rory. Suddenly his eyes widened. "By Jove, you're right! He's just a boy! And the other one's a *girl*! What's going on, David?"

"That's what I'd like to know," Howe's voice said behind them. Rory felt hands grab his arms, holding him fast. He thought he heard Soka whisper "*Run*" but it was too late. They were caught.

"What is this?" Howe asked, stepping in front of them, his face furious. "Some black magic? You're not soldiers. You're not even both men! A Munsee savage and a callow boy. And to think I was worried what you would tell the First Adviser. You will pay for my momentary discomfort, believe me. So tell me, what are you really doing here?"

Rory didn't answer. He was too busy looking around as subtly as he could. Where was Bridget? He couldn't see her anywhere. Maybe she got away. He had to hope so.

"Throw them in the cage!" Howe told his soldiers when Rory and Soka refused to speak. "A few hours in that pit will loosen your tongues. If not, know that I have other, more persuasive methods of coaxing people to talk. Only one of you needs your tongue to speak, after all. Think on that!" He gestured and one of his Hessians threw open the cell door, pointing a musket at the prisoners to keep them at bay while Rory and Soka were thrown in. The Hessian locked the door up again and Howe left, taking most of his soldiers with him. Rory was in shock; he couldn't believe how fast things had turned.

Cornelis ran up to him, his face devastated. "I am so sorry! I didn't realize . . . you know, this is just my luck!" Rory didn't reply, feeling utterly defeated as he glanced around his fellow prisoners. One hope kept him from despairing right then and there: Bridget was free. Hopefully she wouldn't do anything stupid . . .

———

Bridget ran through the hallway of the crew's quarters, feeling horrible about leaving Rory and Soka. But Soka told her to take off, and if she hadn't, she'd be stuck in that cage, too. She had to find a way to bust them out, now. It was time to *Die Hard* it, big-time.

"Bridget! In here!" a small voice called out. She skidded to a halt in front of a small door, where at the bottom, a familiar roach shape was beckoning. She slipped into the room, which was some sort of crew quarters, closing the door behind her.

"They're caught!" she told Fritz, holding back dry sobs as the truth of what just happened washed over her.

"I know," Fritz replied, hopping up onto a small table in the middle of the room. "We've got to get them out of there. But first, we have to make sure you don't get caught. You've still got the paint on your cheeks, so the magic's still working. You just need to change your clothes. Here!"

He pointed to a sailor's striped shirt and white pantaloons, which lay bundled up in the corner. Bridget picked them up gingerly.

"Are you sure these are clean?" she asked, holding the clothes at arm's length. Fritz snorted.

"You're made out of bark and paper," he reminded her impatiently. "I think you can survive a little BO. I'll turn around." He turned his back to her, making Clarence turn around, too, until she'd changed into the sailor outfit. It actually fit her far better than the redcoat uniform, and it was almost as cool. She didn't even have to wear shoes, which was awesome, and the red scarf was an added bonus. Fritz turned back to her and nodded.

"Looking good."

"So what now?" Bridget asked. "Do we take out all the guards and storm the prison cell?"

"Right now *you* don't do anything but stay out of trouble," Fritz instructed her, wagging his insect hand emphatically. "I mean it. I'm going to sneak back into the prison and check up on everyone. I'll be right back. Don't go anywhere!"

Bridget nodded and Fritz hopped up on Clarence's back,

guiding the rat through a hole in the wall. Bridget sat down, trying to be good, but she got bored after about fifteen minutes. Surely it wouldn't hurt to just look around, she told herself. They all thought she was a sailor, and it wasn't as if they were actually *sailing* anywhere, so no one would expect her to actually do any hoisting or jibbing or whatever sailors do, right? So where was the harm?

She tiptoed down the hallway, finding a small ladder leading up to the deck. She quickly scaled it, climbing up onto the deck with a happy sigh. She was glad to be out of that oppressive hallway. This was much better, under the open sky. She spied a group of soldiers standing near the bow, talking in low murmurs. The sailors didn't pay her any heed, going about their business. Bridget stepped back, trying to avoid being noticed and asked to do something nautical.

"Watch it!" a voice cried behind her. Spinning, she came face-to-face with a man in an apron and chef's hat holding a tray with a bottle, a glass, and a large piece of cake. The cook was struggling to keep it all balanced on the tray, and his near collision with Bridget almost pushed it over the edge. The bottle teetered for a moment, and they watched it as it began to fall . . .

Bridget sprang into action, reaching out and catching the bottle before it could break into a thousand pieces on the rough wooden deck. The cook gave her a half smile.

"Nice catch," he said, letting out a relieved breath. "That wine's for the admiral, and he would have thrown me overboard if I'd dropped it."

Bridget cocked her head, a thought popping up. Fritz's voice rose in her head, telling her to stay out of trouble.

"*Sorry, Fritz,*" she whispered.

"Sorry?" the cook said, overhearing her.

"I said, do you need any help?" Bridget growled, adopting her patented low British voice. She held up the bottle. "I can carry this to make sure you don't drop it."

"You'd do that?" The cook looked pathetically grateful. "Then follow me!" He moved past her, heading for a door to the admiral's quarters. She followed obediently, all the while promising Fritz in her head that she wouldn't get into any more trouble. But as they approached the admiral's quarters, she wondered if that was even possible anymore . . .

A FAMILIAR FACE

By Jove, you people are ridiculous!" Teddy Roosevelt exclaimed, pacing back and forth in front of the council. Nicholas had to hide his smile as the council members exchanged scandalized glances. "Our city is torn in two, and you can't even agree on what to do next! We need action, not words!"

"We can't just jump into civil war!" Hamilton replied, his face a thundercloud. "Kieft has an army. This isn't one of your little adventures. This is serious!"

"It's not about Kieft's group of disgruntled spirits," Roosevelt insisted. "It's about the hearts and minds of this city. We need to grab their imaginations, make them believe in our cause! Kieft has a cause: destroy the Munsees. It's a horrible, despicable cause, but it is a cause nonetheless. What is our cause? Save the Munsees? Take down Kieft? What?" The members of the council couldn't meet his eye, uncertain how to answer.

"Come on, dunderheads!" Roosevelt shouted. "We are the good guys! Kieft is trying to tear this city down in his mad quest to destroy the Munsees. He'll burn our beloved home to the ground! We need to protect it! Kieft is a mad dog. His army is a made up of rabble, of dissidents, and we will stamp it out! It's as simple as that!"

Nicholas felt inspired by Roosevelt's words. Even though the council didn't look happy to hear them, he could feel the spirit of action flow through them. Alexa leaned in to his ear.

"Don't you think Roosevelt is underestimating Kieft a little bit?" she muttered. "Kieft isn't just some mad dog. He's the most powerful god in Mannahatta. This won't be an easy fight. Blood will flow."

"At least Roosevelt is doing something," Nicholas replied. A wave of satisfaction washed over him. He'd found his leader, he was sure of it.

Soka glanced around at the filthy prisoners, shocked at how wan and unhealthy everyone looked. Cornelis explained that there were spirits from all boroughs here, as the prison ship was floating in neutral waters. Some of the prisoners had been tortured, she could tell. She shuddered to think what Howe would do to her and Rory. She glanced at him, and he smiled back, trying to be strong. But she could tell how worried he was. There had to be a way out. They just needed to find it.

"I had your package, son," Cornelis was telling Rory. "I knew my luck, so I kept it on my person at all times. But the soldiers took it from me when I reached the ship. I'm sure that damned Howe is reading it right now. I never looked, myself. Adriaen asked me not to, and I never break a promise!"

"But there was a chance you could have learned something we could use against Kieft!" De Vries scolded the patroon, giving Soka some insight into why Van der Donck had handed his prize to the clumsy Cornelis rather than the dashing De Vries. Loyalty was a hard thing to come by.

"Soka! There are some friends I'd like you to meet!" Perewyn's voice came from behind her, and she turned to see the white-haired *pau wau* leading a group of Indians up to meet her. She greeted them warmly, glad to see the faces of her people again, even if they weren't Munsees. Perewyn leaned in to speak softly in her ear.

"They tell me they've seen another Munsee here in the hold."

Soka pulled back in surprise. A Munsee, here? Who had they captured? She scanned the hold, searching for a familiar face. She saw no one she knew, but then one of the Raritan pointed.

"There, he just ducked behind those farmers!"

Soka ran forward, circling around until she could see behind a cluster of Quaker farmhand spirits. A man was sitting there, looking away. He spoke without turning.

"I was hoping you would not see me."

Soka's heart stopped as the man faced her.

"*Tammand* . . ." she whispered.

Indeed, it was her brother, the man who had turned against his own family in his single-minded quest to make the Gods of Manhattan pay for their crimes. He'd even fired an arrow at her, though the act of attacking his sister had broken his spirit. Soka had banished him from her life and her affections, hoping never to see him again. But here he sat.

He looked awful. He'd found a white shirt and pants somewhere, though the white in the shirt had since become a filthy grayish brown—the man who had denounced everything about the newcomers was now dressed like one. His hair was dirty and matted, and his once-proud dog tattoos had retreated to the very edge of his face, like whipped mongrels.

"I am ashamed for you to see me," Tammand said miserably. "I've been hiding since the Trap fell, trying to find my way. It's been so hard—"

"I don't care!" Soka said angrily. "This is what you deserve."

"Tammand? How did you get here?" Rory said as he stepped up beside her.

"Look who it is, the great liberator." Tammand sneered at Rory. "Caught in the rattrap like the rest of us."

"Leave him alone," Soka hissed at her brother. "He freed our people while you almost helped lead them to destruction." She took Rory's hand protectively, as if daring her brother to say more.

"So you've taken that as well, *Sabbeleu*," Tammand spat, eyes narrowing at the sight of Rory holding her hand. "See how the newcomers want everything that is ours, Soka? Their greed is insatiable."

"Just shut up, Tammand," Soka yelled at him. "He has earned what I give him. You took my love for granted and threw it away!"

"I am paying for my pride," Tammand said stiffly. "Rotting in a prison cell with all the people I despise. It is torture, but it is what I deserve. But you, you deserve better than this little boy whose only claim to honor is some gift he was born with. He is not worth a jewel of the Munsees!"

"You . . . you . . . YOU!" Soka sputtered, so angry she

could barely think. She wanted to punch something, or blow something up, and her fingertips tingled as she seethed. Suddenly Tammand yelped as his dog tattoos began to growl, leaping at one another across his nose. They snarled and bit at one another as Tammand fell back in alarm.

"What is happening?" he cried, unable to see the fight breaking out on his own face. Someone else gasped and Soka turned to see a nearby prisoner's hair growing at an alarming rate, pooling in his lap. Against the wall, green shoots began poking out of the ship's hull, growing inward like ivy.

"Are you doing that?" Rory asked her, shocked. Soka had no answer, as alarmed as everyone else. She felt a hand on her shoulder.

"Maybe you should come over here and calm down before the guards take notice," Perewyn's voice said. "I think you're getting a little worked up."

The white-haired medicine man guided her toward the opposite side of the hold, and the shocked prisoners parted before her. Perewyn sat her down, and Rory knelt by her side.

"What happened over there?" Rory asked, but Perewyn waved him off.

"Give us a moment, boy," he said. "She needs time to regain control."

Rory backed off, giving her worried looks. Soka smiled to say it was all right, but inside, she knew this wasn't true at all. She looked across the hold to see if anyone else had been hurt by her burst of magic, but Perewyn sat down in front of her, cutting off her view of the other prisoners.

"I believe I have figured you out," he told her.

"What? Am I cursed?" For that was what it felt like.

"Just calm down," he advised her. "I won't say a thing until you have relaxed a little bit."

Soka breathed, in and out, calming herself. Finally, Perewyn nodded.

"Good. It's quite simple, really. What you did just then . . . that is beyond the powers of any *pau wau* I have ever seen. To call forth magic like that, without words or wampum, it is extraordinary. You could not do this inside the Trap, correct?"

"No, not at all," Soka assured him. "I was still learning basic spells from my mother."

"But then the Trap fell and you felt the land for the first time. What happened then?"

"I became sick, actually," Soka told him, a little embarrassed. "I threw up, repeatedly, and none of my magic worked as before. Eventually, I couldn't make anything happen at all, even after I recovered from my sickness. Until that moment in the caisson, anyway."

"When the voice whispered in your ear," Perewyn prompted.

"Yes. Did she give me some sort of power?"

"No," Perewyn said firmly. "It was there all along. You are very strong, and always have been, I bet, but you did not know it because you were cut off from the land. Your mother might be this strong, as well, though I find it hard to believe. She grew up with the land in her blood, so she would have recognized it and known how to channel it. You, on the other hand, have never felt this power before. You have never felt the *land* before. And it overwhelmed you. Made you sick. You didn't know how to handle such power, so you locked it away, instinctively. Without even knowing it, you cut yourself off from your own abilities. It wasn't all at once. At first, I'm sure some of your spells worked. But the power . . . it was too much. Finally, you cut yourself off completely. Until the caisson."

"Do you know who that woman was?" Soka asked, her eyes wide.

"I have my suspicions, but I will not voice them without more proof. I think I can help you, Soka. I can help you channel your new power and bring it under control. It won't happen all at once, but I know a few simple tricks that can put you on the right path. Will you work with me, right now? We have some time before they return for you."

"Okay," Soka agreed, hope blooming in her chest. "I will try."

Perewyn began to speak, taking her wrists in his hands as he explained what she needed to do. Soka listened, and for the first time since the Trap fell, she began to feel like maybe she could be whole again. It would take work, but it would be worth it if she could help her people and all of Mannahatta with the gift that had been given her.

Admiral Howe barely glanced at Bridget as she placed the bottle of wine onto his desk. The admiral's quarters were pretty nice, she decided, looking around. Curtains on the big windows overlooking the stern of the boat, big comfy chairs in every corner, a large bookcase filled with old, dusty books—everything seemed pretty expensive. Even Howe's desk was fancy—it was made of solid, ornately carved wood, though papers covered the surface. Bridget shuddered to think of all the reading those papers demanded.

She'd been so concerned with looking around, that she hadn't noticed that the cook had already put down his tray and backed out of the room, leaving her alone with the admiral. She started as she realized Howe was staring right at her.

"Looking for something to steal, maybe?" Howe asked her, his eyes hard. Bridget thought fast.

"Oh no, ye matey!" Bridget answered, trying to be as salty as possible. "I'm just a-makin' sure yer happy wit yer rum!"

"But this is wine," Howe said coldly.

"Ah, but to an old sea dog like meself, all spirits are like to rum," Bridget said, mind racing. "Yo-ho-ho and a bottle of rum, ye get me?"

"Is there something wrong with you, boy?" Howe asked. "You sound like an idiot."

"Me mother dropped me on me head when I was a wee lad," Bridget replied, improvising furiously.

"Would you like me to finish the job?" Howe said, and for a terrifying moment Bridget thought he meant it. But the admiral laughed to himself. "You're smart enough to be scared, aren't you, boy. You're an idiot, that is obvious, but you might be the brightest man on this ship besides myself. Here I was, happy to discover that Kieft's man was in fact an impostor, when I come back to my cabin to find this waiting for me." He waved a sheet of paper. "A message, from Kieft, that he will be here this afternoon. No one felt it important to tell me this letter was waiting for me! Even though I have more paper on this desk than I will ever read." Howe lifted a sheaf of papers in the air as an example, and Bridget's heart skipped a beat. She could see the word *Five* written on the top page. Those were from Adriaen's journal! Howe had them!

Excitement at discovering the whereabouts of Adriaen's journal warred in her mind with terror over the news that Kieft would be arriving soon. Kieft would take one look at Rory and it would be all over. She began to back away, hoping to make a speedy escape and try to warn the others. She reached the door and turned to leave.

"Stop right there!" Howe's voice commanded her. She turned back to him, certain she'd been found out. The admiral wagged a finger at her. "All your talk of rum has made me thirsty for harder stuff than wine. Bring me back a bottle. Perhaps that will take the edge off my meeting with Kieft. Go!"

Bridget bowed and ran out of the room as fast as she could. She didn't stop until she reached the far end of the ship, certain Howe was going to realize her deception. When no one came to throw her overboard, she calmed down.

"Bridget!"

Bridget started, almost falling over the side. Fritz was at her feet, waving at her. "You almost frightened me to death!" she scolded the battle roach, who apologized. "Have I got some news for you," she said, proceeding to tell him all about Kieft and Adriaen's journal. Fritz's face turned white at the news that Kieft was coming.

"We have to get off this boat," he said. "I need to talk to the others, down in the hold. Wait here and I'll be back." He disappeared into the floor, leaving her alone, staring out at the sea, hoping no sails appeared over the horizon anytime soon.

Rory sat against the hull, staring at Soka across the crowded hold. She was whispering with the medicine man, who seemed to be trying to teach her something. He wished he could help, but he didn't know how. De Vries had been circulating among the prisoners, with Cornelis eagerly, though clumsily, following, trying to see if they could foment some kind of insurrection, and they'd found a few willing helpers. But the guards didn't seem too worried—obviously knowing what was going on and not caring they watched with amused eyes as the two patroons moved from group to group. That fact didn't really surprise Rory—after all, they were in the middle of the ocean surrounded by enemy soldiers. Where were they going to go?

Rory could see Tammand sitting by himself, far from Soka. The disgraced Munsee retained a little of his haughty demeanor, and the sight of the proud warrior reduced to such a pitiful state made Rory feel bad for the guy, even though he knew he shouldn't. At least the guy's tattoos had stopped fighting one another. Talk about embarrassing . . .

Soka's eyes closed and then, suddenly, an oversize flower shot up from the floorboards, sending the prisoners reeling back. Soka's eyes shot open and her hand flew to her mouth, surprised at her own power.

"What is that?" De Vries asked, stepping up beside Rory as the prisoners buzzed about this strange plant in their midst. Rory tried to quiet them, but it was too late.

"Hey, what are you lot doing?" one of their guards shouted, coming over to the bars to see what the fuss was all about. He spotted the huge flower and whistled. "Will you look at that! That's magic! Who's doing that? The admiral told us to keep an eye out for magic. So stand up, or we'll come in and give you *all* a taste of what's waiting for whoever's making magic in there!"

A few of the prisoners began to glance at Soka, moving away from her. In a moment Rory knew she'd be discovered. He'd decided to step forward and claim responsibility himself, but then Tammand pushed past him, raising his hand.

"That is mine," he told the guards. "I cast the spell to amuse myself."

"Well, that was a mistake, wasn't it," the guard told him, unlocking the cage to step in and grab Tammand.

As they pulled him away, Rory whispered, "Thanks."

Tammand didn't answer, ignoring Rory's gaze as he was led away. Soka came up beside Rory.

"He's trying to win back my respect," she said, her voice worried. "I didn't ask him to. Why does he do these things!"

Perewyn looked worried himself. "We're running out of time. You need to work on controlling yourself or the next time it will be you being led away."

"Rory!" Fritz was back, sneaking around the feet of the prisoners to speak to his friends. Soka and Perewyn leaned in to hear what the roach had to say, followed by the Raritans and the patroons and a few other prisoners. Fritz told them all about Kieft's imminent arrival, as well as the fact that Adriaen's journal was sitting on Howe's desk. They needed a plan, he told them. And they were running out of time.

"Can someone cause a diversion of some kind?" Perewyn asked Fritz. The battle roach shook his head.

"I tried the firecracker trick again upstairs to lure those guards away from you, but they didn't even budge."

"Can Bridget do something?" Soka asked. Rory gave her a look, not happy to involve his sister, but Soka shrugged. "She's good at being noticed, what can I say?"

"I'll see what she and I can come up with," Fritz replied. "What will you do if she does manage to catch the guards' attention?"

Perewyn glanced at Soka. "We'll make magic."

BRIDGET CAUSES
TROUBLE

Now that Roosevelt had declared that the time for action was approaching, Nicholas redoubled his efforts to fill the ranks of the city militia. Lincoln and Simon tagged along as he crisscrossed the island, as did Alexa, though she had her misgivings.

"I just feel like we're moving forward too blindly," she confided to Lincoln. "Many in Kieft's army joined out of fear, or misplaced anger. Are we going to kill them all?"

"They chose their side," Lincoln declared confidently. "They'll get what they deserve!"

"I don't think they understand what side they're on," Alexa replied. "This still revolves around Kieft. I have more faith in Rory discovering the way to end this than Roosevelt and his big battle."

Nicholas proved to be a good speaker, inspiring spirits and gods across Mannahatta with his call to protect their beautiful metropolis. As their ranks swelled, Alexa's fears grew. Was this the only answer—to fight to the death? She worried that this was what Kieft really wanted. To bathe the city in blood. In that case, they were playing right into his hands.

Bridget watched Fritz scurry away on the back of Clarence. So they needed a diversion? She glanced around the deck at the sailors going about their duties while the soldiers stood guard. How was she going to distract them?

A few minutes before Fritz showed up, a pair of redcoats had emerged from below with one of the prisoners. Bridget had been shocked to realize that the prisoner was Tammand! What was he doing here? She didn't get to ask him, as the redcoats marched him right toward the admiral's quarters. She overheard the other soldiers explaining what was going on.

"They caught the savage working magic in the hold," a redcoat had said to his fellows. "The word from above is 'no shamans,' so the admiral is going to question the poor fool and then weigh him down and toss him in the ocean."

Bridget had every reason to hate Soka's brother, but she didn't wish that fate on anyone, even someone who would shoot at his own sister. But before she could think on it any further, Fritz had shown up with his instructions. She'd told him about Tammand then put her mind to the task at hand. Distract, distract, distract. But how?

"Hey, watch yourself!" one of the redcoats said to a sailor who was running past. The sailor glared at the soldiers before returning to his work. "Idiot water monkeys," the redcoat muttered to his friends, who snickered.

"Landlubber blockheads," the sailor quietly remarked to

his fellows, who nodded, rolling their eyes. An idea suddenly sprang into Bridget's head, and she quickly ran to grab her red coat, ready to do what she did best: cause trouble.

She threw on the jacket to appear as a redcoat, sidling up to the soldier who had made the remark. "Cor, guv'nor!" she said in her brilliant Cockney accent. "That's not right what that water monkey just called us!"

"Why, what did he say?" the redcoat asked, his eyes flashing. His friends leaned in to hear.

"He said we're only stationed on this boat 'cause we're not smart enough to be in a real fight. Are we gonna let them talk like that to us, guv'nors?"

The redcoats began to mutter angrily among themselves at this apparent insult. Bridget quickly stepped back, dropping her coat to the floor to return to looking like a sailor. Then she knelt down by the sailor who'd spoken earlier.

"Argh! Did ye hear that, matey?" she said, slipping into her flawless pirate accent. More sailors gathered around as she spoke. "Them landlubbers just said we're such bad sailors we aren't even allowed to work a boat that actually goes anywhere! Those blighters are sayin' we can't run a ship! We gonna take that? Argh!"

The sailors glared at the soldiers, who were glaring right back at them. The first sailor stood, striding up to the redcoat who'd accosted him earlier. "You got something to say?" he said belligerently.

"Do you?" the redcoat spat back, his friends moving in behind him. Bridget quickly threw on her coat and ran to the back of the redcoats.

"Go back to sailing the boat with no sails, you dirty sea dog!"

she called, then dropped her coat and ran around to the back of the sailors. "Why don't you go back to protecting us from all those dangerous seagulls, you musket-for-brains!" The two groups were openly snarling at each other, now, each jostling the other as the insults flew. The first soldier pushed the first sailor, who in turn pushed back. Growing impatient, Bridget called out, "Yer mother's a humpback whale!" and pushed a soldier into the first sailor. That did it. The pushing turned into punching and a full-scale brawl was under way.

Bridget stepped back, watching the fighting spread across the deck. Her brother was right, she thought to herself, she really was a natural-born troublemaker. Amazing, really.

Fritz had returned to the hold, telling Rory and the others about Tammand. Soka's face went white, and Perewyn tried to calm her.

"You need to concentrate on your magic," Rory heard him whisper.

"What kind of diversion is Bridget planning?" De Vries asked Fritz, who shrugged.

"She's a resourceful girl," the battle roach assured him. "She'll think of something good, I'm sure."

A faint sound drifted down from the deck. De Vries cocked his head. "Sounds like a fight," he said as the yelling and cursing grew louder. "A big fight!"

Rory shook his head as the soldiers in the hold walked over to see what the commotion was about. "How does she do it?" he asked no one in particular.

"She's gifted," Fritz replied with a smile.

"Now is our chance," Perewyn said to Soka. "Do what I showed you! You don't need to worry, I am right here."

Nodding, Soka closed her eyes, muttering. Rory watched her anxiously, wishing he could help her. At first nothing seemed to be happening, but then Cornelis gasped.

"Look!" he said loudly, and De Vries had to clamp a hand over his mouth to shut him up. Thankfully the guards were gathered at the foot of the stairs, distracted by the fight on deck. None of them turned to see the small green shoots growing up from the wood floor around the bars that locked the prisoners in. The shoots grew higher and higher, wrapping around the bars. Soka muttered one word particularly strongly and the shoots pulled apart, bending the bars. De Vries turned to the prisoners, who had all gathered behind him.

"We have numbers on our side," he whispered. "Overpower, grab guns, and finish it quickly! Ready . . . go!"

De Vries led them through the now-open bars, launching himself at the distracted guards. They heard him at the last minute, but by then it was too late. He had knocked them both senseless and grabbed their guns.

"Come on!" he said quietly, and led them up onto the deck.

Rory blinked in the light as he stepped onto the deck and into a mass of confusion. The soldiers and sailors were busy grappling with one another as their superiors tried to stop the fight.

"Stop this foolishness before the admiral finishes with the prisoner or there will be hell to pay!" one was saying as he tried to pry apart two combatants. Rory caught sight of Bridget, who was standing in the corner, waving proudly at him.

De Vries raised his gun in the air and shouted, "CHARGE!"

as he led the mass of prisoners into the fray. The redcoats and sailors barely had time to notice their new opponents before the prisoners were on them.

Rory didn't know what to do, but then he spied Bridget waving at him and pointing toward the stern of the boat.

"Tammand!" she mouthed, and Rory broke into a run. There was no way he'd let Soka's brother get killed on his watch, no matter how angry Soka was with him. He dodged the fight as he scampered across the deck, meeting up with Bridget at a door at the back of the ship.

"How did you do this?" he asked her, and she gave an airy shrug.

"Just used my charm!" she replied. "Come on, he's in the admiral's quarters." Bridget led him down a short hall. They burst into the room at the end, diving to the floor in case Howe was waiting for them with a gun. But to their surprise, Howe was worried about someone else.

Tammand lay on the floor, looking stunned as blood ran down a deep cut in his shoulder. Over by his desk, Howe was struggling with someone Rory couldn't quite see, cutlass in hand. Howe swung his assailant around, and Rory was shocked to see the determined but hapless face of Cornelis Melyn.

At first he thought the patroon might have a chance, but his luck betrayed him yet again as Cornelis proceeded to trip over his own feet and fall to the ground, hitting his head on the side of the desk with a loud thud. Rory and Bridget both began running to help Cornelis, but Howe wasn't concerned with the dazed god. Instead he trained his cutlass on Rory.

"You're him, aren't you," Howe said. "The Light. It's the only explanation. And I will be the one to kill you." He stabbed with his sword, hard, but Bridget intercepted it, throwing her arm up to deflect the point. The force of the blow, however, sent the sword straight through Bridget's arm and into the wall, pinning her there. Howe looked at her with confusion.

"You're a tough one," he said, taken aback, before retreating to his desk. He reached behind the desk and pulled out a second cutlass, bringing it to bear on Rory. Rory backed away, tripping over Bridget's leg and landing heavily on the floor next to a chair that had been broken in the fight. He spied a chair leg that had snapped off, and just as Howe chopped down with his sword, Rory grabbed the leg, blocking the blade with the piece of wood. Chips flew off the chair leg as the blade sliced across it, but Rory was able to beat back the attack.

He pushed himself to his feet, holding the chair leg in front of him. Bridget tried desperately to free herself, while Tammand seemed to be out of it completely, perhaps bleeding to death in the corner. Rory was on his own as he faced down a smirking Admiral Howe, and to his surprise, he wasn't afraid.

"A fair fight," Howe said, the sword swaying confidently in his hand. "I like it. Too bad it won't last very long." With that, he launched himself at Rory, bringing his sword down hard. Rory didn't even bother to fight back; he dropped and rolled out of the way. Howe turned, advancing again, before stumbling with a curse.

"Ow!" he cried. He'd strayed too close to Bridget, who'd stomped on his ankle. He kicked back at her and Rory took his chance, leaping to his feet and swinging the chair leg with all his might. But Howe caught sight of the movement out of the corner of his eye, and he quickly brought his sword up to counter the attack. Moving out of range of Bridget's feet, the admiral parried Rory's thrusts expertly, and Rory realized there was no way he could beat this expert swordsman in a fair fight. Good thing he didn't feel the need to fight fair.

Spying a paperweight on the desk, he grabbed it and lobbed the heavy object at Howe's head. The admiral ducked, but the paperweight glanced off his skull, sending him staggering back. Rory picked up some papers that had been under the weight and threw them at Howe, too, trying to make it hard for the admiral to see. Sheets of paper filled the air, and as Howe slashed at them, Rory picked up another sheaf and was about to toss that as well when Bridget cried out.

"Rory, not those!"

Glancing down, Rory realized that he was holding Adriaen van der Donck's journal pages. Blanching, he quickly put them back, but it was too late to look for any more. Howe had cleared a path with his sword and was coming at him again. Rory brought up the chair leg just in time, blocking the sword once, twice, three times, barely keeping the steel from reaching his flesh. But a sick feeling in his stomach told him that his luck was running out. He backed up against the window and Howe moved to follow him and finish the job, but suddenly the admiral stopped short, struggling to move forward. Glancing down, Rory realized that Cornelis had come to and was holding fast to Howe's legs, preventing the man from going anywhere. Howe slashed down at Cornelis, opening cuts all along the patroon's back, but Cornelis would not budge.

Rory knew he'd never have a better opportunity, so he rushed forward, swinging the chair leg with all his strength. Howe caught sight of him too late, and he barely had time to lift the sword before Rory hit it, sending the cutlass flying out of his hand to the floor. Rory leaped after the fallen sword, picking it up near the bookcase and turning back to Howe, weapon in hand.

Howe kicked down hard, and finally pulled free of Cornelis's grasp, reaching down to grab the chair leg Rory had discarded.

"You think you've beaten me?" the admiral said, sneering at him. "I can do more damage with a piece of wood than you can do with a sword, boy. You don't even know how to hold that thing."

Howe swung the chair leg right at Rory's head. Rory instinctively swung back with the sword, expecting the two weapons to collide noisily. But Cornelis wasn't out of the fight yet, and the patroon rolled into Howe's legs, sending the admiral stumbling. The chair leg missed its mark, but to Rory's horror, his sword wasn't going to. It sailed through the air on a collision course with Howe's neck, and Rory knew with a sick certainty that he was about to end a life.

But then a second sword swatted his out of the way and Rory spun to see Tammand standing weakly at his side, the sword that had pinned Bridget to the wall now resting in his hand. Before Rory could say a word, Tammand stepped past him, thrusting the sword through Howe's heart. Howe stared up at the Munsee, disbelieving, before falling over in a lifeless heap at their feet.

"You killed him!" Bridget cried, scrambling to her feet with one arm cradled in the other. "Why did you do that?"

Tammand didn't reply, instead crouching down by Cornelis, who was having trouble sitting up. "You saved my life," he said, though his angry tone was at odds with the sentiment. "Why?"

"It was the right thing to do," Cornelis said, wiping the blood off his lips. "I try to do the right thing, over and over, but it usually doesn't work out the way I want it to. This time, though . . . this time it did. And I'm glad."

Tammand staggered away to lean against the wall. He looked even more lost than he'd been in the prison hold. Being saved by a newcomer threw his whole world out of whack.

"Rory!" Soka stood in the doorway. She noticed her brother, leaning against the wall while blood ran down his tunic. "Tammand! What happened?"

"He saved me," Rory told her.

"Hey!" Bridget cried. "That's not true! You were about to take Howe down yourself before he stopped you and did it himself!"

Rory glanced at Tammand, who wouldn't look at him. "Like I said, he saved me."

BETRAYAL

Tobias sat behind his desk in the upper corner of his bank, going over his ledgers. He glanced up as his door swung open.

"Mr. Prince," he said, nodding as if the intruder were expected. Caesar Prince stepped into the room, closing the door behind him. He tipped his fedora at the God of Banking.

"Tobias," he said, smiling with all his white teeth showing. "I thought I'd find you here. Why aren't you out at Roosevelt Island with Kieft?"

"We may be on the edge of war, Mr. Prince, but that doesn't relieve me of my duties," Tobias replied, nodding at his paperwork. "There is as much money to be made during war as during peace. And it is my job to look after the money."

"Is it really?" Caesar said, cocking his head. "Are you sure?"

"What are you blathering about?" Tobias asked, his voice disinterested.

"J. P. Morgan has been raising a stink about you, you know that?" Caesar said. Tobias shrugged.

"He's always been quite the poor loser."

"He was also the most powerful banker this city has ever known," Caesar said. Tobias shrugged, uncaring. Caesar continued. "Yet you are the God of Banking. Not him. So you must have been far more famous than he was. Yet no one has ever heard of you." Tobias did not answer, bending over his numbers, counting under his breath. Caesar smirked. "You love being the God of Banking, don't you. You're good at it. But what if people were to find out that you aren't who you say you are. That you aren't really a god at all."

"That is slander," Tobias said, though he did not look up from his ledger. In fact, he counted faster and faster, running a finger quickly over the rows of numbers.

"I did some digging. There was a spirit, a clerk, who worked for the last God of Banking two hundred years ago, whose name was Toby. Timothy Reese Toby. Tim to his friends, not that he had any. Tim Toby. I guess T. R. Tobias had more of a godly ring."

"You are talking nonsense," Tobias said. His finger was a blur over his ledger.

"I'm sure I am," Caesar agreed. "Of course, the previous God of Banking died in a battle with the Munsees, and then, suddenly, *you* were God of Banking. And no one questioned it, because how could someone become a god if they didn't earn it? And now no one really remembers where you came from."

"Is that all you came to tell me?" Tobias asked, refusing to raise his head from his work. "Fantastical stories?"

"I think you were Kieft's guinea pig. I think your boss was killed in battle and Kieft proposed a test. Instead of destroying the locket or letting it fade, you would wear it. Just to see what happened. And it made you a god." Tobias picked up a pencil, adding his numbers furiously, ripping holes into his ledger as Caesar continued. "How many of you has he made over the years? How many false gods?"

"I am no false god," Tobias spat, finally looking up with hatred in his eyes. "I am a better God of Banking than this city deserves!"

"Maybe you are," Caesar said. "But you won't be one for long when this gets out. And if Kieft wins? Do you really think he will let you live? You know too many secrets. You were valuable before, but once he's won? He is not one to share power."

"I don't want power," Tobias replied haughtily. "I just want to do my job!"

"Good," Caesar said. "And maybe you can. Here's what I propose. I will keep my mouth shut. I will let you keep doing your job. And soon I will ask a favor. And you will grant me that favor. If you do, no one will ever know what you really are. Deal?"

Tobias stared back at him; his vaunted calm vanished as he faced the end of all he held dear. At last he reluctantly nodded, once, and then bent back over his ledger, counting aloud as if to deny Caesar's very existence. Caesar smiled and backed out of the room, closing the door behind him.

Outside the bank, Caesar walked briskly to a dark corner of the street. There, a figure waited.

"How did he take it?" the figure asked.

"Pretty well, all things considered," Caesar replied. "We'll find out when the time comes. For now, it's back to the scorpion's pit for me!"

"Be careful, Caesar," the figure said, stepping into the light to reveal the concerned face of Peter Stuyvesant. "Kieft is no dummy."

Caesar smiled. "I'm always careful, Peter," he said, tipping his fedora. "But it's nice to know you care."

The former prisoners stood over the sailors and redcoats, who were gathered in a group in the middle of the deck. The revolt had been brutal but quick, and the ship was now theirs. Soka felt a flush of pride as she walked back onto the deck with Rory at her side. She had set this in motion. Her power still didn't feel a hundred percent under her control, but at least it was manageable, if she followed Perewyn's instructions.

She'd left Tammand in the admiral's quarters, where Cornelis was seeing to his wound. She didn't know what to think about what her brother had done. She was happy Rory had been spared the guilt that came with taking another's life, but she couldn't bring herself to forgive Tammand just yet. The wound still hurt.

One of the Raritans ran up to her, his face white. "Come quick!" he ordered. "It is Perewyn! He's been hurt!"

Soka followed him quickly, running to the side of the ship where the medicine man sat, leaning against the railing. Perewyn smiled when he saw her, but she could see right away from his red-stained belly that the wound was serious. She knelt down beside him as Rory stood behind, awkwardly trying to be a comfort to her.

"I am proud of you, Soka," Perewyn whispered, smiling even as he coughed. He wiped his mouth and his hand came away flecked with blood. "So very proud."

"You can't just leave me," Soka cried, her eyes overflowing. "I need your help."

"Don't be scared," Perewyn told her, weakly patting her hand. "You have powerful friends . . . I have done all I can. I am ashamed that we pulled away for all those years. We never should have hid ourselves like frightened children. But it is all right. I am proud, again. I am proud." With that, his eyes grew blank as his hand fell away. Soka bowed her head, tears dripping onto his bloodstained chest. It was she who was proud, she thought fiercely. Proud to have known such a fine man. She would take this pride with her and make it the backbone of everything she was. That was Perewyn's gift to her.

A half hour later, Rory dropped down into the schooner, joining Bridget, Soka, and Fritz on the small sailboat. De Vries and Cornelis had decided to stay behind to guide the ship back to the boroughs. They would use this prison ship in their battle against Kieft, turning it back into the warship it once was and fighting the First Adviser with his own weapons. Tammand also remained on the ship, and he seemed to have awoken from his stupor. He kept staring at Cornelis, amazed that a newcomer god had risked his life for a "savage." Rory could tell the Munsee would be thinking hard about where he stood in the battle to come. But it was the brief conversation that Tammand had with Soka that gave Rory the most hope. He could hear Tammand's promises—that he would win back her respect if not her love. Soka waved him off, but Rory could tell she was touched. Maybe that was a wound that would heal someday. They'd have to wait and see.

Everyone knew Kieft was sailing their way, so the prisoners scurried all over the ship, hoisting the sails and preparing to raise anchor. Rory and his friends would not be aboard, of course—the risk was too great. They would be sailing back to Mannahatta to search for the last piece of Van der Donck's diary. But first they had to read the pages Rory had taken from the admiral's quarters. Once they'd pushed off the side of the ship and were sailing across New York Bay at a decent pace, Rory pulled out the journal. *Five* was the number written on the top page, and Rory thought about what they'd read so far—Adriaen's decision to listen to Kieft's plan to save them after the fading of gods like Peter Minuit; the secret mortality of Kieft's manservant Henry, who might or might not be the Hennessy kids' father; and the start of Kieft, Adriaen, and Henry's journey to some remote place where they would make their plea to the land. The pages Rory was holding were the fifth and last part of Adriaen's journal; the fourth section waited somewhere on Mannahatta, in the home of someone the Fortune Teller had called the Swindler. Well, it wasn't as if he'd never flipped ahead to the last pages of a book before, Rory thought as he began to read aloud.

The pain I feel as I relive this experience cannot be described. I cannot help but feel that Kieft somehow tricked me, tricked all of us. He did not sacrifice as I sacrificed. I sometimes wonder if he knew everything that would happen—if somehow he'd seen what would be taken from both of us. I watch him stride around Mannahatta, drinking in the thanks of our people, and inside I burn. He is a great liar, I can feel it, and by following his lead, I fear I have done great harm. But nonetheless, I must put to paper exactly what happened so the truth will not be forgotten.

After the beast was gone and my tears had slowed, Henry took us farther in. Kieft's eyes had begun to take on a maniacal, covetous look I did not like. But I could not turn back now, not after what had just happened. It was too late for second thoughts.

After an hour's journey, we encountered the most wondrous sight. A beautiful garden, filled with plants the likes of which I had never seen, stretched into the distance. Everything—the trees, the plants, the flowers—they towered over us as if we had somehow shrunk. I had never seen such flora and said so. Kieft smirked at me, lording his superior knowledge.

"Nor would you have," he said, not deigning to look at me. "These have been long gone from the earth. But they live on here, since they are still remembered."

"Remembered by whom?" I asked him.

"By me," a voice cut in, floating out from the garden's interior. I leaped back, pulling out my sword. Henry likewise jumped, arming himself, but Kieft did not move. A pair of giant ferns parted to reveal a beautiful woman, dressed in European finery I had seen only in the portraits of royalty painted years before my birth. What was such a magnificently dressed woman doing here? I turned to see if my companions had any answers, and while Kieft was merely nodding warily at her, Henry's face was white as if he had seen a ghost. Tears welled up in his eyes.

"I'm sorry," he whispered. "I'm so sorry."

"Do you know her?" I asked him, but he did not answer.

"Welcome to my garden," the Lady said, smiling at us. As she looked at each of us, I thought I saw her eyes widen at the sight of Kieft, but I could not be sure. Perhaps I merely wanted her to be as wary of him as I was, especially in light of what happened next.

"What garden is this?" I asked her. "How did it come to be here?"

"This land has been here for far longer than mortal feet have tread upon it," the Lady answered me. "I am the one who remembers and honors all that once lived here. They laid down roots, and I cherish those roots."

"We wish to lay down roots, as well, Lady," I told her. "That is why we're here."

"So you wish to make covenant with me?" the Lady asked, her face unreadable. "You will bear the price of agreement?"

"Not him," Kieft interrupted, pointing at Henry, who flinched at his master's finger. "He is merely here to carry our baggage."

"And yet he was the one who knew the way to my garden, was he not?" the Lady asked, smiling. "Do not worry, I will ask nothing of him. He has already done enough. No, it will be the two of you who will sign our pact. Though"—here she looked troubled, peering intently at Kieft—"are you certain you are able to make such promises?"

"We have brought the offering," Kieft answered quickly; too quickly, I thought. "We carry the prayers of our people inside us."

"You do, I see that," the Lady said, shrugging away her mistrust. I let out a breath I did not know I had been holding—it would have been disaster to be turned away after all we had gone through. The Lady pulled herself up to her full height and addressed both Kieft and me.

"What do you offer me, to bind your people to my soil?"

"We pledge our fidelity to the land, by our promise never to leave the boundaries set by our blood," I intoned, as Kieft had coached me.

"We pledge our respect to the land, by our promise never to murder, by intent or deed, others of our kind," Kieft chanted.

"We pledge our duty to the land, by our promise never to betray the duties given to us by our believers," I finished. These were the promises Kieft had set out—now we had to hope she agreed to them.

The Lady raised her arms to the sky.

"I accept these promises. Now we must bind ourselves to them."

Kieft pulled out his pipe, in which we'd placed a drop of blood from all our fellow gods and spirits. He pulled out a flint and lit a spark in the bowl. He breathed in deeply before passing it to me. I likewise inhaled, fighting not to cough at the acidic taste. Finally, I handed the pipe to the Lady, who sucked in the smoke that was laced with the essence of our people. She finished, lowering the pipe to stare at us through a cloud of smoke.

"And what of the gifts?"

"What gifts?" I asked, confused.

"To complete our deal. The two of you are your people's sponsors. I require gifts to finish our bargain. Did not your guide tell you?"

Henry wouldn't look at me, but even worse was Kieft's total lack of surprise. He'd known all along.

"I give you memory," Kieft said. "My memory of my greatest spells. There is nothing more important to me."

The Lady nodded, reaching out to grasp at the air in front of Kieft's face. He flinched, his jaw going slack, and then he recovered, his face wan.

"Thank you for your gift," the Lady said. "It was nobly given." She turned to me. "And now, you . . .

I could not stand it. Memory? That was what Kieft gave? And I was being asked for even more than the price I had already paid? I knew I should not, but I erupted all the same.

"Have not I given enough?" I yelled. "What more do I have?"

The Lady regarded me for a moment, her face showing more kindness than I would have expected, and then she nodded. "Your gift is also accepted. It was nobly given and will not be forgotten."

She took a step back, smiling at us all. "Our pact is sealed, our agreement made. You are welcome on my shores. You are home. I will remember you."

With that, she turned and disappeared into the lush undergrowth, and I never saw her again.

In the weeks since that day, I have often thought on our sacrifices. What Kieft gave up . . . I do not believe it. I have seen him work great magic since then. He seems to have lost none of his power. This leads me to only one conclusion: somehow he deceived the Lady, and that does not bode well for us all. There will be a reckoning, some day, of that I am sure. I *take solace in the knowledge that our people are saved and we will endure on these new lands. There will be no more Peter Minuits fading into nothing, though some might say we are better off without a God of Shady Dealing. But that is for the mortals to decide, not for us gods. For my part, I hope to live side by side with the Munsees, growing with them, and living in peace in our new home. Then my sacrifice will be worth the pain it has caused me.*

Rory finished reading and let the pages drop. He felt overwhelmed by what he had learned. Looking around, he saw that everyone else seemed equally lost. Soka's eyes were wide, as if something in those pages had struck a chord.

"Kieft is a liar!" Bridget exclaimed. "He lied to that nice Lady!"

"What did Adriaen sacrifice, that is my question," Fritz asked.

"I bet the answer is in the piece of diary we're missing," Rory mused. "I just wish I knew where we could find it."

"The home of the Swindler, that's what the Fortune Teller said?" Fritz asked, and Rory nodded. The battle roach sighed. "Maybe Nicholas and the rest will have some ideas."

"If they can spare the time," Rory muttered, leaning back in the boat to watch the clouds drift by. War was coming; he could taste it in the air. They were running out of time.

They sailed closer to Mannahatta, heading for Battery Park. And there, waiting for them on the shore, was the last person Rory expected to see.

"Dad?"

Peter Hennessy stood on the shore at Battery Park, watching the little boat that held his children float closer and closer. He was about to do something very dangerous, and he could only hope no one got hurt. But he didn't have any choice.

Kieft had been planning to visit the prison ship, but then he received word that the prisoners had revolted, taking over the boat. Askook had used his blood to scry, and he'd spotted Mr. Hennessy's children getting into a schooner to sail back to the mainland. Apparently the prison ship had hoisted sail and escaped into the fog. But Kieft didn't care about that; he just wanted the Light.

Which was what led to Mr. Hennessy being taken to this spot and told to lure his children in. Kieft was sure of his hold over his former lackey despite Mr. Hennessy's recent disobedience; he thought Mr. Hennessy was too weak to rebel, especially since a group of Kieft's gang boys, led by some nasty piece of work called Sly Jimmy, were hiding behind the trees and tourist kiosks. Once the boat landed and his children ran up to meet him, the gang boys would erupt from their hiding places and capture them all.

He glanced to his left, where Sly Jimmy was hiding, The evil-looking boy was running his finger along a knife blade lovingly. Kieft was counting on Mr. Hennessy's fear of his children being hurt to ensure his cooperation; a struggle could definitely end in bloodshed. The thought made him sick.

The kids hopped out of the boat, and ran over to him.

"Dad!" Rory cried. "You're all right!"

In the end, the choice was surprisingly simple. Some risks just had to be taken. Mr. Hennessy opened his mouth and screamed, "It's a trap! Run, kids! Run!"

He'd carry the looks that spread across his children's faces to his grave (if that blessed day ever came). But then the world descended into chaos as the gang boys sprang from their hiding places, and Soka threw her hands back. The lawn exploded as tiny trees sprang up from beneath the earth, knocking the gang boys to the ground. Mr. Hennessy watched the kids run for safety, a smile spreading across his face even as he realized that he'd probably never see open air again.

That smile faded, however, as he watched Sly Jimmy pick up a rock and throw it with all his strength at Rory's fleeing form. The stone hit him squarely on the back of the knee, and Rory dropped to the ground. The gang boys ran up and dragged him back into the newly grown grove of trees, placing a cloth over his mouth until Rory stopped struggling and fell asleep. Peter realized that the other kids wouldn't even realize Rory was gone until they reached Broadway. And by then it would be too late.

He opened his mouth to yell that his son was being taken, but then he felt a cloth slip over his own mouth. He heard Sly Jimmy's voice whisper in his ear, "Good job, boyo." As he fell away into unconsciousness, he felt his world come crashing down around him. He'd failed, just as he always failed. All he could hope for now was that they'd just stick him in some cell until the world ended. Maybe he'd finally get lucky and end right along with it.

THE GREATEST SPY
IN THE WORLD

We need to go get him, now!" Bridget cried.

"And we will!" Teddy Roosevelt declared, gazing around the council room triumphantly. Bridget had been impressed with the god's awesome mustache and cool hat when the Rattle Watch had led her into the council meeting, along with Soka and Fritz. If he could save her brother, he'd really be a god in her book.

They hadn't even realized Rory wasn't with them when they ran from the gang boys. Bridget had been thankful her father had warned them (though why was he there in the first place? That thought she pushed away for another, quieter time). Once they'd noticed his absence, they turned back just in time to see Rory taken away by a large group of boys. Fritz followed them, leaving Bridget and Soka to wait in a state of crazed worry until the Rattle Watch heard where they were and came to take them to City Hall. Fritz returned to report that Rory had been taken to the old smallpox hospital on Roosevelt Island, where Kieft's army was headquartered.

"This is jolly good luck!" Teddy was arguing. "This is the cause we need! To rescue the Light!"

"We can't just go in guns blazing," Whitman explained, his eyes tired. "If they don't attack us first, it'll look like we're the aggressors."

"This is provocation, by Jove!" Roosevelt announced, slamming his fist on the table. "They've stolen a mortal! We are charged, above all, to protect and serve those little blighters! This is our chance to strike a blow! Look, we won't use the Munsee for this attack, so they won't seem like they're fighting against our people. Will that satisfy you? It just means more glory for the rest of us!"

Peter Stuyvesant spoke up. "I don't think this is a good idea. We haven't heard from our spies recently . . ."

"What are we, women?" Roosevelt asked, exasperated. Mrs. Parker coughed, glaring at him. "Sorry. You want to wait for spies? I'm tired of this wishy-washy behavior! Do you want to win this war or not? By gum, I want to win it! I'm a soldier, and soldiers know a time comes when talk is cheap. Now is that time! Are you gonna wait for the old black-eyed bastard to come knocking on your door with a knife in his hand? Or are you gonna take action!"

Bridget felt her heart stir as the council responded to the god's speech. She saw that even Nicholas's eyes were shining. Only Alexa looked worried.

"This is a mistake," she muttered to no one in particular. Bridget just wanted her brother rescued. However they did it was fine with her. But she'd make sure he came home safe and sound.

In his dream, Rory was back in the black-eyed man's dead city.

"I told you I would find you!" the black-eyed man's voice called, and Rory turned to see the man standing triumphantly atop a shiny car, arms outstretched in victory. He jumped to the ground directly in front of Rory. "You thought she could protect you forever, but I proved stronger."

"Who is protecting me?" Rory asked, bewildered. "I don't know what you're talking about."

"I have hunted you, time and time again, and you have slipped away. Do you think you accomplished this through your own power? Come now. You have her blessing. She has chosen you, helped you avoid my grasp. She's still angry with me, of course. This fight is not between you and me. It is between her and me, and you are but a pawn in that struggle. But I have removed you from the chessboard. And now you're mine to do with as I please, and she can do nothing."

Suddenly a roaring sound filled Rory's ears, as if he were standing in a hurricane. The city began to stretch, as if it was paper and the wind was blowing it away. The man with the black eyes fell back, too, under the force of the wind, and he had to shout to be heard.

"You can push me away, but it means nothing!" the black-eyed man screamed, laughing. Rory could tell these words were not meant for him. "I have him now!"

The roaring grew louder and the wind rushed past Rory, hitting the city so hard that the buildings and cars just blew away into nothingness. The man with the black eyes blew away with it, still laughing. There the roaring quieted, leaving Rory floating in nothingness.

"He always was an arrogant fool," a female voice said behind him. Rory spun to come face-to-face with a smiling Soka. But one look in her eyes told him that this was *not* Soka. This was someone else entirely. "He won't bother you anymore," the not-Soka said. "At least, not in your dreams. I finally put my foot down."

"Who are you?" Rory asked.

Not-Soka shrugged. "Just a concerned party in the ongoing story of Rory Hennessy."

"I don't understand what's going on," Rory protested.

"And you may never understand," not-Soka said, patting his cheek as if she were his mother. "That is a mortal's lot in life. But maybe, just maybe, you'll come through anyway. Hope to see you soon!"

"But—" Rory began as the roaring returned and his world was shrouded in black.

———

Rory's head hurt, and he felt ill enough to throw up. He'd awoken to find himself in a strange room, like a hospital room that had long fallen into disuse, lit by the one small window halfway up a wall. The door was locked shut, and no amount of rattling would move it even an inch. That was all bad enough. But the true torture of his predicament had drifted through the wall from the room next door. It began soon after he'd woken up.

"Hello? Hello, is someone there?" the voice had asked.

Incessant, almost manic, like the yapping of a lapdog, it cut through his room like a car alarm. Soon Rory discovered that it was just as irritating. He made the mistake of answering it, and then the voice's words came rushing nonstop.

"Great to meet you, Rory! I'm so glad you're here! It's wonderful, wonderful to meet more soldiers in the fight against tyranny. Down with evil men! My name is Nathan Hale; you may have heard of me. 'I regret that I have but one life to give for my country!' That was me! I was a great spy, you know. Great spy! I really should be the God of Spies. I'm not really sure why that didn't happen. I mean, I'm proud of the godhood I did get, don't get me wrong, but still—God of Spies! That's *so* me! I infiltrated British-held Manhattan during the Revolution! Dressed as a Dutch schoolteacher, I gathered information and struck a blow to the very heart of the British war machine! There was no spy sneakier than I. I could have posed as King George's mother and fooled the monarch himself!"

"So were you sent here to spy for our side?" Rory asked.

"Yes! Peter Stuyvesant himself tasked me with gathering information. He'd been impressed with my last mission, in which, dressed as a Dutch schoolteacher, I followed John Jay's daughter and discovered she'd been seeing a boy behind her father's back—I even got a great look at the boy's face when he caught me in the bushes and beat the stuffing out of me. Stuyvesant knew my talents and sent me on Kieft's trail! So, dressed as a—"

"Let me guess, Dutch schoolteacher," Rory said drily.

"Exactly! Why mess with success? I infiltrated this smallpox hospital, the belly of the beast, as it were, and discovered much about Kieft and his plans before I was caught."

"That's amazing," Rory replied. "How long were you able to poke around before you were discovered?"

"Almost forty-five minutes!" The pride rang in Hale's voice. "A new record for me! And I've been here in this cell ever since."

"Have you tried to escape?"

"Of course not!" Hale sounded horrified. "No, I'm waiting for them to hang me, and then I've got this wonderful speech prepared that will move them all to tears and make them repent of their evil ways. It can't miss!"

"What are you god of, exactly?" Rory asked, a suspicion forming in his mind.

"God of Martyrs," Hale answered, confirming Rory's intuition. "But I should be God of Spies, honestly. I am that sneaky!"

And so it continued. Rory barely had to answer as Hale regaled him with story after story of his spying prowess, each of which involved him being a Dutch schoolteacher and getting caught really, really fast. Rory could tell by the fading light that evening was descending. He tried looking out the window to catch a glimpse of Kieft's army, but his room faced a wall, so he saw nothing but old stone. No one came to his door to check up on him; for all he knew, Kieft had stuck him in this room to rot. He lay down on the old mattress, trying not to think about his father, who had seemingly betrayed him, yet tried to save him in the end. Still, the fact remained that Peter Hennessy had led Kieft's men to Rory and his friends. And for that, Rory didn't know if he'd ever forgive him.

Rory began to have fears of starving to death in this tiny forgotten room while an idiot droned on next door, when something strange happened. A thump sounded outside his room, like something big was hitting the ground, and then his door slowly creaked open.

Rory sat up, his heart in his throat. The doorway was empty, leading out to a dim hallway.

"Hello?" he called out, not too loudly.

"Yes?" Hale answered.

"Not you," Rory said absently, sliding off the bed to creep over to the open door. Cocking his hand into karate-chop position (not that his yellow belt would help him much here), he carefully peered out into the hall.

"What the—" he muttered. A big Hessian in a long blue coat was lying on the floor of the dank hallway, not moving. Rory nudged him once with his toe, ready to leap back if the guard came alive, but nothing happened. The Hessian was either unconscious or dead.

"I've got a friend here, I guess," he said to himself.

"What's going on?" Hale's voice demanded.

"Shh!" Rory hissed through Hale's door.

"How did you get out?" Hale's voice asked, a little quieter.

"I don't know, but I'm out." Rory paused for a moment, weighing the inhumanity of letting someone rot in a prison cell with the annoyance of having this chatterbox along for the ride. It was a tough choice, but finally he sighed, unlocking Hale's door and pushing it open. A handsome man in a black jacket and hose stood on the other side, his open, honest face smiling widely.

"Well done! Now if we meet any of Kieft's men, I am a simple Dutch schoolteacher and you are my son Paco."

"Paco isn't a Dutch name."

"*They* don't know that!"

"Just keep quiet and maybe we can get out of here alive," Rory said, turning to run down the hallway. Hale followed, spouting out more aliases to use when they encountered the enemy.

But, strangely enough, no enemy was to be found. All the hallways, with their flickering lights and damp, peeling wallpaper, were empty. Rory opened a few of the rooms, hoping to free more prisoners, but all of those rooms were empty as well.

"What is going on here?" he wondered aloud, and for once, Hale had nothing to say. Rory found a flight of stairs and carefully made his way down them, peering around a landing just in case. Hale's wooden shoes (he seemed to think all the Dutch wore them) were making a racket, but there was little Rory could do about that. It didn't seem to matter, as there was no one, not a soul, to be found.

"Did they leave?" he asked.

"Maybe they surrendered and we missed it," Hale offered. Not bothering to answer, Rory warily approached a door that led to a courtyard, and looking out, he caught his first glimpse of some other living souls in this dreary place.

Two gang boys, with knives out, were slowly advancing on a poor, weak-looking man in foppish clothing. The man had his back to the far wall, and tears were rolling down his face.

"Please!" he cried. "Please, I have a wife!"

"What a baby," Hale muttered at Rory's side. The gang boys had almost reached the man.

"The high-and-mighty god is crying!" one gang boy said,

smirking. "Not so big now that we've got a knife that'll do you! Yer not long for this world, believe me!"

"I'm not sure if I want his locket," the other boy said. "God of Ornamental Handkerchiefs seems pretty girlie to me."

"Hey, I'll take it," the first one said. "A god is a god, right? And since we caught him snooping around where he shouldn't after everyone else had gone, he's fair game."

"Please! No!" The god was on his knees, tears streaming down his face. Hale snorted in disgust in Rory's ear.

"This cannot continue," he said, grabbing hold of the door handle. Before Rory could stop him, Hale thrust open the door and strode into the courtyard. "Unhand that man! I am but a simple Dutch schoolteacher, but I cannot let you harm him!"

The two gang boys spun, brandishing their knives. Hale immediately threw up his hands. "Okay, okay. You caught me! I'm no schoolteacher. I am Nathan Hale, the famed spy, and I surrender! Do your worst!" The gang boys' jaws dropped, completely unprepared for Hale's unconditional surrender. What came next happened so fast Rory could barely register it. Once his tormentors were distracted, the cornered god's face suddenly changed, the fear dropping away with cunning replacing it. Straightening up, he ran forward, punching one gang boy in the back of the head before sweeping a leg out from underneath the other. He grabbed one of their knives and swiftly stabbed, once, then twice, dispatching both gang boys as quick as a breath. And only a moment had passed.

Hale's arms were still in the air as he stood frozen in astonishment. Looking past him toward the door Rory waited behind, the god spoke up. "You can come out. It's safe now." His voice was strong and steady—nothing at all like the blubbering mess he'd been a few moments before. Rory warily entered the courtyard, stopping beside Hale and nudging him gently.

"You can lower your arms now," he said. Hale grunted, finally dropping his hands to his sides.

"You're Rory Hennessy," the god said, stepping over the dead bodies to walk over to them. "I had heard you'd been captured, but I hadn't been able to locate your room. I had other business to attend to."

"Who are you?" Rory asked.

"My name is Robert Townsend," the god said. "I am God of Spies."

"Impossible!" Hale shouted. "You're the God of Ornate Handkerchiefs! I heard them!"

"That was my cover," Robert said. "Not that it matters now. We're the only ones left in this unholy place."

"Did Stuyvesant send you?" Hale asked, and Robert nodded. "Why? He'd already sent me!"

"The more spies the better, I guess," Robert said, turning away. Rory suddenly realized that Hale had never been the spy. He was the decoy. Now, that was sneaky.

"Where is everyone?" Rory asked.

"I don't know," Robert said. "Kieft just called them all into the courtyard and then led them away. I would have left as well, but I heard you were in the building and I wanted to find you. But before I could do that, I spied these two pieces of scum coming up from the basement, in a hurry, talking about some trap they were setting. They caught me before I could overhear any more, and then you came along."

"What kind of trap?" Rory asked, his stomach sinking.

"I'll find out," Robert said. "You stay here, in case something nasty is waiting in the basement. If I don't return in fifteen minutes, get out of here."

"I'll come with you!" Hale announced, but Robert's steely look beat him back. "Protecting the boy should be our first priority anyway," he muttered as Robert ran off toward the basement.

Ten minutes passed, each minute tenser than the last. Which was why Rory almost screamed when he heard a new voice speak up across the courtyard.

"Rory! You're all right!" It was Fritz, riding in on Clarence. The battle roach stopped at Rory's feet, giving Hale a quick greeting. "I thought I'd have to sneak my way to your cell, but here you are free and clear! Where is everyone?"

"They just left," Rory said.

"Well, I've got a whole army right behind me, so maybe they got wind of that and ran away."

"An army?" Rory asked.

"You bet. When the council heard you'd been kidnapped, Teddy Roosevelt took it as a sign that it was time to attack. They're a few minutes away from storming the place. I was supposed to find your cell so Nicholas and the others could grab you in the confusion. But now it looks like we'll just walk on in unopposed. We might as well just wait here, they'll be showing up any second."

"No!" Rory turned to see Robert running toward him. "It's a trap! The basement is filled with explosives tied to hundreds of god-killing knives! The army will be sliced to pieces in the explosion. Kieft knew you were coming, that's why they left. Come on, we've got no time!"

Rory, Hale, Robert, and Fritz immediately began to run, racing out of the courtyard into an old lobby, past a decomposing front desk, and through the front door into the forest outside. Trees surrounded them, and at first Rory thought they were alone, but then Robert began to scream.

"Fall back! It's a trap! Fall back!"

The bushes rustled as someone stood up, his form barely showing up in the dim of twilight.

"Robert, is that you? What are you talking about?" Rory recognized Stuyvesant's voice.

"The whole place is going to blow! Fall back!" Rory and the others crashed into the trees, and suddenly the forest came alive as hundreds of people began to run alongside Rory. They'd gone maybe a hundred feet when the world seemed to explode, the force pushing Rory forward as if he were a kite in the wind. He hit the ground hard as debris fell around him. Something big landed right on his back and fear shot through him as he thought he was dead. Instead a voice spoke right in his ear.

"I've got you, Rory," Bridget breathed as she used her body to protect him from the flying debris. "I thought you were a goner." And then she burst into tearless sobs.

***

Robert Townsend made his report to the council as the smallpox hospital burned behind them. Thanks to his warning, their army had escaped serious injuries, though some soldiers had been wounded by the shrapnel. Peter Stuyvesant gave Teddy Roosevelt a dirty look, opening his mouth as if to say *I told you so*, but Roosevelt was not one to look back.

"So his whole army is just gone?" he asked. "By Jove, that

is some feat! They could be anywhere! We should have moved quicker!"

"If we'd moved any quicker, we'd have been inside the hospital when it blew," Stuyvesant said sourly.

"And now they could be anywhere!" Roosevelt exclaimed. A murmur ran through the council—no one liked that idea one bit.

"No matter where they may be now," Mrs. Parker said, "they'll be heading toward the park. That's where this will all play out, I promise you."

"I find it more interesting that the foot soldiers, the gang members, have been given knives," Whitman said. "I'd assumed Kieft was only handing those out to sow confusion among our ranks, not to his own grunts. I can't believe that Kieft doesn't know that they don't care who they kill so long as they get a locket."

"Maybe he doesn't care," Mrs. Parker mused.

"Or maybe that's exactly what he wants," Whitman added.

"That's ridiculous," Roosevelt said. "What general *wants* his soldiers killing each other?"

"Someone who doesn't care who's left," Whitman replied. "And those generals are the ones we should be most frightened of, because they will do anything to get what they want."

Rory recounted his adventures in the smallpox hospital to the Rattle Watch.

"Who do you think left the door open?" Soka asked.

"I have no idea," Rory answered. "Whoever it was saved my life. Now, if we could only find that last piece of diary . . ."

"We don't have much time," Nicholas said. "I think Kieft is about to make his big move. I hoped Roosevelt was going to stop him, but now . . ." He glanced at Alexa. "I think Roosevelt just wants to fight, which played right into Kieft's hands! I don't know if Teddy's the answer, anymore. Your quest might end up being the one that saves us all."

"So now we just need to find the home of the Swindler!" Bridget exclaimed.

"Well, what have we found out?" Alexa asked. Rory summarized what they had learned from the sections of Adriaen's journal. When he finished, a queer look came over Alexa's face.

"My father never liked Peter Minuit, you know," she said. "He never liked that the mortal Minuit tried to cheat the Munsees by offering them so little for Manhattan. Of course, Minuit never knew that the Munsees only believed in rent, so in their minds it was never a sale at all. Still, it was an underhanded move. My father felt bad that Minuit faded, of course. But I know he never missed him. The God of Shady Dealings. My dad used to say he was just a thief and a no-good *swindler*."

Bridget gasped at the word and Rory leaned forward eagerly. "So you think Peter Minuit is the Swindler?" he asked. "But he's dead."

"We don't need the guy," Simon mused. "We just need his house. Not that he ever had one."

"Not a house," Fritz said excitedly. "A home. We need to visit what he left behind."

Alexa snapped her fingers, excited.

"His room! It must be in his old room! We have to go to City Hall!"

THE HOME OF THE
SWINDLER

I t is time, Askook," Kieft said. They were standing at the
northern edge of the park, Kieft's army fanning out under
the trees. Kieft was disappointed that his little trap had failed
to destroy the council's troops (although Hearst's flies had seen
them from a distance, someone on the council had instituted
a practice of killing every fly they saw, making the intelligence
spottier and less frequent), but he took solace in the thought
that the pest of a Light had been burned alive. He couldn't
feel the child's dreams anymore, so he could assume that the
wretched boy's little journey had thankfully come to an end
before it could harm Kieft's plans, which he could finally set
in motion. He was not ready to make his main move, though,
not yet. Certain . . . groundwork had to be laid. He nodded to
the snake-faced Munsee at his side, who stood at the head of a
handpicked gang of murderers and thieves. "Are you ready?"

"Of course," Askook said. He slid his thumb across the
blade of his knife and smiled, knowing that tonight would be a
very good night indeed. He led his men into the park, heading
south toward his old home.

Bridget stared around in awe as Alexa led them down the long, dusty passageways hidden beneath City Hall. Even Nicholas seemed impressed by her confident strides through the dimly lit, old halls.

"I've heard of these rooms, but I've never been down here," Nicholas said, giving Alexa a reproachful look. "If you're such an expert, why didn't you ever take me on a tour?"

"Yeah, Alexa," Simon said, smirking. "Why didn't you ever take us down to the eerie rooms of all the dead gods? It's a great birthday-party spot!"

"They're not all dead," Alexa said, pointing at one room to their left whose door was cracked open slightly. From what Bridget could see through the crack, the room seemed clean and airy, with odd, exotic objects lining the walls. A name was painted over the door in ornate black brushstrokes—IRVING. Nicholas stopped, intrigued.

"Is that Washington Irving's room?" he asked. Lincoln bounded by him, heading for the door.

"Let's take a look!" he said, but he didn't get far before Alexa collared him, pulling him back.

"Entering another god's room without permission is forbidden, and, even worse, tacky. Come on!"

She dragged Lincoln along, and the others followed, though Bridget would have tried to sneak a better peek if Rory hadn't been watching her. The passageways seemed endless, with countless intersections and dead ends, but Alexa had no problem steering them onward. Soka looked around with interest, speaking in a low voice to the Hennessy kids.

"We Munsees have nothing like this. It's like a huge temple!"

"My dad wasn't too fond of these rooms, to be honest," Alexa said, overhearing. "He felt like they encouraged the gods to keep secrets from one another."

"The only secret I see is that being a god is no promise of immortality," Nicholas said drily as they walked past more dead, dark rooms. Simon didn't look too happy to hear this, and he held a single china plate to his chest as if it were a security blanket.

"There are plenty of live rooms," Alexa replied. "But we're moving into a deeper part of the hall, where the rooms of the first gods are located. Many of those early gods have been forgotten, so their rooms are lifeless and dark."

"Is my father's room around here?" Nicholas asked, craning his neck to peer ahead.

"Probably," Alexa guessed. "But we're not here for him." She stopped in front of a dark room. The door stood ajar, and by the faint light of the hallway, Bridget could see books piled up on a nice desk, gathering dust. She peered at the name— VAN DER DONCK. Alexa sighed, her eyes red.

"Though he wasn't supposed to, my father would take me down here sometimes, to teach me about how even the gods must be responsible to those they serve. There is no power so great that it can never wane, he would tell me, pointing at all the dead rooms. At first I wondered why he didn't just make that speech in the Portrait Room upstairs, where I could see all the paintings with dead eyes."

"Dead eyes?" Soka asked, confused.

"All the gods have their portraits in the Portrait Room," Nicholas explained to the Munsee girl. "If the eyes of the portrait are alive, then so is the god. If the eyes are dull, lifeless paint, then the god is dead."

"So why not just show me those, right?" Alexa asked. "I realized, eventually, that these rooms were a much stronger lesson. The portraits are just a courtesy, a calling card for the divine. These rooms, however, are a sanctuary, a place that is theirs and only theirs. Some of the gods really do up their rooms, showing them proudly to friends and lackeys. And now look. All that pride come to naught, the rooms empty, the gods forgotten. It was a powerful lesson."

"So now what?" Bridget asked, hoping they'd enter Van der Donck's room and take a look around. But Alexa closed the door, and led them farther down the hall.

"Minuit's room should be around here," she explained, reading the names above the door as she walked by. The names seemed to be all Dutch—Twiller, Van Tienhoven, Rosenvelt. With their doors shut, she couldn't tell which belonged to live gods or dead, forgotten ones. But most of them just *felt* dead.

Finally, Alexa gave a shout and pointed. There it was, above a door that was almost at the end of the hallway—MINUIT.

"Ready?" Nicholas asked them as they gathered around the door. Bridget nodded excitedly.

"Open it already!"

Nicholas nodded to Alexa, who pushed the door inward. They passed into the room of Peter Minuit, to a wholly unexpected sight.

"What is going on?" Alexa asked no one in particular, gazing around in amazement.

"Um, I don't want to ask a stupid question, but I thought

this guy was dead," Bridget said, frowning. "'Cause it's pretty well lit in here, and clean, too."

Indeed, Minuit's room was immaculate, and bright from the lamps glowing in the corners. Fresh-looking maps lined the walls, displaying unfamiliar places with names like New Sweden. It sure didn't look to Bridget like the room of a dead god.

"This is impossible," Alexa said, shaking her head. "Minuit is dead!"

"You don't know everything you think you do, child," a voice said from behind the door. Everyone let out a shout as they jumped back in shock. Lincoln threw closed the door to reveal an easy chair in a hidden corner. Sitting in the easy chair was a woman in a crisp business suit who looked an awful lot like the Fortune Teller. Only this version wasn't fat and gross, nor was she tall and beautiful. She looked middle-aged, of average height and build—wholly unremarkable. But she didn't *feel* unremarkable. In fact, she felt very powerful.

"You!" Rory said, his face white. "What are you doing here? Wait a minute, is this the third door?"

"The third door is not what you think it is," the Fortune Teller said, leaning back in her chair comfortably. "The first two doors are secrets to be uncovered. But the last door finds *you*. The last door is not where you go to ask, it is where you go to *be* asked."

"What are you talking about?" Nicholas asked. "Is Minuit dead or not?"

"That is not for me to say," the Fortune Teller said. "I am here to give you a gift and ask a favor."

She handed Rory a sheaf of papers, the top of which read *Four*. Rory looked like he wanted to punch someone.

"You had it the whole time! Why did you send us on this wild-goose chase?"

"It was anything but," the Fortune Teller said, impervious to Rory's anger. "You asked me your question and I gave you the path to follow to reach your answer. Everything you've done needed to happen in order for you to get to this place. And now the journey culminates with this package, which Adriaen gave to me knowing full well that he would never be able to return to me to retrieve it."

"You're making my head hurt, lady," Simon complained.

"You're a god now, aren't you?" the Fortune Teller shot back. "Try to show a little backbone."

"So you came to us to give us the journal," Rory asked, still confused.

"In part," the Fortune Teller said. "But I am also here to ask something of you."

"What?" Nicholas asked, suspicious.

"Read," the Fortune Teller instructed them. "Then we will talk."

Though Bridget could see the questions burning in her brother's eyes, he held his tongue, picking up the journal and flipping the page.

The journey to our destination began at the mouth of a well-hidden cave by the southern shore of the Collect Pond, not far north of the Commons. Already, the pond that held the drinking water for all of Manhattan was beginning to be polluted—

the color was no longer the clean blue I remembered, but a rather dirty green. I was very much surprised to find that Kieft was not leading the way. Instead, the enigmatic Henry took the point position, lighting a torch and stepping first into the dark cave. Kieft and I followed, each eyeing the other warily as we walked into the black.

Soon the light of day disappeared behind us, and only the flickering of our torches brightened the gloom. After we'd walked through the dark for a bit, we came to a dead end. But Henry was not dismayed. He reached behind a strange symbol, which looked like the Munsee sign for danger, and pulled at a small rock. Suddenly the tunnel began to shake as rocks fell from the ceiling. We crouched down, trying feebly to protect ourselves. When the shaking ceased, we lifted our heads and saw, to our surprise, that the dead end had opened up into another tunnel. Henry strode forward without a second thought and we followed.

This new tunnel felt far older. More Munsee sigils lined the rough rock walls, but I had never seen their like. I had no idea what message was being conveyed, but the quick, almost frightened-looking lines made me nervous. There was something down here more powerful than mere gods, I felt. What it could be, I had no idea.

I do not know how long we journeyed down that ancient tunnel, but soon we began to hear strange sounds all around us. Laughter and the bubbling cries of newborn babes, the rattle of spears and the death moans of old men. Entire lives were being lived as we walked, civilizations rising and falling just beyond the walls of our tunnel, and the sounds grew louder the deeper we went. We began to pass white sticks on the floor of the tunnel—with a start I realized they were bones. Who had died here? I was not afraid of death, myself, as it had already happened to me once. But I could not imagine what the fear would be like for a mortal, hearing the sounds of death all around, unable to escape the knowledge that he, too, would die. I noticed that Henry was staggering as he walked. He touched his forehead, as if needing reassurance. I saw that a reddish-brown concoction had been daubed there. I asked him if it made him invisible.

"There is nothing that can make me invisible to what surrounds us here," he told me, miserable. "But it keeps them at bay."

"Keeps who at bay?" I asked him, looking around the tunnel, bare but for the three of us. Kieft wasn't even looking at us—his black eyes were focused ahead.

"They are not your concern," Henry said stiffly. "You are beyond them. I'll be fine. Just please, leave me be."

And he pushed on, relentless.

Gradually, I noticed a roaring in the distance. We turned a corner and came upon a rushing underground stream. I searched for some sign of how to proceed, but I could see nothing but the rapids.

"Where do we go from here?" I asked Henry. Kieft stepped up behind me and whispered in my ear.

"We go down." And he pushed me, hard, into the river. I thought I heard a shout far behind me as the water sucked me down. I could not see a thing as I was carried along, and I struggled to no avail to control my progress. But I could do *nothing to save myself from what came next. The water pushed me out, over a ledge, and then I was falling.*

I fell for a long time. The water fell with me—I could feel it on my skin moving as I tumbled. Everything was black around me. I had never felt more frightened in my life, not even on the day I died. I could not stop falling. And then my feet hit a floor of water, hard but yielding, and I splashed down into an underground lake, sinking all the way to the bottom. It took me a moment to come to my senses, but then I kicked, hard, pushing myself to the surface. I burst up into the air, violently, gasping with terror. My gasps of fear soon changed, however, to gasps of wonder.

I was floating in a lake inside a huge underground cavern, large enough to hold the entire Manhattan colony ten times over. The water danced all around me, sparkling under the bright twinkle of the most beautiful sight I have ever seen. The ceiling, far above me, glittered with millions of tiny lights, like stars, only brighter, and their glow sent dazzling reflections bouncing off the underground lake onto the jagged walls that lined the shore. I felt as if I'd landed inside a diamond. It made my heart weep to see it.

A splash behind me brought me to my senses. A hole in the ceiling poured water down into the lake—it was through this hole that I had fallen. The splash proved to be Kieft, who soon broke to the surface not far from me. I could not see Henry, and I had my doubts about whether any mortal, no matter their power, could survive such a plummet. I swam for the nearest shore, giving Henry up for dead.

I pulled myself onto soft, dark sand, falling back to collect my wits. Kieft emerged not two feet from me, but to my surprise, he immediately began scrambling for the wall. I scanned the lake, but I could see nothing to be frightened of. I spied a body floating in the water near me. I ran over and pulled it out—it was Henry, and he was deathly pale. I knew he was dead, which was why I was so surprised when he suddenly coughed, turning to vomit water onto the ground. He staggered to his feet, looking as near to death as one can without actually crossing over, but instead of joy at being alive, he looked resigned.

"How did you survive that?" I asked him. He gave me a pained look that I did not understand.

"That was not the part of the journey I was worried about," he told me.

"Then what was?" I asked. Instead of answering me, he glanced over my shoulder and blanched.

"Run for the wall!" he yelled at me, and turned to follow his own advice. I spun to see what had frightened him so. At first I could see nothing. But then I noticed a ripple in the water. Something was coming . . . something big. I only had time to see a flash of white before the water exploded and a creature, as large as a warship, burst out of the lake. I could not make out its form, but I could see its rows and rows of teeth as its jaws opened wide, about to clamp down on me. I would have been swallowed right then and there if Henry hadn't grabbed my belt and pulled me away. The jaws slammed shut a foot from my face, sending a blast of air blowing my hair back like a hurricane wind.

I still could not make out the form of the thing—it was too

big and too close. As I staggered back, I heard Kieft yelling
at Henry.

"Why did you save him?" he screamed. "He was our sacrifice!"

Henry didn't reply, and I had no time to ask him for an explanation as the huge white jaws before me came biting back. I
backed up again, narrowly missing being crushed. But suddenly
I slammed into a wall. Turning, I saw nothing behind me.
Yet I could not move any farther back. Something was holding
me in place. I have since suspected that Kieft was working his
magic to trap me, making certain I would not survive, but at the
time I only knew I could not escape from the monster. I spun
back to face the creature, realizing that I had run out of room
and run out of time. I closed my eyes, waiting for oblivion.

"Adriaen!" a voice screamed. My eyes flew open and there
she was. Pulling herself out of the water like a ghost. My
Marta, my beautiful wife, who must have followed me down
to the gates of hell. She had never trusted Kieft, she was right
not to, and she never was one to ignore her fears. I can still see
her, dripping from her plunge into the lake, running toward me
with fear in her eyes.

"Marta, no!" I screamed, my heart stopping.

"I won't let anything happen to you, you will protect our
people—she told me so," she cried, reaching my side to give me
a kiss. I can still feel her lips on mine, wet with the lake water
and my tears, loving me and saying good-bye. I reached out
to pull her from harm's way, but she danced out of my reach,
turning to the great creature before us, and leaping, willingly,
into its maw.

The scream that ripped from my body as my wife, my love, disappeared forever into the beast's belly, tore part of my soul from my body, I know it. I have never felt whole again since. I can only approach that state when I see my Marta in Alexa's face. Oh, my wife! What was promised to you that you would do such a thing? I fear I will never know the answer.

I dropped to the ground, crying, even as the jaws retreated back into the water. Kieft came up to my side.

"That was supposed to be you," he told me, turning the screw. I felt no surprise. Of course, he meant to sacrifice me. He watched the water with a puzzled expression, as if he couldn't understand how anyone could ever do something so selfless, so loving. Henry came up behind me, placing a tentative hand on my shoulder.

"Come, it isn't far," he said, and I could hear the sympathy in his voice. But I could not move, not yet. I sat still, shaking with grief, and tried to understand how I could have lost so much so quickly. I'll never understand it. But in time, I came to see that without Marta's sacrifice, our bargain would have been made completely by Kieft. And that would have been a disaster. It is small solace, true, but it is something.

Alexa was crying, and Nicholas reached out to comfort her. Everyone had tears running down their cheeks at the sad tale except for the Fortune Teller (and Bridget herself, of course), who watched them all with eyes Bridget couldn't read.

"I never knew . . ." Alexa sobbed. "Father always told me she died in an accident, protecting me. But that . . . that's horrible."

"Nonsense," the Fortune Teller said brusquely. "Someone

had to be sacrificed. Kieft meant it to be your father. But your mother saved him, and if he hadn't given his word to the Agreement, who knows what would have come to pass? Especially since Kieft has proven so faithless–" Here she snarled, showing emotion for the first time.

"Who are you, really?" Nicholas asked, peering at her intently as if trying to see behind her skin.

"I am the Fortune Teller," she replied, straightening her pressed blazer. "Here is my request of you. Kieft's treasure lies in that cavern. He sent it down to a place where no one could retrieve it. But you will find it."

"How?" Rory asked, looking overwhelmed. "It sounds like it's in the middle of the earth! And that fall? It'll kill us for sure—or me, at least. How are we supposed to do this?"

"Just follow the path," the Fortune Teller advised him. "The signposts are all there. Remember, your father—for, as you guessed, Henry is your father—once made his way down there, all by himself, so a mortal can survive. If you follow in his footsteps, you will surely find Kieft's treasure. Now, here is my request of you. When you find Kieft's treasure, you must take only one thing away with you. The rest stays, forever."

"Hey, there's probably some good stuff down there!" Simon declared.

"It was never yours to take," the Fortune Teller told him.

"What about my people's lost magic?" Soka asked. "Kieft has it all written down!"

"You do not need it," the Fortune Teller said. "I promise you."

"I will try to memorize what I can, then," Soka muttered to herself.

Bridget didn't like this. Who knew what they'd find in Kieft's treasure, and if it would contain the spell to save their mother. The Fortune Teller was staring at her brother, as if his answer was the only one that mattered.

"You're asking me to trust you?" Rory asked. "How do I know that I won't have to make some awful choice between the city and my mom? I had to make that kind of choice already, and it hurt like hell." Bridget knew he was talking about the time when Hex the magician forced him to choose between her life and a war between Munsees and gods by opening the Trap too soon. She didn't know if she could make that kind of tough decision.

"You've trusted me so far," the Fortune Teller answered. "Remember, I'm giving you what you asked for."

"Is this really what *I* asked for?" Rory said, then sighed. "Fine. You've got a deal." He stuck out his hand and the Fortune Teller gave it a brisk shake. "So what will you give us in return for following your orders?"

"I will give you two things," the Fortune Teller said. "One now, and one when you have kept your promise."

"What will you give me now?"

"Advice," the Fortune Teller said. "To help you survive the journey. First—Munsee magic will protect you on your journey. Without it, you are doomed. And second—know that the guardian does not require a life to be sated. It just requires a sacrifice."

"Why do you always have to be so cryptic?" Lincoln said, looking cross. "Why not just tell the kid exactly what he needs to do?"

"Because that is what is required," the Fortune Teller told

him. "It must come from you, Rory. Otherwise, she will not listen."

"Who won't listen?" Bridget asked, but the Fortune Teller closed her mouth, unwilling to speak further. Rory nodded, accepting the advice he'd been given.

"It doesn't matter what you tell me or don't tell me," he said. "Nothing you say could scare me away. If this is the only way to stop Kieft and save my mother, I'm going to do it, even if it kills me."

It chilled Bridget to hear him talk this way, and she promised herself, silently, that her brother would never have to go that far. If anyone made a sacrifice to save their mother, it would be her. After all, she thought, scratching her paper arm ruefully, she'd never feel it . . .

They hurried back down the halls, past the rooms of the gods. Alexa led the way, speaking over her shoulder as they ran.

"Something about that cave sounds familiar to me," she said. "I want to check the map room."

"What's the map room?" Rory asked Lincoln, who was nearest him.

"It's pretty cool," Lincoln replied. "See, it's this map in a room." He smirked.

"Oh," Rory said. "I should have guessed that."

Although he wasn't paying much attention to the rooms they raced by on their way out, he could have sworn he heard the thud of a door closing as they passed one section. He pulled up, looking around. Two doors faced each other in this part of the hall, and while one was dead and dark, light was emanating from beneath the door of the other. His heart jolted as a shadow slid across the light under the door. Someone was on the other side! His first instinct was to run, but something made him glance at the name above the door. What he saw there made his heart thud even louder.

BURR.

This was Aaron Burr's room. Hex's room. The fallen god who had tricked him into helping him break into Tobias's bank, who had stolen Bridget's soul, who had set Rory's feet onto this path in the first place. He'd been arrested, held under lock and key in Peter Stuyvesant's barn until the burning of the Stuyvesant farm, during which Burr disappeared. And if this was his room, then was that shadow . . . ?

"What are you doing?" Bridget's voice said loudly in his ear. He jumped a foot in the air, turning quickly to shush her. Everyone was behind her, curious as to why he'd stopped. But when Nicholas saw the name over the door, his face grew grim.

"He wouldn't . . ." Nicholas mused. "He's fallen. It would take unbelievable hubris to claim your room when you've been cast out."

"Desperate people do desperate things," Alexa said thoughtfully. "What should we do?"

"Go in!" Lincoln whispered fiercely. "We can take him!"

"We don't have time," Alexa maintained.

"Yeah," Bridget agreed. "If we're going to get to Kieft's treasure in time, we've got to . . ." She never finished her sentence, as Nicholas quickly clamped a hand over her mouth. But it was too late. The door to Burr's room flew open, revealing the disheveled, dirty, and most of all, hungry face of Aaron Burr.

"You've found it?" he asked, eyes boring into Bridget. Being on the run clearly did not agree with the fallen god. His clothes were in tatters and he looked sickly. "Where?"

"Hello, Hex," Rory cut in, his stomach rolling at having to face his betrayer. "Still running and hiding out, huh?"

"Don't give me that holier-than-thou crap," Burr spat. "This is still my room. I earned this room and they can't take it away."

"Then you should have kept the door shut," Fritz said, shaking his head. "You know we're going to tell the council you're down here, right? You were cast out a long time ago. You lost all these privileges."

Burr sneered. "Tell whom you wish, I'll be long gone." He peered at Rory intently. "You should let me come with you. No one knows Kieft better than I do. Even if you think you know where his treasure is, it will be heavily guarded. I can be useful."

"Do you really think we'd ever trust you again?" Rory asked, incredulous. "You betrayed us over and over, in every way. I could never trust you."

"You have to fight magic with magic," Burr insisted, opening his hand and letting sparks jump from knuckle to knuckle. "Kieft will set traps. I will be able to see those traps and disarm them. I wouldn't ask for much. Just some choice items. I won't do anything you don't ask me to do, I promise."

Soka gave the fallen god a disgusted look. "We don't need you, pretend medicine man. I am with Rory, and I can protect him." She lifted her hand, and clouds formed, raining down on her palm, small jolts of lightning snaking out to zap her fingertips. Burr flinched, gazing at the Munsee girl with new respect. He did not give up that easily, however, turning back to Rory with renewed urgency.

"Rory, all it takes is one false move and this little girl could be killed by one of Kieft's traps," he said. "Let me be the one to take those risks. Let me be the one who risks his life, not your pretty friend. There is no way for you to lose!"

"I *only* lose with you, Hex," Rory told the old man, suddenly tired. "I don't have time for this." With that, he turned to walk away. The others followed, leaving Soka to give the last warning.

"Follow us and you will pay," she promised the old magician. "Understand me?" The lightning licked off her palms onto her fingertips. Burr took a step back, alarmed.

"Who are you, girl?" he asked.

"Stay away," she told him, before turning to follow Rory and the rest. Burr yelled after them, though he did not budge from his door.

"You'll regret walking away from me! You'll regret ever casting me aside. You need me!" But they kept walking, and soon even his echoing voice was a memory.

THE GAME CHANGES

Sooleawa sat in Tackapausha's wigwam, the rest of the elders long gone. The newcomer army was coming to them, convinced that Kieft's army was going to attack the park. The elders had to decide what to do. Even at this moment, they weren't fully agreed. But the night had grown late, and they dispersed. Tackapausha had asked Sooleawa to stay behind, and now she was waiting to hear what he had to say.

"I just want the anger to go away," Tackapausha said, suddenly looking tired. "I thought it would disappear when my son returned to me, but it won't leave me be. Why is that?"

"You've been hurt, deeply," Sooleawa told him. "That kind of hurt is hard to heal. It takes time."

"I feel broken," he said, slumping down. "The newcomers broke me with their lies and their wars."

"It takes more to forgive than many have to offer, I believe," Sooleawa said. "Anger is fire . . . it consumes you and leaves nothing but ash. It tears down our houses and leaves us homeless. Forgiveness, understanding—that is how we build again."

"I fear I am not as strong as you," Tackapausha sighed. "My

anger had burned through me so completely that I am nothing but a shell that can crumble at any time. Part of me wishes to take our battle to Kieft, as I doubt I can survive the wait. Either way, I know I will not survive this last fight. My son will do my forgiving for me."

"Do not speak so," Sooleawa scolded him. "You have more strength than you know."

Tackapausha opened his mouth to reply, but Sooleawa never got to hear his words as just then a ripping sound echoed through the wigwam and a knife appeared in the wall, cutting a hole from the outside. Black figures poured in through the hole, firelight glinting off their knives. Tackapausha didn't have time to fight back as one of the knives found a home in his chest. Sooleawa immediately began to summon a spell, grasping at the wampum she kept in her pouches.

Tackapausha's killer turned to her—it was Askook. She felt no surprise as the snake-faced Munsee approached her. She gripped her wampum, pulling as much magic into her as she could bear, and just as the knife descended she sent herself out, soaring through the air in one last moment of freedom, even as her body fell. She soared on, searching for her children, desperate to say good-bye.

Rory and his friends finally left the underground corridors behind and emerged into City Hall proper. Alexa and Nicholas led the way through the twists and turns of the old building, keeping to the shadows to avoid detection. This didn't seem to be much of a problem, however.

"Where is everybody?" Lincoln asked, gazing around the empty halls in confusion.

"I don't know," Nicholas replied, looking equally confused. "But the map room is off-limits, and anyone we meet would likely keep us from going, so let's not look a gift horse in the mouth. Here we are!"

He pushed through a nondescript door into a dark room, he and Alexa ushering in the rest of them before he closed the door.

"Wow!" Bridget whistled by Rory's side. And Rory had to agree with her. The long room was dark, like a planetarium, though instead of stars, the only light came from what appeared to be a glowing diorama floating a foot above the ground, which took up most of the room.

"It's the whole city!" Bridget cried, running up to get a closer look at the scale-model-size buildings. Rory followed, marveling at the sight. He realized he was actually walking through the diorama, wading through the model as if it were a shallow pond. He passed by the hip-high Statue of Liberty, its torch the size of his fingernail. The Financial District rose up before him, the tall buildings as high as his shoulders. Everything seemed so lifelike, he felt like Godzilla about to attack. Gazing uptown, he could spy the Empire State Building in the middle of the room, and the trees of Central Park beyond that. Everything glowed as if the noon sun shone down on it, even though the room's ceiling was pitch-black. Only one thing was missing.

"Where are the people?" Bridget asked. She had run all the way up to the Village, passing through the buildings as if they were holograms—the most lifelike holograms Rory had ever seen.

Nicholas shrugged. "We're not looking at the city the way it actually is right now. We're looking at our collective memory of the city. When you mash together everyone's memory of a street corner, you're not going to all remember the woman hailing a cab. But you *will* all remember the drugstore with the summer beach display in the window. Understand?"

"I guess," Bridget replied, running up to Midtown. "What about Central Park? Most of you guys never set foot inside it, right?"

"Until a few days ago, Central Park was merely a black, shrouded area in the middle of the map," Alexa replied, walking through the miniature city toward the Brooklyn Bridge and City Hall. "But this map is more than just the city today. Watch." She stretched her arms out, closing her eyes. Suddenly the map began to shift, the buildings melting down into trees, the edges of the island falling into the water, and the land shifting, rising up into hills and falling down into valleys. When the map stopped flowing, the only buildings that were left were clustered at the southern tip, including a fort and a few farms. The rest of the island was covered in trees and bogs, meadows and streams, and a large lake near a long wall that traced the northern line of the settlement.

"What happened?" Rory asked. Alexa opened her eyes and smiled sadly as she glanced around the new map.

"This is the Mannahatta of my youth," she said, running a hand over the lifelike grass that covered the ground near her waist. "I asked the map to remember it with me."

"Why?" Bridget asked.

"When I was small, I used to play by the Collect," she said, reaching down with a finger, gently sinking the tip into the large pond near the wall. "My father didn't like it, but he'd often be busy in City Hall and I'd run off, past the wall that later became Wall Street, up to the pond to throw stones at the ducks. And there was a cave there, a deep cave I never saw the back of, that I liked to play pretend house in, as if I were a cavewoman making a home for her family. My father caught me one day in the cave and I'll never forget how he reacted. It was as if I'd leaped into a bear trap or something. His face was so frightened as he scooped me up and carried me out that you'd think I was playing with rattlesnakes. He made me promise never to enter the cave again, and I didn't, because his fear scared me. Later, other buildings sprang up and I lost sight of the cave, so the temptation disappeared. But I never forgot."

"You think this might be the cave Adriaen entered to go down to the cavern?" Rory asked, hope rising in his heart. Alexa didn't answer, searching the south shore of the pond, then nodding as she reached out with a fingertip to tap at the mouth of a small cave hidden behind some trees.

"That's it," she said firmly. "That's the cave."

"But you said yourself the cave was built over," Rory said. "How can we find it today?"

"Nothing is every really gone in Mannahatta, you know that," Nicholas told him. Alexa nodded.

"You want to know where it is today?" She closed her eyes, and the map began to flow once more. Buildings rose up out of the ground, land emerged from the sea, and hills and valleys smoothed out into avenues and tree-lined streets. Soon the city

Rory knew had returned. But Alexa's outstretched finger had never moved. "It's right here." Rory stepped up to her side. Her finger was pointing at a small pizza place not far north of City Hall.

"You found it!" Bridget cried, hopping up and down.

"She did," Nicholas said, smiling. "Let's go!"

But before they could move, a strange feeling washed over them. Fear, mixed with pain, and unbearable love. Rory bent over double, overwhelmed, and he could see the others were just as overcome. He recognized the presence—he'd felt it before—and the power of it was almost too much for him. But that was nothing compared with Soka, who had collapsed to the floor.

"Mother!" she screamed, tears pouring from her eyes. "Don't leave me!" But despite Soka's cries, the feeling faded, leaving Rory hollow and sad.

"What's going on?" Fritz asked, bewildered.

"It's Sooleawa," Rory replied, feeling shell-shocked and grief-stricken for Soka. "She's gone."

It didn't take long for them to find out what had happened. As they left the map room, they ran right into Walt Whitman, who was running down the hall with Dorothy Parker at his side.

"They launched a sneak attack in the middle of the night," Whitman told them. "Askook, the devil, killed Tackapausha and Sooleawa . . ."

"She's gone," Soka mumbled, pain flashing across her tear-streaked face. Whitman's kind eyes overflowed as Mrs. Parker gave her shoulder a squeeze.

"I'm so sorry," Whitman said, his eyes filling with tears.

"Now my people are left without a *pau wau*," Soka said, and Rory realized, with a sinking sensation, what that would mean.

"And the first real battle is just around the corner," Whitman said. "Though I have no doubt we'll prevail! We have stout hearts and strong leaders!"

"That more than makes up for our lack of guns and swords, I'm sure," Mrs. Parker added drily.

"You should see to your father," Whitman advised Nicholas. "He needs you right now. To be honest, we need all of you right now. This battle is not just for the Munsees. We're fighting for the heart of the city itself!"

After a quick farewell, he and Mrs. Parker continued down the hall, running to meet up with the other leaders to discuss battle plans. Before the Rattle Watch even turned to look at Rory, he knew what was coming. So he beat them to the punch.

"You need to be here," he told them. "Helping your people. I can go alone to the cavern."

"Not alone!" Bridget cried. "I'm coming, too!"

"One of us should go with you," Alexa began, but Fritz cut her off.

"No, your place is with the gods," he said. "They need people they can trust right now. I will go with Rory and Bridget."

"And Soka, right?" Bridget asked, eyes hopeful. But Soka looked away.

"Soka needs to go back to her people," Rory told Bridget. "They'll need her magic to counter Kieft and Askook. That's far more dangerous than where we're going." His eyes glanced over at Soka, the worry rising in his heart. "You will be careful, right?"

"I will if you will," she said tearfully. Bridget stamped her foot.

"But we're supposed to have magic!" she cried. "The Fortune Teller said so!"

"I will give it to you," Soka promised. She looked deep in Rory's eyes, and the pain he saw in her own cut him to the quick. "I will make sure nothing harms you."

Rory forced a smile. He knew it wouldn't be enough, knew it in his heart. But he couldn't let her see. He stepped up and gave her a soft kiss, in front of everyone. "I know you will," he whispered. "I know you will."

Caesar Prince stepped into the small room, frowning as he took in the forlorn figure sleeping on the rough pallet. It hadn't been easy whisking this man away from Kieft and hiding him while Caesar attended to some delicate tasks. It had better be worth it. He turned to the Abbess, who had guided him down to the basement of the abbey and was standing just outside the door.

"How is he?"

"He is a mess," she said sadly.

"Well, we don't have time for his self-pity," Caesar said, though pity is what he felt when he gazed down at the broken man.

"I know," the Abbess said. "Just be gentle. For me."

"I saw your nuns packing up. Going somewhere?"

"The last battle approaches and those of us who remain here must now go to the battlefield, to care for the wounded," the

Abbess said. "There will be many, I can tell." She turned to go. "I will leave you."

"Do something for me, will you?" Caesar asked, grabbing her arm. "If any gods die on your watch, take their lockets and grind them beneath your heel. Don't allow anyone to take them away. Promise me."

She nodded, her eyes wide, and he let her go. She gathered herself with dignity and strode away, leaving Caesar alone with the man. He leaned over the sleeping form.

"Wake up, Harry—or Peter, or Henry, or whatever you're calling yourself nowadays." Caesar poked at the man, who groaned as he woke.

"My head . . ."

"Been drinking?" Caesar asked lightly, showing his bright white teeth.

"Who cares," the man muttered, holding his head as he sat up. "I betrayed Kieft, defied him to his face, and all for naught. He took my son and then the nuns told me that the hospital had blown up. My boy is dead. And it's all my fault."

"Stop it!" Caesar scolded him. "Your son is fine. I opened the door to his cell myself, though it cost me dearly." The man looked up hopefully, then burst into tears. Caesar rolled his eyes at the spectacle. "I've had enough of your woe-is-me prat-tling. I've known you for two hundred and fifty years, through at least ten different names, and the one thing that's never changed is your damned self-pity."

"I'm sorry I'm so predictable," the man said, rubbing his temples with his fingers.

"It stops, today," Caesar announced. "Your boy needs you."

"I couldn't help him." The man's tears welled up. "I couldn't help any of them. I let them all down."

"Do you know what this is?" Caesar asked, pulling out both his lockets from beneath his shirt. The man's eyes widened.

"Two? Who gave you the other one?"

"Kieft." Caesar snorted. "I think he knew I was spying on him, so he decided that rather than try to kill me, he'd make it impossible for me to turn on him. So he gave me this locket."

"Whose is it?" asked the man, peering at the gold necklace.

"The God of Leaders Who Look the Other Way. I've been trying to help Stuyvesant and Whitman and everyone else, but this locket and the duties that come with it won't let me. I'm forced to look the other way. Kieft's ultimate revenge."

"So how is it that you are here?" the man asked, puzzled. "And how did you help my boy?"

"I can't *not* do anything. So I'm breaking the rules and going against my duties, as much as I can, which isn't much, to be honest."

"But that means . . ."

"I will be punished, yes," Caesar said, trying not to think about it. "Harshly. Aaron Burr turned against his duties after the Trap and the land took back its locket. The same might happen to me, or worse. But I can't turn away."

"Why do that to yourself?"

"Because I did a great wrong," Caesar said, his heart heavy. "I built that Trap. I can say I didn't really know what I was doing. That I only meant it as a game, to prove that I could. But I should have known. I was too proud and Kieft used that pride. He told me the Trap would only be up for a short while, and the very fact of its existence would stop the warring between god and Munsee, and I believed him because I wanted to believe him. As I worked with Burr to finish the Trap, I could sense that he knew something I didn't. But I wanted to see it *work*. So I told myself to ignore what was all around me. I used the Munsees' own talismans, the wampum and the Sachem's Belt, to create the way to unlock it, not realizing what an affront it was to pervert those people's magic in such a base way. Such pride! And then the Trap was triggered, and weeks passed, and suddenly the Lights, who I had designated as the only ones who could turn the key, began to disappear. There were never many to begin with, and now, suddenly, there were none at all! And I realized that this was no game. No, this was very real. And it was all my fault. Sure, Kieft and Hamilton, and Burr, and *you*—you all knew exactly what you were doing. But it is my creation. My pride. My crime."

The man groaned, but did not answer. Caesar knelt down to stare into his eyes. "He will kill your son and your daughter, no matter what he promises. Already your wife lies at death's door. What more can be taken from you? You started that family for a reason, did you not? To truly belong, again. And then it all went wrong. You need to make it right. You need to find your way."

"How did you find *your* way?" the man asked, tears running down his cheeks.

"People say I've been underground so long I've lost myself. And they're not too far from the truth. After I helped build the Trap, I went down deeper and deeper, running from what I'd done. And that's when she found me. The lady we both know. She gave me a reason to climb to the surface again. A way to make my wrongs right again. She spoke to me and she spoke to Adriaen, and we gladly placed our trust in her cause. She spoke to you once, too."

"That was a long time ago and I failed her completely," the man said, turning away.

"Your children are traveling to see her," Caesar said. "They don't know it, but that's where they're headed. You need to be by their side when they get there. That's the only way we can beat Kieft and return this city to the mortals who dream it. Henry, your children need you. How many times can you let them down?"

The man stared back up at him, agonizing over what to do. And Caesar waited to see if his sacrifice would not be in vain.

Rory stood in front of the pizza parlor, which had been closed up for the night. The entire street was dark at this late hour, though the streetlights still sent pools of light down to illuminate the sidewalk. Fritz had warned them that they were close to Five Points, the notorious den of thieves, which had been built over the filled-in Collect Pond. The thought of roving bands of nineteenth-century gang members didn't help his sense of unease as he stood there, feeling naked, with only a tiny cockroach and his little sister by his side.

He resisted the urge to touch his forehead, where Soka had drawn a sigil of protection. He knew how strong she'd made it—he felt like he could run through a brick wall and not get bruised, but even though he knew this was probably the "Munsee magic" the Fortune Teller told him he had to bring with him, he couldn't help fearing that it would not be enough.

"Now what?" Bridget asked, getting impatient. "Do we bust in? I can run right through the door . . ."

"They might have an alarm," Rory countered, indecisive.

"I wish Soka could be here!" Bridget whined, kicking at the ground. "That lady said we needed magic and now look at us! We can't even get through a door!"

"We can't stand out here all day," Fritz said by Rory's feet, Clarence shuffling in place under him.

"Where's your little Indian girl?" a voice sneered behind them. They spun to see Hex step out of the shadows. The fallen god had cleaned up a little since they'd seen him under City Hall, but he still looked desperate.

Fritz guided Clarence between the Hennessy kids and Hex. "Get out of here, Burr. You're not wanted."

"Really?" Hex shrugged with exaggerated innocence. "Bridget just said something about needing magic. *Needing* it. And your little magic Munsee friend is no longer among you. So I think there might be a place for me in your little expedition after all . . ."

"You've betrayed my trust over and over again—" Rory began, but Hex put up his hand to cut him off.

"But it's not about you, is it?" he said. "It's about your mother. I may have been hiding out, but I still heard things. I know your mother is deathly ill. I'm sure some of Kieft's stolen magic can cure her. But you will never get close to it if I'm not with you. I see the sigil on your forehead. I know what it means. So you're protected. Well, let me ask you—is there any water on this journey you're taking? Because sigils wash off. And even if it doesn't, even if you're protected all the way to the end, who's to say some other, final trick won't be waiting for you? Kieft is the most dangerous man I've ever met. He'll have provided for every possibility. What good is your protection if the very prize you seek goes up in flames? Can you keep that from happening? Because I can."

"None of this matters," Fritz said. "Because we can't trust you."

"Rory," Hex pleaded with him. "I heard about your stunt in Queens, where you made everyone tell the truth. Do it with me."

Rory didn't want to, but too many of Hex's words had hit home. What if he did need magic, more magic than Soka had given him. What if he needed Hex? He concentrated on his belly, fanning the flames as he sought the truth that no one could avoid.

"Why do you really want to come with us?" he asked, bracing for the painful truth.

"I want to see Kieft pay for all the wrong he's done me," Hex said promptly. "I want to steal his magic and use it against him. I won't hurt you or your family if I can help it. I just want to take Kieft's magic and watch him suffer as I destroy him with it. That will be my ultimate revenge."

Rory regarded Hex, feeling sick as he realized what he had to do. Finally, he nodded. "You can come. But one wrong move and it's over. You can't hurt me, remember? I'm protected."

"I know," Hex said even as Fritz and Bridget both cried their disapproval.

"You can't trust him!" Bridget screamed. "He's a sleazeball!"

"This is a mistake," Fritz told him.

"What else can we do?" Rory asked them. "We will need magic, I know it."

"Soka's spell—" Bridget began, but Rory cut her off.

"Is not enough. I'll do anything to save Mom, even deal with the devil."

"And that's exactly what you're doing," Fritz said darkly. "This will backfire, I guarantee it."

"Do you want to back out, then, Fritz?" Rory asked testily. "Because you can if you want."

"You know I won't," the roach said reproachfully. "I'm in this to the end. But if you think I'm going to stand idly by and let this charlatan pull the wool over your eyes, you're mistaken. I am watching you, Burr."

"I'm not Aaron Burr," Hex said. "Not anymore. All I have left is my magic. All I am now is Hex."

"Then get us in, Hex," Rory said. Hex walked past them, stepping up to the locked door of the pizza parlor. He did something with his hands over the door and it creaked open. Hex turned to them.

"Good?"

"Good," Rory replied, and walked into the pizza place. He knew Bridget and Fritz were exchanging looks behind his back, but he didn't care. A bargain with the devil was the least of his worries right now.

They made their way into the basement, where they figured the cave would be. Pizza boxes and crates of flour and tomato sauce lined the walls, while a cooler in the back held big containers of cheese. At first Rory couldn't find any sign of the cave, but then he noticed the back wall.

The bricks there were discolored, as if something damp was

behind them. Rory poked at them. "These are loose!" he called back behind him. "We need a crowbar."

"Out of the way!"

He moved just as Bridget came flying past him, running full force into the wall. Rory had to cover his head as bricks went flying everywhere, and dust rose up to obscure the wall. He and Hex stepped forward, waving the dust away to reveal a huge hole in the wall. Bridget lay on the ground on the other side, covered in broken bricks.

"Thanks, Bridge," Rory said drily as he helped her up.

"It was fun!" she answered brightly, hopping to her feet.

"I think this is it, all right," Fritz said, riding halfway down the tunnel they'd uncovered. They followed him into the rough-hewn passage, lighting a torch Rory had brought along. Hex snapped his fingers, and a soft glowing orb appeared by his head to light his way.

"Show-off," Bridget muttered. The rough stone walls of the passage dripped with greenish water, leading down to dark moss which lined the floor.

"We're close to the water table," Hex said. "They could fill in the pond, but they couldn't keep out the water which fed it. Come on."

He walked on through the dark tunnel. Fritz rode up to keep pace with the fallen god, unwilling to let him out of his sight. Bridget gave Rory a look.

"I hope you know what you're doing, bro," she said. Rory didn't reply as they moved deeper into the tunnel.

THE FORGOTTEN STATION

Nicholas watched the beat-up and dispirited army march through the park, still recovering from the near debacle at the smallpox hospital. Teddy Roosevelt and the council had agreed that Kieft was most likely coming for the Munsees, so they were heading to the center of the park to the most easily defensible spot—Belvedere Castle.

The castle loomed before them as they crossed the Great Lawn. Built to resemble something from a fairy tale, Belvedere Castle housed a bird museum and the weather station for New York City. It was never meant to be a real stronghold. But it was built on a hill overlooking the wide expanse of the Great Lawn, with Turtle Pond right beneath serving as a moat. The castle was the only structure in the park from which they could realistically defend themselves against Kieft, so that was where they would gather.

A somber Buckongahelas waited for them on the ramparts, his wife, Abigail, by his side. Wampage stood nearby with a Munsee named Chogan. At the sight of Chogan, Soka, who'd accompanied them, ran to him, sobbing in his arms.

"It's all right," Chogan consoled her. "She would have wanted you to be strong."

"Kieft is coming," Buckongahelas told them after their greetings. "We have heard from the forts up north that they've seen people moving through the trees. We are ready to fight. Are you?" He glanced out at the army from Mannahatta, which did not look impressive.

"They're just a little banged up," Teddy Roosevelt assured him. "I've been bucking up their spirits on the way here. They'll be fine!"

"If you say so," Abigail Hamilton said, though she looked dubious. Her father did not look hopeful, either. In fact, none of the council members, save Teddy, seemed convinced of their army's readiness.

"All we ask is that you fight with us," Buckongahelas said. "As hard as we will fight with you."

"Nicholas, may I speak with you?" Peter Stuyvesant asked, pulling his son aside. "Nicholas, you have to do something."

"Me?" Nicholas pulled back in surprise. "What do you mean?"

"Alexa told me how you've been searching for the right leader to inspire us, and how you thought Teddy was that man. Well, he isn't. The troops hear him talk about glory and bull like that and they fear he doesn't value their lives. And though it pains me to say it, I'm not the answer, either. I'm too dour. Hamilton is too divisive. No, there's only one person they all respect. You."

"What are you talking about?" Nicholas asked.

"You recruited most of them," his father told him. "They saw someone who wasn't a god, who could never be a god, ready to die for his city, and that awakened something in them. Some pride, maybe. A sense of being a part of something bigger. *You* are the leader you've been looking for. Now go talk to your men. They need you."

Peter patted Nicholas on the shoulder, then pulled him into an embrace. Holding back tears, Nicholas nodded. "I'll try."

He climbed the ramparts, overlooking his army. The council members and the Munsee elders stopped talking as he began to speak.

"I am not a god," he said. This caught the army's attention and they stared back at him intently. "I will never be a god. And I don't care. Some of you are gods, some aren't. Some of you are immortal, some aren't. But we are all a part of this city. We watch over it and keep it safe. That is why we are here. Kieft wants to kill this city. He is a murderer. He may promise riches and power and divinity, but all he delivers is death. And we are all that stands in the way of that death. And he knows that and he is afraid. That is why he tried to trick us at the smallpox hospital, to lure us into a trap. Because he is afraid of us. Because we belong here, and he doesn't. We are a part of this city, and he isn't. This city created *us* and loves *us* and needs *us*, not him. And when he comes here with his knives, the city will reject him. I know you're hurt and tired, but every stone, every blade of grass, every slab of concrete, every shining building in the distance wants us to win! Everything is with us! Can't you feel that?" The soldiers began to nod, standing up and clapping their hands. "Can't you feel how *right* we are? How *wrong* he is? He wants to tear down our home. And we are not going to let him! Who's with me?" Cheers erupted in the crowd. "I said, who's with me!" Louder cheers as the Munsees joined in. Soon everyone was stamping their feet. Glancing over, Nicholas spied the council members nodding, and even Roosevelt had a smile on his face.

"Nice speech," Alexa said, patting his arm. "I hope you're right." Nicholas smiled wanly as he looked out across the cheering crowd. He'd better be right. Or they were all going to regret it.

It didn't take long for Rory's small party to reach the dead end. As described in Adriaen's journal, a strange symbol sat in the middle of the wall. To Rory it looked like some kind of lizard. Hex did not hesitate; he walked right up to the sigil and put his hand on it, mumbling. After a moment a rumbling began to echo down the tunnel. Stones began to fall from the ceiling, and Rory belatedly remembered what happened next.

"Fall back!" Fritz cried at him, and Rory immediately turned and ran down the tunnel, away from the falling stones. The entire world seemed to shake as he fell to the ground, covering his head with his hands. Thankfully, nothing landed on his skull, and when the shaking stopped, he pushed himself to his feet and ran back down the hall to see if everyone was all right.

The wall had opened up, and the tunnel continued on the other side. Bridget was pushing herself out from under a mound of rocks, while Fritz rode Clarence out from behind a small outcropping. Hex had already started walking down the tunnel, and he turned back with an impatient look on his face.

"Come on," he called. A sly smile spread across his face. "Told you you needed me."

"You almost killed us!" Fritz scolded him, riding up to his feet. "Next time you want to do some hocus-pocus, give us a warning!"

"You got it, boss," Hex told Fritz, smirking. Rory didn't like the magician's attitude one bit—but he also didn't know how else he'd have opened that wall. He helped Bridget, who looked no worse for the wear, to her feet and followed Hex down into the new tunnel. He heard Bridget muttering behind him.

"Didn't need no stupid magic. I could have run through that wall, too. Stupid Hex and his stupid magic."

Rory smiled and walked on.

This tunnel felt older, with strange scribbles on the walls. Hex touched one, before pulling back with a hiss.

"Don't go near these," he warned. "They're older than the Munsees, I'll tell you that much. Much older. But they still hold a great deal of power."

Rory stayed to the middle of the tunnel, eyeing the strange markings warily. They looked like nothing he'd ever seen before—not pictures, not words, nothing. He was so busy studying them he tripped over something. Lighting the ground with his torch, he spied something white lying under his feet. He kicked at it, then backed away—it was an old, human bone.

"What *is* this place?" he asked out loud.

"Somewhere you don't linger," Hex replied, walking faster. Rory, Bridget, and Fritz followed, moving as quickly as possible.

After a while, something strange began to happen. It started as strange sounds seemingly drifting in from the other side of the tunnel wall. Rory thought he heard someone crying, and someone else laughing uproariously. What was on the other side of the wall? Then he remembered Adriaen mentioning something similar in his journal. He'd simply walked past these sounds without incident—there was no need to worry. But then Rory saw something Adriaen never mentioned, something horrifying.

Three bodyless heads of ancient women were floating down the tunnel toward him. Their faces were ruined—Rory could see bone through their skin, their stringy hair fell out in clumps as they floated, and their eyes were bloodred. He froze, praying the heads wouldn't see him.

"Why did you stop?" Bridget asked at his side, worried.

"Can't you see them?" Rory whispered, avoiding the women's gazes.

"See what?" Bridget asked. Her voice seemed to grab the women's attention—their eyes swiveled in their sockets to fix on Rory, and their thin, cracked lips split into evil smiles.

"Yum!" one of them muttered, smacking her lips. Rory stumbled back as the heads made a beeline for him, mouths opening with hunger. He tripped over his own feet, falling to the ground as the heads dove toward him, ready to eat . . .

"Rory, what's wrong!" Bridget was crying, shaking him. The heads filled his vision—he could smell the rot on their breath and see their yellow, jagged teeth.

"Close your eyes!" Hex's voice commanded, and Rory was glad to comply. The last thing he wanted to do was watch himself get eaten. He curled up, eyes jammed shut, waiting for the pain to begin. But it never did.

"What did you see?" Hex's voice in his ear asked.

"Something horrible," he replied, trying not to cry. Why wasn't he dead yet?

"It isn't real, Rory," Fritz was saying by his feet. "There's nothing there."

Rory didn't move, refusing to open his eyes. He could still see the ancient faces hungrily attacking him.

"Rory, none of it is real," Hex said, helping him up. Rory opened one eye—the tunnel was clear.

"What was that?" he asked.

"I don't know," Hex answered. "But it must only affect mortals. Which means you're not the only one who is going to have to endure apparitions."

As if in response, Bridget squealed, pointing. "The dolls! They're marching toward me! You won't get me!" She began to punch at the air and kick with her steel-tipped boots at nothing at all. "Stay back, Beanie Babies!"

"We need to keep moving," Hex said. "How long did Adriaen say they were in the tunnel?"

"A long time," Rory replied miserably.

"Then the sooner we start moving again, the better," Fritz said, before gasping. "Empty armor! Stalking me!"

"Come on," Hex said, and walked on ahead. Rory grabbed his sister, who was still shadowboxing the air, and moved on down the tunnel.

He lost track of the number of apparitions that assaulted him. Everything from creatures out of his nightmares, to the kids from school, ghoulishly undead, threatening to eat him alive, to the Rattle Watch, overwhelming him with tales of despair about their losing battle against Kieft. Rory could barely take it, but he walked on.

From the sound of it, Bridget and Fritz were having trouble as well. Even Clarence had to be restrained from running headlong into the wall to escape some imagined predator. With every new ghostly attack, Rory's resolve weakened.

"How can anyone survive this?" he wondered aloud.

"You're being tested," Hex replied.

"I don't know how much more I can take." Rory averted his eyes from the sight of his second-grade teacher laughing at him as she chewed on a severed hand. She threw it at him and he shut his eyes, certain he'd feel the dead, clammy thing hit him square in the face—which it never did, of course.

"It looks like you won't have to," Hex said suddenly. "Look."

Rory opened his eyes and gasped. The tunnel had collapsed, sealing off the way forward. "No!"

"This looks new," Fritz said, swatting at something invisible as he rode up to the cave-in. "Yeah, it definitely happened recently."

"Did Kieft do this?" Rory asked.

"No," Hex replied, inspecting the rubble. "I think it was probably the earthquake."

"But Kieft didn't bring his treasure down here until after the Trap fell, so this cave-in must have been waiting for him, too," Rory said. "Where did he go from here? Did he dig through?"

Before anyone could answer, Bridget let out a yell. She ran past Rory and hurtled herself, full speed, into the rubble. Unsurprisingly, she bounced right off, landing hard on the ground as some stones crumbled away to reveal . . . more stones.

"Worth a shot," she mumbled.

"It was, actually." Fritz pointed to the side wall, whose stones had loosened at the impact of Bridget's collision to reveal a hole. Rory stepped forward and pulled the stones free, uncovering a second tunnel.

"I guess Kieft decided to make his own tunnel," Hex said, peering down the new passage. "It looks like he just blasted his way through with magic. Now, *that* is power."

"Do you think he left any traps?" Rory asked, gazing down the new tunnel.

"Only one way to find out," Hex said, climbing through the hole. "Coming?" No one had a better idea, so they all climbed through the hole, leaving the apparitions behind.

The going was much easier now that they weren't being constantly attacked by apparitions, but Rory was worried about traps, keeping his eye out for anything in the floor or ceiling. But it seemed as if Kieft thought no one could follow him, for it wasn't long before they arrived safely at another pile of rocks blocking their way. Pulling a few aside, they peered through a jagged hole into what looked like a storeroom. The room was old and dusty, with nothing but an old broom in the corner. A door sat in the wall opposite them. Bridget immediately climbed into the room, reaching for the door.

"Wait!" Rory called as they climbed in after her. "We don't know what's on the other side."

"Do you have any better ideas?" she asked him, and turned the knob to throw open the door. Light fell on their faces as they stepped through, coming face-to-face with something they never thought they'd see down here.

"What is this place?" Rory breathed, gazing around in wonder.

"I couldn't even begin to guess," Fritz replied.

The room they'd discovered did not belong underground.

It stretched out in both directions like a long, opulent ballroom. Paintings lined the walls, flanked by lush red curtains. A grand piano sat slightly elevated at one end, its black finish covered in dust. Nearby stood a large, ornate fountain, light playing off the water inside to send shifting patterns dancing across the walls. Peering closer, Rory could make out small goldfish. How they remained alive down here, he had no idea. Gaslight torches lined the walls, flickering slightly; a few were crooked and one of them no longer burned at all. Above it all, glittering like a falling star halted only yards from hitting the earth, floated a magnificent glass chandelier. Three times as large as the piano, it presided over the room like a frozen sun.

They cautiously creeped into the ballroom, peering around in disbelief. Every step seemed to echo as they ventured farther into the opulent room. Richly upholstered chairs surrounded them, dusty and ancient, but Rory had no desire to sit down. Whatever this place was, he didn't want to be delayed in it while his time ticked away into nothing.

They reached a flight of stairs, which led down to a landing. The landing led to a large circular opening cut into the wall, flanked by two bronze statues Rory recognized as Mercury, messenger of the Roman gods (the winged hat gave it away). Etched into the stone above the opening were the words PNEUMATIC (1870) TRANSIT.

"So you're back, you miscreants!" a voice yelled at them, making them jump. "You'll find it hard to do your thieving with a bullet in your chest!"

Rory spun around to see a figure holding a long silver gun at them. He immediately put up his hands.

"We don't want any trouble," he told the figure.

"I'll have you know I'm a powerful magician," Hex said, his voice low and dangerous. "You don't want to mess with my powers!"

"You don't want to mess with my bullets!" the figure answered. "You did enough when you stole my train!"

"We didn't steal anything!" Bridget cried. "We just got here!"

"What kind of fool do you think I am?" The figure stepped closer and the light fell on his face. Rory's jaw dropped as he recognized who it was.

"Mr. Beach!" he said. The man holding a gun on them was none other than Alfred Beach, God of Subways, who had picked up Rory when he was lost in the subway tunnels after the earthquake. "It's me, Rory Hennessy!"

Alfred squinted, peering closely at Rory. "Why, so it is! Why did you steal my train?"

"We didn't steal anything, I promise," Rory answered. "We just stumbled across your place, here, completely by accident."

"Then who's been stealing my train?" Alfred asked, looking peeved as he lowered his gun. "I'd really thought I'd caught the culprit. Oh well, I'm glad it wasn't you. You seemed like a nice enough fellow."

Rory introduced his companions to the tall, thin god with the delicate mustache. Alfred shook all their hands, apologizing for his rude welcome.

"What is this place?" Bridget asked. Alfred smiled at the wonder in her voice.

"This was the very first subway station in New York," he said, throwing his arms open wide. "I built it back in 1870, in secret, since Boss Tweed wasn't too keen on a subway he didn't control. This was the waiting room, where people could await their train in comfort."

Rory glanced around the opulent room. "Not bad."

"That's what I thought. But Tweed shut me down. It'd be thirty years before the city got its subway, and my invention lay hidden here, underground, forgotten."

"Is your train on the other side?" Hex asked, pointing to the circular opening.

Alfred nodded. "Or at least it had better be," he said, frowning. "Last week, I stopped by to check on her after I dropped Verrazano off at the surface, and the train was gone! Someone had stolen her! I went ballistic, searching everywhere for it, but by the time I returned to the station, the train was back in its place. Though I could tell someone had used her. A joyride, I guessed. Though who would want to take a joyride in the place where that train goes is beyond me."

Rory turned to Fritz and mouthed, "Kieft stole it!" Fritz nodded—the same thought had obviously occurred to him.

"What does *pneumatic* mean?" Bridget asked, reading the sign above the entrance.

"Let me show you," Alfred replied, smiling at the girl's interest.

He led them down the steps to what proved to be the entrance to a tunnel. A short subway car sat on rails in the middle of the tunnel; it was the same circular shape as the tunnel, its sides barely clearing the walls and ceiling. It was much smaller than a normal subway car, and the light from its headlamps barely pierced the gloomy dark ahead of it.

"Is that a fan?" Fritz asked, looking behind them. Indeed,

a huge fan sat across from them, pointed down the tunnel.

"Of course," Alfred said. "*Pneumatic* means 'air' after all. Didn't I tell you, Rory, that I would show you the first subway car I built? Well, here she is! Ain't she a beaut?"

"She is," Bridget agreed, running up to stare in the windows. "All the seats have cushions!"

'Of course." Alfred smiled. "This ride was meant to be a luxury, after all."

"Where does it go?" Hex added, his eyes glinting in the dim light.

"Well, that's the thing," Alfred said, shrugging. "It really doesn't go anywhere. This was my first exploration project. I've gone deeper down with this girl than with any of my other cars. I'd probably still be digging if I hadn't reached a dead end. Now I explore with my other subway trains, trying to find other ways down."

"So whoever stole this train rode it down to a dead end and then drove it back?" Hex asked, clearly believing there was more to the story.

"Well, *dead end* is a strong term," Alfred admitted. "I actually hit an underground stream. I tried to follow it, but it went too deep, even for me. I sometimes ride this old girl down there, to sit by its shore and think about where it goes, but I can't bring myself to follow it to its end. Some secrets are meant to be kept, I believe."

"Can you take us there?" Rory asked Alfred.

"Are you sure you didn't steal this train?" The inventor narrowed his eyes.

"That place you can't bring yourself to go?" Rory asked. "That's where I need to be. Please?"

Alfred gave Rory a piercing look then nodded. "Why don't you climb aboard?" he said. "You're in for a treat."

"Good work," Hex mumbled to Rory as they climbed into the train. The car was small but comfortable, with cushioned seats lining each side. Small windows interrupted the curved wall, looking out onto the black tunnel. "So Kieft took the train in order to bring his treasure to the cavern."

"I'm just glad we won't have to walk with those horrible illusions," Rory muttered back. Hex laughed and Rory started, realizing he'd been dropping his guard with the traitorous ex-god. He'd have to be cautious or Hex would take advantage of him.

They took their seats as Alfred climbed into a chair at the head. "Hold on!" he said brightly. "This is a ride like no other!" He pushed a button and a large door began to close off one end of the tunnel, creating an airtight seal. There was a whirring sound as the fan began to spin, blowing air fiercely at the car. Finally, with a wrench, the car gave way under the onslaught and rolled down the tunnel with increasing speed. The light of the station soon disappeared and they were shooting forward through the dark, propelled faster and faster by the fierce gale behind them.

It was eerie to be traveling without engines; the only sound was of the wind propelling them forward. At first Rory couldn't speak; the roaring in his ears was too great. On and on they rode, until the roaring faded and they were simply rolling along, shooting through the tunnel like a bullet. The end was somewhere up ahead, but Rory had no idea when they'd reach it.

Rory tried looking out the window, and initially he couldn't see a thing. But then they burst out of the narrow tunnel into a huge open space, and the light from the train bounced off the walls to illuminate the whole area. The rails ran through the middle of the cavern, carrying the train over a deep, seemingly bottomless drop. Rory didn't know how Alfred could have built these rails hanging over nothing, and he didn't want to know. He just wanted to get to the other side without tipping over.

They reached the far wall, diving into another tunnel. This time, Rory could see some space on either side. And then he realized why. Something was coming up alongside, a light, and he leaned forward to see more clearly. At last he realized that a train was overtaking them on the tracks that ran alongside.

"There's another train there!" he told Alfred. "I thought no one else traveled this deep underground!"

"Well, that's not exactly true," Alfred admitted. By now, the train had reached them, and gradually, it began to pass by. The metal-and-glass skin of this more modern train couldn't have been more than two feet away, so Rory peered across the short distance into the windows as they slid by. He heard Bridget gasp and he drew back in shock; Alfred's voice, suddenly dead serious, came from behind.

"Don't worry, kids. It will be gone in a moment. That train is not for you."

The train roared alongside slowly but inexorably, on its way to who knows where. Inside the weakly lit train, every inch of space overflowed with people. Hundreds of them. They filled each car like commuters at rush hour, thrust into one another, stacked like dead fish. But it was the faces that scared Rory. Those horrible, horrible faces. The cars passed by like a hellish amusement-park ride, allowing Rory a good long look at every nasty expression, every ghoulish head. Human faces, at least at one time, but changed. Sallow, sickly, festering, yellow-eyed, disintegrating, and most of all, dead faces still dripping dirt from the grave.

It seemed to take forever, but finally the last car passed out of sight, returning the tunnel to black, and Rory could breathe again. It never crossed his mind to ask Alfred about the story behind that train, and Bridget never asked, either. He had a sneaking suspicion he already knew the answer. He prayed he'd never have to ride it.

Finally, the car they were in rolled to a stop. The silence was deafening as Rory looked around at his companions.

"I guess we get out," he said. Alfred shrugged, looking a bit spooked.

"You can if you want. There's nothing there but the river. I don't think I'll go with you, actually. Is that all right?"

Rory nodded. He walked to the door, opening it and climbing down to the tunnel floor. He spied a smaller, much older tunnel entrance lit up by the train's headlights. There was a roaring in the distance that sounded like a river. Bridget dropped to his side, giving an elaborate shudder.

"That was a freaky ride," she said. "I hope we don't have to go back that way."

Rory didn't answer. He just hoped they got to go back at all. Hex climbed down beside them and Clarence leaped to the ground at their feet, Fritz upon his back. Rory took a deep breath.

"Let's go take a look," he said, and walked into the tunnel.

The tunnel itself was very short, and the lights from the train behind them illuminated the entire way. Familiar sigils lined the walls—this must be the end of that long-destroyed passage Adriaen had walked down so many centuries earlier. Thankfully, they soon reached the end and were standing on the shore of the river, watching the water rush by.

"This looks familiar," Fritz said, and Rory agreed. The arching rocks overhead, the swiftly moving water dimly lit by glowing plants below . . . the feeling of déjà vu was overwhelming.

"This was the river we floated down on that dead alligator when we escaped from the bank!" Rory realized. He avoided looking at Hex—it had been the magician's fault they were on the run in the first place. Instead, he remembered what lay ahead. "This ends in that horrible waterfall. That must be the place where Adriaen said he plunged in his journal!"

And to think, Rory had been there, unknowing, and he'd almost taken that same fall. He shuddered to think about it.

"So what now?" Bridget asked. "We jump in?"

"I'm not jumping in there," Fritz said firmly. "I'll drown in a second."

"We can take the canoe," Hex offered. Rory turned in surprise, but it was true. An old canoe, just like the Munsees used, was leaning against the side of the tunnel. It was free of dust, so it couldn't have been there long.

"Kieft must have left this here," Fritz mused. "Maybe he planned to come back."

"Or maybe he had more stuff he wanted to send down," Bridget guessed.

"Either way, it's a boon for us," Hex said. "We can ride that to the waterfall. I can put protection around it so, if we're lucky, we'll all survive the fall."

"Are you really going to try to protect all of us?" Rory asked, willing the truth from the fallen god. Hex smiled wearily.

"Of course. I promise." He bent over the canoe, muttering to himself, as Rory watched. He knew in his heart he couldn't trust the man, but everything seemed okay so far.

"Rory, I'm a little scared," Bridget confided, speaking softly so Hex couldn't hear. "How far do you think we'll fall, anyway? How dark will it be?"

"Don't worry," Rory reassured her. "I'll hold on to you the whole time. You'll never be alone."

"Promise?"

"Promise."

Hex was finished with the canoe, and he and Rory dragged it to the river's edge. Fritz climbed up into one pocket of Rory's pants and Clarence took the other pocket.

"I don't like this," the roach said, and Rory could hear the fear in his voice. He himself was just as frightened—this was the part of Adriaen's story that had worried him most of all. How could he survive it? He thought of the sigil on his forehead. Maybe it would protect him. He hoped so. He just had to hand himself over to fate.

They sat in the canoe, which Hex pushed into the river with his paddle. Immediately, the water took them, pulling them along quickly. The jagged walls of the cave flew by as the river carried them toward an increasingly louder roar. Rory glanced up, noticing the same arrow painted on the ceiling he'd seen on his last trip down this river, the arrow he now knew pointed the way to the cavern far below. The roaring drowned out everything as the waterfall came closer and closer. Bridget let out a cry, grabbing Rory with both hands. Rory clutched the sides of the canoe as he saw the blackness approach. He had just enough time to whisper a small prayer, and then the canoe hit the falls. He reached for his sister as they bounced over the side, and then they were flying out into the void before falling, falling, falling forever into the black nothingness below.

THE SACRIFICE

Kieft's army appeared as if from thin air.

Soka was meeting with Chogan when a scout came running in with the news. The entire army had just shown up on the north end of the Great Lawn, standing on earthworks that came rising from the ground as the scout watched. It was a stunning display of Kieft's magic and it left all of them shaken, Soka most of all. How could she fight that? She wasn't her mother.

With Tackapausha's death, Buckongahelas had taken over the Munsee war preparations. Wampage stood apart, giving his advice but not taking charge. Soka asked him why while the others were busy with their plans.

"I am not the future, here," he told her. "That is Buckongahelas and you. I will leave the war plans to you. I have a different mission."

He would not elaborate, and Soka did not press him. She had enough to worry about.

For one thing, Teddy Roosevelt was being impetuous again. He wanted to attack, right away, and surprise the enemy. "We need to bloody them," he argued. "To show them we mean business. Take a few lives and the rest fall at our feet."

"No killing," Buckongahelas said firmly. Roosevelt blinked in surprise.

"What are you talking about?"

"There is nowhere else for us to go," the Munsee war leader said. "This is our home. We cannot baptize our home in blood. How can we live in peace surrounded by people who remember all the lives we ended? How can we forgive them for the lives they took? If we descend into killing, we will never have peace."

"The sentiment is well and good, young man," Teddy said. "But Kieft's army isn't going to just throw down their weapons and cry uncle!"

"Kieft, that's who matters," Nicholas said. "We need to get to him and the rest will crumble."

"Good luck with that." Simon snorted.

"How will we keep them at bay while we try to get Kieft without Sooleawa?" Chogan asked, the round Munsee tanner still raw from Sooleawa's death. "She was the difference."

Wampage glanced at Soka. "We have a worthy successor here in our midst."

Soka sighed, facing them as proudly as she could. "I will find a way," she promised. "I am not my mother, but I will find a way."

She wished she felt as confident as she sounded. But she would find a way.

Kieft stood with Tobias, staring out across the Great Lawn as the sun began to rise. His army milled about at his feet, uncertain about the battle ahead. He had certain spirits moving through the crowd, telling stories of Munsee atrocities, trying to keep the anger high. Soon the bloodlust would set in and they would need no encouragement. Soon the lockets would litter the field like shells on a beach, and he'd simply have to reach down and pick them up.

"Look at them all," he muttered to Tobias. "Sheep, waiting to be slaughtered. Have you decided which lockets you'd like for yourself?"

"I have all I need hanging around my neck," Tobias answered, his voice bored.

"Right answer." Kieft laughed. "That is how you survive, Tobias. You have everything you want already. But will you fight to keep it?"

"To the death," Tobias snarled, and Kieft's eyebrow lifted, surprised at Tobias's emotion. He smiled; it was good to know the god cared about something. Kieft turned to his little group of gang members, led by Sly Jimmy, who were standing nearby, and gestured for them to approach.

"You have your knives?" he asked them.

"You bet," Sly Jimmy said, smirking.

"When the battle starts, I want you all to kill any god who falls."

"On our side, too?" Jimmy asked.

"On *either* side," Kieft stressed. He didn't care which gods died, so long as they died. "The more gods you kill, the angrier and more fearful the other gods will get. You are my little angels of war. Once the battle begins, I want the blood to flow."

"What about the lockets?" one of the other gang members asked. "Can we keep 'em?"

Kieft reached out and grabbed the gang boy's neck, snapping it with a twist. The boy's limp body fell to the ground as the others watched in silent horror.

"Anyone else want to ask a stupid question?" he said quietly. "What do you do with the lockets?"

Jimmy gulped. "We bring them to you."

"Good. Now go, ready yourselves for the fight."

Sly Jimmy and his boys ran off as quickly as they could, leaving the still body of their comrade on the ground at Kieft's feet. Kieft stared across the field for a moment, watching the small figures run back and forth along the ramparts of Belvedere Castle. Excitement ran up his spine. After four hundred years, his day had finally arrived. The morning air had never smelled sweeter.

Bridget's eyes fluttered open. She was staring at the bottom of the canoe, where a small pool of water had gathered around her feet. She remembered falling, and clutching at her brother, but then everything went black. Had she passed out? Maybe her brain just couldn't take all that falling and shut down for a while. Pretty smart, her brain.

She could hear the sound of falling water nearby, and the canoe rocked gently in place, so she was floating in something. She rolled over, wincing at the paper hair that fluttered to the floor—that must have been some landing. Lying on her back, she looked up—and felt her breath catch in her chest.

High above her, stretching out into the distance, twinkled the lights. They glowed from the very stone of the ceiling of this huge cavern they'd fallen into, like millions of veins of blue and green. The cavern itself seemed larger than her eyes could see. Sitting up, she could just make out the slope of the other side, far off into the distance. And beneath her, reflecting the sparkling blue and green like an ocean at sunset, was a large lake, softly shimmering. The water rocked them gently, after their violent landing. The hole they had fallen through opened up hundreds of feet above the lake, water flowing steadily down into the basin.

A groan beside her brought her back to the moment. Rory was just coming to, sitting up slowly while rubbing the back of his head.

"What happened?"

"You passed out from the fall," Hex said. The two-faced magician sat at the back of the canoe, watching them. "It was too much for your mortal brains to take."

"Even Fritz?" Bridget asked, looking around for the battle roach. She found him poking his way out of Rory's pocket, pulling off his helmet while shaking his head to clear it.

"Even me," he said wryly. Clarence climbed out of Rory's other pocket to run up to his master, licking the roach in a rare sign of devotion. Fritz laughed, fending off the rodent. "I'm fine, boy. We're all fine."

"So nobody remembers the fall?" Bridget asked.

"No, I was awake," Hex informed her. "I received no blessed relief from the plummet. It was because of me that our canoe wasn't shattered. A quick spell righted it before it plunged into the lake."

"Of course, we only have your word for that," Fritz pointed out. Hex merely shrugged. It really bothered Bridget that her brother had let this liar come along—she tried to watch him, but during the time they'd been knocked out, the sneak could have done anything.

Rory turned to Bridget, his hand flying to his forehead. "Is it still there?" Bridget squinted, trying to see past the blue and green playing across his face. *Phew*—Soka's mark still sat on Rory's forehead. Hex could try to take credit for their survival all he wanted, but Bridget knew in the space where her heart used to be that it had been Soka's skills that saved their lives.

"I've been scanning the shores, searching for the treasure," Hex was saying. Bridget peered into the distance, but she couldn't see much beyond the sparkly water. Hex seemed to have a similar problem. "So far, I haven't seen any trace," he said, looking peeved.

"Maybe it sank to the bottom of the lake," Fritz offered. "After all, Kieft just sent it down in canoes, right? It's just as safe under all this water as it would be on the shore."

"I don't believe it," Hex replied, dismissing Fritz's words with a wave. "Kieft cares about his secrets too much. He'd make certain the treasure was retrievable. We just can't see it."

"Should we paddle around?" Rory asked, glancing across the lake.

"What about the monster?" Bridget cut in, since no one else was saying anything. "What are we going to do about that?"

"I've seen no sign of a monster," Hex said. "Maybe it's no longer here."

"No, it's here, somewhere, I can feel it," Rory said firmly, and the urgency in his voice made Bridget shudder. "We should get out of the water."

"But in which direction?" Hex asked, gesturing to include the wide expanse around them.

"Well, didn't Kieft stick the treasure in canoes?" Bridget asked. "That's what we think, right? So if they didn't sink, then wouldn't they float in the same direction we're floating right now? You can't argue with basic fourth-grade science!"

"That's the only science you know," Rory teased her, though she could tell her brother agreed with her. Hex didn't say anything, but he reached down to pull out a paddle that had been fastened to the bottom of the boat. He handed it to her.

"You're the only one who won't get tired," he said. Bridget made a face at him, but took the paddle and dipped it into the water, first on one side, then the other. They moved forward in the same direction they'd been floating, cutting through the still lake toward the shore. As they came nearer to the shore, Bridget could make out a white band of sand that she assumed was a beach. As they approached it, she gave a happy shout at the sight of some dark forms bobbing in the water.

"There they are!" Fritz announced. He glanced up to Bridget with a proud look on his tiny face. "Good thinking!" Bridget was glad her paper skin didn't allow her to blush.

They pulled up alongside the canoes, which had drifted up against the beach. Hex was the first to hop out, sinking into the lake up to his knees. Without even glancing to see if the others were following, he splashed over to the canoes and began to paw through their contents.

"Hey, wait for us!" Bridget cried, angry at the greedy ex-god. But Hex ignored her, muttering as he tore through Kieft's treasure. Rory jumped out of the boat and pulled it up onto the shore as Bridget reached out her hand to Fritz and Clarence. Holding them up high in her palm, she climbed out of the canoe onto the soft, white beach and, together with Rory, ran over to see what Hex had found.

She counted a dozen canoes floating in the water, bouncing up against one another. Most of the canoes held boxes, many of which had split open, probably during the fall into the lake. Strange items spilled out—gold figurines and strange symbols and old books. She spied a dried-up little head rolling in the corner of one canoe, while another held a life-size gold statue of a pharaoh. Hex was mumbling to himself as he rummaged through the booty.

"Egyptian, Sumerian, African, Tibetan, Incan, voodoo . . . look at all the cultures he's stolen from! So much magic! This is amazing!"

"No wonder he's so powerful," Fritz said, gazing into the canoes from his place on Bridget's hand. "He took from everyone."

"Think of what I could learn," Hex was saying, his eyes shining with greed.

"What about the Munsee magic?" Rory reminded him sharply. "Do you see any sign of those parchment pages?"

"Look for pages with the Munsee sigils," Hex advised him, all the while digging through the ancient artifacts himself. Rory poked around, flipping through books and loose pages, trying to find signs he recognized.

Bridget walked down to the canoes at the far end. She noticed Fritz wasn't even glancing at the loot; his eyes scanned the lake. "What are you looking for?" she asked.

"We're not alone down here, remember?" he reminded her. "The quicker we find whatever we're supposed to and get out of here, the better."

Of course . . . the monster. Bridget had almost forgotten in the excitement over the treasure. She ran to the last canoe, which held the strangest cargo—a long metal box, sealed up. Another wooden box sat at its foot, and this box had broken open, spilling out what looked like a rolled-up poster. Placing Fritz and Clarence into the canoe, she picked up the roll, feeling rough canvas, and unrolled it. She shouted in alarm, dropping the canvas into the canoe as she fell back into the sand.

"Bridget, be quiet!" Fritz hissed as Rory and Hex came running over. "You'll attract the wrong kind of attention!"

"It was staring at me!" she cried. "Right at me!"

Hex grabbed the canvas and unrolled it. His brow furrowed in perplexity at what he saw. "I don't understand how this can be." He showed the others the painting, for it was a painting. A portrait, of a narrow-faced man with large ears and a big, bushy beard. It looked like any portrait, except for the eyes. They seemed to pop out as if someone were standing right behind the painting, looking through. The eyes were alive.

"This is a god portrait," Hex said, confused. "This should be up in the Portrait Room. It looks familiar . . . I didn't know you could take those portraits off the wall, especially when the god was still alive, as this one obviously is."

Bridget could see a name written small in the corner of the painting. She leaned in and read it aloud. "Peter Minuit." She glanced up in confusion. "But he's dead!"

"I know," Hex said, looking like he wished he could drop the thing. "I've seen this before! But the portrait I saw, the one hanging in the Portrait Room, has dead eyes. That's how everyone knew he was gone."

"It looks like he isn't gone, after all," Fritz said. "Kieft must have switched the portraits."

"But why?" Rory asked. "To get the gods to make the Agreement with the land? To make it seem like the newcomers were fading away?"

"They *were* fading away," Hex replied. "It wasn't only Minuit. Many of the gods grew weak and the mortals from whom they sprang were dying out as well. No, this wasn't about the Agreement, I bet. This was something else. Could he have . . . no, not even Kieft would dare that." He glanced at the large, metal box. "Or would he?" Hex stepped over to the box, running his hands along the smooth metal surface.

"What are you thinking?" Rory asked uncertainly. "What's in the box?"

Hex didn't reply. Instead, he closed his eyes and began to chant. After a moment the box began to glow softly until finally, the top popped open. Hex's jaw dropped at what he saw.

"I don't believe it . . ."

Bridget ran over to Hex's side, and her jaw joined Hex's on the floor. Inside the box lay the body of a man, senseless but still breathing. He was dressed in old Dutch clothing, and his beard was matted and dirty. Bridget recognized him right away, given that she'd just been staring at his portrait.

"What is Peter Minuit's body doing in a box among Kieft's treasure?" Fritz asked. "I don't understand."

Rory bent over the body and lifted the chain around its neck up to take a good look at the locket. Bridget shuddered—it was like fooling with a corpse and she didn't like it. Rory turned and showed them the necklace—half the gold locket was gone.

"Do you think Kieft took it?"

"I don't know how he could," Hex said. "That's supposed to be impossible."

They stood there, staring at the body, wondering what it could mean, until finally Hex turned away. "We've got to grab as much stuff as we can and get out of here before that creature of yours shows up," he said, walking back to the other canoes. Rory ran to his side.

"No! We're only supposed to take one thing away. And that's gonna be the spell to save my mom!"

"I made no such promises," Hex said, picking up a small idol. Rory grabbed it out of his hands and threw it back into the canoe.

"I promised!" he said. "If you want to bring any magic out with you, you better start memorizing some spells."

"Don't you talk to me like that, you little brat!" Hex yelled, his voice echoing across the lake. Fritz hissed at him to quiet down, but the fallen god ignored the roach. "I told you I would help you in return for magic to humble Kieft, and I will take that magic! You have no right to keep me from my spoils!"

"That wasn't the deal," Rory began, but Hex cut him off.

"I don't care about your deal!" he shouted.

"Shut up!" Fritz told them. "Do you hear that?"

They immediately quieted, looking around in sudden fear. Bridget thought she heard a splash in the distance, but it could have been no more than the falling water. She peered intently across the glittering lake, looking for some sign of the creature. At first she saw nothing, then a flash of white broke the surface, just for a moment, sending a chill down her spine.

"I see it," she said, fear gripping her. "We've got to get out of here."

"Not yet!" Rory said. He ran up to the canoes and began tearing through the treasure, tossing things left and right. Hex joined him, grabbing things and putting them into his pockets. Bridget could hear something coming now—soft splashes as something big briefly broke the surface of the lake.

"It's coming, guys," she said. "Hurry up!"

She could see it clearly now. A long strip of white gliding through the water like a snake. Was that what it was? A huge water snake? What *was* this monster? She really didn't want to find out. She quickly turned to scan the wall, looking for a way out. She saw nothing but rock in every direction.

"Just leave it!" Fritz cried, no longer caring about being quiet. Bridget turned back and gasped. The white thing was closer than ever, cutting through the water like a submarine, and it was very, very big.

"Come on, Rory!" she cried, terror overwhelming her. "It's almost here!"

Rory let out a triumphant shout and lifted a bundle of bound parchment into the air. "I found it, Bridge! These are Munsee spells! Mom's gonna be all right!"

But as he stood there waving the book in the air, something rose up in the water behind him. Bridget's fear became unbearable as the huge white creature emerged from the lake. It had a long jaw filled with razor-sharp teeth, and its eyes rose up on either side like attic windows. She realized she knew exactly what it was, but Fritz said the words first.

"Oh my God!" the roach breathed. "It's the Albino Alligator."

Bridget was flabbergasted. She'd heard stories about the

Albino Alligator—Mr. Little used to tell tales of the giant reptile patrolling the sewers under the streets. Supposedly some
kid had dropped a baby alligator into a manhole, and it grew up
down in the sewers, white as snow since it never saw the light
of day, preying on anyone who walked underground. There was
no such alligator, of course, but it made for a scary tale. But
this creature was more than some stupid story. This creature
was a monster.

The huge white alligator, easily the size of a tour bus, burst
out of the water with jaws open. For a moment Bridget was
afraid she'd lost her brother for good. But Rory heard the
creature just in time, leaping aside just as its mammoth jaws
clamped down. Its head landed with a crash on the beach where
Rory had just been standing, and a few of the canoes were
crushed beneath its weight.

"Get out of there, Rory," Bridget screamed. But Rory hit
the ground hard, lying in the sand with the wind knocked out
of him, the book of Munsee magic clutched tight to his chest.
Bridget knew he was wearing Soka's protective rune, but she
didn't think that tiny little smudge was going to work against
something so mammoth. So she did the only thing she could
thing of: she ran straight for her brother, ready to save the
day.

She reached his side just as the giant reptile pulled back
for another assault. If it weren't for the putrid stench wafting
from its mouth, she'd have thought it was some animatronic
creature from Disney World. Its shiny, wet scales were too
huge, its mammoth eyeballs spinning in sockets too large, to
be alive. But its teeth were extremely real, and they were dripping with saliva as the alligator pushed off with its giant, scaly,

clawed feet. It made another lunge for the two of them. Bridget grabbed her brother and pulled him to his feet. She leaped forward, carrying him, just as the alligator lunged. Its giant mouth smacked down on her feet, and she heard something crunch beneath the force of those huge smackers. She yanked herself free, hobbling forward, Rory now helping her.

"Your foot!" he shouted, and she glanced back. An entire piece of her foot had been bitten off, toes and all. She was down to one steel-top. But she didn't let it stop her, balancing on the back of her heels as they scrambled away from the shore.

A loud rush of flame rang through the cavern and they spun to see that Hex was fighting back. He'd grabbed one of the Incan idols and was breathing through the back of its head, making fire shoot out its mouth. The alligator reared back, though the lick of flame seemed pitiful compared with the power of the huge reptile. It gave Hex enough time, however, to run toward the last canoe.

He reached into the large box and pulled out the senseless body of Peter Minuit.

"What are you doing?" Fritz yelled.

"The only way to get the beast to leave us alone is to offer a sacrifice, isn't that what you told me?" Hex screamed back. "Who would you rather it be? One of you or this poor, unconscious fool?" He dragged the body free of the canoe, dropping it on the beach.

"Wait a second," Bridget called out. "This isn't right! We can't just feed that guy to the alligator."

"You have a better idea?" Hex yelled. The alligator had regained its senses, and Bridget could see it was readying for another assault. She knew what Hex was doing was wrong—but

Rory and Fritz stood frozen, unable to act. She knew she'd regret this later, but she had to do what was right.

She ran at Hex, grabbing the body of Peter Minuit by the legs and pulling him away. Hex scowled at her, trying to pull the body back toward the lake.

"You're going to get us all killed!" Hex screamed.

"We can't just kill him in cold blood," Bridget screamed back. "It's not right!"

"I don't care!" He lifted the Incan idol and blew a quick breath through it, sending a flame right toward her face. She fell back, beating at her skin furiously. Thankfully, the fire didn't catch, but by the time she could see again, Hex had almost reached the alligator.

"Here, take this and leave us alone!" he cried out, and the Albino Alligator crouched, as if ready to take the offering.

"NO!" a voice yelled out. A form burst out of the water on the other side of the alligator and ran right at Hex. It was a man, disheveled and drenched, and he grabbed Minuit from a disbelieving Hex and dragged the senseless god to safety.

"What did you do?" Hex screamed at the man, running over to him. The man who'd saved Minuit turned to face him and Bridget realized who he was.

"Dad . . . ?"

She glanced over at Rory to make sure she wasn't dreaming, but he was just as astonished as she. Peter Hennessy stood toe-to-toe with Hex, preventing the magician from taking Minuit to the alligator.

"Harry Meester?" Hex said, jaw dropping as he recognized Bridget's father. "What are you doing here?"

"You can't do this, Burr," Bridget's dad said. "It won't work."

"Of course it will work," Hex said. "It's a sacrifice."

"No, it isn't," Mr. Hennessy insisted. "A sacrifice has to mean something. Killing someone you've never met before means nothing, at least nothing good. All you'll accomplish is destroying the one piece of proof you have that Kieft is living a huge lie."

"What are you talking about?" Hex asked. "Who are you to decide this?"

"Believe me, I know," Mr. Hennessy said. He turned to Rory. "Rory, this has to be *your* sacrifice. It's the only way."

"No!" Bridget cried, hobbling to her brother's side. "I won't let him!"

"So I have to die, is that what you're saying?" Rory asked. Bridget glanced at the water, where the alligator was gathering its wits and getting ready for another rush.

"No, of course not!" Dad replied, his face turning white. "I would never allow that. But you need to give something up."

"What?" Rory asked, his face frightened and confused. Dad pointed to the book.

"Those spells were never meant to be written down. It was wrong of Kieft to steal them. You need to let them go."

"No!" Rory screamed, tears running down his cheeks. "If I don't bring this back with me, Mom's gonna die!"

"She won't!" Dad replied. "You're not down here to get that book of magic, believe me. It's meaningless."

"Guys, it's coming back!" Bridget warned as she watched the alligator crouch.

"Rory, the Fortune Teller did say that if you follow the path she laid out for you, your mother will live," Fritz reminded him.

"But I already have the answer right here," Rory said, shaking the book as tears welled up in his eyes. "I can't throw it away on some stupid blind hope!"

"But, Rory, it's not just about your mother," Mr. Hennessy said. "Do you want her waking up to the shell of a city? A city ruled by Willem Kieft? She might not be able to see it, but she will feel it. Every mortal will. And you will have to live with that. I have faced this challenge, Rory, and I have failed miserably, so please, listen to me. Or you will regret it for the rest of your life."

"Rory, watch out!" Bridget cried. The giant alligator came lumbering up the beach like a monster truck, leaping in the air with its jaws open wide, heading right for a terrified Rory. Rory stood frozen for a moment, out of reach of everyone's help, but then he pulled his arm back and threw the book of Munsee magic deep within the beast's maw before rolling to safety.

The alligator landed heavily on the beach in their midst, sending sand showering over everyone as its mouth closed with a snap. It was close enough to all of them that, if it wanted to, it could have simply reached out and swallowed them all. Bridget stared up at those huge white scales, the massive muscles gliding beneath them, and she felt overwhelmed with awe. She felt certain that they were all dead.

But the Albino Alligator did not attack again. Instead, it slithered backward down the sand, leaving a huge gash on the beach in its wake. It crunched over a canoe or two as it retreated, driving their contents deep into the ground, before dipping back into the lake, tail first. The last thing to disappear under the water was its huge, white head, with its long, evil-looking snout bristling with teeth, until only its beady eyes poked up like periscopes, the ripples in the water the only indication of the massive creature's presence. Finally, they, too, disappeared.

Rory dropped to his knees, tears streaming down his face. Mr. Hennessy hesitantly stepped toward him.

"You did the right thing, son," he said, and Bridget's heart ached to hear those words.

"Why are you doing this to me?" Rory said bitterly, wiping his eyes. "You just show up again, telling me to throw away the only chance I had of saving Mom's life, and that if I do, she'll end up saved anyway. Maybe. I threw away my chance for a maybe."

"In this life, that's usually all you get," Mr. Hennessy said softly. He reached out a hand to touch his son's shoulder, then stopped, uncertain. Bridget couldn't stand it. She ran to them, practically bowling her dad over as she clutched him with one arm and Rory with the other. If she could have cried, she would have drowned them both. Instead, she sobbed without tears, feeling her father stroke her thin, paper hair and whisper that he loved her. She never wanted to let go.

But they couldn't stand there forever, and her dad finally stepped back, releasing her but still keeping one arm flung over her shoulder. She happily burrowed into his side.

"How did you get here?" Hex demanded. "You came from nowhere!"

"I knew you'd be here," Mr. Hennessy told them. "A friend tipped me off. So I raced here as fast as I could, by a path only

I knew. I've been here before, you see—a few times. But this will be the last time. I can't run anymore. I'm ready to end this madness once and for all."

"So what now?" Hex asked.

"Yeah, I was only allowed to take away one thing," Rory said. "And that thing is gone, eaten by that monster. But I don't want anything else."

"I think the fire-breathing idol might be useful," Hex urged, looking over the rest of the treasure with greedy eyes. But Dad pointed to the prone body of Peter Minuit.

"We're taking him. He's the key to the whole thing. Come on, the way isn't far. There's someone I want you to meet."

THE BATTLE FOR
MANNAHATTA

Nicholas wasn't certain how it started. They'd taken their positions inside Belvedere Castle. He'd suggested putting some archers on the island in the middle of Turtle Pond, but Soka vetoed the idea. Maybe she knew something he didn't. They'd find out soon enough.

They could see Kieft's army across the long lawn. The day was cloudy, and as Nicholas watched, it grew cloudier still. He heard Soka mutter behind him.

"He's calling the clouds. How is he doing that?" She looked fascinated and perplexed. But Nicholas had long ago given up on trying to explain Kieft's power.

He glanced around at the troops. The Munsees were at the ready, grasping their spears and bows. He spied people from all over the five boroughs—the Red Legged Devils and Marylanders from Brooklyn, gods and spirits of all races from Queens, the entire Yankees baseball team holding their bats like clubs—even battle roaches with Captain Liv at their head. She caught his eye and saluted. He saluted back. So many making a stand—so many lives that could be lost. But what choice did they have?

The clouds had completely covered the sky, turning the morning into a dark, gloomy affair. Nicholas shifted uncertainly, staring out of the ramparts. Suddenly a wave of intense fear washed over him. It was magic, he knew it, and he opened his mouth to cry a warning. But it was too late, as arrows filled the sky, horses burst out of the trees on each side of the castle, and in a moment they were overrun.

The Cowboys came from one side, the Hessians from the other, and soon everyone was fighting for their life. With a loud "Tallyho!" Teddy Roosevelt leaped atop his horse, leading his men into the thick of the fight. Buckongahelas let out a war cry, echoed by his warriors, as they charged into the rising tide of battle. Nicholas grabbed his sword, ducking as a mobster shot a bullet into the rampart he'd just been occupying, and he entered the fray, determined to keep the enemy at bay.

Alexa struggled to fight her way through the crush of enemies. She'd found herself with soldiers from two regiments from Breuckelen: the Red Legged Devils and the Marylanders, led by a pair of colonels called Smallwood and Wood. They proved to be fierce fighters, but they were all finding it difficult to push the enemy back when they weren't allowed to kill.

"Damn these rules!" Colonel Smallwood cried, smacking a Hessian on the head with the butt of his musket while dodging a knife thrust. "Guns were made for shooting, blast it!"

But looking around, Alexa could see the wisdom in not killing their opponents. For every angry, hate-filled god attacking her, she spied a scared, lost god who didn't look like he rightly understood how he came to be on this battlefield. Such was the power of Kieft's fear campaign. It made enemies of friends and killers of neighbors. She didn't want to draw their blood. But there were so many. How could they hope to survive if they couldn't protect themselves?

"Ms. Van der Donck!" Colonel Wood cried, pointing with his sword. "Watch out!"

Turning, Alexa spied a familiar horseman, bearing down on her with a gun pointed at her head. "You can't run anymore!" James DeLancey cried, readying to fire. Alexa froze—she had nowhere to go. But then, out of the fighting mess rode another horseman, who barreled into DeLancey, sending him crashing to the ground, where Colonel Smallwood quickly rendered him unconscious with a thump of his musket butt.

"Good show!" Smallwood said to her savior. "What's your name, soldier?"

"Sergeant Peacock, sir!" the man cried, saluting. "Happy to finally see battle, at long last! The War of 1812 has nothing on this! I'm off to find Private Kinderhook, my partner in arms. He was hiding under a bush, last I checked, but I don't want him to miss all the glory!"

With that, Sergeant Peacock rode back into battle before Alexa could thank him. She looked around; the fighting seemed to be growing more intense. Despite their best efforts, bodies already littered the ground. She didn't know how they were going to survive this. Taking a deep breath, she prepared to dive back into the fight.

Suddenly another wave of fear overcame her. All around, her companions fell to the ground, paralyzed by this new attack

and helpless before their enemies. Even as she struggled to regain her feet, she knew this had to be one of Kieft's tricks. She
prayed that Soka could counter it before it was too late.

Soka felt the magic wash over her. Kieft was going all out,
blinding some defenders, sending apparitions at others, all
the while sending waves of fear washing over her troops. His
armies climbed over the ramparts to take advantage of the confusion. She quickly pushed back against the magic, clearing the
minds of her army before they could be overrun. More waves
of magic followed and she strained to contain them all. But still
the battle raged on.

She felt overwhelmed. She could keep pushing back the fear,
but what could she do against all this slaughter? Then she felt
it. A mind, at the edge of her consciousness, barely awake.
What was it? She closed her eyes, delving deeper, trying to find
this mind. Right before she was about to give up, she found it,
so large she could barely understand it, so slow she could barely
speak to it. But speak to it she did. And when it heard what she
had to say, it grew very angry indeed.

With a burst, the island in the middle of Turtle Pond exploded out of the water to reveal . . . a giant turtle. The turtle
had been the island all along. It answered Soka's call and began
to attack the enemy soldiers, driving them back from the walls
of the castle.

The awakening of the turtle gave Soka an idea. She sent
her mind out, calling to all of the creatures of the land, asking
them to help protect it. A screech came from above her as a
giant owl swooped down, flying into battle with beak snapping.

The ground began to rumble as coyotes and bears and even a mastodon lumbered out of the trees to join in the fight. The animals were coming to life to protect their land, and under Soka's direction, what began as a rout turned into a fair fight. But still, the battle continued, with no end in sight . . .

Lincoln didn't know where his friends had disappeared to. When the battle started, Teddy Roosevelt had charged into the fray, and Lincoln had eagerly followed. When he finally looked around, however, he couldn't find the rest of the Rattle Watch. Swallowing his fear, he focused on keeping the attackers away from the castle. On and on he fought, dodging knives and bullets while trying to keep from killing anyone. The fighting never seemed to let up.

Suddenly a giant turtle that seemed to show up out of no-where crashed down on a group of Brokers of Tobias, smashing them into metal bits. Lincoln staggered away, his heart beating a mile a minute. This battle wasn't as cool as he thought it would be. In fact, it was pretty darn scary. But he was a fighter, so he'd man up and fight.

"I give up!" he heard somone shout, and spun to see Nathan Hale with his arms in the air. Before him, a vampire lawyer readied himself to spring. Lincoln quickly launched himself at Hale, pulling him to the ground. The vampire lawyer jumped at them, teeth bared, but a Munsee dog met him in midflight, and fought him off. Lincoln turned to Hale.

"Are you crazy!" he said.

"I was just about to complete my ingenious plan to infiltrate the enemy stronghold," Hale replied peevishly. "Now please, you don't know me. I'm a Dutch schoolteacher." He pushed himself to his feet and immediately put his hands in the air. "I give up!" A rush of fighting bodies raced by and Lincoln lost sight of the idiot. He shook his head. You couldn't help everyone.

Looking around, he spied Babe Ruth smacking people on the head with his baseball bat and then standing still for a moment, admiring his shot. War was crazy, Lincoln decided. A horse trotted in front of him, bearing Roosevelt, who seemed unafraid of the battle raging around him. Lincoln wished he could be like him. So brave and proud and courageous. Roosevelt's very presence seemed to lift the soldiers' spirits.

Suddenly Roosevelt flinched, falling back off his horse. Lincoln ran to his side, horrified to see a bullet hole in the god's chest. "Sir, are you all right?"

"Damned sharpshooters!" Roosevelt coughed. He pointed to a hill, where Lincoln could see men training their guns on the battling armies. "I will go show them the back of my hand!" He coughed.

"You're in no shape to go back into battle, sir," Lincoln told him.

"Nonsense! I'm a god! This is but a scratch!"

"You may be a god, but you're still wounded," Lincoln said. He turned to a nearby World War II soldier. "Excuse me, could you take him to the nuns?" The soldier helped Roosevelt to his feet, ready to take him to the medics. Lincoln glanced around. His comrades seemed to have lost some of their spark. He realized that the sight of Roosevelt being shot down must have shaken them. They couldn't lose their focus! He wouldn't let them. He turned back to Roosevelt. "Give me your hat! And your jacket! And your monocle! We need Teddy Roosevelt, and I'm gonna give them Teddy Roosevelt."

"I hate to tell you this, son," Roosevelt wheezed. "But you're black!"

"Details!" Lincoln scoffed, donning Roosevelt's clothing and climbing into the saddle, his sword raised high. "Tallyho!" he yelled, and the soldiers around him raised their swords in return, glad to see their leader was all right. He flicked the reins, guiding the horse through the battlefield, trying to look general-esque, while, inside, he was just praying he didn't get a bullet in the chest.

The sharpshooter reloaded his gun, calmly placing the bullets in the chamber one by one. In his mortal life, he had spent about a week in Europe during World War II before deciding that life was better back home, where he wasn't getting shot at. He'd promptly deserted, sneaking back to New York. He spent the next year drinking away his shame at local bars before getting run down in the street one drunken evening by a passing taxi.

It wasn't until the call went out for shooters that he discovered that it wasn't the battle that bothered him. It was being in the middle of the battle. He was perfectly happy sitting up on this hill, out of harm's way, taking shots at poor saps all the way across the field. He lined up his rifle, sighting some idiot dressed up in a ridiculous Teddy Roosevelt outfit, trying to rally his troops from the back of a horse that was far too big for him. *Sorry guy,* he thought as he started to squeeze the trigger. *Better you than me.*

Suddenly something dropped directly onto his face. He fell backward, screaming as he realized that a giant cockroach was clinging to his chin.

"Looks like your shooting days are over," the roach said. The shooter could see his fellow gunmen being overrun by battle roaches, led by a girl roach with no helmet who was riding a sleek rat. She shouted at the roach on his face.

"Sergeant Kiffer! Stop messing around and take him out!"

"Yes, ma'am!" the giant roach yelled. It slammed its insect head into the shooter's forehead, and the man swiftly lost consciousness, leaving yet another battle to be fought on without him.

William Randolph Hearst sat under the trees, watching the battle with glee in his eyes. The smoke from the muskets and cannons stung his eyes, but he didn't mind. Every bullet that found a home was a headline, each fallen spirit a heartrending story. His newspaper fed on spilled blood and lost lives, and the next edition was going to be a fat one indeed.

He watched Kieft's sharpshooters being overrun by battle roaches, but felt no alarm. Victory, defeat, neither really mattered to him. He followed Kieft because Kieft promised war, but now that war was a reality, he needed no one. Swords rang and bodies fell and Hearst watched it all, writing the evening edition in his head.

He was so engrossed in the drama that he never noticed the gang boy creeping up behind him with knife drawn. The boy was a Dead Rabbit, but he wanted to be so much more. Like

Hearst, he didn't care who won or lost the battle. He only wanted the spoils.

With a flash of metal, Hearst fell to the dirt, his last head-line destined to remain unwritten. The gang boy grabbed the fallen god's locket and ran, leaving Hearst bleeding in the dust. His obituary better make the front page, Hearst thought. And then he was gone.

The battle raged on, in wave after wave of attack and coun-terattack. Kieft watched it all—his army gaining ground, the enemy army fighting back, blood spilling all the while—and he threw back his head and laughed and laughed.

Family History

Peter Minuit's body wasn't the lightest in the world, but together, Rory and his father managed to carry it across the beach to the stone wall. Out of the corner of his eye, Rory spied Bridget hobbling along, half of her foot missing. Hex trotted up to her, holding out a piece of torn papier-mâché.

"This was on the beach by the water," Hex said. "I believe it belongs to you."

"Not anymore," Bridget said sourly. "It's been torn off."

"Allow me." Hex knelt down like a clerk in a shoestore. He mumbled some words as he placed the piece of papier-mâché onto Bridget's foot as if he were Prince Charming fitting Cinderella with her glass slipper. When he finished, her foot was whole again.

"Wow," she said, admiring the restoration. "Thanks."

"No problem," Hex replied. "I used to do that for Toy when he had accidents."

Bridget's face went cold. "You know Jason died last week, right? He gave his life to help Rory free the Munsees."

"I heard that, yes," Hex said, looking away.

"You treated him like a servant. You even called him Toy! He was your son!"

"He wasn't my son," Hex said, still not looking at her. "I found him when he was a baby, and I recognized his gifts. So I adopted him."

"Stole him, you mean," Fritz cut in, riding up.

"I saved him," Hex insisted. "He would have been taken like all the other Lights if it weren't for me. I treated him like my own."

"If that's how you treat your own, then I'm glad you never had any real kids!" Bridget scolded him.

"I don't think anyone here is an advertisement for perfect fathers," Hex replied, glancing at Mr. Hennessy.

They approached a cave mouth right in the middle of the wall. Fritz rode up to it, turning back to them to say with exasperation in his voice, "Why didn't we just run over here in the first place? That great beast would never have gotten to us in here!"

"It wasn't there earlier," Mr. Hennessy replied, his voice tired. "Believe me, I've been down here before, and that cave has never appeared until after the alligator is sated."

"Why did you come down to this place the first time?" Rory asked, puffing from carrying Minuit's body.

"It's a long story," Mr. Hennessy said. "Longer than the time it takes to get to where we're going."

"You and your secrets," Rory said, anger welling up. "I don't know who you are, what you are, I don't even know your real name!"

"It's Henry," his dad said. "Like you read in Adriaen's journal. That was my real name."

"Oh," Rory replied, taken aback. "Nice to finally meet you, Henry."

"Don't be sarcastic, it doesn't suit you," Henry told him. Rory opened his mouth to retort, but he heard his sister giggling at their father's words and he decided to let it go.

They passed into the cave, which soon led to a long, dimly lit passage. Hex's ball of light danced back and forth as they walked in silence. Something was about to happen, they all knew it, and the weight of that knowledge made talk seem unnecessary.

They finally approached a light at the end of the tunnel and emerged into a beautiful garden, the very garden Adriaen had described in his journal, Rory guessed. The garden stretched off into the distance, with huge plants and trees growing in lush abundance. The air was warm, like the inside of the jungle house at the zoo. Gazing up, Rory couldn't even see the ceiling. Warm, sweet light poured down over everything like golden honey. Just a breath of the air loosened Rory's back, easing his worries. But even though the sweet smells and soothing light calmed him, he did not feel comfortable. He could sense that he was not really welcome in this garden—no mortals were. It was not their place.

They walked a little ways into the garden until they reached a small clearing inside a circle of tall palm trees. They gently placed Peter Minuit's body on the ground and looked around.

"Now what?" Fritz asked.

"Now we wait," Henry replied.

"Wait for what?" Hex asked.

"For *her*," Henry said, nodding behind them. They spun around and Rory felt his heart jump.

"Mom?" Bridget whispered at his side. And it *was* their mother who was emerging from the trees in a long white dress, barefoot and smiling. Even as Rory's heart was aching at the sight of his mother, he could hear his father sighing.

"This is not fair," Henry said.

"I wear the shapes required of me," Rory and Bridget's mother said, and Rory knew right away that it wasn't really her. The voice coming out of their mother's mouth was low and earthy, barely a human voice at all. He could hear the rhythms of the water as she spoke; the eternal patience of the mountains colored every word.

"You're not our mother!" Bridget accused.

"No, I'm not," said the woman who wore their mother's face. "I am wearing the shape of what is at stake for you."

"So who are you really?" Fritz asked, riding toward the woman. "Are you a god?"

"Mortals believe their gods are everything," the woman said, smiling at Fritz's question. "Yet your gods only care for mortals. I do not spring from any mind, nor do I require worship to survive. I was what the first mortals felt when they knew they were being watched over, but they had to create their own protectors, since I did not give them the attention they felt they deserved. I have so much to protect"—here she gestured to include the entire garden—"and so had no time to devote solely to them. Mortals are so needy."

"So you watch over plants and stuff?" Bridget asked.

"I watch over everything," the woman replied. "I remember everything. I recall the winners and the losers, the victories and the defeats. And my memories became a place all on their own. Mannahatta was not created by the Munsees—I simply allowed them to live there. And I eventually allowed the new-comers to thrive, as well. They are all boats floating on my ocean, and their gods are the wind in their sails. But without my blessing, they would all drown."

"Are you the Fortune Teller, too?" Rory asked, a suspicion forming in his brain.

"No," the woman said, laughing softly. "But she and I walk in the same direction."

"She sent us down here," Rory continued. "She told me how to get here and what to do."

"And you have performed admirably." His mother's face smiled. "You are my champion after all. All the Lights were born to be my champions."

"Why?" Rory asked. "I can't really do anything."

"You see the truth," the woman replied. "That is the cur-rency I value. You take my truth and disperse it among your people. All of you have heeded my call, though you did not know it. It is not an easy thing, as your father can tell you."

"Do we have to speak of this?" their dad asked, his voice miserable.

"Of course," the woman replied. "I think it is time for your story to be told."

"But I wouldn't know where to begin!" their father pro-tested.

"You can begin with your name," the woman instructed him.

"It's Henry, right?" Rory asked, suddenly feeling bad for the man. The woman shook her head.

"Your full name, Henry."

Henry took a deep breath and turned to face his children.

"My name is Henry Hudson."

Rory felt the world roll as he staggered back.

"*The* Henry Hudson?" he asked, astounded.

"Yes, *the* Henry Hudson," Henry said, sighing.

"So you *are* a god," Bridget whispered.

"No, I'm not," Henry replied. "I'm mortal and have been for over four hundred and thirty years. Because of this woman, here." He nodded to the woman who wore their mother's face.

"What happened?" Rory asked, glancing at her placid face. He noticed out of the corner of his eye that Hex was staring at Henry, his face a mixture of awe and fear.

"I guess I should begin at the beginning," Henry Hudson said. "I was a proud man, when I was young. I did not like listening to others, I went my own way against the council of those wiser than I, and I never asked for anyone's opinion but my own. My employers hired me to find the way to the West Indies, and I became obsessed with that one purpose. I knew that the way to the Orient lay across the western sea, the mighty Atlantic. I had already tried to go east north of Russia, but I barely survived the voyage. The New World would be the answer, I knew it in my bones. Verrazano, who I believe you've met, wrote of a large river north of Virginia. I thought for sure it would lead me through the continent and out into the Pacific. The Dutch believed in my theory, so they gave me the *Halve Maen* to prove it. I took on a crew that included my young son and we set sail for the New World.

"I can still remember the day I set eyes on the river that would later bear my name. So wide and deep—I was certain it would lead me to the fabled riches of the East. I didn't even bother to stop on the small island I sailed by on my way upriver, the island the natives called *Mannahatta*. But soon my hopes were dashed as the river grew narrow and shallow and eventually petered out completely. I sailed back downriver in poor spirits, not sure what to do next.

"It was then that I decided to make landfall on the long island at the head of the bay. One of the sachems we'd met upriver had spoken of great magic to be found there, and I wanted to see it for myself. I wasn't a big believer in magic, but I'd do anything if I thought it might help me get what I wanted. I disembarked and traveled into the island, looking for the magic.

"At first I found nothing but some friendly members of the local tribe—the Munsee. I ate and slept in their company, enjoying their hospitality and their tales. They had a medicine woman, her name was Alsoomse, who was truly a great woman—one of the most powerful magicians I have ever met. She told me that my presence was requested. By whom she would not say. I followed her to a glade, where I came face-to-face with the wife I'd left behind! But it was not her: it was the Lady we are sitting with now, who had taken my wife's form. She wished to see me, to ask a favor. She asked that I not tell anyone about her island, or the land around it. She wished to keep the newcomers away as long as possible. If I agreed to do that, she would give me a rune of protection, which would help me in my journeys. I agreed. Why would I tell anyone about her land? I didn't care about the New World. I wanted to get to the Far East. It was an easy promise to make.

"I went back to my ship, told my crew to keep quiet about Mannahatta in return for a healthy amount of gold supplied by the Lady, and we sailed back to Europe.

"But I did not keep my promise. In my effort to drum up more money for another expedition, I began to brag about the new lands I'd already discovered. Anything to be able to sail after my obsession again. My crew likewise told everyone about the beautiful river and its surrounding land. We all proved faithless. I have sailed on the ghost shop *Halve Maen*, and I know that they have paid for their sins as I have paid. But at the time, I got what I wanted: another ship at my disposal. But at what cost? I did not care. I was going to sail to the West Indies if it killed me.

"This time I went for a northern route, above what is now Canada. I thought the eternal sunshine of the arctic summers would melt the ice away, leaving me with a clear passage to the East. I was wrong.

"We soon discovered that the long days of the northern summers did not lead to melted ice. In fact, ice surrounded us at every turn. The voyage was arduous and long, and soon my crew began to grumble as food became hard to find. I pushed on, however, partly because of my obsession, and partly because the rune on my forehead protected me. I did not fear the way I should have. So I kept pushing and pushing, right up until the day my crew mutinied, placing me and my most loyal sailors onto an ice floe and sailing back toward England.

"And there I should have died, but for this damn rune on my forehead. Instead I had to watch my men die, one by one, and something in me broke. I washed the rune from my skin, ready to follow my men into death. But still I did not die! Months passed, and though I should have perished, I continued living. When that ice floe floated to the mainland, I began to walk. I trekked across the tundra, down through the forests of Canada, all the way to the mighty river.

"At long last, I reached the island. I marched into the very forest where I'd met the Lady, shouting for her to come to me. Instead, Alsoomse found me. She bore a message from the Lady. I was to follow the path down to her garden, where we would meet.

"I followed the path, which led to a raging underground river, which in turn carried me down to the underground lake. Then the creature attacked. I had never seen an alligator before, so I didn't know that was what it was, but it terrified me. I started throwing things at it, trying to drive it away, and without thinking, I tossed a bundle of letters I carried from my wife into its hungry mouth. It swallowed the last link between me and my beloved family, and then it disappeared back into the lake.

"Overcome, I fell to the beach and sobbed. Eventually, I spied the cave in the wall, and I staggered down the tunnel to this very garden, where the Lady was waiting. She still wore my wife's face, and I could not bear to look at her. I collapsed, refusing to meet her gaze. She did not care. She was relentless. I had broken my promise, she told me. The Europeans were coming, and they'd be here within the century. I begged her for death, to end my guilt, but she refused. Instead, she told me that I was cursed to remain alive through the long years, to witness what my faithlessness had wrought. I would suffer until the day I could redeem myself. Which I soon found myself unable to do.

"Eventually, the Dutch arrived to colonize, and soon after came Willem Kieft. One day he discovered me in the woods, and recognizing that I was special in some way, he captured me. He tortured me, using methods I cannot bear to relate, and found, to his delight, that I could not die. So he pushed me well past the point of death, over and over, using all the black arts he'd mastered over the years, until I broke again, this time so completely that I could not cross him if I tried. The memory of the agony he inflicted on me was too great. He owned me, completely.

"Through me he learned about Mannahatta. He forced me to show it all to him, and then he went one step further. He hunted down Alsoomse, and captured her. He forced her to tell him every secret she knew, until finally she died, passing beyond the spirit world to someplace I will never see. I wanted to stop him, but I couldn't. He was too strong. And with Alsoomse's magic, he was more powerful than ever.

"Now that he had the Munsees' magical secrets, he wanted them gone so that only he would know them. He began to make up lies about the Munsees, preparing for a slaughter. I wanted to expose Kieft, but in the end I couldn't do it. I was too frightened of the pain to speak. And the Munsees died for my weakness.

"Kieft was finally arrested, of course. But on the night before he was to be sent back to Amsterdam, he came to me. He wanted one last thing from me—my immortality. Using some black art I am glad not to know, he ripped out a tiny piece of my spirit, sending it deep inside himself. The pain was beyond belief. And from that moment on we were bonded. So long as I lived, he would live. And I could not die. So he could not die.

"The next day he sailed away to Amsterdam, and when I heard that the ship had sunk, I felt no peace. For I knew he wasn't dead. And, sure enough fifty years later, he returned, disguised, and he sought me out. He had a new plan, you see. He noticed all the gods that were popping up. Verrazano, Minuit, Van der Donck. He wanted their power. I don't know how he managed it, but somehow he made a spell, using Munsee magic he'd ripped from poor Alsoomse, to create a knife. This wasn't the same kind of knife he later made, though it was an early prototype. This knife could do one thing—it could steal the power of a god.

"He then set out to trap a god—Peter Minuit must have been the first one he happened upon. The gods had a tenuous grip on the spirit world at this point, and Kieft knew no one would miss Minuit, who was no match for Kieft's magic. He sliced that poor Minuit's locket in two and placed it around his own neck. It didn't make him a god, but it gave him the appearance of one. His own power easily helped maintain the illusion. He hid Minuit's body away and switched the god's portrait in the Portrait Room, covering all the bases.

"So now Kieft had joined the ranks of the gods, but it would mean nothing if the newcomers faded from Mannahatta. He knew from my tale that the Lady had not wanted the Europeans to come. He realized that the land needed to be appeased. The newcomer gods needed to prove they would respect the land. So he came up with the idea of a compact, an Agreement with the land. He forced me to lead him and Van der Donck down to this very garden. Secretly, I was sure we would all be destroyed by the Lady. But I was mistaken."

"Though Kieft's intentions might have been foul," the woman said, interrupting Henry's story, "I could tell that the others truly wished to honor me. They wanted to be a part of

Mannahatta, just as the Munsees did centuries earlier. The Agreement itself was nobly offered, proving that the newcomers deserved to be remembered by me. Of course, if Kieft had sacrificed Adriaen as he'd planned, I would not have made any agreement. But I knew by then that the newcomers should be allowed the chance to make an honest pact, so I arranged for Adriaen to survive."

"An honest pact?" Henry said, shaking his head. "There was nothing honest about Kieft. You thought you were neutralizing him by taking his magic away, as his sacrifice, but he'd already removed it himself. He'd stuck it in my head! He simply took it back from me—painfully I might add—when we returned to the surface. I not only made sure Kieft lived forever, but I helped him become a god and I made sure he held on to all his magic. Plus, now all the gods were tied to rules that he himself *did not have to follow*! He wasn't a god, not really, so he could go anywhere, and more importantly, kill anyone he pleased.

"Of course, he still hadn't worked out how to kill a god. The Munsees could do it, but he couldn't. It took him a few centuries, but he finally figured it out. And the day of reckoning is at hand.

"So now you understand my shame. This is all my fault. If I had kept my word in the first place, I would have long passed on and none of this would be happening. Instead, war is breaking out and Kieft is threatening the very fabric of Mannahatta. All because I was too weak."

"But the time has come for the redemption you were promised," the woman told him. "Kieft is collecting godhoods, gathering all the power up for himself. If he has his way, he will be the only divine figure left in all of Mannahatta. I will not let that happen. Rory, I have something I must ask of you. Expose Kieft for what he is—a liar, a thief, and most certainly *not* a god. Minuit's body will be proof. You must hurry, the fighting has already begun."

"Why will they listen to me?" Rory asked, still reeling from the story he'd just heard. "I'm just a mortal."

"You carry the power of the Sachem's Belt inside you," the woman told him. "That belt was created by Alsoomse herself. Use it to *make* them believe you."

Rory took a deep breath. He could do this. Kieft was going down, and Rory would be the one to see that he did. No matter what.

HONOR AMONG THIEVES

Soka's mind hovered over the battlefield as she did her best to save her people. The animals had come at her call, and they were doing significant damage. But too many good spirits and gods were being overwhelmed by their enemies—she'd seen more than a few fall. The battle right outside Turtle Pond was especially fierce, with Nicholas Stuyvesant and Buckongahelas fearlessly leading their men into close combat with Kieft's soldiers. Toward the outskirts of the battlefield, Soka spied bodies upon bodies, strewn about like sticks, and to her horror, shadows crawled among them. Looking closer, she realized that the gang boys were methodically moving from body to body, taking their lockets. Sometimes a god still breathed, at which point a knife would flash and the god's life would be ended on the spot. To Soka's horror, she saw these cowardly murderers killing gods on their own side, as well as hers. It didn't matter to the gang boys—they just wanted the lockets.

She was about to intervene, when she heard screams. Returning her attention to the battle by the pond, she was just in time to see Nicholas thrashing about, a terrified expression on his face as he clawed at the air. Soka felt the power surrounding him and she quickly rushed in, pushing the malevolent force away. Nicholas regained his senses, just in time to evade a crooked cop's billy club. Alexa ran up and knocked the cop unconscious, and both Rattle Watchers reentered the fray.

Determined to take the fight to the enemy, Soka followed the power to its source, far across the Great Lawn in the shadow of the far trees. Askook stood there, wolves surrounding him like guardians as he knelt over a pool of blood and worked his will on the tide of battle. Soka knew she needed to do something to contain this traitor's power, but she felt stretched so thin. There was hardly anything left. She was too weak.

Then she felt it, surrounding her. A presence, a strength, flowing up from the earth and enveloping her, replenishing much of the power that she had expended. At first she thought it was the Lady, coming to her aid a second time, but something, a breath of wind, touched her cheek, and suddenly she could feel her mother's love, giving her everything she would ever need, as she always had done. Soka pushed a portion of her renewed strength toward Askook, holding his will at bay. She felt his fury, beating at her, but she did not break. She knew she was not strong enough to keep him back forever, but for the time being, he was contained. Her mother's presence faded, sinking back into the earth, but Soka had no time to mourn its passing. Too many lives begged for her protection. She concentrated on the fight with redoubled efforts.

On the ramparts of Belvedere Castle, Soka stood tall, eyes closed, as her mind worked its will on the battle. If any saw the tears falling unchecked down her cheeks, they did not say a word.

Rory didn't know how they made their way back to the surface. One minute they were in the garden and the next they were standing at the edge of the Great Lawn in the middle of a war.

"What's going on?" Bridget asked, gazing around in wonder. "Is that a giant turtle?"

Rory could barely see for all the fighting. Belvedere Castle rose in the distance, and he could discern the Munsee and their friends holding off the enemy.

"Where's Hex?" he asked, looking around. The magician was nowhere in sight.

"He ran off the minute we arrived," his father said. "Though he'll be disappointed to find the Lady didn't let him keep any of the treasure he stole."

Rory didn't mourn the loss of the fallen god—though he could have used his magic in this final battle. He looked around, finally spotting Kieft standing on a hill, smiling as he observed the fruits of his labor.

"Can you expose him from here?" Fritz asked Rory.

"I don't know what I'm supposed to do!" Rory admitted.

"We confront him," Henry said, setting his shoulders. "We can't do this in the shadows. We confront him on the hill, where everyone can see, and you expose him from there."

"But he'll kill us!" Fritz yelled.

"Leave that to me," Henry said. But before Rory could take a step, arms encircled him from behind, holding him fast. Look-

ing around in a panic, he saw Bridget, his father, and even Fritz
in the clutches of the last creatures he ever wanted to see—the
Brokers of Tobias. There, out of the trees, strolled Tobias himself, waddling his way to them. At his side walked Boss Tweed
and Mrs. Astor.

"Look what we have here," Tobias said, his calm truly dis-
turbing in the face of all the fighting. "Now, this is a prize."

He glanced down at Peter Minuit's senseless body, lying on
the grass where Henry had dropped it. "And what is this?"

Rory saw his chance. "Your master is not who he says he
is! Kieft is a mortal who stole his power! He took his godhood
from Peter Minuit! That's Peter right there! Kieft has been
lying to you and he plans on taking everyone's power for his
own!"

"What are you talking about?" Tweed asked, his face troubled.

"Kieft isn't a god?" Mrs. Astor said, horrified. "How can
that be?"

"Does it matter?" Tobias said, shrugging. "He is just as
powerful."

"Of course it matters!" Mrs. Astor spat. "There is too
much . . . *democracy* going on around here! Lowly spirits becoming gods. *Mortals* becoming gods! That is not the Mannahatta I want to live in!"

"Then walk away," said Caesar Prince, stepping out of the
trees.

"I knew it!" Tweed said, pointing a finger. "You were never
on our side."

"Are you happy with how this is turning out?" Caesar asked,
ignoring Tweed's accusation. "When this is over, will you feel

safe?" Rory thought he saw Tweed flinch. Caesar continued: "Are you sure you want to live in Kieft's new world?"

"You're just trying to trick us," Mrs. Astor accused him.

"What if Kieft wins?" Tweed asked, more pragmatically. "Where will that leave us?"

"Dead, most likely," Caesar replied. "No matter what you do, Kieft will kill you, or one of your own lackeys will do it in order to claim that juicy locket around your neck. You can't win. So walk away and let the Light do what he must. Tobias!" Caesar stared at the God of Banking intently. "You know what you have to do, Tobias. Just walk away."

Both Tweed and Mrs. Astor turned to Tobias, whose face had gone white. To Rory's shock, the God of Banking, Kieft's most loyal supporter, nodded at his Brokers, who dropped their arms, releasing their prisoners. The rotund god then turned and walked away, disappearing into the trees with his green monsters on his heels. Tweed and Mrs. Astor looked as shocked as Rory felt, but Tobias's retreat pushed them into action; they quickly ran off in the direction of the park exit, leaving the battlefield for good.

Caesar turned to Rory and his companions with a twinkle in his eye. "Kieft inspires a lot of things—fear, for example—but loyalty is not one of them. Oh dear." He grabbed at his neck, and when he pulled his hand away, he held two lockets dangling from his fingers.

"Oh no," Henry said, his eyes sorrowful.

"It's all right," Caesar assured them, smiling his toothy smile. "I knew it would come to this."

"What happened?" Rory asked, confused.

"I turned my back on my godly duties one time too many,

and I lost my godhood. See?" He lifted his hand up, and the lockets dissolved into the air, blowing away on the breeze. "It's a small price to pay to right my wrongs."

"You're not going to die, are you?" Bridget asked, her voice sorrowful.

"Oh no. I'm still a spirit," Caesar said. "I'm just a fallen god. It's okay. I follow a different master now. I pledged myself to her long ago, and now that I've cut my ties with my past, I can devote myself to her causes. You will be seeing me again, I'm sure. Now go make my sacrifice worthwhile, Rory. Go bring us all the truth."

With that, the fallen god disappeared into the trees.

Sly Jimmy was running up the hill, his arms weighed down with hundreds of lockets. Blood covered his coat, and his cheeks were stained red. Not all of the blood had come from dying gods—a few of his boys had tried to take lockets for themselves, and Jimmy dealt with them quickly and harshly. The last thing he needed was for any of those evil bastards to become gods.

Kieft waited at the top of the newly created hill, surveying the battle with delight. Jimmy ran up to him, holding out the spoils.

"Here you go, boss," he said, forcing a big smile. "Quite a haul, if I do say so myself!"

Kieft didn't bother to answer. Instead, he scooped up the lockets and dropped them around his neck, one by one. With each new necklace, he seemed to glow brighter, until Jimmy could barely look at him. The rest of Mannahatta seemed to recede behind Kieft's magnificence. Sly Jimmy felt a very real terror bloom in his belly. Would he *see*?

Kieft stared down at him and frowned. "You are wearing something that does not belong to you." Sly Jimmy almost wet himself as he began to stammer.

"It's just a small one!" he protested, backing away. "God of Moderately Successful Sandwich Shops. It's nothing! Just a little souvenir."

Kieft stepped forward, and he seemed to cover the many feet between them in a single stride. A flash of steel glittered from his hand and Jimmy's luck finally ran out. He fell back, the gash in his chest first trickling, then gushing, blood—a spreading river covering his stained shirt with one last coat of red. Kieft leaned over him and watched him die without emotion.

"If it makes you feel any better," the black-eyed god said, as casually as if they were talking over a mug of beer, "I was going to kill you anyway once the battle was through. So you only lost a few hours at the most."

Sly Jimmy didn't have the strength to answer. He closed his eyes, fleeing the battle and all his sins forever.

THE TRUTH

Rory half ran, half stumbled toward the newly made hill in the center of the Great Lawn, where Kieft stood directing the battle. Bridget and his father followed close behind, Henry carrying the limp body of Minuit over one shoulder while Fritz rode Clarence close on Rory's heels. Rory could feel it, the finality of this last confrontation, and the fear in his chest threatened to overwhelm him. But there was no room for second thoughts, not anymore. He reached the bottom of the hill, his family around him, and called up as loudly as he could muster.

"Kieft! I am here for you!"

Any bravado in him fled, however, as the old sorcerer turned his deep black eyes on him.

Kieft could taste the victory as he watched the two armies battle it out on the lawn, in the trees, and on the ramparts of Belvedere Castle. He did not care who killed whom and how many died. Every knife thrust on either side brought him closer to the day he'd been planning for ever since he set foot on this backward isle, three hundred and fifty years ago. Almost every plan he'd laid had gone his way—these naive gods had been fooled, the Munsees had been fooled, even that damned Lady had bought into the lies he told. Setbacks, small and inconsequential, had occasionally popped up, but they were never more than brief detours on the journey to this day. It might take a few years to finish off the stragglers, but soon he'd complete the task he set out to perform—kill the gods in Mannahatta and take their power for his own.

Already he wore a hundred lockets, easily. Soon he'd have thousands more. As a mortal, he did not need to follow the rules that came with these necklaces, rules that he, ironically, helped put in place. He owed the people of this city nothing but his contempt. The mortals of New York would cry out for their guardians, their protectors to watch over them. And he would not answer. He was no servant, no. He would be master and the mortals would bow to him, and him alone.

"Kieft! I am here for you!"

Startled, Kieft glanced down at the foot of the hill . . . and froze. There stood the Light, who was supposed to have been killed in the smallpox-hospital explosion. And even worse, there stood Henry Hudson, somehow defiant, glaring up at his master like an angry little boy. Kieft would have to punish him for his insolence. But then he received the worst shock of the day. Over Henry's shoulder lay the limp body of Peter Minuit. His secret! It was too soon! His ties to his army were strong, but not strong enough to survive this revelation. No one must know that he'd stolen his power, that he was not, in fact, a god at all. His triumph depended on it.

Kieft immediately sent out the call to all those who were near him—the hill must be protected! Immediately, his nearest troops turned from their enemies and ran for the Light and his companions. But this was not enough. Everyone who knew his secret had to be destroyed. He didn't even need Minuit anymore, now that he had gathered so many lockets. There might be craftier ways to deal with them, but now was not the time for subtlety. Gathering every last drop of power within him, he sent his magic, all of it, raw and explosive, hurtling toward the four figures standing at the base of the hill. Henry would survive—he always did—and with him, Kieft's immortality, but Kieft needed to make certain there was nothing left of the others but ash and bone.

Soka felt the power building on the hill even as she struggled to contain Askook. She knew in an instant what it meant—Kieft was making his move. Disentangling a corner of her mind from her battle, she glanced in the First Adviser's direction, just in time to see him cast the whole of his power right at Rory and his companions.

Horrified, she immediately dropped her fight with Askook, leaving the Munsee magician free to do what he pleased. She sent a call to the Rattle Watch, warning them of Rory's plight, before sending her thoughts speeding toward the hill with all her strength, praying she wasn't too late.

All Bridget saw was the big bad guy giving Rory the hairy eyeball, and then the air got all staticky and charged, like a lightning storm was about to break. Her father gave a panicked shout and grabbed her arm.

"Get in front of him," he screamed, pulling her, and she didn't need to be told twice. Rory had to be protected from whatever sorcerer shenanigans Kieft sent his way. She pushed her brother to the ground, throwing herself between him and Kieft, while her father did the same for the limp body of Minuit. At first nothing happened and she felt foolish. But then the world began to burn.

"AGHHH!" She couldn't contain the scream inside. This was the first pain she'd felt in her paper body, and it overwhelmed her. She smelled the heavy smoke of a campfire and realized that her body was on fire. Her paper hair, her paper skin, all of it was burning merrily like she was a starter log for a Christmas fire. She could see her hands begin to turn black as her paper skin curled beneath the heat. *This is it,* she thought, less frightened than she thought she'd be. *I'm a goner.*

But then the fire suddenly stopped as if someone just blew it out. She felt a presence wash over her, soothing her, and she recognized it.

"Soka!"

Others are coming, with knives, Soka's voice whispered in her ear. *I've doused your fire but you must fight! I will hold back Kieft. Rory, you must do what you came here to do, and soon!*

Bridget climbed to her feet. Her body was blackened and curled like . . . well, like burned paper. But she could still hold herself together to protect her brother.

Rory was pushing himself to his feet, unharmed but clearly shell-shocked. Their dad seemed likewise unscathed, though his clothes hung in tatters. Rory's eyes filled with tears as he looked at Bridget, but she pointed at him, wagging her finger vigorously.

"Don't you wig out on me, mister!" she scolded him. "You've got a job to do!" She glanced up at Kieft, who seemed to be struggling with an unseen force, and she smiled tightly. Soka was doing her job.

"Here they come!" Fritz cried, pointing all around. All manner of enemies were converging on them, from every side. Bridget squared her burned shoulders, ready to do battle. One mean-looking vampire lawyer launched himself at her, teeth bared, but right before he reached her, a plate appeared, colliding with his face. The vampire went down in a spineless heap.

"Bull's-eye!" Simon yelled as the Rattle Watch ran to the Hennessys' side.

"Are you okay?" Alexa asked as Nicholas and Lincoln immediately joined Henry and Fritz in fending off the attacking horde. Bridget nodded, glancing down at the broken plate.

"I thought you had to protect the good china?" she asked Simon, who was readying another beautiful piece of crockery for flight.

"It's for a good cause!" He tossed the plate, knocking back a gang boy who was just about to hit Henry in the back. Bridget laughed and turned to Rory, who was standing, frozen, staring around him in fear.

"Why aren't you doing anything?" she asked her brother, turning to punch a crazed hippie in the face. Rory's eyes were wide with fright.

"I don't know what to do!" he confessed.

"You better think up something soon," she told him. "We

can't hold off these goons forever!" It was true—though they were fighting ferociously, even Bridget could tell there were just too many enemies. Rory had better do something, and quick.

Askook felt Sooleawa's whelp flee, and suddenly he could work his will again. He didn't know why Soka had pulled back, nor did he care. Anger burning inside, he sent his mind racing over the Great Lawn, toward the ramparts of Belvedere Castle, searching for the upstart who dared try to thwart his will.

There she stood, eyes closed, swaying as Chogan and other Munsee elders surrounded her, keeping watch over their new *pau wau*. Askook sneered. As if this little girl could hope to match his power, which he'd nurtured for centuries. He gathered himself, ready to obliterate Soka with one thought.

Suddenly pain exploded in him, and he felt something tear. Something was very, very wrong. Fear raced through him as he flew back the way he came, returning as quickly as he could to the clearing where his body waited. As he approached, he was horrified to see his wolves being scattered by a pack of spirit dogs. And in their midst stood a tall, proud Munsee warrior holding a copper spear as he towered over Askook's prone body. As Askook flew nearer to his body, the warrior glanced up and smiled grimly.

"You do not deserve to die cleanly," Wampage said, and lifted his other hand, from which dangled a pair of snakes writhing and hissing with fury. Horrified, Askook floated down to his body, coming face-to-face with his bleeding cheeks.

"Give me back my snakes!" he screamed, diving into his

body. But it was too late. Wampage dropped the snakes to the dirt and ground them beneath his heel. Askook awoke in his own body to feel it dying. His tattoos had held a significant part of his life force. They had made his magic stronger, but now they were his downfall. As the snakes died, so did he. He fell back, feeling the life slipping away from him. Wampage bent over him, his face grim.

"That is for Sooleawa," he said, and walked away, leaving Askook to slip into the dark to which he had sent so many souls. As his final thoughts faded, one horrifying realization rushed over him. *They are waiting for me!* And then he was gone.

Rory stood in the eye of the storm, magic swirling about his head as Kieft strove to break through Soka's protection. His father fought on one side of him, his sister on the other. Spread out around him, Nicholas, Alexa, Lincoln, and Simon kept the tide of enemies at bay, while Fritz, Bridget, and his father stayed close to fend off those who broke through. They all fought for him, to buy him time . . . to do what? Rory wanted to scream with frustration. What was he supposed to do now?

He returned his attention to Kieft, who stood at the very top of his little magic-born hill. The First Adviser's eyes bore down on him, striving to reach him through Soka's shield, and Rory knew his time was almost up. Soon Soka's strength would fail and her protection would melt away, leaving him exposed and weak. He already felt weak. Kieft was so strong, so powerful in every way, while Rory was nothing but a weak little boy a breath away from his end. How could he beat such a powerful sorcerer? The Lady seemed to think he could do it, so there must be some weak point, a chink in the armor. But *what*?

Rory concentrated on the First Adviser, blocking out the cries of battle and the smell of sweat and blood, trying to focus in on the truth. Kieft was so powerful . . . Rory could almost see the tendrils of power winding out from him, reaching out to his armies. They pulsated, black and hungry, and the sight of them made Rory nauseous with fear. But then it dawned on him—the power running through those conduits only flowed in one direction. The tendrils sucked and sucked, draining everything in their path, without sending anything back. Kieft took and took, but he did not give. He was only connected to the world until he sucked it dry. Then he was alone, surrounded by the drained corpses of those he betrayed with promises of power and protection, safety and revenge. And that made him a liar. His promises were tricks, sleights of hand. And Rory saw through all the tricks. It was time for everyone else to see through them, too.

Rory reached inside, pulling from a deep well of power that could have been deposited there with the destruction of the Sachem's Belt, or could have been inside him all along. He drew more and more, until he almost burst. Then he sent the power out to Kieft, and tried to draw the truth right out of the First Adviser's heart.

Kieft's eyes widened as he realized what was happening, but the old liar had no idea how to stop it. Rory sucked out every last drop of truth and then sent it down the long, black tendrils of power, forcing Kieft's own magic to flow in the opposite direction, sending the truth along with it. Within seconds, every last spirit and god knew Kieft's secrets.

The truth burst into their hearts full-blown, into every last member of Kieft's army, and as one their weapons fell to the ground as they felt the truth wash over them. Kieft had never planned to let any of them live. He had no desire to share power with anyone. His fondest wish—the driving force behind this entire war—was to stand over the dry, empty husks of every god and spirit in Mannahatta, every last locket hanging from his neck. Then he would be the last god, the only god, and everything would be his. He would not even have to pay homage to the Lady—Rory showed them the body of Minuit, still alive after all these centuries, and gave them the truth about Kieft's crimes. Every spirit and god on the battlefield gasped at the implications—Kieft was mortal, and thus not bound by the Agreement. He could, and would, watch laughing as the mortals descended into anarchy and madness, abandoned by their gods forever. Kieft would drink and eat of their despair, until they had nothing left, until only death could stop the pain. And finally, with everything rotten and dead around him, Kieft would leave, and make his way to the next city, and it would start all over again.

As Kieft himself stood by, helpless, his true feelings—his hunger, his disdain, his terrifying ambition—flowed into his army. And one by one, they shrank into themselves, dropping their weapons, backing away from the fight, and surrendering without protest. A cheer went up all over the battle-torn Great Lawn as the enemy fell apart, unable to bear the sight of their leader's true face. The attackers around Rory receded—leaving Rory and his friends alone to face down Kieft, who stood shaking with fury as his army melted away.

"You are spineless fools," Kieft yelled after his retreating army. "This is not the truth. This is a lie. He's lying to you!

The Munsees are the ones coming to take your lives, your place in the natural order of things. I am offering you power, divinity, everything you ever wanted! We cannot turn back now or the savages win!" At that moment he noticed that his captains, his great allies, were joining in the retreat. They turned their backs on him and left him to his fate. The First Adviser had never looked so . . . powerless.

He turned to Rory, who stood swaying on his feet from his exertions, and Kieft's vast anger focused on the boy before him. "I don't need magic to hurt you, boy. I don't need an army. I only need one thing." He pulled out a large, glittering knife, and Rory's heart leaped with fear. "Your victory will be ashes in your mouth," Kieft shouted, and threw the knife into Rory's heart.

Rory gasped, but then realized he felt no pain. He glanced down. It wasn't his heart, after all. Instead, it was his father who had acted when everyone else stood frozen, stepping in front of his son and taking the blade meant for Rory's heart into his own.

Henry stumbled, falling back into Rory's arms, driving the boy to his knees.

"Dad!" Bridget cried, throwing herself at his side, the ashes from her charred face falling like tears on her father's mortally wounded chest. Henry Hudson stared up at his children, the fear, the self-loathing, the haunted pain gone from his eyes. He smiled, strong and sure in his final moments.

Kieft began to laugh. "What a poor excuse for a trick, Henry! You cannot die! You have betrayed the Lady and she will punish you forever. You cannot pretend otherwise!"

"She . . ." Henry began to cough, blood bubbling up on

his lips. Bridget cried her ashen tears even harder as Rory held his father close. Henry tried again. "The Lady . . . she has forgiven me. She told me, when she sent me up here with you, that I have earned her forgiveness. But I told her I didn't care." He coughed again, and Rory wiped the blood away from his mouth with his sleeve. "I don't need her forgiveness. I need . . . I need my children's. Because I am so, so sorry. So, so sorry." He repeated it again, each time it grew fainter.

"Stop playing games, Henry!" Kieft's voice was less sure now. Fear began to color the edges.

"I forgive you, Daddy!" Bridget cried, clutching her father's body. "Please don't leave me! I love you! I forgive you!"

Henry began to smile and his eyes closed. His time was running out. Rory opened his mouth . . . and at first nothing came out. He felt the anger bubble inside him—all the years he'd hated his father, all the years he'd blamed him for his mother's tired eyes and weary life—all that anger screamed to the surface . . . and then softly drifted away. All that remained was pain, but a good pain. A sorrowful, gnawing, heartbroken, clean pain. His father was dying—and Rory loved him.

"I forgive you, too," he whispered in his father's ear. "I love you."

At first he thought it was too late, that his father had gone to his death believing his son never loved him. But then Henry smiled, whispering weakly, *"Thank you . . ."* And then he was gone.

"No!" The cry came not from Rory or Bridget, but from Kieft. They turned to see the black-eyed man, destroyer of gods and would-be ruler of Mannahatta, running around the top of the hill like a crazy person, clutching at the lockets around his neck as he desperately tried to pull them free.

"What's he doing?" Nicholas asked.

"He's no longer immortal now that Henry is dead," Fritz said, a smile creeping across his face. "And mortals cannot wear the lockets of the gods. That power was never meant for them. He stole a few centuries' worth of godhood, but now he has to pay for what he took."

Kieft's clawing grew frantic as he fell to his knees. Smoke, dirty and gray, began to ooze from his neck, until they could barely see him. A stench drifted their way, of disease and dead flesh, and Kieft's cries grew strangled and soft. He fell back, his body seeming to just fall apart like wet, moldy paper, as if he'd been decomposing for centuries. His cries weakened until they could hear him no more. The twitching of his limbs slowed, and then ceased completely, and then they could no longer pick out the shape of his body. It collapsed in on itself, with a sigh, and when the smoke finally cleared, the only parts of Kieft that remained were the hundreds of gold lockets piled up where his neck used to be. The black-eyed man himself was gone, swallowed up by the green earth.

Nicholas was the first to move, walking up to the lockets and sifting through them with his toe. Rory and Bridget watched from their father's side as Alexa and Lincoln joined him. Simon took a step forward, before letting out a cry. Reaching up to his neck, he lifted his locket, which melted through his fingers.

"I'm free!" Simon whispered, his voice a mixture of relief

and regret. "I guess I threw one plate too many. Oh well. Who wants to be a stupid god, anyway? Too much work!" He ran over to the other Rattle Watchers, leaving the crumbling remains of his fleeting godhood behind in the grass.

Alexa stood next to Nicholas as he leaned over to poke through the lockets. "You can take one," she said hesitantly. "You'd be a better god than most. They would finally take you seriously. They'd listen to you. You could make a difference."

Nicholas pondered for a second, then straightened up, standing tall. "It's over," he told her, then brought his heel down on the lockets, grinding them into dust.

HELLO AND GOOD-BYE

Rory and Bridget sat on either side of body of the father they'd just started getting to know. The Rattle Watch and Soka walked up behind them, and Soka put her arm around Rory's shoulders.

"Come away," she whispered. "It's over."

But then something strange began to happen. The wind picked up, throwing dirt into their eyes. When they could see again, Henry Hudson stood before them, looking shocked.

"Am I dead?" he asked. Rory and Bridget could only nod. "Then what is this?"

Nicholas stepped forward. "What is around your neck?" Henry looked down and lifted a gold locket. Rory's mouth dropped open.

"You're a god!"

"Well, it makes sense, if you think about it," Alexa mused. "Henry Hudson's name is on everything. If anyone is remembered, it's you, sir."

"I guess I'll be around a little longer than I thought," Henry said, smiling. He opened his arms and took his children in, where they should always have been.

~~~~~~~~~~

A bonfire burned merrily in the middle of the Munsee village as the victorious army celebrated the survival of their beloved city. Munsees and gods sang together while battle roaches and children of the gods swapped tales of their valor in battle. Kieft's army had melted away, disappearing back into Manna-hatta, and while some advocated searching them out to punish them, the Council of Twelve declared that there was to be no retribution. They would begin this new era of friendship with the Munsees with a general amnesty so that their joined future could begin with peace.

Rory sat on a small hill overlooking the celebration. Bridget had put on a robe to cover her burned body, but she was laughing and describing her battle with the Albino Alligator to a group of children of the gods led by Jane van Cortlandt, who looked at her with shining eyes as if Bridget were a god herself. Bridget pulled out her sword and waved it around at the imaginary monster.

"It was bigger than a house!" she declared, glorying in the dropped jaws surrounding her. "But I saw the fear in its eyes when it realized it was up against Malibu Death Barbie!"

Rory smiled. Bridget deserved the glory. Nearby, Fritz sat next to his wife, Liv, her head resting on his shoulder as they watched the festivities. Earlier, Fritz had taken Rory and Bridget aside, holding back tears.

"I couldn't be prouder of you if I were your own dad," he said, choking up. Bawling, Bridget bent over and tried to hug him, though putting her arms around an inch-long insect wasn't easy. Rory settled for some heartfelt thanks.

"Thank you for being there for me, Fritz," he said, a tear running down his cheek. "I needed that more than you'll ever know." Fritz had to ride away before he got too emotional.

Rory scanned the party, catching a familiar face here and there. Soka's brother, Tammand, stood in a far corner, David de Vries by his side. Rory heard that they'd sailed up the Hudson on the HMS *Jersey*, stopping a British warship from firing on the battle in the park. He was glad Tammand had been able to redeem himself. It was a relief to put their enmity behind them. Tammand noticed Rory watching him and glared at him. Okay, *mostly* behind them.

Rory spied Wampage standing uncomfortably in a group of Munsees led by an animated Chogan. Rory knew it would take some time for Wampage to feel comfortable among his people again. Chogan said something to the group, slapping Wampage on the back as they all doubled over with laughter. Rory thought he saw a hint of a smile on Wampage's face. Maybe it wouldn't take as long as he feared. The solitary warrior deserved to go home again. He'd waited so long.

Rory's father walked by, looking a little shell-shocked as Walt Whitman led him around, introducing the newest god to all the gods and spirits. Henry caught his son's eye as he passed, smiling at him and shrugging. Rory smiled back, still not sure what to make of his newly returned dad. That was one change that would take some getting used to. His dad was a god . . . As Bridget had already mentioned at least five times, there could be advantages to that . . .

Rory glanced over at a group of gods that included Peter

Stuyvesant, Alexander Hamilton, and a wounded Teddy Roosevelt, his arm in a sling. Nicholas stood in their midst, looking overwhelmed.

"I say, old boys," Roosevelt was declaiming. "There should be a place for a chap like Nicholas in the council! To represent those nongods, as it were."

"I don't know if that's such a good idea," Hamilton Fish began, but Peter Stuyvesant cut him off.

"It's a damned fine idea!" he announced. "And it's about time! It's true this city has gone to the dogs since my day, but you have to move with the times, or so they tell me. And there is no one better suited than my own blood! You'd be fools not to appoint him, even if he is an opinionated do-gooder!"

"Thanks, Father," Nicholas said, grinning. "From you, that means everything."

Smiling, Rory turned his attention to Lincoln and Simon, who were exchanging war stories by the fire.

"You're crazy," Lincoln was saying. "Of course you'll miss being a god!"

"Not one bit!" Simon replied. "It's too much work. Do you know how much a stack of plates weighs? It was torture!"

"I don't know," Lincoln replied. "For a few hours, I got to be Teddy Roosevelt. Everyone cheered and fought harder when I rode by. I was pretty much a god, and it felt really good."

"You weren't a god," Alexa said, strolling up. "You were an idiot who was lucky he wasn't killed. But you were both very brave." She raised her glass, saluting them. "To the brave members of the Rattle Watch!"

"To the Rattle Watch!" Simon and Lincoln chorused, raising their glasses. Nicholas walked over, his own glass raised as well as he shared a satisfied smile with Alexa.

"To the Rattle Watch," he said, and turned to face Rory across the way, his glass in the air. The rest of the Watch turned to salute him as well. Rory nodded his thanks, his eyes stinging as he blinked away tears.

As they all went back to their conversations, Rory felt suddenly alone. Looking around at all the gods and Indians, spirits and creatures, he realized that he couldn't stay in this place. He was still a mortal. He had a life waiting for him in the real Manhattan, and there was no place for battle roaches and albino alligators there. He had to go to school, and do homework and one day get a job and live a normal life. He couldn't be the crazy guy going on about talking statues and invisible ships. He had to go and be normal.

"Why are you hiding over here, Pretty Nose?" a lightly mocking voice said behind him. Soka sat down next to him, intertwining her arm with his. "You saved the day. You should be in the center of it all, soaking in the accolades."

"I'm fine out here," he said, sighing.

"You don't look fine," Soka said. "In fact, you look like you're moping! It's not a good look for you."

"I'm just taking it all in before I have to go back," he said sadly.

"Back where?" Soka asked, furrowing her brow. "You live up the street."

"Back to normal life. I can't live like this forever. Straddling two worlds, one of which no one else can see."

"They can if you show them," Soka reminded him.

"But I can't do that," he replied. "It's too dangerous. I've got to stay the only one who—"

"Oh, just stop it!" Soka said, shaking her head. "You are not alone, Rory Hennessy! You have a sister who loves you, a mother who would do anything for you, and a father who's returned from the dead! You have friends who care about you, even if you can't take them outside the city limits. You belong in Mannahatta, *and* you belong in Manhattan. People straddle two worlds all the time. Look at me. I'm a Munsee girl in love with a pale-faced Irish boy. People think I'm crazy! But I know it's definitely worth it." With that, she leaned over and kissed him, and as he folded her into his arms, Rory knew that he'd never be alone again.

It was close to midnight when Rory and Bridget finally reached their house. They'd stopped by the cave in Inwood Hill Park, but while Bridget's body was still there watched over by a jubilant Tucket, their mother's had disappeared. They weren't worried, however. They knew the Lady would keep her promise. Bridget had to let go of her paper body (which was pretty much toast, anyway). As she leaned over her mortal face, she realized she'd grown so used to being strong, to being Malibu Death Barbie, that she was scared to be the normal, everyday Bridget. That was why she couldn't leave her body before. Because she couldn't let go.

But she didn't want to stay a child forever. And she was tired of not being able to cry. So she leaned over her body and let go. Her mortal eyes fluttered open and she was home. As she watched, her old paper body collapsed in on itself, falling into a pile of ash and burned paper. She felt a pang in her heart, but she was ready to move on.

Now the two of them burst into their apartment, running for the bedroom with Tucket on their heels.

"Mom!" they cried. "Mom, we're home."

No one answered and their hearts were in their mouths until they flung open the bedroom door to reveal their mother, eyes blinking from sleep, sitting up in her bed.

"I've had a real humdinger of a dream," she said, rubbing her eyes. "I'm glad I'm awake."

Rory and Bridget ran to the bed to envelop her in their arms, a family again.

"Me too," Rory said. "Me too."

Read all of the
GODS OF MANHATTAN
adventures!

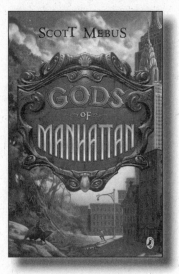

978-0-14-241307-4

978-0-14-241645-7